IN LIFE

ONE MAN'S STORY OF LIFE FROM THE APPALACHIA TO VIETNAM AND BEYOND.

PART 1, THE BEGINNING

To Kathy

David C Shaffer

BY DAVID C. SHAFFER

Outskirts Press, Inc.
Denver, Colorado

Outskirts Press, Inc.
http://www.outskirtspress.com

ISBN: 978-1-4327-6715-0

Library of Congress Control Number: 2010939972

Outskirts Press and the "OP" logo are trademarks belonging to Outskirts Press, Inc.

PRINTED IN THE UNITED STATES OF AMERICA

Dear Readers,

Names, dates, places, and incidents in this book have been changed or omitted for a variety of reasons, including but not limited to the security, safety, and wellbeing of the people, places or agencies involved.

Any resemblance to anyone living or dead is purely coincidental. I will leave it up to you the reader to realize what is what, who is who, and where is where.

With this in mind this book is listed as a work of fictionalized **biography.**

Have fun and enjoy,

The Author

Chapter 1

Even at this time of night it is hot. The air surrounding us is heavy with moisture. It's almost like trying to inhale under water in a hot tub. Not only that, but tension is all around. It is one of those anxious nights when all the men in my A-team are uptight and ready for anything. We all know something is about ready to break loose. The jungle is alive with the sounds of lizards, frogs, rock apes, and jungle birds, which only reminds us we are a long way from home. As we await the coming dawn, our thoughts drift back to home and our return there, but our eyes and ears never leave the present tense of 'The Nam'. We know that the intense training we received, as members of the Special Forces would soon be put to the test and that is what we want. As elite members of S.O.G. we are ready to fight that clandestine war that we were trained to fight.

Separate from the conventional and unconventional operations of Special Forces are the clandestine operations of Military Assistance Command Vietnam / Studies and Observations Group (MACV/SOG). This is a cover name to disguise the real function and name. Special Operations Group better describes us more accurately. Working closely with CIA, SOG carries out clandestine operations all over Southeast Asia. These missions include cross border operations into Burma, Cambodia, Laos, North Vietnam and the provinces of Yunnan, Kwangsi, Kwangtung, and the Island of Hainan in China. Our mission is to carry out intelligence gathering raids on the enemy's safe havens, searches for POW's along with executing rescue missions, including the kidnapping or assassination of key enemy personnel, and the retrieval of sensitive documents or equipment. What we do is unusually hazardous. For example, a number of night HALO (High-Altitude bailout, Low-Opening) parachute jumps are made into very remote areas.

We are waging a top-secret war, which you don't read about in the papers back home. Only a select few even know of our existence. Our standing orders are not to be seen. Our true identity is classified top secret. If contact is made, we are to take no prisoners, leave no survivors. If caught, our government will disavow any knowledge of our existence. If captured, we face torture and inevitable death. We are therefore ready to die to prevent that. It is something like "Mission Impossible" except this is for real.

As we move, we give the impression of predators stalking their prey through the teeming jungle. Each mans a study in motion, soldiers moving almost imperceptibly through the thick cove of vegetation. We vigilantly step, pause to look around and listen. Eyes moving back and forth, scrutinizing every color and contour for any irregularity in the symmetry of the jungle around us. Each step is measured, deliberately placed, carefully measured. Always surveying the ground for trip wires, as thin as silk, tautly strung a few inches above the jungle floor, and sections of detonator cord beneath the rotting leaves. All of our senses finely tuned to near perfection. Every nerve ending, every muscle readies in anticipation. We are treading on the very edge of life or death. This is where the mind functions smoother. Your thoughts are more lucid, your reflexes more adroit. The gentle rustling of the palms, the snap of a twig, and the faint whiff of Vietnamese sweat all could spell danger. All the skills you have acquired from months of living in the jungle are brought to bear even the ominous feeling of being watched by an invisible set of eyes. All of this comes together to manifest the raw survival instincts of the human animal.

We'd been humping for six grueling days through the sweltering heat, sometimes cutting our way through the almost impenetrable jungle so dense it is nearly claustrophobic. We have to avoid enemy contact, which means we have to stay off the footpaths. In our way stands thick clusters of bamboo, enormous palm fronds and broad leaves the size of elephant ears. Overhead, the dense foliage of the trees are entwined with twisting vines that seem to be struggling to choke the life out of their hosts. Only rarely does a splinter of sunlight break the eternal shadows to reach the moist jungle floor.

Occasionally, the dense jungle would give way to fields of razor sharp sawgrass. Which could slice through our nylon web gear, and our clothes leaving lacerations in our skin which can quickly fester in this moist heat. Adding to the misery are the ever present clouds of mosquitoes swarming about our head, bussing and darting like a squadron of tiny dive bombers looking for a place to feed, and the needle-sharp thorns of the "gitcha" vines that claw at our skin and clothing.

Through this teeming vegetation we slowly slash our way,

trying to follow a long abandoned animal trail, or make it look like some of the locals have passed. Through skill and good luck, we have avoided Charlie thus far, even though the area is infested with V.C. and N.V.A. Units. In fact, the military command had suspended all ground operations in this AO because 35 grunts had been waxed over the last couple of weeks. However, an exception is made in our case in response to the desperate plea of a Montagnard chief for help in setting up a local force to clear the V.C. out of his territory. That's one of the things that Special Forces are trained to do, and to say the least we do it very well.

The clouds that covered the sky have parted allowing the full moon to shine down on us making it easy to see the landscape. The valley below is wide and deep with a river running through it like a snake slithering back and forth between the hills. The vegetation on the hills has a denseness that makes it impossible to see the trail we have traveled. I'm starting to think that this is the time Charlie would like to pull an ambush. I don't want to think about that. I have taken all the normal precautions to have a safe area around us.

So I put my mind in reverse and go back in time to when I was five years old. It was just before my Mom and Dad sent me to live with my Dad's parents in a very small town in southeast Kentucky high in the Appalachian Mountains. Being from an old southern family, it is our belief that the first born son is to become the head of the family and responsible for the history and traditions.

Since I was the first born male, it was my lot in life to move to Kentucky. Where I was to grow up and learn about the land, family history and carry on a long list of commitments. Our family has lived on the same plot of land since 1779. This land was granted free and clear to us, because of our military contribution in making this a free country. During the War of Independence, my great whatever grandfather came to America to command an Army of Prussian Troops. In the old country there had been bad blood between the Hessians and the Prussians. So when the Hessians sided with the British, he decided to bring his troop of Prussians to help George Washington win the War of Independence. Or so the story goes. I think it was more to just kill Hessians. From then till now every generation has had the first born son in uniform, fighting in every war this country had been in. For that reason, we did side with the Confederacy (the correct side) in the war of Northern Aggression (Civil War as it is known in the North).

The distant staccato of small arms fire snaps me back to Nam. It comes from the hill across the way and is followed by a fire-fight between an Army platoon (in the wrong place at the wrong time) and a company of VC. We sit and watch the tracers going back and forth between the two groups. They look like little red and green fireworks. In a way, it's fun to have a ringside seat at a fire fight and not having to think you are going to be pulled into it. Knowing we are safe, I let my mind drift back to my youth.

I started to think about my last summer in New York City before my big move to live in Kentucky. Having grown up on the Lower Westside of New York City wasn't all that bad at first. I still have cherished childhood memories of games of stickball, tag and kick the can played in the street in front of our home. The Lower Westside was a mosaic of brick, stone and wood, which housed a melting pot of cultures. Our neighborhood was a mixture of Irish, German, Swedish, Italian, and Jew. Other ethnic and racial neighborhoods that had fallen on harder times surrounded it. This included the lower class slums and tenements, the rundown ghetto of blacks and Spanish Harlem.

The neighborhood had reached its twilight years and was on its first tentative steps towards decline. The cancerous spread of ghetto poverty, crime, and despair had started to eat away at the fabric of our village.

It had been a close knit community of family, friends, and neighbors, but even that was starting to unravel. Though a few struggled in silence to resist its inevitable fate, the fight was hopeless. But I was a young and innocent boy; I never saw any of this.

Our block had an almost old-world feel about it. Our brownstone row house faced into a street whose cobblestones occasionally peeked through the well-worn blacktop. By the curb stood wrought iron lampposts that looked like walking canes which held white globes of glass to light the sidewalk by night. Across the street was a pawnshop whose shelves were strewn with the discards of strangers. Who seemed to come and go at all hours of the day? Behind whose dingy windows laid a treasure trove to a small boy. Inside were displays of discarded jewelry, gem set rings, knickknacks, gold watches, knives of all types, big and small, and guns. The walls were hung with guitars, tarnished brass instruments, and old suitcases. Shelves and counters were crammed with old dusty radios, typewriters, sporting goods, and a host of other mysterious objects.

Across the street and down at the corner was an old Jewish Delicatessen, which had been the same location forever. It was an oasis of mouth-watering delights to me. Its counters and shelves displayed a tantalizing array of foods, which tempted the taste buds. There were a couple of tables with red and white checkered tablecloths and cane back chairs for the customers to eat at. Overhead was a hammered pattered lead ceiling with several large fans, which gently stirred all the appetizing smells into one tantalizing aroma. The old plank floor was well worn by years of steady traffic. I will never forget the appetizing aromas. Everything smelled so good, the pastrami, gefiltefish, whitefish, lox, bagels, rye bread, matzo balls, stuffed cabbage, potato kugels, kosher meats, imported cheeses, hot mustards, horseradish, pungent spices, and spicy dill pickles in a large barrel. But most of all I liked the sweet smells of the pastries, blintzes, cheesecakes, kugelhops, fruit filled strudels, and the donuts.

Sometimes Abe (the old man who owned the deli and an old family friend of my Moms parents) would stop me in the morning to give me a bagel covered cream cheese and lox to eat. Frequently I would stop by in the afternoon to sweep out the store or do any other odd job in exchange for a mouth-watering treat.

My grandparents on my Mom's side came to this country from Sweden. They settled in this area when my Mom was 2 years old. Grandpa had been a carpenter and did some work for Abe. They soon became friends and stayed friends.

It was one of those sweltering summer afternoons when you could fry an egg on the heavy steel doors, which cover the opening in the sidewalk for the dumb-waiters. Here and there, men were sitting on their front steps reading the newspapers or smoking cigarettes, while women leaned out open windows to share the latest gossip.

I was sitting on the front steps of the old brownstone apartment building we lived in. It was one of the common brownstones you see on the lower West Side of New York City. The night was a very hot and sticky one. The street gang in this block was known as the Alphas and the gang that was the most trouble for them was the 13 th Streeters. There was trouble between them going back to the time of their fathers and grandfathers. There was a no-mans land between them that had been setup right after the big fights of the early 1940's. I was told that six kids had been killed in one of those fights that went on and on for about three weeks. Down at the corner the fireplug had just been opened, so I went to cool off in the water that was spraying into the street.

As I walked close to the corner (which was in no-mans land) I could tell that the 13th Streeters were the ones who opened the plug. It had been safe for us young kids to go anywhere, but for some reason this time I was jumped. They knocked me to the ground and kicked me about five times. I was yelling all the time. Until they picked me up and told me that if Sonny did not stop messing around with Manney's sister, no one in the Alphas or anyone that lived there would be safe. My yelling had caused a stir in the people sitting on the steps in front of my house. Just then five of the Alphas ran down the street. The 13th Streeters saw them coming, dropped me and took one last kick at me. By this time I had some of my wits about me so I grabbed one of their legs, and sank my teeth into the calf muscle. The guy I had a hold of fell on top of me and started to swing a pipe at me. He was just about to hit me in the head when Sonny grabbed his arm and put him on his back. Two other Alphas took hold of him and held him down. Sonny helped me up and told me to go ahead and hit him for what they did to me. I took the pipe, but was told not to use it. So I kicked the squirming 13th Streeter right square in the groin, twice. He immediately clutched his groin, curled up in a fetal position, and groaned in agony. The Alphas picked him up and heaved him into the bed of a passing pickup truck that had slowed to turn the corner.

As we walked back to the steps Sonny asked what happened to trigger the fight. I yelled, "You helped me not knowing what it was about. What if I had started it? Would you have helped me then?"

"Yes, we would have. We have a code of honor. If any of our people are in trouble for any reason we will help them out. If we find out they were wrong we will straighten them out." Sonny answered.

"I'm not one of your people." I said.

"Yes you are, you live on our turf, and are friends with my kid brother Ed. So what was it about?" I told him everything they said and his face went purple with anger and screamed that "this means war."

Sonny and about ten of the Alphas went right over to Manney's apartment that was three flights up a dimly lit stairwell. The building was a dilapidated cockroach-infested tenement building with the paint peeling and holes punched in the plaster walls. On cue, they burst into Manney's living room and took turns beating him to a bloody pulp. Before leaving, several Alphas drug him out of the apartment and tossed him down the stairwell. We then retreated, leaving him lying crumpled and unconscious at the bottom of the stairs. He ended up spending 14 days in Bellevue Hospital with a fractured jaw, cracked ribs, a broken arm, and numerous contusions and lacerations. After that, he was never the same. He walked with a limp, and the right side of his face was partially paralyzed.

That started a gang war that lasted for over a year and a half, with each side trading blows by ambushing rival gang members.

They would be jumped from alleys or stopped in the subways, dragged into a dark place and thumped in revenge. Even with all the violence there was never a gun used.

This was my brutal initiation into the ways of the street, thus ending my youthful innocence.

Every other summer I would return to New York City to see my Mom and sometimes my Dad. My father was a Navy lifer, and for that reason was seldom home. He was a strict disciplinarian. Had he been around, he would have put a stop to my running around real quick. My Mom on the other hand was a loving, doting mother, but I was simply too strong-willed for her to control. After several summer trips back to NYC, I started carrying a switchblade for protection. I became streetwise, learning to fend for myself, always pushing back when pushed. In later years things changed. Blacks moved in and tried to take over. That is when guns started to show-up. Zip guns at first then the real thing. I was shot three times and stabbed repeatedly in gang fights, but managed to survive. Maybe, if my Dad had been around more, I wouldn't have been into what I was when I was back in NYC. It was funny but over time I had became two different people. I was just a country boy when I was home in Kentucky, but on my trips back to New York City I would become just another one of the kids of the street.

Chapter 2

I am rudely snapped back to the Nam by a tap on my arm. It's Mike. He tells me that someone is coming down the hill and heading right at us. If we open fire on them we will give away our position. I tell Mike to hold tight and see what happens.

Mike is the teams' heavy weapons expert (besides being my XO). Because of his tanned skin, blond hair, and blue eyes, he could have passed for a California surfer instead of being from Philly. His dad was an Army Officer and had Mike take R.O.T.C. at the University of Colorado, where he graduated first in his class in mining. He was also an All-American Running Back. He married his college sweetheart (Linda) after Special Forces training and spent his leave as a honeymoon. They made an odd looking couple because he is over six feet tall and she is just five feet tall in high heels. Veto was his best man and the rest of the team went to the wedding.

Mike and Veto went to the same high school in Philly. Mike was in tenth grade when Veto was in the seventh when they met. The Senior High kids would work with the kids just entering

Junior High. Mike was Veto's big brother through school. He helped him make the football team that year. I think it was Veto's suggestion that Mike would be interested in SF. Veto would write Mike in College, about The Nam and share his thoughts about re-enlisting for SF when he returned to the states. We would sit around at base camp and Mike would say. It's Veto's fault that he is here eating bugs and stuff instead of being at home with his wife. It is all said in fun, they are good friends.

Veto is the youngest of eight kids, five girls and three boys. He looks like one of those Roman statues of an athlete you see in museums. Tall, well built with dark hair, dark eyes and a Roman nose. From the time he was ten, he was the only boy living at home. One of his brothers (Mario) was in the Navy; the other (Tony) was married and lived Newark. Mario (the one in the Navy) would tell all kinds of stories about his world travels when he was back on Newark. Veto looked forward to seeing the world after school but did not like ships or anything to do with large bodies of water. After high school he went to a junior college for two years, and then enlisted in the Army. After his first tour in The Nam with the First Cavalry, he reenlisted for Special Forces.

There are more shots fired on the other side of the valley, which draw our attention. Veto crawls over to tell Mike and me that the people that were coming towards us have now changed their trek so as to head over to the other side of the valley. I tell Mike and Veto to return to their positions and stay sharp. In short order, I do not follow my own orders and find myself slipping back in time again.

It is now six years later and my third summer trip back in New York for a month to see my Mom, Dad and now two brothers. I would not have returned this year had it not been for my new brother being born. He was born during the school year so this was my first chance to see them. I return to the Big Apple, and it's the Fourth of July. I get to spend time with the old gang, of which I'm a full member. I had been writing to them during the school year to stay in touch (plus my two week visits every other year) to learn all that was going on with them. We had talked about going down to the docks to watch the fireworks that were to be set off over the lower end of Manhattan Island.

I meet up with them and received a good old ribbing about the way I now talk. I do have a southern accent.

The docks had always been a kind of a cross between a war zone and no-mans land. On this night, there were guys with the girls from about five different street gangs down by what we called our spot. All was fine till Manney's half brother said something to Sonny about Ellen, Manney's sister. I don't really know what happened then. The next thing I remember was floating in the Hudson River (back then you could swim in it) looking up at the pier. Bob H. threw down a rope for me to climb back up. When I arrived at the top I could not believe what I saw. Padro was sitting up against one of the pillars and the top of his head was a hammer sticking out of it. I jumped over the edge of the pier really quick and was ready to run when Bob H. called out for help. Bob H. had three of the Streeters hanging on him. I grabbed one of them and just as he spun around I saw he had a shiv. The shiv (knife) was pointing at my gut. I went down and took hold of the first thing that came to my hand and swung at him. It was dark, the city did not keep up the lights on the docks and this one had not been used in some years so it was in need of repair. Not only were all the lights broken but also the pier was coming apart in places. The first thing I had put my hands on was a piece of the pier, a board about three feet long with some rusty nails in it, and I hit him in the side at the middle of the arm. The arm that was hit was the arm holding the shiv. One of the nails ripped a hole in his biceps causing him to drop the shiv. As he stepped forward to retrieve the shiv his foot went through the pier. At this, I picked up the shiv and fell on him putting the shiv into his back just below his rib cage. Then his blood spurted out on to my hand and arm. This was the first time I had been bloodied. It felt warm and sticky, with the slight taste and odor of copper. The only thing that was going on in my head was, do I run or stay and continue to fight?

The answer came from the people around me before I had a chance to make up my mind. A shot rang out and Pete fell with a hole in his chest. Everyone hit the ground and I started to crawl for what small cover there was on the pier. The topside of the pier had nothing on it bigger then a breadbox for cover. The only place for me to go was to go down one of the ladders leading to the river below. As I headed for one of the ladders it came into my head that if someone was out for me I would be an open target hanging out there for the entire world to see. In the dark I could tell that just under the pier was a cat walk running across to the other side and it met with one that ran from the end of the pier back to the shore.

That catwalk looked like the best way out of this mess, so down I went. As I was about to reach for the rail of the catwalk something hit me on the back. I put my hand into my belt and pulled my knife ready to cut who ever it was. Looking back I learned it as one of the Alphas who was following me. I said to him as we ducked under the pier real quick, that he was lucky I did not cut him. We then took two or three steps in under the pier and stopped to see if we were followed. In the time it took to be positive no one was following us we heard five shots ring out and three people went into the river. I don't think the ones that went into the river were shot because they started to swim for the next pier.

It was darker down under the pier than on top and had a lot more crap for you to trip over. The only light came down through the holes in the pier, giving the area strange lighting. As we worked our way towards the shore we could hear the fighting above us. It was very hard to walk on the catwalk, you were either stepping over something laying in your path or going over a place that had no floor to it.

At one place where the light came down through a big hole the guy with me, Larry, jumped like he was going to jump into the river. There on the catwalk in front of us was a river rat the size of a large cat. He sat up and looked at us like we were going to try to take over his kingdom down under that pier. I no more wanted to stay there then I wanted to kiss Jacks sister and Jacks sister was so ugly I can't explain it in this book. Larry pulled out a zipgun and was ready to shoot the rat when I grabbed hold of his arm to stop him.

He looked at me and said, "What did you do that for?"

"If you had pulled that trigger you might as well run up a red flag and tell the world we are down here with no way out. I don't want all those S.O.B's to know where we are, do you?"

He said "no" he didn't and asked what we were to do. I found this very funny for he was about six years older then me. As we started to look for something we could pick up and throw at the rat, a member of the Satans fell through the hole in the pier. He landed on the rat so hard that they both went right through the catwalk and into the river. When he came up to the surface of the water he still had that rat on his back. Boy did he take off swimming for the shore.

I turned to Larry and said, "Well no more rats to think about."

The hole they left behind was too large to cross without help. Larry went back to the place the catwalks crossed and pulled up two long planks. They covered the hole just right. As we approached close to the shore the sound of the cops coming was getting close. We just looked at one another. Put our hands up in the air as much as to say "now what." In looking closer, we could see that just to the south of where the pier met the shore there was an opening to a storm drain.

I should probably explain here what the area of the pier and the shore looked like. The pier sat about fifteen feet off the water with the catwalk system about five feet under the supports for the pier surface. The shore was a stone wall that came straight up out of the water vertically to a point that was level with the top of the pier. At the place where the supports meet the stone wall, the stones were missing to let the pier supports sit on the wall under the top planks of the pier. Part way down was a place where the stone wall was thicker than at the top so as to form a walk way that went over to the next pier and to a set of stones steps leading up to street level. This stone walkway went under the pier at the same level as the catwalk.

We looked at one another trying to figure out if we could make the drain before being seen by either the cops or the other gangs. Two people going into the river on the other side of the pier answered our question. This caused everyone to look over that side, giving us time to run for the storm drain. We made it, we said as soon as we were in the drain.

I said, "Let's stay here and watch what happens."

Larry wanted to follow the drain back up under the city until he found a manhole to come up out of. I decided to stay and see what happened to the others guys we left behind on the pier.

He took off back down the drain and I found a way to sit and watch the fireworks on the pier. As I looked out to see what was up, I could tell that the cops must be close. I don't know why, but whenever the cops arrived everyone knows it and splits. The only ones left on the pier were the ones that could not runaway for one reason or another. The cops, like the fools they were, drove out on to the pier not thinking how old and rotten it was. Lucky for them no car fell through all the way. I say all the way, because the second car onto the pier broke through with its front wheels and was left hanging by its frame and back wheels. That was the fastest I ever saw cops move. They jumped out both doors and ran to the edge of the pier and looked back like they expected to see their car taking a dive into the Hudson River. The cops in the first car saw their comrades running away from the car and ran after them. They came to the side of the pier by the storm drain and started to talk to one another.

The one who looked like a sergeant said, "What is going on here? Why did you run from your unit like that?"

One of the two officers in the car that went through the hole said, "We thought that they were going to receive an unexpected dunking in the river."

The one called Sarge looked back at the car and said, "How did you do that?"

"I don't know all of a sudden the nose of the unit started to go down and the tail went up. We did not stick around to see what would happen next. I just put the parking brake on and ran. Now what do you think we should do, Sarge"

By this time all the kids had scattered to other parts of the city, so the only people on the pier were the cops. As was common of the New York cops there were more cops then there had been kids. And that was more then I cared to count. It was like watching an old Keystone cops movie to see them try to procure their car back up on to the pier. The first try consisted of one cop with a rope tied to his middle getting into the car to try to back it up. All this did was make a lot of smoke from the tires burning on the old wood. I started to laugh, but stopped myself because I did not want to be found. Next they tied a rope from a third car to the stuck one and tried to pull it out. This did not work, so the cop that was in the stuck car before, returned behind the wheel and tried to back up while the other car tried to pull. All this did was make more smoke. I was having a hard time not laughing at this. Next they backed the paddy wagon out onto the pier. Boy, was that a mistake. It started to break through the pier just as soon as it drove on to it. Lucky for the cops this time, for the paddy wagon would have gone through if it were not for the pier supports. It had all its wheels spinning in midair. The only thing holding it up from going in the river was the two pier supports holding up the front and back bumper. At this point I could not help but laugh. Not one cop heard me because they were all making noise, running around like chickens with their heads cut off. The chief showed up and started to scream at his men making things worse. Now they had one truck (the paddy wagon) and one car in holes in the pier. They also had two other cars on the pier that they could not back off because of what had happened behind it.

I was having such a hard time not busting out laughing, it was best for me to leave. Turning and going the way Larry went was the only way out. I couldn't go out and up the steps to the street with all the cops around. It was dark and damp in that drain with just enough light to see where you were going. I walked for what seemed like miles, with no sign of a way out. At every bend the rats would make noise and run as I almost stepped on them.

As I went around a bend, there was Larry coming back my way. "What are you doing here", was all either of us could say.

I told Larry about what was going on at the pier and that they would be at it for a long time. Larry said that he did not find a manhole he could open. We were heading east and if we could keep going that way we would come out on the East Side of town. As we went further in, the smellier it became and the more we felt lost. Then we saw the light at the end of the tunnel. As we approached closer we could hear a lot of noise. It was where we went in, we had gone in a big circle.

In looking out to see what was going on, I could see that the cops had obtained one of those large cranes that are used on construction jobs. They had put a sling under the paddy wagon and were lifting it up and putting it down onto the street by the pier.

I said to Larry, "It looks like they will be out of here soon. So let's stay here till they are gone." We sat down to watch the fun like typical sidewalk superintendents.

The next car started to back up and almost went into the hole left by the truck. The crane operator started to laugh and was told to be quiet. The chief was mad enough without that. The chief and two other cops were looking over the car that was stuck to see how to remove it from the pier. They called the crane operator over to ask him how he wanted to do it. He walked around the car a couple of times.

"The only way to get this car out without dropping it in the river is to put a sling on the back axle and lift it straight up. I only hope the axle is in good and solid" the crane operator told the Chief.

The Chief, with a look of fear on his face asked if there was any other way. "No, if we try to lift it with one sling around the middle it could fall either front or back, and there is no way to place a sling around the front and back so we can lift it like we did the truck. There is nothing for us to stand on to put a front sling on it. I am surprised it did not slide on into the river with that much of the front end down that hole."

They followed the crane operator's idea and put the sling around the back axle. As the crane started to lift the back end the front started to slide. The more they lifted the back end the further the front end went into the hole. The car was almost perpendicular and over half of it was in the hole when the rear axle started to let go. All the cops on the pier just stood and watched. The car did a flip and went into the river on its roof. As the axle let go, the crane jumped and looked like it was trying to do a dance on the street. The operator jumped out and ran for cover.

I said to Larry, "Boy am I glad we don't have to count on them for help."

It took about another hour before they were gone leaving the car in the river, or would it be more correct to say stuck in the mud. The first thing I wanted to do since the trunk of the car was above water was to see what we could obtain from it. Larry wanted to just split the scene before the cops returned. I gave in and we took off for the clubhouse.

When we were back at the clubhouse all the other guys were talking about what could have happened to us. I told them all about the catwalk escape and the funny things the keystone cops were doing, and about the cop car still in the river. Sonny started to tell us about the running fight they had with the 13th Streeters up until the subway cop pulled a Joe Pig and clubbed one of the 13th Streeters. As it turned out it was a good night after all, for we signed a pact with the Satans and the Lords to work together against the Streeters. The Streeters were not only going after us, but also them. It seemed that all the girls that lived on Streeters turf wanted nothing to do with them. They were going out with guys from outside their turf. This all started when one of the girls became infected with VD from one of the Streeters. This was a no-no back when you as a guy had to look long and hard to find a girl that would do anything, and then had to keep it secret.

I spent the next two days covering my tracks, because my father had returned home when I was out running from the cops. My mom did not care where I was, so long as I did not get put in the slammer. Now my dad was different, when he was home he would send us out of the house but wanted to know what we were up to. That made it difficult to run with the gang and not piss off my dad for being one of those "hoodlums" as he put it. Especially since it was expected of me to be the one that was to carry on the family name and history. Not to mention the fact that it was predestined I was to go on to the U.S. Military Academy like my grandfather and his grandfather and three generations before them. Only my father was a traitor and went to the Naval Academy. Oh well it happens in the best of families.

Chapter 3

Wham! Wham! I'm snapped back to Nam by an air strike that is hitting the other hill in the area of Charlie. I look around me to see if anyone is looking at me. No one is, so I turned my attention to the other hill only to have one of the guys asks, "Say, what were you thinking about? You were not here with us for sometime."

I turn and ask, "What time is it?"

Mike answers, "0530 hours, Sir"

A flash of light catches my attention. Looking out across the valley I see phosphorus airbursts blossom above the ground creating an umbrella of white streamers that make their way to the jungle floor below, followed quickly by four fast-movers dives out of the clouds. Pop, pop as they are peppering the slope with a chain of orange flashes followed in seconds by a rapid succession of explosions. This seemed to quiet things down.

Nam life has two sides to it, one of utter boredom, the other of maddening fear. If anyone tells you that they were not scared. Just laugh at them, for we all were scared from time to time.

There are no atheists in combat. Everyone to a man at some point has looked up and said. "God Help Me! "

The night is really dragging on, and I am getting tired and want to sleep, but one of my worst enemies, the bugs, keep me awake. All the repellent and mosquito netting in Southeast Asia cannot stop the hoards of flying, creeping, crawling, biting, stinging, and buzzing things that come out at night. The bugs are as thick as flies on a garbage truck in July and the mosquito's sound like a flight of B-52's going overhead. As I cover my self with repellent and put up my net to stem the tide a little, my mind drifts back to Kentucky and my life there.

My hometown in Kentucky is very small. It is so small the one and only town welcome sign has two sides. One side tells you welcome and the other tells you thank-you for coming to our town. There is no population listed because if more than five people leave town to go shopping the number would be way off.

The town has a General Store (by name and what it is) built in 1794. It sits on the southeast corner of the uncontrolled crossroads. There is a covered wooden sidewalk out front with benches by the front wall to sit on. As you open the door, you see there's a place inside to sit around the potbelly stove where one can hear tales of the past. This is the place for people to meet and spread the local gossip. Electric power has arrived in town, and the store now has a soda machine.

My Uncle Lennie owns the General Store. He is a second cousin once removed on my great-grandmother side. He fits the part of a hillbilly to a tee. Every time you go in to the store, there he is in his bib overalls, plaid shirt and shit kickers. There is a well-used handkerchief in the top pocket of his overalls that he takes out often to wipe his nose or forehead. His beard is down to the top of his bibs. The beard will have that morning's breakfast in it until lunch. He does wash his hands often and can count to ten. Most of the people in the valley have an account with him. His son Bubba goes out the second of every month to collect on the accounts. Bubba does not work, so this is his way to help his dad by collecting on the accounts. He has been known to come back to the store with baskets of eggs, sacks of corn, slabs of beef or pork, crates of chickens and other things. The barter system is alive and well in there here parts.

The post office is built across the street to west of the General Store. It was completed in about 1850. The red brick of the building still looks like they were just laid. There is a hitching rail out front to tie-up your horse. There's a wooden sidewalk like the general store, just no benches. Inside there is an open counter to buy stamps and other mailing supplies. There are mailboxes behind the counter for those that come to town for their mail. You do not even have to tell him who you are. He has your mail ready to hand you as you come in the door. The postmaster must have been here since the turn of the century. He has a long gray beard and white hair. He talks slow and like all of us has the talk of a southerner. You can ask him about anyone within 30 miles, and he can tell you all about him or her and their kin. It is said that he delivered the mail by wagon till one summer when a lighting storm spooked his horse. He was thrown from the wagon just before it went over the edge near the top of one of the mountains. It took almost five hours till someone went looking for him. They found his dead horse and busted up wagon about 500 feet down the mountain in a creek bed. A search party was sent to find him. He was found knocked out and bleeding. He was in the hospital six weeks before he was up and about. That is when he became the postmaster. He still to this day walks with a limp and has limited use of his left arm. Oh, by the way he is also related to my family by marriage. We call him Uncle Leroy.

In the back of the Post Office there is a large room with the windows blacked out, a high tin ceiling and three ceiling fans that run on slow day in and day out. The floor is unfinished wood that creaks when you walk on it. The smell of stale cigarette smoke, electrical sparks, and old coffee hangs in the air. There is some-one here 24 hours a day, seven days a week, and 52 weeks a year.

There is a steel door on a short wall to the left of a long wall covered with maps broken up into odd shaped blocks. In front of the wall at the other end of the room is a half glass wall. In the center of that wall is a frosted glass door.

The longest wall is filled with a big odd-looking setup. It looks like a box sitting on end on top a desk. The box looks like some-one has drilled a bunch of holes in. All the holes were drilled in a neat orderly manner. Equally spaced top to bottom, side to side. They are fitted with what looks like copper collar. Above each hole on the front is a small red light, which light blinks when it wants a plug placed in the hole. There are hundreds of wires exit-ing out the back, over the top and in to the attic.

There is a small shelf sitting in front of the box with holes in it. It is at the right height and back far enough to sit at with your arms resting on the desk. On this shelf is a panel that sits at an angle so the operator can see it. This panel has hundreds of four-inch long ¼ inch round copper looking plugs sticking up out of it. Above each plug is a small white light. Coming out the bottom of each plug is a wire that goes back under the table. As a red light illuminates in the upper panel the person working there takes the plug at the far right of the lower panel with the yellow strip and plugs it in where the red light is lit and asks if they can help. There are six of these plugs, plugged in to six of the holes on the box at all times. I never learned why. This monstrous looking thing is made of dark wood that is well polished.

This is our local phone exchange. It is one of the local phone co-ops that fill the need down here in the sticks. Not everyone has a phone so you learn to think of it as your phone company. Mary Lou, the person in charge is my Grandmother's niece. She took over from her mom who passed away last year in the flood.

We all still have the crank phones. Two short cranks for the operator. Three short and one long will have every one on the party line picking up to help. To place a call just crank twice and tell the operator who you want to reach. In just two shakes of a lamb's tail, you are talking to them. If you wanted to place a long distance call (anywhere outside the valley) you would crank twice. When Mary Lou would come on you would give her the number and hang up. It could take anywhere from five minutes to a day later. She would call you back and connect you to the number you wanted. If your luck was with you the call might last long enough to complete what you wanted to say. The big problem with this type of a system is anyone on your party line can overhear all you have to say (so you do not say a lot). Oh! There is another little problem. That is you can only have one phone and it is bolted to a wall in your house. Standing up to talk has its advantages. One for sure, you don't want to talk for long. Holding the earpiece to your ear with one hand and holding the mouthpiece with the other standing sure get old quick.

The gas station was built in late 1933 with a one bay shop. It has a roof that goes from the front of the building out over the two gas pumps. John, my grandfathers' brother owns the station.

John had gone to Detroit Michigan to learn auto repair as part of a program from General Motors. When he returned Albert, (my grandfather) loaned him the money to build and start the station. The station was looked at as a way to improve the area north of the Gap, hire locals and let us not mention to help John and his family (a wife and six children).

The cinder blocks used to build it were trucked in from Tennessee and the tin roof came from Virginia. The wood came from a mill in Kentucky, as did the plumbing and electrical. This was done to give business to other relatives that really needed the boost in the hard times they faced as part of the Great Depression. Most if not all the laborers were hired from the area. If it could come from or be done by a relative or a local all the better as my grandfather would say.

In part it was from the Tennessee Valley Authority (TVA) that Albert learned the TVA would be using the main road south through the Cumberland Cap to Tennessee. They would be moving men, equipment and supplies to build the dams as part of the TVA project. This would open a steady flow of people; cars, trucks and money thought the valley.

There is a cut off from the main road leading south to the Cumberland Cap that takes you back into the hills. To say we were in the hills is an understatement.

The area was very hilly with very few homes. Most of them were just one or two room shacks, with no running water or electricity. The local industry now is coal mining or timber. There are still some share croppers around but not like it use to be. Most of the people are poor and pick-up odd jobs to survive or drive into the bigger towns 20 to 30 miles away for a low paying job.

The roads are mostly dirt, following old animal paths or

Indian trails. They bend back and forth around the mountains, up and downhill and are narrow with no guardrails to keep you on the road.

My folks had been one of the first settlers in this area and have a lot of land. The nearest house to ours is over three miles away by road. We are at the head of the holler. So there are mountains on three sides of our place. There is a creek that runs across the place that at one time was used to float pine logs down to a sawmill. The old mill is now gone but the water wheel is still there. The dam to direct the water to the mill makes a nice little lake for swimming. It's secluded, so it is perfect to go skinny-dipping. Which we would take advantage of whenever it was warm. (When I say we, I am talking about my friends and classmates from school, both boys and girls.)

The first log cabin built and most of the outbuildings are still in use. What was the slave quarters is now migrant workers housing. The groundskeeper and his wife use the cabin. Jerome is not only the groundskeeper but also helps to oversee the migrants that come into pick the tobacco. We grow a type of tobacco that is picked leaf by leaf through the season. Our land is divided into thirds. Two thirds grow tobacco and the last third grows cotton. We rotate the planting to rebuild the soil. His wife is the cook for the main house. Offellia (the cook) is a descendent of one of the free slaves from the plantation. If you look at a bottle of Aunt Jemima Maple Syrup you would know what she looks like.

Yes we had slaves. Like most Plantations in the south, we did not mistreat them. We gave them food, clothing and had a doctor come in every two weeks to help them just as he helped us. If someone were injured he would be called in for both slave and family alike. The visiting schoolteacher came by once a week to teach the slave and family children to read and count. We lived by the one in seven rule. The one in seven rule was a rule that a slave works for you six days a week. On the seventh day he or she can work for you for pay or he can work for someone other then you for pay or he can do nothing. If he or she works and saves up the original price you paid for him or her. He or she then brings you that amount and he or she and any offspring they may have had is then free. Of the 6,800 slaves that worked our land 6,500 were free at the start of The War of Northern Aggression (Civil War as it was called in the North).

At the end of the war it was our freed slaves that drove off the carpetbaggers and saved our place from being stolen. A little known fact is the "Constitution of the Confederacy" outlawed the importation of slaves. It figured that in a short period of time all slaves would be free.

The main house was built in 1884. It is of the antebellum style. There are porches on both the first and second floor that circled the house. Large white columns hold up the porches with an arch over the main entrance. If you opened the double front doors and looked down the hall to the back you would see the double back door. This is sometime called a run through hall because we could ride a horse in the front door and out the back door (Which I did several times). The staircase to the second floor is one of the half circle types that lead to a balcony on three sides of the second level. The ceiling on the main floor is 14 feet high and the second floor is 12 feet high. The first floor has two rooms to the right as you come in the front door. These are the front parlor and the dining room. To the left are three rooms. The first is a sitting room. Next is the ladies parlor and last is the game room or as some would say the gentleman's smoking room. The second floor has two rooms to the right. One being the Masters bedroom the second being the Mistresses bedroom. To the left are three bedrooms. I had the front bedroom. The windows are of the type that goes from floor to ceiling. The bottom half would open over the top half giving you a walkway to the porch. We have no screens on the windows because at night even in summer it would cool down to where there are very few bugs. Our beds are all four-posters with netting to close in the summer and drapes to close in the winter. A fireplace heats every room. There is no running water in the main house. But a two story outhouse was added to the back of the house with an entrance off each floor a back porch. I say outhouse, as that is what it looks like. It has running water and all the things a regular bathroom has.

The cooking is done in a separate building called a cook-house. This keeps the heat and smells out of the main house. Not to mention the fact that there were wood fires used to do the cooking. From time to time a kitchen fire would or could happen. Being in a separate building this would save the main house from being burned down. As it did a couple of time over the years.

The house sits about a mile back from the road and has a willow tree lined driveway. We do not let cars or trucks drive up to the house, but will meet people coming to see us by horse and wagon. All deliveries and outgoing tobacco are loaded and unloaded by way of a back road that keeps them away from the fields. We do not allow any motorized equipment in the field. Horse or mule power does all the work. This is done to keep the fumes and any leaking oil or gas out of the fields to avoid con-taminating the crops.

I have made some friends but not a lot, as the school is just a two-classroom schoolhouse. It was built in 1889 with wood and labor donated by the people of the valley, so the children could be schooled, as it says on the plaque by the front door. There is a bell tower on the roof that calls the class in. The school has a barn with stables and a coral for the horses. Several of the parents supply the hay and grain for the horses. Each day a student that rides to school would have the chore to pump the water for the horses into the large trough in the coral. Each rider then had the responsibility to care for and to see that his or her horse had a bucket of water and grain through out the day.

Once inside the school there is a large area as you came in the front door. In this area are open front cubbyholes built into the walls. This is where you would hang up your coat. This area is where the wood burning stove is that heats the place as we are high in the Appalachian Mountains and it does cool down in the winter. The room off to the right is 1st through 6th grade and 7th through 12th is in the room to the left. The desks are set in three rows of two seats to each to the front and to the back of the room. There is a large space halfway back to separate the grades. The desks and chairs are of wood and very hard on the bottom. The floors are made of wide planks and are well worn from years of use. The walls and outside of the building are white washed every summer. By the end of the school year the inside walls have taken on a dull light gray color from the soot from fire in the stove.

I started in a class of nine students, which went to 16 in the fourth grade and then graduated, with a class of 12 after losing four in ninth grade. The eight boys and four girls in my class were more like cousins, and several were, then anything else. Even though we were all friends. I did not look at the girls like they were "girls". They were more like one of the gang. We would hang out together and do things. We'd play baseball and football in the schoolyard or in someone's backyard. We would also just hang out with each other in town. In the summer, we'd all go down to the creek and go skinny-dipping. I did not think anything of us all being nude. I must have carried this over into my summer trips to New York, because I never had a girlfriend or even gave it a thought. My Mom would ask my Dad about this, and Dad would tell her not to worry I was in a small town and thing were different, and would be OK.

Being from the oldest family in town, I was able to get away with a lot. My Great Uncle was the Mayor of the next town over and most of the people in the area are related in some way or another. My grandfather taught me to ride a horse by the time I was four years old. I love to ride and it is not uncommon for me to ride to town (12 miles one way) for supplies. To be on horseback and ride the hills was a way for me to be alone, away from life. I love the woods and all of nature. When I was in the third grade, I would ride to school everyday. About half the kids would ride to school. If I were to take the bus to school it would take about an hour and a half ride to school and the same back home. But going by horseback it took about 15 minutes. In fourth grade we were allowed to have a pistol strapped to our hip. I became a crack shot by the age of seven. Mostly black powder pistol or mussel loading rifles. To this day there has never been a problem with carrying a gun to school because you learn from a young age how and when to use it. If you have a problem with someone you just take care of it in other ways. A good fistfight is just that. We are allowed to carry a pistol because of the wildlife that was in the woods going over the hills to school. There were and still are deer, bear, snakes, and wild boar in the area. This part of Kentucky has several very large areas of state and federal parks and game preservers.

We did not have any of the crap classes the schools have now. We had only the three R's. School was to learn not play. If you wanted art, music, or anything like that you could take the school bus after classes were out to the big town school and back later. I took the bus starting in 7th grade to take part in the sport of Rodeo. One of my chores was to break the young horses to saddle so I was a good rider.

School started at 8:00 am with lunchtime of noon. The school day would end at 4:00 PM and then home to chores. It is a simple life. I learned how to live off the land and do things for myself.

Chapter 4

My body feels like I am on a boat, as if the ground moved under me, bringing me back to Nam. "What is going on now!" comes out of my mouth as I jump back to reality.

I start to give the order to saddle up, when Mike says, "What, what is that? Can you hear it?"

We stop to listen. There is an ominous sound like the slow roll of a large kettledrum off in the distance. Then we start to feel it. The earth begins to tremble. The sound of rolling thunder is walking its way down the valley. It is an Arc Light strike. Bombers so far up you can not see or hear them unleashing their racks of devastation. A half-mile wide swath erupts up the valley from us. Each payload pulverizing the jungle, gouging crates, flinging tons of dirt and trees into the morning mist. As the parallel rows come closer, the sledgehammer blows rock on the ground under our feet.

I yell to John, "Call S.O.G. OPS, tell them we are here before we eat one of those sticks of bombs."

I know that by calling in I risk compromising our position,

but I don't want any of us lost to friendly fire. I never understood how anything that would take your life could be considered friendly.

John Hanraddy is one of the best RTO's in all of Southeast Asia. His 6'-7" frame carries a large share of responsibility in maintaining our radio link, using an AN-109, with the outside world. This muscular hulk of a man who could intimidate people without even trying is an easy going, calm, and composed person. Although he has the potential to explode in a violent fury if sufficiently provoked. He is soft spoken with thoughtful blue eyes. The sun, wind, and snow on his family ranch in Wyoming have sculpted his character, and face. Until he was drafted, he had never ventured more then a hundred miles from the horse ranch he was born on. His loyalty and fiercely protective nature is an indispensable asset to the team.

As John relays the message, the ground splitting devastation continues to narrow the gap between the last explosion and where we stand. Anxious seconds pass before John yells, "It's O.K. they said the pilots had received the word. OPS said not to worry; they were told that a friendly village was near to our local."

With that, the bombing run stops. A silence settles over us while overhead, at 30,000 feet the silent killers return to their bases on Guam leaving only a vapor trail to show their passing.

With that message received we decide to saddle up and start down the other side of the hill to meet the village chief. The sun is just about to the top the hill to our east as we start down into the valley. It is light for sometime before the sun starts to heat up the air and we use that light to start our trek. In the valley below, there is a large river that makes a U shaped bend forming an island with a 50-meter wide 100-meter long strip of open low marsh covered land connecting it to the mainland. It is on this peninsula that we are to meet the chief. I don't like the looks of it. If we are caught out on that peninsula we could be trapped. There is a small hill, on the mainland, just to the south of the strip of open land. We set up on that hill and send a small team out to make it look like we are on the peninsula. When they returned, we sat back to wait for something to happen.

The sun is now high over the hilltop and the temperature is going up. To me, it seems like the only difference between the days and the nights are that most of the bugs only come out at night. It did cool down a little when the sun went down, but not enough to make a whole lot of difference. I find some shade and sit back with a breeze blowing across me. This little hill is a good place to rest for you can see 360 degrees around you. The land around us is a bunch of rice paddies with our little hill sitting at a place where three dikes form a cross. To the north the land slopes off to the riverbed and the other directions there is just a patchwork of rice paddies for a least 300 meters.

A few of us take out some balls of glutinous rice from our rucksacks and eat a late morning snack. We don't eat c-rats. Instead we rely on rice balls with raisins inside. C-rats are just too heavy to hump through the bush, taste bad and the effect they have on your body odors could get you killed. You can tell by the smell of a man's sweat if he has been eating C-rats. The V.C. would even go so far as to dig up the holes we have buried our shit in to check its smell. If we want to stay alive, we have to remain as elusive as quicksilver, so we eat like the locals so as to smell like them. But besides the practical reasons there other aesthetic factors. It is a rare GI that savors the taste that comes out of one of those olive drab cans. There is an almost universal loathing for meals like ham and lima beans. I remember the first case of C-rats I ever had. I was turned off to them even before I open the first can. On the box was printed, "Manufactured by Pillsbury Corporation, Minneapolis, Minnesota, February, 1945", which meant I was one year old when they were packaged.

We are in position to meet the chief one-day early so most of the day is spent cleaning weapons, keeping watch on the peninsula and general relaxation. After I have put an L.P. out near where the trail opens onto the open low land, and all the men know what they are to do. I'm brought back to my thoughts. This time about that trip to Sweden and try to rest and sleep.

The summer of my 16th year was a very good one for me. When my last class was out for the summer, I went to New York City to see my Mom, my brothers and my Mom's parents. I was to go to Sweden that summer to meet my relatives on that side of the family. My Mom, her brother and parents came to the United States when she was two. Her brother was killed by a taxicab three years later and they never recovered from the loss.

I was to fly to Sweden. I had packed weeks before it was time to go. My Mom had received money from my grandparents, (her mother and father) to buy me new clothes and things I would need for the trip. I put on a suit, not the first time, nor the last, but also not a common thing for me to do, which was so uncomfortable. I did not like to dress up so to say. My normal way to dress was dungarees, T-shirt and engineers boots when in New York. I changed to cowboy boots the rest of the time. In the winter I added a leather jacket. So this having a suit and tie on was totally out of character for me. I guess it was more an act of desperation then anything else which prompted them to send me to Sweden for the summer.

When I was in New York City I was with the gang, and when in Kentucky I was what one could be called a "redneck". Quite a difference I know. My Mom wanted me to be more like the upper crust of New York. My Dad was raised just like me. So it was ok with him, as he was also the first born male. Dad would say to Mom every time she started on the subject of me being a redneck. "May, the boy will be all right. I was raised the same way and turned out OK. Didn't I?"

But even the best-laid plans go haywire, and so did theirs. Their plans to reform me would start to backfire as soon as I boarded the plane.

We took a cab out to the airport. While at the airport we lost our way and spent about a 1/2 hr. looking for Scandinavian Air Service, the airline I was to fly on. I finally asked one of the airport cops, (You know one of those rent a pig's) and he told us we had to go over to the International Terminal for my flight. The International Terminal was a long way off and my three suitcases were heavy.

I asked, "Can we please have a sky cap take the bags for us?"

Mom said "NO" and rented one of the carts the airport has. (How come every time you push one of those carts, just like a cart in the food store, they have a wankey wheel that is square and will not turn the way you want it to)

We made it to the S.A.S. gate with about 30 minutes to spare. My grandparents had purchased a first class ticket for me, so we went to the first class lounge. This was pretty special considering my Mom folks came to this country with nothing. They went through Ellis Island, and entered as legal immigrants, learned English, adopted the ways and customs of the U.S.A., as all should do. They became successful and wealthy and then helped others to do the same.

The people in the first class lounge were very nice to us and even offered us a drink. Mom said "No thank-you" but I said "yes to a Pepsi". Mom asked how much that would be and was told that all drinks in the first class lounge were free to the people going on the flight. I said, "Is that true of booze also?" The steward said "yes but I could not have any, at least not till we were in the plane and airborne."

The Flight left right on time and soared out over the Atlantic. Looking back on the big city I felt relief. To me New York was one of my homes even with all the trouble and pains it caused. (That's not true, it was not the city that caused the pain so much as some of the people in it) I felt relief when I realized that I would not have to put up with my Dad's Bullshit about the gangs and who they are.

As the big silver bird headed northeast I said to myself, "What have you placed yourself in the middle of now?" The reason for this was I was going to spend the summer with my maternal grandparents going all over Sweden, visiting all my relatives. My mother and her parents came to the U.S.A. by themselves leaving all the rest of the relatives over there. I had looked forward to this trip with mixed emotions. I wanted to see Sweden and meet all of my Mom's family, but did not want to be stuck sitting around with the old people shooting the bull. I wanted to be able to get out and meet some of those Swedish girls we all heard about.

I was just about to dose off when the stewardess came around with the drinks. She asked me what I wanted. All I had up to this point was beer and moon shine so my choice was a bourbon and water. (That is the drink of choice in Kentucky) It was real good so when she came back I asked for a second. The seat next to me was empty and there were only about thirteen people in first class. Three older couples, two men in suits talking about some deal they made in the states, and a man with his wife and kids. His daughter looked about my age and not too bad looking. This was to be an eight-hour flight and I thought why should I spend it alone went through my head. On my first trip to the head, (navy name for toilet,) I said "Hi" and smiled at her. She was sitting two seats back and on the other side of the plane. The only reason to go by her was to go to the head. To do that again, too soon, would be too obvious, so what now. In about ten minutes they served dinner and another drink if you wanted it. I was starting to feel the first two, so it was coffee for me.

While eating dinner and thinking about how I could talk to this girl two seats back, something strange happened. She went forward to the galley and came back with a big class of milk. As she was about to pass the seat next to me, I was sitting by the window; she stopped and asks if she could sit down. (Man, Oh Man, this is too good to be true went flashing through my mind) I stammered and said "yeee yes." Her next words came as more of a shock to me.

"I asked my dad if I could sit up here with you, so I would have someone to talk to. My brothers are only 12 and 10. He said it was Ok with him if you do not mind. Do you mind if I sit with you."

"No I don't mind" came out of my mouth so fast that I was afraid of scaring her off.

"My name is Brit, Brit Anderson, what is your name?"

She was a sculptured, Scandinavian beauty with honey blond hair which flowed to her waist. Her face was silken smooth, with azure blue eyes, thin, soft lips, and a smile that radiated a graceful beauty. Brit was voluptuous even at the age of sixteen, long legged, and warmly wise to the ways of the world. In total loss of mind I could not remember my name for what seemed like hours.

Then I said, "My name is Eric."

As we talk it came to me that she did not talk like everyone back home. She sounded different some how. After we sat there and talked for about an hour, the stewardess came around with more drinks for everyone. Brit asked for something I never heard of. "A Pepsi for me, please," was my answer.

Brit asked, after the stewardess left, "Don't you drink? " (What do you say now went through my mind) The only answer that came into my head was, "Yes I do." (I was looking for a more intelligent answer then that, but could not find one)

As we sat there I came to know my first Swedish girl, no not in a physical or biblical way but as a person. We also found out that we would be in Uppsala at the same time. It was decided that we were to meet and have an evening out on the town. She was from Uppsala and wanted to show me the town. I was to find out later that Brit had more then one way in mind.

The lights in the plane went down so people could slip off for some sleep. The Flight took off at 7:20 p.m. and was due to land in Stockholm at 9:30 a.m. the next day. It was now about 11:30 by my watch and with the lights turned down, the plane took on an air of quiet. Brit and myself found that we were whispering to one another. Sometime during the night we both drifted off to sleep leaning on one another. The lights came back up, accompanied by some light music. I looked at my watch only to find that it was only 2:00 a.m. The speaker came to life to inform us that we were behind schedule and would be landing in Stockholm at 10:00 a.m. This is dumb, why wake us up at 2:00 a.m. to tell us that we will be landing at 10:00 a.m. was my comment. The stewardess started to bring breakfast around and asked what we would like.

I asked, "Why are we having breakfast at 2:00 a.m." only to be told that it was now 8:00 a.m. in Stockholm. (Did I feel dumb?) Brit asked if this was my first trip.

"Yes and no, yes by myself, and no because I have traveled with my family." As we were in our final approach to Stockholm, Brit took hold of my hand and said "be in Uppsala on time, for we would have a time not to forget."

In the airport were my Grandparents and my Uncle Ulf and his wife Anaka. As we were looking for the luggage to come down the baggage ramp Brit's brother came over to me and handed me a slip of paper with Brit's phone number on it. The next, (slow and boring) week was spent in Stockholm with all the old people just sitting around day in and day out. I wanted to move be out and do something. You see just sitting around was not for me.

Ten days later, we left for Lapland. Lapland is in the very northern part of Sweden, where the sun never sets in the summer, or comes up in winter. This is where my great grandmother lived. My great grandmother lived with two of her sons and their wives and their children tending a reindeer herd. They did not have electricity, indoor plumbing, or running water. A wood burning stove heated the house and the water came from an ice-cold stream running through the back yard. The outhouse was about 100 yards from the house and you could freeze your butt off if you sat too long. They kept the seat for the outhouse in the kitchen by the stove, so when you had to go you could have a warm place to put your butt. Great grandmother did all the cooking and housework for the family. I liked it up there except for the cold.

In the middle of summer it never warmed up. Part of the family would be out with the reindeer, while the rest of them would be sleeping because they had to keep an eye on the reindeer. We rode reindeer or went for rides in a sled pulled by reindeer. The landscape was mostly just open flatland, but it had a charm about it that was hard to describe. It was now getting close to the time we were to go to Uppsala and my excitement was on the rise.

We rode down to town in the reindeer sleds, and arrived in the train station just in time to have dinner before going on the train. Grandpa went to check on our compartments. When he came back we could tell he was mad about something. He told us that we did have two compartments, one for them and one for me. The problem was that they were in two different cars on the train.

Grandma asked, "How did that happen?" The numbers were in order but there was a split between cars between the two compartments. (To myself I gave a cheer. The one that was for me was next to the dining and bar cars. Oh goody!)

We had a nice dinner and before we boarded the train, my great grandmother, she was 102 years old then, gave me a long coat made from reindeer hide. That was the warmest coat I ever had. I will tell you this, that coat never was on my back in the states. You would be laughed off the streets of N.Y. in something like that.

The train pulled out on time and the long trip to Uppsala was started. We went to the dining car for a late night bite to eat about 9:00 PM and then went back to our compartments. On the way back Grandpa gave me ten crowns, a crown is a Swedish dollar, and said, "Have fun but stay out of trouble." Having changed clothes and cleaned up, it was close to 10:30 when I walked into the bar. There was an empty table just inside the door and about eight feet from the bar, so that is where I sat down. It is a good place to see who comes in and who is at the bar went through my mind.

The barmaid did not speak English, one more thing in my favor. It was my plan to try and have some lady who spoke English to offer to help me out. With great difficulty I received my first drink and settled back to watch the people. Just then, in through the door came one of the most beautiful ladies I had ever seen. She was about 5'5" and slender in the right places and not so slender in just the right places. From what I had seen, most of the young women in Sweden had tits that looked like they were trying to burst out of the bra they were in. That is if they are in a bra at all. Her hair was blond, eyes were blue, and her skin looked oh so soft. She had on a thin white blouse over a very dark blue skirt. She sat down six feet from me at the end of the bar, so I had a side view of her. I called the barmaid over to try to order another drink. She did not understand what my order was, so we went round and round trying to make it clear. The blond at the bar was watching what was going on. As we were getting nowhere the barmaid went over and said something to the bartender.

The blond stood up and came over to my table and asked if she could help. "Yes, please!" was my almost instant response. "Please do." Can you tell them a screwdriver please? She talked to the barmaid and the barmaid said something back. The blond turned and asked me what went into a screwdriver.

I said, "It is made with Vodka and orange juice."

She stood up, went to the bar and told the bartender, only to have him say something to her. She came back and sat down.

"They don't have any orange juice." "Would you like anything else." She said. "A rum and coke will do." I said. She turned and told the bartender.

"My name is Eric. What is yours?"

A big smile came to her face and she said "Anna." Anna asked if I was from America.

I told her "Yes I am" and asked "Why?" She said "Because" and left it at that. We sat and talked and drank till 1:00 am.

Anna asked, "How would you like a cup of coffee?" In looking around it was becoming a very full place and we were starting to have trouble hearing one another over all the noise so my answer was "yes."

The dining car was closed so she said that she had a travel pot in her compartment and we could go there if I liked. Do I like, flashed before my eyes? "OK, if it is all right with you," was my come back.

Anna's compartment was in the same car as mine. She opened the door and told me to take a seat on the bed. The compartments on this train were just like the ones you see in the old movies. The seats are on one side. The other side had a dresser to put your things in and on that side was a door leading to the next compartment. Set in to the corner opposite the window is small bathroom. Under the window was a table that folded out. At night the porter would come and change the seats into a bed and pull down an upper bunk if needed. Anna was traveling alone so only one bunk was made up.

She located the pot and started the coffee. "It is difficult to fold up the bed and with the bed out you can not use the table so do you mind having your coffee on the bed?" She asked.

I said "No, not at all if you don't mind." I was not even thinking about the table. We drank that pot of coffee and started another, all the time just talking about her country and mine. We started out sitting on opposite ends of the bed from one another, but as the time went on we move closer to each other. I hate to admit this, but it is true, she made the first move.

Anna was with the Swedish Travel and Information Department, and traveled all over Sweden and Europe. She had been hired for the job right after graduation. The Swedish school system is a lot different from ours. They start out at a younger age then we do. I found out that she was 22 and never married. I learned a lot that night and not just about her life either. Breakfast was at 7:00 and I just made it back to my compartment in time to clean up and meet my grandparents.

The dining car was full when we arrived there so we stood in line. We were to be next when a place for two opened. I told Grandma and Grandpa to go ahead, I would take the next table. Behind me were a man and his wife and two kids. The next table was for four so I let them go. I was no dummy for behind them was Anna.

Anna and I had a nice breakfast for two and a long talk after. It was set that we were to meet in Stockholm one week before I was to head back to the states. I was returning to the states by boat and had told Anna that last night. She wanted us to meet before I left to give me something so I would not forget her. It would have been impossible to forget her, but I readily agreed. My grandparents were returning to the states by plane and their flight left one week before my boat did. I was to stay with relatives in Stockholm till leaving for Goteborg to board the boat. We hoped that we could spend that week together. This trip was turning out better then I thought it would. Just in case something happened and we didn't get to see each other we exchanged addresses and phone numbers. With that it was time to go pack to leave for the train. We would be in Uppsala in 1/2 hr.

Chapter 5

There is a hand at my mouth and a voice in my ear that snaps me back to reality. I look up and see its Mike.

Mike says, "There is a VC patrol coming over the ridge behind us."

"What time is it Mike?"

"0700 Sir."

We are well dug in on the top of this small hill that overlooks the near ground and most of the valley. The kill zone around us is about 200 meters, then the ground cover becomes heavy with low vegetation, but a man standing can be seen out to a distance of about 400 meters. We did not disturb the ground around us but left a trail out onto the peninsula.

I say to Mike "Let's see if they fall into our trap." "Phil, go check with Veto and see if he is ready."

Veto as my demolition's expert had set up some fireworks for anyone crossing the strip of land connecting the island with the mainland. Phil came back and reported that all is in readiness.

Phil is the team's light & heavy equipment specialist plus

being the demolition expert. After high school Phil started work at a Chevy dealer, as a grease monkey, and worked his way up to shop foreman in just sixteen months. His girl had a flower shop that she was going to sell to help him start an auto dealership of his own. One day he came home from work and told her he was going in the Army for the bennies. Phil went onto explain to her all the ways the Army would help after he left the Army. He sent almost his entire pay home for Carol to put in the account they opened to save for the auto dealership. In a letter Phil received from Carol, she told him he could come home now, because they had enough for the auto franchise and building. When Phil read the letter, he started to laugh. He then told us about what she said and all of us had a laugh out of it too.

Sometimes when we were under fire Phil would start to laugh and say "I'm leaving now, Carol said I could come home." Phil could have passed for James Dean except Phil is taller. Phil acts like Dean too, especially like the part Dean played in the movie Rebel Without A Cause.

We sit back to watch what was to happen next. The VC, to this point, has not seen us so we stay still and wait for them to make the first move. It is just about lunchtime when the main body of VC comes into view crossing the ridge. The lay of the land is such, that after crossing the open ridge of the mountain you would drop under a two or three layer canopy of tree branches. Under that canopy, it is a dusk type lighting with the smell of rotting wood and leaves all around. It never dries out in there, even in the dry season. The trees drop water from their leaves and moisture runs down their trunks. On the ground are thousands of leeches. They look like little buggy whips hunching across the ground. They move by stretching out their thin long worm like bodies. They then plant their head and hunch up their backs pulling their back ends up to meet their head only to stretch out again, and again. They do all of this only to feed on any warm-blooded host they can crawl upon. If you have to take cover they will crawl all over you looking for a place to attach themselves to feed on your blood. After a long hard walk you come out into an area that has fewer trees and from time to time you can be seen.

The main body of VC is now about 100 to 120 meters out from the strip of land we start to call Florida. If they stay to the trail they are following they will be on Florida at a time that will put the sun in their eyes if they look at our location. I say a small prayer that they would follow the false trail out to Florida.

Doc starts to signal me like crazy over the commo net about something and points to the north side of Florida. He is pointing out that the village chief has moved into an area just to the north of Florida and in a place to put Charlie between a rock and a hard place. How do I let the Chief know we are over on this hill without Charlie knowing?

Doc (Michael Patrick O'Leary) is our resident intellectual. His thick Boston accent and his high brow comments are just a hoot to hear over the explosions and retorts of weapons fire. He, like so many others, had entered the Army for the GI Bill so he could finish his education. His dream is to finish college and go onto Harvard Medical School. Doc has a look of someone forty-five even though he is just twenty-two. His once bright blue eyes have lost their luster and taken on the 10,000-yard stare. His once soft brown hair is now streaked with coarse gray hair. His face is etched with lines of stress and anger from having to work medical miracles. Not only on us, but also the local people who Charlie went after for helping us or who Charlie thought were helping us. The VC would torture and or mutilate the senior citizens and children. Women and young girls were gang raped and beaten. I watched him help people that should have been dead and he did it with a lot of love. I only hope his young wife will be able to recognize him when it is time to DEROS back to Boston.

I once had Doc dig a slug out of my leg in the middle of a firefight. In the dark of night, he came across an open field to get to me and then would not hear of leaving the slug in until the battle was over. The bullet had hit an artery. Doc said that if he did not stop the bleeding I would be dead in two hours. He took two slugs in the arm that night while fixing up my leg and never stopped what he was doing.

Our Kit Carson Scout, Dou, comes crawling over to me pointing out that if he went to the west he could circle around the peninsula as Charlie came in from the east. There are shallow points in the river north and south of our location that were hidden from view and he could go that way to tell the Chief our plan. I told him to move it and make it quick and quiet. We would hold our fire till Charlie was on Florida, or until the chief's men open fire. Dou took off with the message and we kept an eye on Charlie.

Dou Van Tran is a typical Vietnamese, small, slight of build, about 20 years old. He is a North Vietnamese that moved south as soon as he could. At the age of ten he saw his parents killed by the NVA. The NVA then raped his three sisters. All ten of them slept only to wake and rape the girls again. Dou was tied to a tree and made to watch. The NVA said it was because his family was helping Americans. After the second time the men had their way with the girls they killed them and took Dou to a reeducation camp. He escaped five years later and took an oath to hunt out the Communists and drive them out of his country. Dou is now one of the best scouts we have.

It seemed like forever before Dou was back with one of the chief's men. As Dou comes up to me he says, "Dai Uy. This is Nep. He comes to talk for his Chief." We whisper about what we are planing to do and what the chief has to say. The chief wants us to fire the first shot if possible. That way he would not open up before Charlie had gone into the trap. I have Veto tell the chief's men about the trip wire traps and claymores on Florida. With that information Dou and Nep take off back to the chief and I settle back to wait. It seems like more time is spent waiting then doing. Not that I am complaining for the doing can and often is dangerous.

Whammm! The first set of claymores goes off, then the second. As Charlie starts to run for cover we open up on him from the south and southeast. As the first claymores explode, Roy and Doc move to the east to have a better field of fire to cut off more of the eastern end of Florida. My mind flashes, I hope Dou and Nep made it back.

Roy is the team Engineering Sergeant and is cross-trained in Intelligence. Roy comes from a small town just outside of Detroit where his mom and dad work on the assembly line for Chevy.

There are some people who said Roy and I could have been identical twins. But I don't agree, first off he is about six inches taller then me, second he does not have the muscular mass I do, and lastly he has a big nose.

He was going to the University of Michigan to become an engineer in the automobile field. But due to cut backs on hours at Chevy his folks could no longer afford sending him to college. He dropped out of school and took a job at a quick lube shop hoping to save money to go back to college. But Uncle Sam stepped into change Roy's plans again.

The chief's men moved into position to the north and northwest. We have Florida surrounded, except for a place at the western most point of the peninsula. We did not put anyone there because of the high palisades. The low strip of sand before the heavy tree line on the peninsula is now red with the blood of the VC. The first set of claymores had allowed the first two or three groups go through and then the fourth group trips them, cutting the main body in half. This then sends Charlie running back for the mainland only to run into the second set of claymores, which are on remotes. The Chief's men and our men open fire on the VC driving them back onto the peninsula. We now have them right where we want them.

A fast call goes out for an air strike on Florida. We held Charlie on Florida for about 20 minutes with heavy firepower, only to sit back and let the fast movers come in for the kill. The first of the F-4s came in from the east low and fast and open up with all they have. Man, it looks like every tree and bush on Florida is being put through a meat grinder as the second and third birds come across. They then climb and roll out for a second pass. This time the first two ships lay down two tanks on the outside edges of Florida, only to be followed by the third ship doing the center strip. As the tanks hit the ground there came that unmistakable sound. There is a dull thud that is followed by a great whooshing sound. That sound is the sound of napalm in use. A strong wind develops as vivid orange flames jump skyward. A blast furnace like heat covers the area as the mixture of naphthalene, palm oil and gasoline burns. The blast consumes hundreds upon thousands of cubic feet of oxygen taking our breath away momentarily. The fast movers then climb out and cross the hills to the east.

We look for any sign of life on that burning strip of land only to see smoke and flame. The sight reminded me of the look of the abandoned strip mines in West Virginia that had burned.

I'm now in contact with the Montagnard Chief, Lok by name, so we setup a CP on this small hill and place our men in a commo net using PRR-9's around Florida to wait for it to stop burning. The heat from Florida just adds the heat of the day. The combination of the two is just the pits, that napalm burns so hot that you can feel the heat almost two hundred meters away. It's not only the heat that makes this night so bad but also the smell. If you have never smelled the smell of human flesh burning you don't want to.

The place burns throughout the night and just before sun up the last of the fires go out. Florida now looks like a steak that was put in the broiler and left too long.

I send a message to Lok that at 0930 we will move out and check Florida for anything of use and to take the ears of the KIA's if any could be found. Working the way we do, we are paid a bounty of $50.00 for each right ear we take in. Don't think our government pays this bounty, for they do not. In all truth the U.S. forces in Viet Nam are told not to take part in this. We however are not under the control of the U.S. Military in Viet Nam. SOG doesn't take its orders from Saigon. They come from Langley, Virginia (the CIA), The Joint Chiefs of Staff, or the White House.

At 0930 our point man followed by a six-man contingency of Lok's man move out. We follow at about a 100-meter distance.

The smell was worse the closer we were to Florida so I take out a spare T-shirt, wet it with my canteen, and tie it over my mouth and nose. As the lead party crosses the sandy strip a shot rings out from the peninsula stopping the team in its tracks. (How could anyone be alive in the burned out hellhole?)

Then a second shot goes whizzing by and we all knew in an instant. The shots did not come from on the peninsula, but from the rear of our position. I signal for two of my men to back track and check it out as we take cover. The jungle where the shots came from is so dense we can not see a thing except the muzzle flash. It looks like it is just one dink firing at us. Our point man and his party moved out onto the peninsula as we took pot shots at the flash. The jungle erupts in a shower of bark, leaves, dirt and other junk.

It looks like a frag has exploded off. Roy and Doc came back with an ear to tell us that in all the excitement last night we missed one dink. He set himself up in a tree to wait till we moved in. Doc is laughing so hard he can hardly stand it. When he stops laughing he tells us that dink had a 61 and dropped it the wrong way and took himself out.

Veto and the first team are on Florida and find nothing to salvage. The place is a total burn. We take a count and come up with 32 ears but little else. At the western end we come across a tunnel that looks like it at one time went down and under the river. Now it is full of water and crap. In the center of the peninsula we find a pile of dead gooks, under the pile we find a map with many markings on it.

"Look at this Dou, What do you think it is?" I said.

On the map is an outline that looks like Florida. There is also a series of dotted lines running from where we are, to what looks like a village four klicks to the west. One dotted line looks like it starts from where we found the first tunnel. Lok comes walking over to meet me. He is a man of about 70 years that looks like he could go another 70. His round face is wrinkled and weathered to a dark brown and his once black hair is now mostly silver. His hands are gnarled and dark but with a strong grip.

I greet him and show him the map. Lok takes the map and starts to scream at his men. Dou tells me that Lok is mad at his men for not knowing about the tunnel. The tunnel runs into his brother's village, and by the looks of this map a lot more places then that. As a joke I say it looked like a map of the New York City Subway System. Dou points out that for us to find this map is a great embarrassment to the chief. He is in charge of this valley. It is for him to know all that goes on and to have us find this map makes him to lose face.

The Montagnard's are a proud people and to lose face is the worst thing that can happen, especially for the Chief in front of an American he asked to help him. After he calms down we go through the rest of the peninsula with the map as a guide.

The map shows three other tunnels entrances that we have to check out. The first is in the center of the peninsula almost under the pile of gooks where the map was found. This one is sealed off by dirt that more than likely fell in during the air strike.

The second is on the north side about half way down. It has about five dead gooks just inside the entrance, all burned to a crisp, and is blocked just after them. Doc bends down and cuts off an ear from each for the bounty.

The next and last one is on the south side almost opposite the point where we spent the night. This one is open and has no sign of anyone going down it in a long time. The map shows that it runs from this point, to a point that is about 80 meters to the rear of the hill our CP is on and to the east side of the rice paddy. Doc being the smallest of us, besides me, is sent down into it with two of Lok's men. (I do not envy them at all, for the tunnels the VC dig are small, dark, and stink like a latrine on a hot day) It should take them about 1 1/2 hrs to come out at the other end.

"Let's pack up and be there when they come out." I say.

The map shows no cross tunnels or forks in the one they went down into so, it should be an easy trip for them. Little did I know what was to come. We make it to the spot on the map and found the trap door that hid the exit. The door is a heavy sheet of steel that looked like it came off a downed bird. It's concealed with vines and branches woven into a mat and in turn covered with dirt and the same ground cover as is in the area. The cover, after being checked for booby traps is lifted open. The stench that came up out of that hole would be enough to gag a maggot. I sent one of Lok's men down to see how far he can see with a light. He came back up and told us that it is about a five-meter drop to the bottom, and then it runs off in a northeasterly direction. This did not coincide with what the map showed but that is nothing to worry about, for none of the VC maps are done to any scale. We drop a flare down to help Doc find the way and sit back to wait. It is getting to be about lunchtime when Lok and his son Twan come over to where we are sitting.

Twan is typical of his people in build, lean and leathery, a compact little man with a reddish brown color, who stands only about chest high to me. He has a friendly, melon-round face accented by dark, discerning eyes, a pug nose, and a disarming smile which shows more gum then teeth. Like his father, Twan exuded a fierce sense of loyalty for his brothers in arms and an uncompromising hatred for his foes. He was born in the village of Ba-Choa, where we are going to help his people fight off the commie hoard.

They are carrying two big baskets each. The closer they come the worse the smell.

Lok asks, "Would you and your men please join us for a bite to eat."

To say no would be an insult so I say, "Ok let's eat."

I don't know how I ever progressed to the point of being able to eat, keep down, and the most amusing part, like this Yard delicacy. Whatever this stuff is or called, it smells like rotten fish, dirty gym socks, and a beer fart all rolled into one. I am to find out later that the smell is from Nuoc-mam, and the people here use it on everything.

"Lok, What do you think will help you overcome the Cong in your area?" I ask.

"You, green hats, teach us to do, we no need ARVN help. We have no problem if left to kill Cong with you. Problem only when Saigon sends ARVN to try to help. ARVN only take rice and things then run away when Cong come. They afraid to fight. We lose more to ARVN then Cong when ARVN here."

Lok's answer is something we have heard from a lot of the village chiefs. It seems that there is more trouble than just between the north and the south. It has now been 2 1/2 hrs since Doc went down into the tunnel.

"Say Lok, will you send two of your men down to see if they can find out what happened to Doc and the others." I ask.

His son jumps up and says he wants to go. I look at Lok, who just smiles. I then tell Twan to take two men and my cricket.

"If you hear someone coming at you, click this twice, if you receive a reply of three clicks, click once, that will be Doc's group.

If that's not the reply or you hear no reply, waste them." Just before he drops down the hole he asks for a torch to light his way.

"With the smell that's coming out of the ground, is it safe to have an open flame down there?" asks John.

Lok answers and says, "That's Cong's light."

It is now back to the same old game, sit and wait. Start to remember the times before the Army, before the killing, before not knowing if life is all it is cracked up to be.

Chapter 6

Istart to think about what will happen to me next, when the train arrived in Uppsala on time and to a large crowd of people waiting for it.

My grandmother pointed out my aunts and uncles as we pulled in. The ride to the house was about a 1/2 hr away and we went right by the street where Brit lived. I asked what was planned for that night. "Nothing except relaxing." was my aunt's answer.

"Do you remember me telling you about the girl I met on the plane? Well, I would like to call her if it is all right with you?"

Aunt Helen asked what her name was. "It is Brit Anderson; I think her father is Henry." Aunt Helen then asked if they lived on Strengness Street.

"Yes they do, I have the address right here. Let's see, its 1256 Strengness. Do you know them?" I said hoping they did and were friends. Aunt Helen told my grandparents that the Anderson family was one of the best families in town and had been in the same house for four generations.

"Are they friends of yours?" Grandpa asked.

"We know one another. I remember about two years ago they lost one of their children in a boating accident and Uncle Paul did the funeral. We had a nice talk then and have been friends since, you could say." Aunt Helen told us.

"So is it alright for me to call her later."

"I don't mind if your grandparents don't." Aunt Helen said.

"Do you mind Grandma?"

"No since Helen and Paul know her parents and think she is from a good family."

Now I could not wait to arrive at their house, but I had to cool my heels until after lunch. The anticipation of that call had me on pins and needles. I could not eat or think. It was right after lunch, I gave Brit a call to see when we could meet. We planned to go to a movie that night. We both asked if it was all right, and were told it would be ok. The time went so slow, it appeared that all the clocks had stopped. As soon as dinner was over I asked if I could go. Grandma said, "Yes" and asked if I needed a ride to the Anderson's?

"No Grandma, Brit asked me to call as soon as we were done. "She will come over for me." I told my Grandmother.

Five minutes after the call to her she was at the front door ready to go. As I was going out the front door I said, "Bye will see you later. Hope not to be too late", and with that we were gone.

"What time do you have to be in?" Brit asked.

"Who knows, they gave me a key and said to have fun."

"We will have a lot of fun and more. OK!"

"Whatever you say, just so long as it does not leave any marks."

I was pleasantly surprised to see that she was driving. As we walked over to the car, Brit asked if I wanted to drive. "No you drive, I don't know my way around and you people drive on the wrong side of the road."

Brit's car was a small Saab. She drove like we were in the middle of a Grand Prix race, but then so did everyone around us. The movies in Sweden are different than in the states. When we went inside the theater, I was shocked by the numerous commercials on contraception and personal hygiene products for both men and woman. The sexually liberated climate of Sweden was a radical change from my past. Then came the main show with the coming attractions after that. The movie we went to see was a very dumb thing about some train robbery and the chase after the robbers. It was in Swedish and had no subtitles. I knew Swedish but did not want her to know that. That way when people talked about me they would not know I understood what they were saying. (You can learn a lot when people do not think you understand) Brit would laugh at something and I would have to ask what was going on. After the movie, we went to a coffee shop.

Once in the coffee shop I asked, "What was all that funny?"

Brit said, "Oh I am sorry I forgot that you don't understand that much Swedish."

Little did she know that Swedish was the first language I learned.

"Well I guess I must make it up to you."

And she did. We spent just about everyday with one another for almost a month. We went for walks around the lake. Took sauna baths and ran out to jump into the lake. Boy was that a shock. Leave the hot sauna covered with perspiration only to jump into a cold lake. We also took out her parent's sailboat and I learned how to sail. Skinny-dipping with Brit was different then with the old gang back in Kentucky. She was all female and not ashamed to show it. Here again I had another chance to grow up even more. We never spent a night with each other, but that was ok.

I also had the chance to go with her and her parents to visit the Saab Factory. Her dad Henry was going to pick up his new Saab. He had a plane so I had a chance to fly in a small aircraft for the first time. Henry asked me if I would like to sit up front with him. Boy did I jump at that. I sat in the left seat and could not believe how much fun it was. I think that is what started me thinking about learning to fly.

When we arrived at the plant, Henry asked. "Can we have a tour of the plant? This young man is from the United States and I would like to have him see how we do things here in Sweden."

The man he asked told us to have a seat in his office and he would check with the plant manager. His secretary came just after he left and asked if we would like some coffee. I said nothing till Henry and the rest said yes. I also would like some. About two minutes later she rolled in a cart with coffee and some small cakes. We helped ourselves to the treats and sat back to relax.

It was about ten minutes later the man Henry asked came in with another man dressed in clean coveralls and a hardhat. "I would like to introduce you to Doctor Ollie Johanson. He is our head of production and he will escort you around the plant."

Henry stood up took his hand and said, "I would like to thank you for this opportunity. We are very happy you are doing this for us."

Doctor Johanson replied. "It is my pleasure to be able to show you and your family around. You say the young man with you is from America?"

Henry says, "Yes he is over here to visit family. His mother was born in Sweden and moved to America as a young girl. I find it interesting your name and her maiden name are the same."

Doctor Johanson turns to me and asks, "Where was you mother born."

I answer saying, "I believe she was born in Strangnas."

Doctor Johanson looks up, tells me that is where his family is from, and asks. "What is your Grandfather's first name?"

I tell him my grandfather is Eric just like me. "He married Greta Olson, had two children Albert and Mybrit. Albert was killed shortly after they moved to America."

Doctor Johanson takes a step back and asks. "Do you know if your Grandfather was in the Swedish Calvary?"

"Yes I do. He tells stories about it and how hard it was in winter."

With very pleased look on his face he steps forward and takes my hand shaking it. He then says. "Welcome to Sweden Cousin Eric. Is your Grandfather still alive?"

"Yes I tell him. "I am in Sweden with my Grandparents."

Doctor Johanson hands me his card and asks if I would please ask my Grandfather to call him. "Yes I will," I say.

We leave the office and are taken to the assembly plant. For the next two hours we are shown every step in the building of a Saab. Then it's on to the test track to be shown how they test the safety and performance of the Saab. I am given a ride around the test track and asked if I would like to drive. Of course I would love too! I came out so fast I was embarrassed. After a couple of laps around the track I parked the car and said thank-you for the ride and test drive.

After the test track we went back to the showroom so Henry could get his car. On the way Brit took my hand and said.

"Eric I did not know you could drive like that. You looked like you have raced sports cars before." I tell her "no I have not. Just driving around the hills in Kentucky."

"Well from now on you drive when we go out". Brit tells me. I tell her I can not because I do not have a valid driving permit for Sweden.

Back in the showroom Henry's new Saab is sitting on the de-livery room floor. It is all polished up, gleaming in the sunlight. As we walk over to look at the car the first man we meet hands Henry the keys to the car and tells him the gas tank is full and ready to go. But first here are some gifts for you. He hands Henry a dark blue canvas bag about the size of a small suitcase.

As this is going on, Doctor Johanson comes over and takes my arm leading me away from the group.

"Eric I have something's to give you. Do not open this till you are home." He tells me as he hands me a large cardboard box. "Also if you would like to come back anytime just call me and I will meet you."

I say "thank-you" shake his hand and return the group stand-ing around the new car. As Henry starts opening the car door on the right side I ask if I can put the box Doctor Johanson gave me in the trunk. Henry looks at me like I am crazy.

Brit speaks, "Father he means the boot."

He hands her the keys and says, "Ok." Brit's mom enters on the left side, while Brit and I get in the back seat. Henry starts the car as two men open the large doors in front of us so we can drive out of the building. We head to the airfield and everyone is excited about the way the new car smells, drives, and looks. I am confused as to how we are going to get the car and airplane back to Uppsala. I do not say anything, as I do not want to look nervous.

At the airport, Henry gets out and tells me to come with him. I do and as we walk toward the plane I look back to see Brit and her Mom getting in the front seat of the car and driving off. Ok so I am to fly back to the Uppsala airport. I would not have said "No" to this arrangement. On the flight back Henry asks me about my home in America, and about what I am going to do in the future. I tell him about my family and what is expected of me. He tells me it is good to follow family tradition. As we are approaching the airport for landing I see the house I am staying in, the lake Brit and I sailed on and swam in. It all looks so different from the air. I think now I have to get up in an airplane in Kentucky to see what our home looks like from the air. Do they give flying lessons at the airport back home? If they do how much will it cost? And how old do you have to be to learn to fly?

After we land Henry drives me back to my Aunts house. As we stop out front he tells me Brit will bring the box over in the morning. He tells me goodnight and that he will see me tomorrow. I tell him how nice it was that he took me along. That I had a great time and how much I enjoyed the trip in the plane.

He then says to me. "No, thank you. If it had not been for you and meeting one of your relatives I would never have able to see that much of the Saab factory or have received the gifts I did. I know that from now on there will be a different greeting whenever I buy a new Saab. That Saab is the fifth new one I have picked up, and I was never treated like that. They do know the people that pickup their cars by flying in by plane. I know this because when I make the arrangements to buy a new Saab they ask if I want to pick it up like last time. Now there will be a note about what happened this time in the file about my buying habits. So thank-you. Eric."

When I went in to the house I told everyone about the day and meeting Doctor Johanson. I gave the card to Grandpa and asked if he knew who he was. Grandpa had a little smile on his face. He then told me. "Yes he did". Also he was happy to get the card as he had lost touch with that side of the family since the death of Doctor Johanson's dad. I then went to bed and fell a sleep very quickly. I have a dream about flying that was very vivid. The only thing was I did not have a plane. I was flying.

The next morning the phone rang and my Aunt answered it. She came into the kitchen and told me it was Brit and she wanted to know when you could meet her.

"Grandma may I go out with Brit today? We will be leaving in two days and I would like to see her."

Grandma tells me "yes I may but I have to be back for dinner, as we will be going out to eat." She then went on to say that I could ask Brit to join us if I like. I was thinking that that was a dumb question. "Yes if she can go I will ask. Thank you." I tell Grandma.

With that said I call Brit and ask if she can go with us tonight. Brit tells me to hold on and puts the phone down. It seen like it takes her forever till she is back on the phone.

"Yes I can go with you. Can you get away now?"

"Yes I can." I tell her. "I will start walking your way, you start my way and we will meet in the middle."

She stops and says, "No you stay there. I will be there shortly. Pack your swimsuit and a nice outfit."

"I do not wear outfits. I am a MAN and MEN do not wear outfits. I will bring along a clean shirt and pants."

"Ok!" Brit answers, "Yes that will be fine."

We head out for a day of sailing, swimming, and time spent

on the lake. About lunchtime, we return to the dock and change into our good duds.

I ask, "Why are we dressed up?"

Brit tells me she has a surprise for me. We drive out of town and around the lake to the Castle. I asked about once when we were on the lake. As we drive up to the front of it I see there is a parking lot with a couple of very expensive cars parked in it. Brit pulls into a parking spot between a Rolls Royce and a Bentley. Her little Saab looks out of place. I get out and go around the car to open her door only to be beat to it by a young man in an Old Swedish costume. He then tells us to follow him to reception. (I wonder what is going on here...) Inside the Castle, a young lady also dressed in costume meets us; she asks if we have a reservation.

Brit tells her. "Yes we do, it is in the name of Henry Anderson."

"Oh! Yes we do have that reservation. Please follow me."

We are led to a very large room with tables set for a meal. I am impressed with this place. It looks just like the Castles you see in movies. Except this is real. Our table is by large windows that overlook the lake. The table is set with large silver plates, crystal glassware, and what looks like way too much silverware for just one meal. Everything here looks like it came straight out of the times of the knights. Or should I say the Vikings.

The meal is like none I have had before. The servers' keep bringing more and more different dishes of all kind of things to eat. As soon as one item is finished they bring something new. There must have been six different settings of things to eat. Plus four different beverages to drink. Before the last setting was presented. That was a setting of several pastries, coffee, brandy, and finally a mint. After this lunch I did not think I could eat for a week. After sitting for a time to relax Brit started to get up and from nowhere an elderly man stepped behind her to help with the very large and heavy chair. I looked behind me only to see someone there to pull my chair out also.

Both Brit and I said, "Tack så mycket.

The two people said, "Varsågod." Brit started to leave and I was moving to take hold of her arm.

As I touch her arm she turned and asks if something was wrong. With a question in my voice I said, "Yes, what about the bill for that great meal?"

"Oh, that. It was taken care of before we arrived for lunch. My Dad ordered this for us as a way to say thank-you for yester-day." Brit answered

"What happened yesterday?" I ask.

"Don't you remember how we were treated at the Saab plant? That only happened because you were with us and my Dad will never forget it. He was so happy he called his partner and just went on and on about you and the treatment we received." Brit answered.

"Stop, it was nothing; I did not do a thing." I answered.

We then drove back to my Aunt's house. When we arrived there Brit said she has to go home and get ready for tonight. I say it is only 2:00 and dinner will not be until 8:00. Brit tells me she knows. My Aunt Laya had called her in the morning and told her.

I ask, "What else did she tell you?" She tells me that I will find out later. "Ok, but I do not like secrets. See you later."

After going in the house, I find my Grandmother and Aunt Laya in the dining room having coffee.

"Grandma, what is going on? Brit tells me she was called and told about tonight."

Aunt Laya tells me. "Don't worry dear it is nothing. It was just the arrangement for tonight. Now why don't you just relax till later?"

I say "Ok" and go to my room. I am happy to be here and able to take and a nap after that meal is just what I need. I fall asleep and do not dream.

There is someone knocking on my door saying, "Eric it's time to get ready. The bathroom is empty and you need to get a move on." With a confused feeling I sit up. On the back of the door is my good suit, a clean freshly pressed shirt and tie. My cowboy boots have been polished and placed by the dresser. A robe is on the bed with a clean towel. So I go to the bathroom and shower, return to my room and for the first time look at the clock to see if I need to dress now. To my surprise it is 7:45. I must have been asleep since 2:30. That is over five hours. Was I that tired? Must have been. After dressing I go down to see what is going on.

Everyone is dressed and having a drink. Brit is sitting on a chair by the table with a cup of coffee. She looks up and says. "Hi sleepy head. Did you have a nice nap?"

"Yes I did, I think." In my head I was thinking it would have been better with you next to me. "Aunt Laya tells me she would like introduce me to meet her son Johan and his wife Becca. They will be going with us tonight." So I have asked Brit if she would mind driving also as our car would be full. After meeting Johan and Becca, we all go out to get in our cars. To my surprise Brit is driving the new Saab. We drive from Uppsala to Stockholm. A distance of about 70 Km and with Brit driving it took just about 50 min.

Once in Stockholm we went to a place called Berns. Berns is a very old restaurant that was just wonderful. As we entered the restaurant and went to the desk to check in. Grandpa told the man at the desk who we were and was told the rest of our party was in the red room and to follow him. At our table we meet Doctor Johanson, his wife Ake and their two sons Adolph and Bjorn. Doctor Johanson stood as we approached the table. With a huge smile on his face he told us how happy he was that we could make it.

Grandpa told him he was glad he had the opportunity to see him and his family again after so long a time and apologized for losing touch with him after his father's death. He then thanked Brit for taking me along on the trip to the Saab Plant. Only to have Doctor Johanson tell Brit thanks also. Brit turned red and said, "you are welcome." Most of the conversation was about what had happened in the lost time. How everyone was doing and just generally about life on both sides of the Atlantic.

After the meal and about two hours of conversation Brit asked if we could be excused to just see Stockholm. We were told we could and to have a good time. Bjorn who lived in Stockholm told us of several places to go and where we should avoid. He also offered to put us up for the night if we did not want to drive back to Uppsala later. Grandpa told us that would be "ok with him and he would let Brit's folk's know where we were." Brit said " thank-you" and that she had already told her folks that she might not be home until tomorrow.

Bjorn gave Brit a key and told her where the house was. He went on to say there were two empty bedrooms on the second floor at the end of the hall. He then winked and said, "Have fun." As we left the restaurant Brit took my hand and smiled telling me she did not have any underwear on under her dress. I laughed and told her I do have underwear on.

We toured Stockholm until four in the morning before going to Bjorn House. Bjorn had a very nice home just on the outskirts of Stockholm. It had a small yard with a lot of plants. The house was warm and inviting.

We had a good sleep and left for Uppsala about noon. The drive back was nice as I had a chance to relax and look at the world around us. We did not talk much as we both knew I would be leaving soon. That was sad. Back in Uppsala Brit dropped me off and told me she would be by for me at about 7:00 and better be ready. I said "ok" and exited the car. There was no one in the house. Everyone was on the back deck so I went out to say "hi." Grandpa asked if I had a good time and told me "thank-you for putting him and in touch with Ollie." I told him that was "ok" and I was glad I could do it. I ask if it was all right if Brit and I went out tonight. I was told yes. I then went upstairs and fell on to the bed. Sleep was on me before I could undress. All I took off was my boots.

At 6:00 I awoke and changed my clothes and went down to the kitchen for something to drink. There was a note on the ice-box telling me the rest had gone out and would not be back till late. To have good time and remember we would be leaving for Stockholm in the morning. At precisely 7:00 Brit came in and asked if I was ready. I said "yes" and asked if I was dress properly for what she had in mind. Her answer surprises me. Her answer was it would be better if I was naked but that I had on for now would do. WHAT DID SHE HAVE IN MIND??

We started out by going to a coffee shop for two cups of coffee to go, some small cakes and a large bag of cookies. We then went out to the end of a fishing dock and sat on the edge of the pier. We talked, drank coffee, ate the cakes and shot wooden matches into the water. It was arranged that the next time she came to America we would meet up. I told her if I get back to Sweden after college we would meet again. (Little did I know we would both be married by the next time we would meet) We did other things that night and we were both very sad when Brit dropped me off at my Aunts.

When it came time to take my grandparents to the airport I did not want to leave Uppsala or Brit. On the way to Stockholm I almost asked if I could stay in Uppsala till I had to board on the boat. As I sat there in the back seat it came to mind that Anna was in Stockholm waiting for me, or at least I hoped she was. I had told Brit that I would ask if I could return to Uppsala with my aunt and uncle and leave for Goteborg from there. A plan was set in my mind that if Anna was not in Stockholm and I was stood up I would call Brit and have her come retrieve me. Brit had already asked her parents if I could stay with them till my boat left and she would drive me down to set sail for America. They told us that they would love to have me stay. But if I was not able to, I was welcome to come back next year and spend the summer with them.

We arrived at the airport and went straight to the gate that was for their flight. It was about a 20-minute wait till they had to board the flight, so I went and called Anna. There was no answer at her house. So the next call went to her office number. No answer at her office number also. Is this getting stood up? Went through my head. I returned to the family group, sat down and tried to become involved with what was going on.

My grandmother was talking to my aunt saying, "I think it would be a good idea to have Eric live in Sweden and go to school over here.

"New York has street gangs and he could become a gang member. Be into some of that evil and turn bad. The back woods living in Kentucky could cause him to become like his father."

I do not know what they are saying about my Dad but looking back now I am so glad the movie Deliverance had not come out yet. I looked around to see which aunt and uncle she was talking to. There were four aunts and uncles sitting around at that time and I wondered which one would it be. It would be nice to stay, but I have a lot of friends in New York, and I love Kentucky. The open air, the woods, and the way of life of the south. What would I have here in Sweden? SEX. That is not what life is all about.

Grandma said, "We can't do it now, your mother and father have not been asked." That is good because I do not want to stay here indefinitely, went through my mind.

"Grandma, I have things I need to do back In Kentucky. My Papaw needs me back on the Plantation. Let's talk about this when we are all together back in the states. OK?"

The speaker came to life and told us that Flight 237 to New York would be leaving an hour late. As we sat there I was just half listening to what was now being said and was thinking about Brit and Anna. I asked to be excused and went to call Anna again. There was still no answer at her home or office. I have obviously been stood up went through my mind. The gift shop was open so in I went to look around for something to give to my grandmother to take to my parents from me. It would be at least another two and 1/2 weeks before my boat docked in New York. After finding something for Mom and Dad I went to use the phone one more time. There still is no answer. I said good-by to my grandparents and stood at the window to watch the plane takeoff. We were to go to lunch next and that would give me time to try one more time to call Anna. If she weren't home or at her office this time I would ask to go back to Uppsala.

My aunts and uncles said that they would be in the restaurant in the main terminal building. I said "Ok, and that I would be there after the plane was airborne" and I made a phone call. A feeling of sadness came over me as I watched their plane leave. I don't know if it was just because they were leaving or because of not getting a hold of Anna. As I turned around to go the restaurant, after trying to call Anna one more time, there she stood in all her loveliness. Boy was I happy then. Anna said that she was worried that she might be too late. There was a hint of sadness in her voice that she might have missed me at the airport. She tells me, her flight back from France had just arrived late and she ran all the way over in hopes I would still be here. I said that I did not remember telling her what flight they were on.

Anna told me with a big smile "No you did not; you only told me that they were leaving on the 29th of September, and you would call after they left."

"So how did you know?" was my reply.

"I looked it up in one of the books at my office and saw that there were only two flights to New York today, one now and one at 11:00 tonight." She said sheepishly.

Ok what is it that has changed me? I think to myself. For the first time in my life I have two women thinking about me. Or at least that I know about. Not only two women, but also two gorgeous ones. What happened? I am just this country boy from Appalachia. Yes I spent some summers in New York but not with the upper crust. I am nothing special. Can life back home be the same? Will the girls look different to me now? I hope not.

"Ok, now what do we do from here? How do I extract myself away from my Aunts and Uncles? What do you suggest Anna?"

Her face took on a look of question and she said "Let's just go tell them I am going to show you around the city."

My reply was "How do I explain you?"

Anna handed me a card that introduced her as a member of the Swedish Tourist board and said. "If you give them this card and tell them we met on the train between Lapland and Uppsala. Then tell them that at that time you asked me to show you around after your grandparents left and it was me you called."

"All right, I think that will work, thanks for the help." I quipped as we walked to the restaurant to face my relatives.

The restaurant was one of those places you only find in Europe. It had mirrors on the ceiling and the back wall. There was a large fountain in the middle of the room with small tables around it. The front or long side of the room was one big window looking out over the runways with the sea behind it. The place had a sense of space and openness about it. The floor was marble or polished stone and had no floor coverings so the place was noisy. In looking around, I found them sitting at one of the few tables that sat more than four people. When we arrived at the table, I introduced Anna to each person seated at the table. While I was doing the introductions the bus boy put another chair at the table.

This was the second most uncomfortable chair I ever sat on.

They were made of wire with a very small pad for a seat. We had lunch of pickled herring and other sick stuff, I did not eat much. I had asked for a hamburger thinking this is an airport and they should have food a tourist would like. But no they did not. We talked about the things Anna should show me and what was around to do. After we excused ourselves to leave, my Aunt Helen, who lived in Stockholm, handed me a key to their house and gave Anna the address. She also told me what bedroom I was to have and where to find it, as they would probably be asleep when I came in. Little did I know that when we went to Goteborg a week later I would have spent the best week of my life to that point seeing the town by day and having a ball by night. This woman taught me about being a man in more ways then one and spoiled me for the women that were to follow back in the states. She treated me like a King and it was easy to give her pleasure. We spent a lot of time just being with one another, not talking or doing anything except being with one another. As I boarded the boat a week later I wanted to cry, but held it in for a man is not to cry. We were to meet again next spring when Anna was to be in New York for a convention.

The boat ride back to the states started out real slow for me because my mind was back in Sweden with Brit or Anna most of the time. The people who run the boat for the Swedish American Lines worked hard to keep you entertained. They had movies, card games, skeet shooting and a lot more. All this was going on around me, while my mind was sad for leaving a good life behind and looking ahead to going back to the streets of the city. The second day out we ran straight into a hurricane. At breakfast that day, there were only about 100 in the dining room that had held about 600 the day before. The food was plentiful and I ate too much. After breakfast I went to the captain and asked if I could come up to the bridge and take some pictures out the front windows. The captain said, "fine so long as I stay out of the way." As I stood looking out the front windows. The sea covered the bow to a point halfway between the bow and where I stood. Then in the next minute the only thing you could see beyond the bow was sky. The ship would take a nosedive and then stand up on it stern and every time the bow went down, the stern would come up out of the water with the ship's propellers running wild. The man at the wheel was fighting to keep the nose of the ship straight into the wind, so as not to roll the ship over. There was also a man at the thing that controls the speed of the ship and when the bow went down he would signal to the engine room to cut power. Then the bow would go up he signaled for power to climb the wave in front of us.

I did not stay long on the bridge, for I did not want to be in the way. On the way back down to the main bar there were about six kids my age sitting by one of the TV's that were on the ship. I stopped to talk to them and see what they were up to. That started a group friendship that would last till we docked in New York. At lunch and dinner that day there were only about 30 people, so us kids all sat at one table and joked with the people serving the food. We had a Dining Room Steward (Peter) that was one of the good guys that would bring us all kinds of treats that were left over because of so few people were eating. We partied for the next seven days. I became a good friend with a Danish girl named Ingrid and several other people on that trip. Ingrid was a very good-looking girl, short blond hair and the prettiest gold colored eyes I have ever seen. The last night out we had a party to end the trip. The Wine Steward, who's name I can not remember, served ten bottles of Asti Spumante to the seven of us and at midnight we all put or names and addresses on slips of paper and put them into all the empty bottles to throw overboard.

It is a very somber service when you throw the bottles overboard, one by one to the God of the Sea. You ask Poseidon (the God of the Sea) to see to it that the bottles reach shore for someone to find and send each of us a note to tell us where they were found.

The next morning we docked in New York. This was supposed to be a happy time but for me it was a sad time. For the first time in my life I spent a summer looking at the opposite sex as if they were opposite. I looked at girls differently, more then just one of the gang. Would this carryover when I was back in Kentucky. Could I still go skinny-dipping with them? Little did I know?

I asked, "When are we going home?' My mother then informed me that we would be going home to our new home in the morning.

I asked "Why?"

Dad spoke up and told me about his job and the move to Lansdale, Pa. And they wanted me to see the new house and town. My father had left the Navy, and taken a job in a small town outside Philly (Philadelphia). As I discovered later, it was one of those typical small towns trying to be a big town without the history. And now I would be spending my summer going to a place full of Yankees. Not even the good kind of Yankees you find in New York City. In this new town, if you could put more then two words together in a sentence, you were a genius.

I could not sleep that night. My mind was full of all types of things. One was that I would not have the chance to say good-bye to the gang in New York. Another was that Anna was to be in New York next spring. Ingrid lived in the Bronx and I could be there in thirty minutes from where we had lived. Summers were not going to be the same. Unless I could talk Mom and Dad into letting me spend some of my summer time with Grandma and Grandpa in New York.

In the morning, I asked if I could have one day to say good-bye to all my friends in the city. Mom told me "yes but I had to be back at Grandmas by 4:00 so we could arrive in Lansdale before it was too late in the day." I spent what was the hardest day I ever had in my life up to that point. The gang was sad, but being the guys they were not one of them broke down. I was told that I was, and always would be, one of them. Whenever I returned to the city, all I had to do was just look them up. The last person I went to see before leaving was Ingrid. At her house we sat and talked for most of the afternoon. She told me that the next time I come to see my grandparents, I had to see her. She told me that we could write or talk on the phone. If need be I could call collect. I said I would ask if she could come down to Kentucky to visit. I did not have the heart to tell her about our backwoods phone system and how everyone in town and for a good ways around would be on their phone listening in.

The afternoon went by so fast that it was 3:30 before I knew it. I had to call my mom, because to travel from the Bronx to Long Island where my grandparents live would take over an hour with two subway changes. Mom understood and told me to give the directions to my Dad for Ingrid's house and they would pick me up there, seeing how close she lived to the George Washington Bridge, and that was the way we would be going to Lansdale. After I told Dad the directions to Ingrid's we went to her room till my parents were due to pick me up. It was in her room, that day, that I had my introductions to the best of the Danish Delights.

The trip to Lansdale was a long one. It seemed like that trip took longer then it did to fly to Sweden.

We spanned the George Washington Bridge, drove across New Jersey, around Philadelphia, only to head north on the PA. Turnpike in to what looked like oblivion. As we turned off the PA. Turnpike and started to drive to the house, I could not believe my eyes. There were people dressed all in black driving horse drawn wagons. There were also nice looking farms but they had no power lines or telephone lines going to house or barn. So this was supposed to be the affluent North?

I asked about what I saw and was told those were Amish people. They do not believe in electricity or any of the modern conveniences. I spent the longest week of my life in that town. It was depressing and boring. For a town its size it had less to do then a town one quarter its size down home in KY. The people were not friendly. No one said "Hi" as you passed on the street. In the shops the clerks would look the other way rather then offer a hand of help, the people taking your money acted like they were doing you a favor. If you were to say anything to someone they would look at you as if to kill. Not everyone is that way but you are hard pressed to find the ones that are not

On Saturday the five us drive to Philadelphia for my flight to Kentucky. By now Kentucky was my home and where I wanted to be. I had to work hard to finish High School. Not to mention all the interviews, the tests and the exams it would take to pass in order to go the Academy.

This was to be My Senior Year. Lots of work and studying. Back home in Kentucky I found that things had not changed.

It was still the same slow, easy pace it had always been. Skinny-dipping made no difference. The girls still held no interest sexually. Not that they were unattractive, just they were themselves. I had to study a lot and have my self-ready for what was to come. September till November was time for the crops and horses.

December and January were spent getting all the paper work done to go on to the rest of my life. Late January I found out that our class as invited to graduate with the big school Corbin. They had a class of over 700 and invited our school to join in. I did not want to do that. We took a vote in school and by one vote we were to graduate with them. Boy was I happy to find out I had to be someplace other then here for that. The down side was we were also invited to take part in their Prom. Which to my dismay I would be home for. My first thought was to invite Ingrid to the Prom. After driving to Corbin, which had a regular phone system without party lines, I called Ingrid only to find out she and her family had returned to Denmark for the winter.

In February, with my birthday money I purchased a 1960 Austin Healey Sprite and had a ball with it. I loved that car and wanted to have some fun with it. It was not the type of car you would use for "running shine." So I looked for something to do with it. I found there were sports car clubs for people with them. I went to a meeting, and found they have events just for this type of car. The first sports car event I took part in was a Rally. Sports Car Rallies are a timed event. At the start they give you a list of instructions called clues. The clues were like, turn left after the red barn, or take the left at the fork in the road. While you are trying to follow the instructions you are also told that your speed limit is 26 mph for so far and then change to 42 mph for so long or some other speed. It is not easy and if you lost you way you would have to make up the lost time, so you speed. To do it right it takes two people. One to drive and look for the clues and another person to do the navigation as to speed and distance while also looking for clues. I have to have someone to navigate for me so I ask the only person good with math and reading. He is an old friend by the name of Joe. His nickname is Moon. We call him Moon because he looks like a Moon, he is as tall as big around, and his choice of fun things to do is moon people from the back seat of his family car.

I remember one summer several years before then the four guys from school were out for some fun. We had Bo's Jeep with the top off and were roping outhouses. There were and still are a lot of outhouses still in use in the hills. We had roped and pulled over several. Till this one time the rope became stuck when the outhouse fell over. Moon jumped out, ran back to release it.

Just as Moon had the rope loose to the outhouse, the old hillbilly that lived there came out his back door with a shotgun. He fired into the air to scare us off. It worked and Moon started to run but ran the wrong way. In his attempt to return back to the jeep Moon ran right in to the open hole the outhouse sat over. Splash. The old hillbilly put his arms in the air turned laughing and went back into the shack he called home. I went to the stinking hole and looked down at Moon. He was clawing at the wall of the hole trying to climb out.

When he saw me he said, "Please throw me the rope." I undid the rope and sent one end down to him.

The other end being tied to the Jeep. We pulled him out. He was covered in a very thick, reeking goo. There was no way we would let Moon back in the Jeep so we made Moon walk to the river to wash off.

February to May went quick. There were a couple of Sports Car Rallies. Two races around road cones in a big parking lot. I was still too young to apply for a license to race so that was the extent of what I could do. I also attended the meetings for the SCCA (Sports Car Club of America) it was at one of the SCCA meeting I was introduced to Rita. Rita was a very attractive girl from Corbin. She was in the class from Corbin that was to share their Prom and Graduation. When she found out I was in that class she asked me to the Prom. Man what is this? What is happening? I said "ok" only to be nice and to see what all the hoopla about a Prom was over. We did a couple of rallies before the Prom. Had dinner at the SCCA meeting but nothing more.

The night of the Prom was coming and I was not happy to find out I had to be in a monkey suit. Papaw tells me I need to have flowers for my date. DATE!! This is a date??? When did it become a date? Papaw tells me the minute I said "yes to Rita to go with her."

"Ok so where do I obtain the flowers? Can I pick them from out front of the house?

At this point Mamaw steps in and says "NO! You need to find out what color her dress is and then go down to your Uncle Ken and have him make up an arrangement for you. Call Rita and ask what color her dress is and if she want a pin on or strap flower thing."

Man this is a lot more then I asked for. Is there anyway I can extract myself from this? Is there anything else I should know about this date thing? Mamaw tells me that the Prom is second only to the wedding for a lady. It is very important day in the life of a young lady. I had to be a true Southern Gentleman with her.

Open doors for her and ask if she needs or would like anything. But above you have to dance with her. Do not leave her alone. Make her think she is all there is for the evening.

All goes well till after the Prom. Her friends are having an after the prom party and she want to go. Little did I know that beer, booze, boats, and a lot of so called fun was to be involved. I am driving down to Norris, TN as she is stripping out of her gown from the Prom. There is not much room in a sports car but she makes it. Rita is down to the suit she came in to the world in. Trying to put her body into a pair of jeans and tee shirt. After she is dressed she tells me to pull over and she will drive so I can change. I look at her with a look of question on my face.

Rita asks, "Did you not bring a change of clothes?"

"No, I did not, no one told me I needed to."

Rita then asks if I have underwear. "Yes I do." I answer. Her next question is a real strange one.

"Are they Boxer or briefs?"

"I am in Boxers."

"Good then you will be ok just take off your shirt and pants when we get there."

As we round the last corner before the lakeside cabin that belongs to Rita's Uncle. A cop car goes by a high rate of speed. He has every light on and the siren going full blast. I look at Rita to see a look of fear and concern. We pull into the driveway and park in front of the garage. With a slight sound of worry Rita takes my hand and pulls me toward the front door of the cabin. Out of her jeans pocket she pulls a key and opens the door. The cabin is dark as we enter.

She reaches for a light only to hear "Don't turn the lights on."

"Rita is that you" is the voice that sounds like it is coming from no where and everywhere at the sometimes.

I ask. "Ok what is going on?" The voice comes back the police are raiding an after Prom Party at Donnelley's place. They have cars on the road, boats on the water and there was a plane overhead not long ago. "How did you get here without being stopped?" The voice asked.

"I came down the old shine road." I answered.

"Rita, go open the garage and have your date put the car inside."

After we had put the car in the garage and closed the door I looked outside and down the road. Just around the next bend you could see flashing light from a large number of police cars. Upon returning to the house I was met by a man about 25 years old. Tall, good looking, clean-shaven and with a nice pair of jeans on. Rita introduces me to her cousin from Atlanta. He had come up for the summer to visit. He told us about what was going on around the corner.

It seems the party had started with a bonfire and about 50 kids racing around the lake when one of them ran into the dock next door to the party house. The people that owned the dock had called the police and an ambulance for the three people in the boat. He did not know who the people in the boat were but they were taken away in the ambulance some time ago. Nate, Rita's cousin had counted over 15 cops speeding down the road. They had been there for over an hour when five left only to return about an hour later. The couple on the other side of the party had called him about 30 min. before we came in. They told him the police were going door to door asking question and check to see if anyone was trying to hide from them.

Nate then told me to go upstairs to the second room on the

right and change into some jeans and a tee shirt. I asked "why?" "Because they may come here and you do not want them to see you dressed as if you were just coming from the Prom. It could cause trouble."

I said, "Thanks I do not need that now. I am due to leave for the Academy in a short time."

Rita looks at me and asks. "The Academy? What Academy are you going to?"

"West Point." I tell her. Both Rita and Nate look at each other and then back at me with a look of surprise and shock.

There is then a knock at the door. Nate opens the door to find three policemen standing there. They ask if then can come in. Nate tells them "yes come in." The first asks if anyone other then the three of us are in the house? Nate tells him no.

He them asks, "What are we doing here?" Rita tells him "we are here to say goodbye to Eric pointing at me. He is leaving for West Point Military Academy in a few days and we wanted to have a little time to say goodbye." The cop then asks how long we have been in the house.

Both Nate and Rita say for sometime "The cabin belongs to Tom Evens, my uncle and we have his permission to be here. Would you like to call him? I have his number right here."

"That will not be needed as we have a list of the owner and it checks. Do any of you know what was going on down the road?" said the cop.

Nate answers "no," "but I was wondering what had happened? A lot of police cars have gone by. I think I also saw an ambulance."

The cop tells him. There was a Prom Party that got out of hand. A boat was wrecked and three people had to be taken to the hospital. One boy may not make it the other boy and the girl was thrown out and has minor injuries. They will be all right.

I could tell Rita wanted to ask who they were so I spoke up quickly and said that is a shame taking Rita's hand to keep her quiet. The cops ask if we had been drinking. Again, I spoke up and told him "Rita and I were underage and did not drink. Nate told the cop he had a beer or two but was not driving till morning."

One of the cops came over close to Rita and me. I knew he wanted to smell us to see if he could tell we had been drinking. My luck was with me. I knew we had not so I did not step back and let him get very close to us. I did not say anything just let him check for himself. He put out his hand as he got close and took my hand and gave it a shake. He then told me congratulations for getting in the Military Academy turned and the two of them left the cabin.

As they were going back to their car, I followed them and asked, "If it would be safe to leave in the morning, " I was told, "Yes, to stay in the cabin till then, and to have a good evening." As I turned to return to the cabin. I hear one tell the other we need more good kids like that. Little did they know?

We spent most of the night sitting on the deck over looking the lake and talked. Nothing in particular, just about life and what we were going to do later in life. Early the next morning I returned home leaving Rita with Nate. I did not go to the graduation. But spent the little time I had left cleaning up the loose ends of my life in Kentucky. Saying goodbye to my friends and family. I also stopped by the schoolhouse for one last look and to thank my teachers.

That summer I had to report to college. My grandfather went with me, as he was an alumnus of the Academy. I would have to leave my prized possession (my car) at home with them as I would have no free time to use it.

The next four years were long and hard. Lots of class work, marching, discipline, and physical training. The one bright spot was the spring and fall mixers, as they were known. At that time the Academy was an all-male school. Therefore, they would hold these get-togethers where the young ladies from a nearby all-girls school would come over for a dance.

In the fall of my first year, I met Debbie. We were told not to spend our time with just one girl. But for some reason Debbie and I hit it off. We would dance with each other. Follow the rules and move on to dance with someone else only to return back together for another dance. Then the spring mixer the next year we meet as planned. This time was the same except she slipped me a note with her name and address both at school and home. This started a letter writing romance that lasted four years. This was punctuated by our semi-annual meeting at the mixers. In my last year at the Academy I asked her to be my bride. We were married two weeks after graduation. It was a very special wedding. A full military wedding held in the Chapel at the Academy. My parents, both sets of grandparents and two brothers came to the wedding. Her folks were there too. It was even better since my Dad being a Naval Academy grad came to what he called the "enemy territory." Debbie had graduated the year before and was now in Medical School.

Having a 30-day leave we went to Barbados for our honeymoon. Upon our return, it was time for me to start my flight training, which I had signed up for thinking it would be fun. I knew I would be going to Viet Nam and being in a flight unit would give me a clean bed to sleep in plus three square meals a day. I'm assigned to Fort Walters, TX for primary Helicopter Training. Debbie was pregnant and stayed behind to finish her studies. After Primary Flight I was sent to advance flight at Hunter-Stewart Ga. where I learned to fly the UH1B "skid" and the AH1A "Cobra" Helicopters.

In March I was told I have a daughter. I am also told that mother and daughter doing well. We named her Ingrid. Debbie did know about the girl I met on the return trip from Sweden. Debbie and my mom were the best of friends so a Swedish name was a nice idea, besides Debbie liked the name.

Chapter 7

Just before receiving my wings in May, I found out that a Chopper pilot in Nam does not live too long, this is second only in short life span to a door gunner. I looked around at what the Army had to offer that would help me live longer. I found out that was Special Forces. The longest life was with the best. The fifty-one week training you go through gives you a lot of skill to stay alive.

I signed up and was given a thirty day leave before having to report for Special Forces Training. Since I had taken Parachute training in my second summer at the Academy that was out of the way. I had a good time at home with Debbie and our daughter Ingrid. My wife had never been to Kentucky so we take a week and go south. It being late May early June the weather was perfect for being outdoors. Debbie being a city gal had never been on a Plantation or for that matter seen the wilderness as it was around our place. She was surprised at how much there was to see. A little put back by the wilderness way of life. Her family had servants but not like the ones that worked for us. The pickers were in the field picking the tobacco leaves. She did not know how much work went into being a tobacco farmer. I had to explain to her about the different types of tobacco and that we grew the kind that had to be picked leaf by leaf as they matured. Not the type that was grown to maturity, chopped, dried and shipped to make cigarettes. Ours was for cigars. Our small town was another. Debbie thought it was a museum of some kind. She told me it looked like we had stepped back in time. As we drive north up the back roads. The mountains, the people and the vast open spaces take us back to a time when this was a new country and how life has changed.

One very sad morning Debbie takes me to the airport on her way to the hospital. So off I go to start a new facet of my life. Fort Benning is a hot, humid, and dusty place. The barracks are old and creak with every little breeze. There are 500 men packed in the buildings. There is no air conditioning to cool you at night or during the day. Not that we had a whole lot of time in the barracks. The first month was hell. Up at 0400, breakfast at 0500, and inspection of the barracks and you at 0530. Then run in formation to the PT field for an hour of hard exercise. Then run in formation to the classroom for instruction. After class run in formation to the company area for instruction on the rest of the day, dismissed for 30 minutes to use the latrine and wash for lunch. Back to the company area to form up to run to the mess hall for lunch. Boy this sure reminds me of the Academy. The only difference is here we run and run. We do not march or walk only run. By my second month I was used to it. It was not so bad. As the third month starts I receive a letter from Debbie telling me she is with child. I do not tell anyone of this, as it is hard enough to keep your mind on what is expected of you without that distraction going around.

At morning formation in last February of 1967, the First Sergeant informs the 457 men assembled that I am, as of early this morning the father of a baby boy. He tells me to stay and dismisses the group to morning cleanup. After everyone is gone I am told to follow him into the office. Now what did I do wrong goes through my head as I'm following him into the office. As I enter the front part of the office the company commander walks up to me to congratulate me.

He starts with, "We had a phone call from West Point at 0330 this morning to inform this command of birth of your son. Mom and baby were doing fine. I went over you record after hearing the news. I did not know you were a West Point Grad, or that you are also a Helicopter Pilot. This week is when we pick the team leaders for the 12 man A-teams. I do not want you to volunteer for that." (Volunteer went through my mind. I learned a long time ago not to volunteer for anything in a situation like this)

"The last three months of your training will be mostly field-work. Of the 500 men that started this class, you and 24 others are all that are left. That gives me two A-teams with one man leftover. I would like you to be the B-team leader. In that capacity you will be in the field with both teams coordinating them. It is a harder position to handle. I know you can do it. Your record with us is exemplary, above reproach. Will you accept this position?"

"Sir if I may ask, what effect will this have on team ` after graduation?"

The Colonels reply, "It will have no effect on the assignments. What it will do is put you in line for a promotion. You will graduate with the rank of Captain. The team assignment will be made on a basis of M.O.S and need of the service. If you except, you will work closely with the people in this office and have the experience of group command. Not to mention the add skill of administration. We have found that the only way to receiving any promotions above Colonel you need to have spent time in Administration. For some reason beyond me the regular army brass look for admin skills in the ranks of General. That is if you plan to stay that long. What is your answer?"

"Yes sir, I will accept the position. But I must inform you my spelling skills are poorly lacking. I had to have someone check everything that I was required to write at the Academy." I answered.

"Good, we will inform the command center and make the announcement at tomorrow mornings formation. I will have the First Sergeant check your work and help you improve those skills." I chuckle to myself, thinking so many have tried to do just but to no avail.

"You are to say nothing to anyone about this. Do you understand?"

"Yes Sir, I do Sir."

The Colonel then tells me to go into his office and the First Sergeant will put a call through to the hospital at West Point so I may speak to my wife. I am also told that I am to be dismissed from the first morning class and the instructor for that class will give me the notes so I may keep up the good work I have been doing.

"Thank-you sir." I say with a salute and turn to his office to await the call to Debbie.

In the next three weeks I am worked to exhaustion. Lots of fieldwork. Testing on all of our training. With two weeks to go we are now down to 20 men to graduate. It is now the time to meet our teammates. Sign the documents pertaining to the clear-ances we are given. It is like signing your life away all over again. To break any of the rules, to say anything you are told not to say is to face a court-martial as a traitor to the country. After being give my Green Beret and Orders it is home to my now one larger family for 30 days.

I knew I was going to Viet Nam and would be gone 2 years. So I tried to make the most of this time without giving Debbie too much to worry about. The news was all about how the war was going and that we were having high counts of American death. Just before being shipped out to the Nam I told my family I would be back. I had a great time with my daughter, new son we named Eric Charles Howard the IV and my wife. It was SO good as a matter of fact, that when I left for the Nam, Debbie was with child again.

Thud. It is more the ground moving then anything else that has me back in Nam. I look up. Not that I believe in God as much as I know there is a God, and think what harm can it do and it may do some good, and say "thanks." Thanks for snapping me back from thinking about my wife, children and the one that was born while I was here. I love them, but cannot spend time with them just yet as I have a job to do. I do hope to be able to return home in one piece and spend time with her and see the new boy we named Eric Frances Howard the III. A second thud shook the ground and we all run to the tunnel mouth to see what is going on. I knew it was from the tunnel because there is no smoke or dirt flying around above ground.

Looking down into what appears to be an open grave we are intent on listening for any sounds of life. The only sound that can be heard is the sound of running water.

Veto looks up and says." Do you think they set off a frag and dropped the river bed down on themselves?"

"I hope not. Let's take a look." With that said, I slide down the hole only to hit the bottom and not be able to move into the tunnel, because Twan and his men coming back block the way.

Upon climbing out I say, "What is going on down in that sewer?" With great fear in his eyes, Twan says that they had gone in about fifty meters to a long slope. After the slope, the tunnel ran a ways back till it opened into a large open room with several smaller rooms off it. The large room was full with about a ton of ammunition and enough stuff to supply a Division of NVA.

"What about Doc and the people who were with him? Did you see them? What was the explosion?" I want answers and I want them now.

Twan looked up at me and said "I see someone light fuse on ammunition and run to other side. I not know who it is."

"If that was Doc, could he have made it back to the other end? I am going to go back to Florida to see if Doc comes out that end. Twan, you and your people stay here with Phil, Mike and Roy. John, you and Veto come with me."

John besides being my RTO is also a medic. I want him with me in case someone is wounded. As we start out to cross the sand strip back to Florida. I yell, "Someone is coming up from the tunnel. See him John?" I ask.

"Yes and that is not one of our men."

We open up. Between the three of us stitching slugs across his chest, we cut the gook in half. Veto bends over and takes an ear. Down the hole I go, only to find it so dark I can't see a hand in front of my face. I turn back to the opening and yell up to John.

"John drop me a flare."

With a white flare in front of me, I am one good target for Charlie. Turning in the direction of the large room, I see that the tunnel goes down at a slight grade of about ten Degrees. John comes down behind me, only to grab hold of me.

"The floor is nothing but mud John, so watch your step and don't walk too close." I say.

There is now two of us moving down in this black hole. Quiet is all around us. The only sound I hear is my own heartbeat and my breathing. "John can you hear my heartbeat?"

"No way, all I can hear is my own."

"Listen! Sounds like someone coming at us from the front."

With that, John turns to the entrance and signals Veto to stay put, Charlie is coming. I did aside step into what looks like a small cave cut in the sidewall of the tunnel. This must have been a guard post at one time. There is a wooden seat built in the back wall and a shelf cut out of the right sidewall. On the shelf is a crude wooden bowl. Also a cup made from an old c-rat can.

"These dinks will use anything we throw away." John states. He then goes on to say that he only hopes it was a throw away and not one that was taken from a dead GI. The floor is nothing but mud, mud about four to six inches deep, so I stuck the flare in the mud to hide the light.

First one VC then another go by on the dead run. I look for John, but in the darkness of the tunnel, I cannot see him. I reached out for him only to find he is not there. My first thought is that he went after them. But no he would have let me know. Just then a flare comes to life from back down the tunnel. I look up only to see John standing over the last of the two VC, with the VC's head in his hand and the rest of him on the floor with blood pumping from the severed neck. He has used a garret to take off the Cong's head without making a sound.

We would now have to fight if anyone were to be following his comrades. I say this because there is no place to hide the body. John and I look at one another, because we can see a light coming up the tunnel. It is coming from the same direction the VC came from. With the sound and light of approaching people, I go back into my hiding place. John takes the VC and sits him up, putting his head back in place. With the VC sitting up, John lays down behind him so as to be hidden from view.

We are ready to take out whomever it is coming up out of the tunnel. As the light becomes closer we take up firing positions with our weapons on semi-auto. With the weapon on semi-auto the use of ammo would be less. The light is close now just around a bend in the tunnel.

As the person with the light is just about to step into the line of fire a voice comes to my ear and I scream to John " DON'T FIRE IT'S DOC."

As Doc comes closer to us, we could see that he has a look of both fear and anger on his face. For me to see a look of fear in his face meant something was very wrong. As a SOG team we have been through a lot, seen a lot and done a lot.

"Doc, what is back down there? Is it that bad?"

"Well Sir, it is like this, there is enough stuff back there to keep the U.S. Army in supplies for the next year. There is food, ammo, uniforms, medical supplies and heavy weapons to keep this situation hot for a long time. On top of that there must be 100 or more bodies in neat piles off in what looks like a torture room. It looks like a scene from one of those camps the Germans had in W.W.II to rid themselves of the Jews." To hear

Doc talk like this surprises me.

Doc, on a mission before, had to work medical miracles to put several local people who had been tortured by the N.V.A. I say back together in literal terms and for some there was nothing, nothing he could do except make their last few minutes on earth as painless as possible. There were small children and young women. One young woman about 12 years old had been staked to the ground spread eagle. Then raped by 40 VC in front of her mother. After being raped they put bamboo sticks up both her lower openings and then one down her throat. The mother was then staked out and every bone in her body broken one at a time. In Doc's eye is just the start of a tear. It must have been real bad back down that tunnel.

"Let's go take a look at what is down that way, and what we will need to destroy it." I say to Veto, who has now joined us.

As we arrive at the area of the supplies, I am overwhelmed. First by the sight of all the supplies and second by the smell of death that hangs in the air like a great cloud. Not only is there a smell, but also a presence of death. Almost like the torture and death that had taken place here had taken on a life of its own. With a sense of urgency we retrace our steps to where we entered this world of death and disfigurement.

Once back on the surface Veto and I sit down and put together what we need to render useless all that is down in that huge tunnel system.

"If all that goes off at once we had better be well out of this area." Veto states with such calm that the Yards have no idea what we found under where we are sitting. I place a call to Roy to bring Lok over here. I tell him to leave.

If Lok had seen the atrocities we saw. He would have placed

fifty of his men there to watch over that end of the tunnel. Then Lok would have taken off his brother's head in front of all of his brothers' family. It's that old face thing that these people have, or maybe just maybe his brother is a VC. It would not be the first time or the last time that a family member turned.

John says "We should we tell Lok about what we found."

"You might be right, tell him to find his brother and meet us at the tunnel entrance." I say, as Veto and I pack up and move out to the mouth of the tunnel.

Lok and this guy came over to us just as we are about to enter the tunnel. The guy with Lok looks real scared. The closer to the tunnel they move the more the guy looks like he is going to run. Dou and John walk up to them and stand on either side of the new guy.

Veto and I walk over and Lok says, "This is my brother, Yep."

Yep looks nothing like his brother. This man looks like he has not worked a day in his life. His hands are like that of a fine lady, soft and without a mark on them. His face is round and full. He looks to be as round as he is tall with short fat legs that do not carry his weight well. His feet look out of place. They look like they are too small for him. He waddles and must stop often to catch his breath.

Doc walks up and starts to tell Lok about what we found in the tunnel system. The more Doc tells Lok, the madder Lok becomes. At one point Lok takes hold of Yep and screams something at him. He screams so fast that we cannot understand much of what he is saying. The only thing that makes any sense is when he calls Yep a VC. Lok asks if he and Yep can go down and see what we have found.

"Yes, you can, but we are going to plant explosives to destroy all that is down there." I tell him.

As we walk away, Doc asks if Lok was told about the bodies in that torture chamber.

"No and I don't want to tell him."

If I was to tell him now, the impact of what he is about to see will be lost, and if this brother has no idea of what has gone on here it will be lost on him too.

I leave Mike and Phil topside on the hill, where our C.P. is, along with the fifty of Lok's men. Roy and Doc are to stay here at the mouth of the tunnel with about one hundred of Lok's men. We set up a commo net between the two topside groups. I am not positive if the AN-109s will work underground. It is time for Veto, John, and I to move into the tunnel to destroy the cache that we found. The tunnel is darker then I remembered it, as we go down to plant the explosives. It looks darker. Could be because of what we know is down here. I have a very strong feeling I am walking into an open grave.

Lok with Yep behind him and several of Lok's men in back of them follow us. As we go further into the tunnel I become aware of a smell. A strong smell of what best I can describe as a combination of rotting vegetation and food, along with decomposing human bodies and years of human waste sitting in a damp closed off place. The further in we go the stronger and stronger the smell becomes.

I turn to Veto and say, "I don't remember that smell last time I was down here."

We moved to the point where John had wasted the VC and the sight of him made Yep try to turn and run. Lok's men turn him around and push him on.

Veto asks if I knew the way. "Yes I do, we were here before don't you remember. We were the only ones who went beyond this point." Lok speaks up and says, "one of the men with him was with Doc and he can lead the way."

To me, this could be one of the worst case scenarios to follow, because there is no way to know who or what is just around the next bend or down any one of a number of side tunnels. As we pass a side tunnel John fires his M-79 down it. It would have been nice to have a commo line with us, but Tran the yard on point, drops down and is very still as all of us follow suit. I move slowly to the front. The bend is just in front of me when there is a large flash of light followed by an ear splitting crack. The flash and sound come from Veto's 12 gauge. He is up in a kneeling position firing at a small group of NVA that are using the cross tunnel. I look up and say "thanks". Veto's 12 gauge is a pump action with the barrel cut down to the front stock. The rear stock has been replaced by a pistol grip looking thing and he has a sling to carry it, so he can swing it up to fire fast. Veto and I move down each of the cross tunnels about 30 meters setup a demo pack in each to close them down. As the main body moves out, Veto and I run back out of the cross tunnel and blow them.

To my surprise there is no dust and the main tunnel shows no sign of problems. In front of us now is the large room. We start to set our demo packs and take inventory. As we are doing this Lok is taking his brother around asking how all this could be here. Lok is mad and Dou has trouble telling us everything Lok is saying to Yep. The jest of it is that Yep is either the dumbest person on earth or a VC. Just then Twan found the torture chamber and let out a scream that could be heard back to Saigon. All of us ran to see what is going, only to find Twan out cold on the floor. Lok became very angry at what he saw. He grabbed Yep and threw him into the room. Then grabbing one of the weapons from the stacks, pointing it at Yep and pulling the trigger. Only to hear click, click. Lucky for Yep there is no ammo in it. This only makes Lok madder; his face is beet red and the veins in his neck look like they could burst any second. To calm Lok down, I tell him that he should send someone back for some of his men.

He looks at me and asks "Why?"

I answer, "To retrieve as many of these weapons as your people can use or will need. We are only going to destroy them and you might as well have some use out of them." He sends two of his men back to ask for as many men as can be spared from above.

Lok then turns his attention to Yep. Yep is still sitting where Lok had thrown him, too scared to move. Lok has him tied up in the usual way. That is with his elbows tied together behind his back. He then put him on top of one of the stacks of bodies. Lok wants to know how Yep could not know of this. Some of the people in the piles came from his village or were family members to people of his village. Yep at this point received enough courage to just spit in Lok's face and say that the North will win and he wanted to be on the winning side. Lok is in a rage and can hardly control himself. He shakes as he asks if we have an extra demo pack.

Veto answers saying that we have two that we were going to put in this room and you can have one if it is used in this room. The demo packs we are going to use in here are incendiary type and will burn all this to nothing.

Lok answers "That good, I want Yep to sit on it. That is what

Yep need for what he do to our people. Just look around, you think I wrong?"

Yep is then bound about the feet, his hands tied to his feet and placed so he can see the demo pack but not so close as to do anything about it. "You now ask help from whoever you pray too. I no longer know you. I ask that the souls of these people who lay here come after you now and after you die." Lok says as he leaves. Twan left a light so Yep can see the bodies and the charge that is to take him to meet his ancestors.

There must be about 100 people taking weapons and ammo up to the surface. Veto has all the charges on a 30-minute de-lay fuse, and tells every one to "Di-Di Mau" out of here. The charges are now set. We make the surface with ten minutes to go. The hill our CP is on is a safe place to go and watch the fireworks. The track from Florida to the CP takes six minutes. I take up a position so as to see both entrances to the tun-nels. The one behind us that was closed by the river coming down in it and the one that we used to mine the underground chambers.

KABOOM!! The whole area moves, there is a new hill begin-ning to erupt. It starts to form just to the east of where Florida and the main land meet. As the hill grows, smoke and flames come out of the entrance on Florida. The ground on top of the new hill splits. Smoke, flame, and all kinds of nasty stuff come out of it. The land then falls into a huge crater. A lot of small val-leys form, running in five directions from the large crater. There is a second explosion part way up the mountain to the east. A second hill forms only to split with more smoke, flame, and junk coming out of the ground. There must have been second cache of ammo up there.

"It looks like Charlie has been in this area a long time." Veto states. Lok is both mad and confused. He cannot understand how his brother could do this to his people.

On the way to Lok's village, he asks me if I think we have put a stop to the VC in this area.

I answer "No not a stop, but we have given him a hard blow. It will take sometime before he can operate in this area again. You now have enough weapons and ammo to protect yourself for some time. We will teach you to use and care for them."

For the next three weeks, we take his people through the care and feeding of the weapons that they have. Veto spends time with Twan teaching him now to set up demolitions. John took three others and showed them the use of the radios. Doc helped the sick and old people of the village and showed them how to care for themselves. We dug a water system and showed them how to put in latrines.

Doc says, "If we teach these people how to take care of themselves we can go and not worry about them. We are here to teach the people to take care of themselves and leave them to it. Give a man food and he will starve when it is gone. But teach a man how to grow food and he will not go hungry."

We take Lok's men out on patrol in groups of ten to teach them to do it for themselves. We spend a lot of time with them and their family. Life is easy and fun living with these people. Time goes by fast and the weeks turn into months. The horrors of war slowly slip from our minds in this small village hidden away from the modern world. The village is a very peaceful haven in a world gone mad.

"All good things must come to an end and so must this. The choppers will be into pick us up in the morning." I tell Lok.

Lok had his people throw a little party for us that night. We drink the local wine, a very strong wine, and eat till we are full. The fire that was used to cook the food is just about out when the choppers come into pick us up. I look at Lok and his son Twan as we lift out. There are tears in their eyes as there are in mine.

Chapter 8

We have been back in our base camp now for almost three months and the only things we are given to do is short three to seven day missions. Nothing beyond going out to bring in a village chief or recover a piece of equipment that could be lost to the VC. My team becomes very itchy just sitting around. Not only itchy from boredom but also because all around us are the sounds of the night that come out of the jungle like they have a life of their own. Outside the wire, all is dark and you can just feel that Charlie is sitting out there watching and planning. In camp we feel trapped, open to attack, uncovered, lacking the ability to use the stealth we have learned. Out in the bush we can move unseen. The bush is our element.

This team of mine is lean, mean, and mobile unencumbered by the standard equipment of larger Army units. We operate on the very forward edge of military involvement in Southeast Asia. We carry out covert operations deep in enemy territory for months at a time, often well beyond the protection of our artillery or air support. Instead, we use a proven repertoire of jungle skills perfected in guerrilla warfare. The jungle is our element. We have learned to use it to our advantage. We are masters of camouflage, and expert in the deadly art of stealth and sabotage. Out in the bush, we live off the land and exist in the same manor as the Viet Cong. We play his game by our rules in order to survive and win.

I lay on my bunk thinking about our last real mission. Real in that it took us over the fence and into harms way. It was the one to Lok's village. I have spent the last two months going over and over it. I keep looking for something we did wrong. Between the heat, high humidity, and worry over that mission, I do not sleep. I don't want a black mark on my record. It is my intention to stay in the Army. Move up through the ranks. To prove to my Dad that I am better then he thinks I am. Not finding an answer, I remove myself from the bunk, dress, and leave my hooch.

I head across the compound, pursued by the ever-present waves of mosquitoes, which fly about my head paying no attention to the oily repellent that coats my bare skin. I stop outside the mess tent to light up a cigarette, then open the screen door and enter. Except for John sitting at one of the tables hunched over a cup of coffee, as if meditating its contents, the mess tent is empty. Naked light bulbs suspended by their cord bath him in an eerie glow, which accentuate his solitary setting. I go up to the ever-present coffeepot and take a cup. As I slid, up a chair and join him in a late night cup of coffee. John glances up with that unspoken look as if to say, "need to unwind too, huh?"

I am not alone in bearing the pent-up tension, which weighs upon each of us. I take a measured sip of coffee. Then break the silence with the question, which haunts each of us, especially when you are getting ready to lay your life on the line.

"Do you really think those people back in the world under-stand what it's like here."

In his matter of fact way, John gives a blunt answer "In my opinion, NO!"

He pulls a folded letter from his shirt pocket, looks at it with a quiet sigh, tucks it back into his fatigues, and says, "I just received this letter from Sue. In it, she said that an old school friend of hers told her that I would come back from Nam an animal. She told Sue that when I come home she had better watch out for me. Sue asked her "why." She told Sue that a friend whose husband had been in Nam. And when he came home all he did was beat up on her, drank a lot and did drugs."

As I listen to his concerns, I cannot help thinking that if we were not dreading a "Dear John" letter from our wives or girlfriends. We were privately fearing that the brutality of 'Nam would warp us in such a way that we, too, would never be the same when we return to the world.

I say to John "We have seen and done too much over here not to be different then when we left the states, but that is no reason to think we will go back and be like that."

"But Eric, she thinks I will and that is what upsets me."

To console him and possibly myself. "John if I were you, I would not think about it. First of all, if you don't act that way she will see it. Secondly, we may not return back for you to find out. Say did I tell you about what my Mom said in her last letter?" I ask John.

"No you did not. What did she have to say?"

"She said that one of the guys I use to hang around with in New York City came by the house to see how I was doing. He told her he received the address from Abe at the Deli. He scared my Mom out of her wits. He had on dirty jeans, black motorcycle boots, and a black leather motorcycle jacket with a rag over it that was flying the patch of the Hell's Angles. He stopped to see how I was doing and ask for my address over here. He told her he was in Nam for one year and had only been back state side for half a year. My Mom said that she hoped I did not end up riding with them when I was back in the states."

I look at my watch to see it is about 0300 Hrs. I say, "You know if we want to be ready for whatever this war is to throw at us I need to sleep."

Dawn came early that morning, or so it appeared to me due to my lack of sleep, lighting the jungle canopy with the first golden rays of the coming day. It is one of those mornings you both love and hate. You love it because the sun is bright and the world is alive with color. You hate it because the early morning heat is only promising the day would only be hotter. I did not have any chow this morning and I am now ready to eat my web gear. Most of this morning is spent getting the gear ready. It is hard to prepare for something when you don't know what you are going to be doing or even where you are going to do it.

I have the team meet with me in my hooch. We talk about what has been going and brainstorm about the last big mission. Time goes by and we head off to the mess tent through the stifling humidity, and the brain baking heat of mid-day, protected only by the shade of our green berets. I feel like I am slowly drowning in my own sweat-soaked fatigues. It is that sweltering time, between the monsoon season and the coming dry season, when the air is so saturated with water vapor it is like breathing inside a steam room at the health club. For months, we have endured the driving rains and drizzle. Almost daily there are towering green-black thunderheads massing over the mountains to our west before the winds drive them over us. Heavy green-black clouds that release slanted sheets of torrential rain. Those eerie looking green tinted clouds that drop millions of incoming droplets that hit the ground like miniature bombs. But the last rains of monsoon have begun to subside; leaving in their wake rotting material, mildew, mold, and occasional small puddles which would quickly evaporate. The ground bakes fast in the sun and soon turns dry as cardboard. Then the intolerable dust takes over coating everything with layers of red dust with the consistency of sifted flower.

As we go into the mess tent the hollow "thoomp-thoomping" of incoming mail interrupts the small talk. Call it "hard core" or simply battlefield indifference, but none of us are going to let Charlie inconvenience us. Some of us silently count off "one-one thousand, two-one thousand, three..." in the back of our minds. Others try to second guess the pattern of impact and take bets on it, while others simply ignore the disruption altogether. Besides, the V.C. have been regularly lobbing in a somewhat predictable pattern of harassment rounds, primarily aiming at the commo bunker, fuel dump, and the latrines. Yes I said the latrines. Why the latrines I will never know, but maybe they think that's where we are the most vulnerable, or maybe Charlie takes some perverted pleasure in blowing fifty-five gallon drums of crap all over the compound. Usually, he did little short of stirring up the dirt and showering the camp with another layer of dust.

This is one of the best meals I have had while in the army. I have finally convinced the Mess Sergeant to use smoked ham instead of sugar cured crap. I also taught them how to make biscuits and gravy. We eat till we are full and then some, for we know that once out on the mission we have to eat off the land. We are lucky as usual in that the mess cooks did not return, to clean up, till after we are done. After chow I go to the Command tent to obtain the supply list for our stay in camp.

Mike, my second in command, came looking for me. He looks like he has just seen a ghost when he finds me.

"Mike what is going on? I didn't think anything could scare you."

Mike looks me straight in the eye and says. "Man there is this chaplain over in our area asking if any of our people want to have confession or last rites."

That did it, I am mad. The simmering contempt I feel for some rear area ass holes suddenly erupts into a blood-boiling rage. I half run across the compound looking for my prey. When I found the chaplain, I grab him by the shirt and amidst a torrent of obscenities I jerk him across the compound only to throw him into the base commander's tent. At the base command tent I am steaming. The chaplain is standing there in his rumpled fatigues trying to regain some semblance of professionalism as I launch into a blistering tirade.

"Who sent this *#&%$% &^%$# over to my area. I don't want some R.E.M.F scaring my men. We all know that we may not make it back. We don't need some R.A.M.F. making it worse. If one of my men wants to talk to a chaplain they can go to him."

I don't want any of these people in my team area. It is not that I hate God or chaplains, I just don't want them cramming their religion down our throats or making death seem any more imminent than it has to be. Besides, I have confidence in the odds of us making it if we rely upon our training more then I do in such factors of providence.

The base commander Colonel P. L. Lee says he will look into it and that I am to stick around. There is a briefing session coming up and I am to be there.

As the chaplain is leaving, he turns to me and in very sheepish voice says. "Sir, I am sorry. I did not think it was wrong of me to see if your men wanted to talk with me. It is my job in this base to provide spiritual guidance. I will not go into your area again unless I am asked to."

"Chaplain I am also sorry for the way I treated you and some of the things I may have said. You see we work under a lot of pressure and have to just sit in this base not knowing when or if we will be back in the bush. It's hard for people like us that are more at home out there." I say to him.

I then ask him. "How long have you been in camp?"

"Sir, I have only been in country three months and at this base two weeks. I need to learn more about your type of unit and what I am able to do without inflaming the passion of the people around here. I came to this base from a supply base near Saigon. There is a world of differences between the two. The people stationed here do have a more intense aura about them. Do your people know they can come to me?"

The Chaplain asked Colonel Lee. "Yes Chaplain they do. I did not think to have an orientation meeting with you. The last Chaplain we had here was with us for sometime and had come from another SOG camp."

The chaplain asks. "Where did he go from here? I would like to speak with him about this?"

Colonel Lee looks at me, and then looks back at the Chaplain. "Chaplain, he went out with a team and never came back. To this day we do not know what happened to him or the team he went with. That was two months ago." When that was said the Chaplain just turned hung his head and walked out very slowly.

As I go into the briefing room the MP's stop me to check to see who I am and to be positive I am who I say I am. In the briefing room there is one full Colonel, Colonel T.S. Poerts, two Lieutenant Colonels, Q.E. Tate and D.H. Stone. There is also a guy in a white suit, dark tie, and mirrored sunglasses. I am shown to a chair, told that two other men are due and to have a cup of coffee if I want. It is hot in the tent and coffee does not sound too good at that point, so I ask for something cold. Just then a real cool breeze comes into the tent. The MP's have set up this cooler fan in the back of the tent. Not more then two or three minutes pass and in comes this General, looking like an ad for West Point in his starch-creased fatigues, spit-polished boots, and four black stars embroidered on his collar. He mounts the platform and starts to talk when his aide says something to him. He becomes very upset and sits down. There is a commotion in the back of the tent so I turn around to see. There are three of the mess cooks with large buckets of ice. In the buckets are Coke bottles. Boy, talk about being knocked over with a feather. I have not seen a Coke in a coon's age. The cook's pass throughout the tent handing the Cokes out to anyone that wants one. They open the bottle and ask if you want a glass. Who would want a glass? I think only to see the guys in suits; the General and his aide take a glass. In my mind I think go figure. As they get to me the head cook bends over and tells me he had put 12 aside for my team. I tell him "thank-you they will love it". The coke bottle is covered with frost as it is handed to me. The first slug of coke goes down with a tingle. Boy this has to be the best coke I have ever had was all that was on my mind. Lost is the pleasure of now slowly sipping this wonder I am not aware of time slipping by.

About ten minutes later, two MP's with another guy in a suit walks in. This guy has a black briefcase chained to his wrist. He walks straight up to the general and asks him for the key. The general hands him the key he had in the front pocket of his shirt. The case is opened so the general can take the some papers out of the case. The general, with papers in hand looks straight at me. I am the lowest rank in the room, and felt out of place. He cocks his head slightly and asks the bird colonel if I am the officer assigned to lead the mission. He tells him I am.

"Captain, are you and your men ready?"

I stand to attention and say. "YES SIR, we are Sir."

"Captain, Do you know where you and your men are going?"

" No Sir, I do not, Sir."

"Captain I will be giving you an envelope that you are not to open it till you are 25 minutes from your jump point, do you understand?"

"YES SIR."

"The operation is code-named "Night Flight" You and your men are to go over to the security shed and turn in anything that may link you or any of your men to the U.S.A. You are to have nothing that is U.S. made, no identification, and most of all you must be totally positive that no one has any personal items. Do you understand?"

"Yes Sir."

"I gave orders that you and your men are not to be fed any food made by our people. You and your men will be taken to a special camp shortly. We have it set up to prepare you for this mission. You will eat only local food cooked by local people. The weapons you are to carry will be weapons we have taken from the V.C. The exact time of departure from the camp will be given to you only one hour before takeoff. Do you have any questions?"

"NO SIR, All is understood, Sir."

"If you do have any questions later Mr. Jones (we all know the cloak and dagger cover-up is a little too melodramatic if not outright hokey, but if he and the General get off on it. Who am I to interfere) will be in your camp to help. He is not informed as to the mission only the information needed to prepare you to start the mission and information on your equipment. Captain Howard good luck and good hunting." He then gives me a big salute and leaves the tent.

Colonel Poerts comes up to me and tells me. "You and your men are to be on the flight line at 1900 hrs. You are not to talk about what was said inside this tent. Your men are to be told nothing till you are airborne and on our way. Do you understand?"

"Yes Sir!" is my answer (but in my head is that small voice saying here we go again).

This is not the first time I have been in a briefing like this one. My mind jumps back about nine months to the last one like this. It was just before we went out for a little walk in the woods, as the General put it. It was a HALO drop over the Yunnan province of Red China that borders North Vietnam. It was basically a recon mission to photograph a North Vietnamese training camp for high-ranking officers. It took us five and half months to walk out of there, and then we only barely made it out with our lives.

On the way back to my area, Roy meets me. "Ok Eric, what happened? It took a long time for you to return after that thing with The Chaplain?"

" Roy, we have a mission. I can not say more at this time. Get the men together please." With everyone in my tent I say. "We have a mission I can not tell you anything about it other then we will move to a training camp at 1900 hrs or when we leave for the mission itself for now. So just sit tight. When I know more then that I will tell you about it. I can say we are not in trouble and this is our time to relax."

It is exactly one week to the day since we arrived at the special camp the General had for us that we are told to move out. At 1800 hours we are told to move out to the flight line. We have not received any mail or had any contact with the outside world in all that time. We do not know where we are going. All we know is that we are wearing uniforms that are not the standard issue. We are to carrying Communist made weapons. All the food we eat, all the smokes we have are from the locals. (Oh how I want a good American smoke or some C-rats) As we go out to board the bird for the flight to who knows where, we are stopped and searched. I am told that it is done so no one will have anything on them to link them to the U. S.

In anger, I state, "We know we have been here before."

With all the precautions, you might think we are on a secret mission to infiltrate the Soviet Union. Well anyway we all load onto the plane with no more problems. The general and his two friends in suits come onto the plane, shake hands with each of us, and tell us to have a good trip. Man, I still wonder if the REMF's know what life in this part of the world is like without their air conditioning, Officers Clubs, and all the other frivolous things they have from back in the states.

Then the pilot and crew board, the cargo master retracts the tailramp. We stash our gear and settle in for the flight as the engines roar to life. In moments, our C-130 is rolling down the runway fighting to become airborne. We bank out and head for our destination somewhere above the DMZ in a circular route, which takes us over the central highlands before we veer out over the South China Sea to loop back in over North Vietnam and onto our jump off point. I slip off into a half sleep dreaming about home.

The monotonous drone of the planes engines and several hours pass before the pilot's voice comes over the speaker saying 25 min. till jump off. This is when my nerves become raw. I start to think about all that has happened up to now. I try not to think about what is going to happen. This is the hardest time for me. Once we jump clear into the night sky of North Vietnam, my mind will click into high gear. My all-consuming thoughts will be the mission and my men.

These men have been with me all through AIT and fifteen hard months in "The Nam." We have cultivated guts and glory, an esprit de corps seldom rivaled. Each of us is a specialist with a primary and secondary M.O.S. that only adds to our overall proficiency. We are a TEAM in all meanings of the word. We have grown to instinctively anticipate the reflexes of one another as if they are our own. We are men who share an unspoken bond of camaraderie forged in the crucible of combat.

Our camaraderie came about in the midst of mutually shared misery and uncertainty. This compelled us in some mysterious way to care for one another with such a depth of selfless love that we would have laid down our own lives for one another in a firefight or simply shared the contents of a letter or a care package from home.

The pressures of war force us together, but other factors back home accelerate the process. Political dissent, student riots, and peace marches combine with the turbulence of the '60's only to encourage the steady erosion of national support for a war that is increasingly seen as immoral and unjust. From the halls of Congress to college campuses, from student to homemaker, it becomes increasingly popular to distance yourself from the war and those who are fighting in it. A man who forty-eight hours earlier had been humping through hostile jungle or been crossing fields of fire in a muddy rice paddy are spit at and greeted with taunts of "baby killer" and "murderer" upon arriving at their home airport for the first time. It is the men coming home that face the full brunt of national contempt. This is especially galling for those who have laid their lives on the line in the patriotic conviction that they are doing what is right and honorable. It is the stress of combat, as much as the mood back home, which forces us together as a team.

As a member of this team my job is not only team leader, but also demo expert and light weapons expert. I do still fly a chopper now and then, just to stay current and keep my rating. It is time to open that ugly brown envelope with the orders in it. I'm one who never likes to open this brown envelope. It always meant that we are going to be put in harms way. This time out we are to take and hold an NVR camp. The camp is suspected to be a transfer point for all heavy troop movement in the sector. Our local support is to come from a Montagnard group. I always like working with the "Yards." Most of the isolated Montagnard villagers just want to be left alone to continue their time-honored rhythms of life, which reaches back to the dawn of time. But some like Lok are wise enough to see that their villages are not remote enough. There can be no peace until their enemies are driven out. Some like Lok see the path to deliverance through the small Special Forces teams who are only too willing to come and live among them in their villages.

My team and I spent our first year in country living among the Bru and Matla Montagnard tribes and have grown very close; we have even been adopted as blood brothers into their tribe and have been given the coveted brass bracelet of brotherhood. Living in their isolated mountain villages they have little contact with the outside world. They tend to be suspicious of strangers, but once they take you into their hearts, they will do anything for you. They are tough hard fighters. This group of "yards" is the same ones we had spent part of our first year in country living with. I am only to have 25 men to take and hold an NVR camp and that makes me feel like we are being put out on the line to dry. That is nothing new to a Special Operations Group. You become accustomed to being told that your government will not acknowledge you if the enemy takes you, dead or alive. I check my watch, take a final glance at our orders, tuck the N.V.A. map into my pack and burn the rest in a special container that was put on board for just that reason.

Chapter 9

In the training camp I overhear Mr. Jones talking to one of his friends. He said that we are to have a party just before we take off. His friend asks him why? Mr. Jones tells him "We don't expect any of these men to come back." (I just wish I could erase that statement out of my head. Oh! By the way, we never did have that party)

The red light comes on; it bathes the cabin in a soft reddish hue amidst the raucous clamor of a buzzer that jolts the team into a state of readiness. We stand up and move, ready to file out the door. I take one last look at the map and it hits me like a ton of bricks. We are jumping into the same area as before. Oh Boy!!!

As I prepare to jump, I am faced with one of the things in my life that has two effects on me. One is to have a feeling of high anxiety and the other a real trip of excitement. I am anxious that I might lose some of my men. The excitement comes from knowing I am to face death and it is in my hands to live or die. I am the type of person that if it is not dangerous it is not fun.

That is why I am in Special Forces in the second place, first place is survive and return home to my wife and children. I now have both son and daughter.

Looking out of the door all that can be seen is an orange glow from a small fire on the ground. The Yards are to set a small campfire in the clearing that we are to land in. All the light that can be seen is from that fire. I know the tribal chief and am confident that he would not light a fire if the V.C. were in the area. As we start our first pass over the area a blue light flashes on and off. That blue light is our signal to prepare to jump in. Adrenaline is pumping through my veins as I prepare to bailout. Each of us gives his gear a quick check to make sure everything is secure and then checks the gear of the man next to him. The green light flicks on and out the door we go like spent rounds out the ejector port. We tumble out into the turbulent wake of the departing props, twisting in erratic somersaults before the snap of the shroud lines and muffled billowing of nylon jerk us into a graceful descent. All is quiet as we float down through the velvet blackness towards the clearing below. We land in a tight pattern and quickly gather up our chutes for burial.

The signal fire the Yards have lit is larger than it seemed from the air. Its flames are crackling and spitting sparks, bathing the entire clearing in an eerie orange glow which silhouettes us against the night shadows. I am happy to see Twan. Twan is the son of Lok, the village chief of Ba-Choa, where we had lived for three months. His father has entrusted him and his yard detachment to give us back-up support. Twan grabs my arm and pulls me to cover. Once out of the clearing he tells me that one of his runners has just made contact with a V.C. patrol out to the north. It looks like they heard our approach and they are now coming to have a look see. I signal to Mike to form up a guard to the north. Man, am I glad we do not have to talk, for the V.C. are on us just like that. The head of one of the Yards explodes like a pumpkin hit with a baseball bat and then all hell brakes lose. There are grenades going off, people screaming in pain all around us.

Twan says in broken English "V.C., V.C. Come. Hurry now!"

The chaos is compounded by the blood-curdling screams and moaning of wounded men scattered in the dark undergrowth. Twan taps me on the shoulder and points down. I cannot believe my eyes. I barely make out the black mouth of a tunnel opening which disappears into the jungle floor in front of me. Twan has set up our landing site a few feet away from an abandoned tunnel complex for an emergency escape route in case we were to have the VC hit us. With a signal to my men to follow, I descend into the hole. Only a few meters into the tunnel, the firing above ground takes on a strange muffled sound like listening through earplugs. I can barely hear the final retorts as the last Yard drops into the hole and quickly camouflages the opening. At first the earth slopes downward before leveling off. It is an eerie feeling crawling through the darkness of one of Charlie's tunnels. It is pitch black, damp, and reeks with a nauseating stench of defecation and urine. The tunnel is cool and dank in its perpetual darkness. Twan is leading us through the underground maze with a small flashlight. We have to walk hunched over because the ceiling is only about four feet high with roots poking through the moist earth. The low, earthen tunnels are constructed to accommodate the small, slender frame of the Vietnamese, and not the average American. Trying to negotiate the cramped confines, unable to turn around, sandwiched between others with fear closing in around you is almost unbearable. In this black hole, claustrophobic madness is ever present. It takes extreme mental discipline to fight back a touch of panic, which threatens to overcome us as we go deeper into the silent darkness. These clammy tunnels are the perfect breeding grounds for bacteria, parasites, and microorganisms, which could thrive on our moist bodies. Besides this the tunnels are often infested with other vermin which can make life miserable. In the blackness, you never know what is lurking in crevices, crawling on roots, or lining the walls. It could be fire ants, poisonous centipedes, fist-sized spiders, pit vipers, or rabid rats. I can handle a lot of things, but this is taxing my limits of endurance. This tunnel is a lot smaller then the ones we found on Florida.

We keep slipping because negotiating the tunnel floor is like trying to walk on polished ice. None of us want to know what the crude sewer is caked with, even though it does not take much imagination. We must have traveled about a half a mile through this system before we start up a steep incline. The slimy ascent is even harder going but we press on, only too willing to emerge into the fresh night air. I am relieved to look up at the tops of the trees instead of up at the bottoms of their roots.

Twan tells us to stay put because he wants to find out how the V.C. knew we were coming. I ask if he has anyone new in his village. Since we last saw Twan he has move away from his father Lok to start his own village. His new Village is named Ba-Ngu, which is about 15 klicks from his Dad's village.

Twan says, "Yes about two weeks ago a family in his village have relatives come to visit and they are still there."

We take cover and give Twan two days to return with the answer. If trouble is to start we are to go down into the tunnel and go to the left at the Y. I do not want to go back down into that hole in the ground for all the tea in china. We set up a night defensive position and settle in. Just about the time everyone is settled, the bush to our right starts to rustle. The noise sounds like it is circling us about every hour. This keeps up for about two hours, only to stop and leave us in silence. Then just before dawn it starts again only to come in closer and closer. No one wants to move or make a sound that might give away our position. I sent one of the two Yards that are still with me out to take a look-see. When the sound is in back of us, I send Nik out to the front. The sound continues around till it arrives at a point just about where Nik is to be. I try to see what is going on, but the undergrowth is too thick. You can not see five feet in front of you. No one wants even to breathe for fear of what might happen. I look over at Mike with a look of question on my face. Before Mike can do anything there comes a loud noise. (Like being inside a lion's den at feeding time.)

All at once Nik comes running back like a man that just seen Satan himself. What scares me is what is right in back of Nik. That has to be the biggest cat I have ever seen. That tiger must be at least ten feet long, if not more. What do I do now? I was not trained to fight a 600-lb. cat, and I never liked cats anyway. You have this tiger coming at you and you dare not fire a round for Charlie is out there looking for you. I do a stupid thing and take out my knife. What good would that do? I can just see me wrestling with a tiger like Tarzan, stabbing away like mad as he shreds my body with his claws.

Nik is just about to our line when the cat lunges and brings him down in mid-stride before tearing half of Nik's side out with a flesh-ripping bite. The tiger turns and looks me straight in the eye with a menacing look. He emits a low, guttural growl with a fearless snarl, which exposes rows of dagger-like fangs. He settles slightly back on is haunches and compresses his body in preparation to pounce. I fumble for a grenade and am ready to pitch it when this shaft whooshes by my right ear. It hits that tiger between the eyes and down he goes. I look over my shoulder and into the business end of a crossbow. I then turn around to see what happened to that cat, only to find that if I put my hand out I can hit him on the nose. After this event the next two days are spent in boredom. But we do have fresh meat to eat.

At noon on the second day, Twan comes back with the heads of two people hanging from a pole. One is a man about 20 years old; the other is a woman about the same age. Their eyes are open and the face of the woman has a look of fear like I have not seen before. The man's face is that of a person who hated the people that he saw before death took him. His lips are curled in a snarl and the eyes have a look of hate that is hard to describe. Twan tells me that the V.C. now knows we are in the area and we must call off the mission.

I say "NO. I have never quit on anything and I am not going to start now."

Twan informs me that the V.C. has put twice the personnel as is common on duty at the outpost and it would be insane to try to take it. Do you want to go ahead anyway? Is that the question? Not only on his lips but also his face.

I say, "I do and nothing is going to stop me." Mike comes over to see what is going on and hears what Twan is saying.

Mike looks at me in a strange way and asks what my problem is.

You see up to this point, I was not one to want to put my men in a place of undue danger. There is danger on all of our missions, but I am one who looks out for his men and this is not like me. I say to Mike that I see no reason to not go ahead with the mission, but if it would make him feel better I would send a message back with a runner.

On each mission we have a predetermined emergency transmitter site (ETS) for message transfer in case there is a problem and this one is no different. It is set up to protect us, as well as, the incoming support group, which is to take over after we clear and take over the area. That makes Mike feel more at ease. I code a message and have Twan send a runner back to the ETS with it. Just to be on the safe side I have a second runner follow the first. He also is carrying the same message. The second messenger follows about one hour later. I know what the answer is going to be, but to keep Mike and the other men happy I send the message anyway.

During the next three days we have a running fight with the V.C. They would find us and hit us with all they have and we would fight back to cover our melting into the jungle. Then we would lay an ambush for them and kick hell out of them for a time. The plan was to use the Yards in a diversifying move. The Yards were to hit The V.C. from the northwest and pull them into following them while we moved out to the east. This was done to give us a clear shot back to the contact point. The Yards open up on the V.C. just after midnight on the fourth night of our running battle. There are tracers all over the place but none from the V.C. camp. What's gone wrong? I send two of my men into see what is going on. They return to inform me that the V.C. have Di-Di Maued out leaving a small contingent of men in camp and the main body has pulled out to the southwest.

I send Doc with five Yards to the original contact point, while the rest of us follow the V.C. It takes about an hour and a half for us to come up on the rear elements of the V.C. They are taking no precautions at all so we almost walk into them. The plan is to see if we can take one of them alive to find out what is going on and why they are pulling out of the area. Mike and Veto are to go up the left side of the V.C. and try to distract the last two or three of them, while John and I go up the right side with six of the Yards. At a given point in the trail Mike and his group are to make contact.

The V.C. do just opposite to what they normally do. The front of the group takes off running, while the back five dig into fight and protects the rear of the fleeing group. The firing is very heavy from their position. This is like no action I have ever seen the V.C. take. They are fighting like they have to hold this section of ground at all costs. We hit them from three sides at once with all we have. The battle rages on for almost an hour, with the loss of six of the Yards.

I have Twan on one side of me and this little guy on the other. At one point in the fight a grenade comes rolling into our position. The little guy to my right just jumps on top of it. Lucky for him it does not go off. He picks it up looks at it and starts to laugh like crazy. He then shows it to us. The V.C. are so freaked, he has not pulled the pin. As he stands here showing us the grenade a bullet went in the right side of his head and explodes out the left side. This showering the ground and every thing close to him with blood and brain tissue. The fight just seems to drag on, one side taking the upper hand, then the other. I find life in Nam has only two styles. One you are bored to tears. The other you are scared out of you skull. In this set to we are having is just like that, one minute bored the next minute scared. All of a sudden all firing from the VC stops, the only sound is our weapons going off. I call a cease-fire and all is "dead" still. Not even the common noise of the jungle is to be heard. The peace is welcome and we all stop to catch our breath. The longer there is silence the more nervous we become.

What happens next, I thought only happened in kid's books. There right in front of my eyes are four V.C. with their hands in the air asking to be taken prisoner. That is unheard of. The V.C. would fight to the death instead of giving in. But here are four of them. One is waving a stick with a piece of white cloth tied to it. They are repeating over and over, "Chieu hoi, chieu hoi" in shrill, high-pitched voices, which border on sounding whine.

Some of the Yards stand up to cover them, while I motion with hand signals and shouts of "Di-Di Mau, Di-Di Maui" for them to move faster.

They are scared and plead nonstop for us not to kill them, but to take them prisoner. Not only did they give up, but also they are willing to talk. In front of me is the enemy. The ones who killed the little guy who was willing to give his life on a grenade for me. The enemy that has killed 12 of the Yards that worked with us. My anger is more then I can take. I want to kill them with my bare hands, which I can do and have done. I take one step at them and I am stopped by that small voice in my head. The voice says that to kill these unarmed men is wrong and I am not to do that. Even now God has that small voice in my head trying to keep me straight. I don't always listen to it, but it is there.

The Yards then truss them up with their elbows tied together behind their backs. They are made to sit on their haunches in the typical Vietnamese fashion, when one of the Cong starts to talk real fast. I have to stop him and call our interpreter, John, over to see what he had to say. He is scared, but not of us. I want to know the reason for his fear. The Cong do not fear Americans, they hate us. I ask why they were left behind to die. The one in command, Doung by name, says because they were ordered to stay back and hold us up so the main body could move away. This is not normal so I ask why. I'm told that they have three Chinese advisors with them that do not want to be found out. My next question is why did they surrender? The answer is startling to say the least. It looks like the Chinese have made their lives miserable through constant drilling, indoctrination, and back breaking labor. The Chinese have stripped them of all their personal belongings, burned their villages, press-ganged them into service, and lied to them about the reasons they are fighting the south. Doung has a brother living in the south who has told him a completely differ-ent story from what the Chinese are saying. Doung also says he and about ten of his comrades have spent the last month looking for a way to escape from the Chinese.

If that is so, I ask him, "Why didn't you stop fighting after the others pulled out and just give yourself up."

He says they were scared. They were told to keep fighting un-til reinforcements came back for them. They were also told that others were left behind to keep an eye on them.

"Why did you give up now then?" I ask.

"Because we are out of ammunition and had nothing to lose. If we did not show the white flag your men would kill us. We didn't know if others were there or not so we took that chance."

Our Kit Carson Scout Dou asks about the base camp that we are to take. Doung says that until recently, it had only contained two companies of Viet Cong, but it has been reinforced with four NVA companies and one company of Chinese regulars.

These are not the black pajama-clad peasants in conical hats, wearing tire-sole sandals, and carrying vintage rifles, which the Viet Minh had captured from the French. These are the crack, battle-seasoned regulars armed with the most modern of weapons the commies have to offer. I am relieved to have learned this now instead of later. If we were to try to take our objective in the way we planned we would be walking into a death trap. I now have four VC and don't know what to do with them.

The Yards want to kill them. I have Dou ask them if they want to join with us.

Their answer "Yes they do." Twan asks me if I trust them. What else is there for me to do? Normally, we would have little choice but to let the Yards have their way under the circumstances. But they have been so cooperative and sincere in their hatred of the North Vietnamese and their allies, that I have little choice but to take them with us.

"Dou, I want to tell you to thing about this. An ancient Chinese thinker named Sun Tzu once wrote a book call THE ART OF WAR. We can learn a lot from his writing and one point he made is very true. That point is to keep your friends close and your enemies even closer. Do you understand?"

Dou answers. "Yes I do understand. What said I order them untied before heading out?"

Chapter 10

We turned around and head back the way we came hoping to meet up with Doc. My mind is asking all types of questions, but not getting any answers. I cannot figure out how we were so lucky, not to walk into that mess. After four klicks, we finally link up with Doc. His face is pained and drained of color from a hard hump through the jungle. He is out of breath and drenched in sweat. All I can obtain from him is that about two klicks out from our original contact point, he ran across three companies of North Vietnamese regulars with about ten Chinese officers headed in our direction. Again, we have been spared from walking into a no-win situation. Our good fortune is holding out. With a renewed sense of urgency, we double back to the ETS for a message transfer hoping we can send an emergency call to arrange a lift out before all hell breaks loose.

As we get close to the ETS, we see signs that a battle has taken place. From the stench, it does not take long to find the fly-infested bodies of the two runners we sent ahead. They are both tied to trees with their arms and legs stretched out or at least as much of them as is left. It looks like they were tortured for whatever information they had. Trem, the younger of the two had both his eyes carved out and the skin peeled off his back with what smells like nothing in this world smeared on him. He is stripped naked and castrated. The other man is even in worse shape. It looks as if a V.C. has forcefully pulled his left arm off. Every bone in his body is broken and not just once. His tongue is ripped out of his mouth and his teeth kicked in.

After finding this grisly discovery, my immediate concern is whether the V.C. has uncovered our emergency transmitter. I say a silent prayer to myself asking that the radio will still be here so we can make contact. We need to lift the hell out of this mess. I don't know what I will do if it is gone. It is our only link to the outside. I dig it out of the hole it was buried in, unwrap it and send the code set up message. Nothing happens, so I send again. Still nothing, so I start to check the unit. Just as I turn it over, it crackles and comes to life. Mike by now has our message encoded. With the message sent, a quick response comes into call back in six hours.

We saddle up and start moving in a direct line away from the last known contact with the enemy. We want to put as much real estate between them and us as possible. This part of Southeast Asia is not one of the best for fast travel. Everywhere you go is either dense rain forest of large trees, bamboo stands and tangled undergrowth or open rice paddies, swamps or some steep hills to climb. We are in a hurry because the more real estate we have between them and us, the better chance we have of a safe lift out. Just a head of us comes one of the worst possible situations that could have come up. A river is not one of the things you like to see at a time like this, but there one is. It looks like it is 100 meters across and swift moving. The tree line comes down to the very edge of the water leaving no way to tell what or who is on the other side. This side is no better, all along the shore dense jungle runs right up to the waters edge. To cross is not only mandatory, but also dangerous. It has to be done to put Charlie off our trail. At least until we can set up an ambush.

Twan and one of his men steps into the fast running muddy water and goes straight under. We look for them to come up, but they do not. I think what a way to end ones life after going through so much at the hands of Charlie. Just at that instant about 20 meters down stream Twan comes up. He tries to swim to the other side to no avail. The current pushes him down stream faster the he makes headway. I call him back to our side of the river. Now we have lost one man and still need to find a way across this river.

I send five Yards and Veto up stream and Doc with five Yards down stream with instructions to go two hours out, or until they find a crossing then return. An ambush is then set up in case Charlie comes to cross the river before our teams return. The sun is just about to go behind the hill to our west when contact with one of our patrols is made. It is Veto's group coming in fast. Mike clears a way through the ambush. The Yards are so jumpy they just might shoot first and ask questions later. Veto reports that there is no way to cross up stream. There is a company of NVA heading downstream about four clicks behind him. It is time for us to bugout. We go downstream in hopes of making contact with Doc and his group. After about 30 minutes of humping, we meet up with Doc. They are wet, but not with just sweat, and excited. Doc reports that they have found a way across and the best part no contact was made with hostile forces.

Doc takes the point along with one of the Yards that had been with him. The pace picks up when Veto tells Doc about the company of N.V.A. following us about four clicks back. Twan suggests we send out a small team to leave a false trail. Twan adds that if we make it look like we are a small team on recon it might lure them off our real trail. Then we can set up an ambush at the river. Word is sent up to Doc to fall back and meet with Twan and me. When Doc meets up with us, Twan asks about the lay of the land on the other side of the river. Doc tells him there is a steep slope up from the river of about 25 meters with little to no ground cover for about 100 meters. I ask if he has been on the other side. "Yes he had and he left two of his men over there to control the high ground."

"Good, but how did you know we would cross at that point" I ask. He did not have an answer.

It is time to call in for instructions, John codes up a message asking for a lift out, and gives a map location of a hill about two clicks to the rear of the river crossing. The message is sent, and we are told to be at the pick up point in 24 hrs.

"That may be too long!" Is the only comment that is going around. We know that the N.V.R. will be overtaking us in about four hours, and we do not know if we can hold them off that long. I ask Twan, if he would send about ten of his men away from the river.

"Yes, but why?" he asks.

"To do what you suggested, which will give us time to set up an ambush and to add time, so we are open for the lift off."

The team is split with ten of the Yards going away from the river, while the main body heads for the river crossing in an around about way to also add some time. We have no trouble hiding our trail for there is foliage in this part of the jungle. The jungle is so thick that if you took one step off the open trail you might not find your way back to it. Twan's men start to replace all moved or trampled undergrowth to cover our passing. The other group does the same, but not to the extent that they cannot be followed. The N.V.R. are not stupid, and they would not follow an open trail only one that looks like someone is trying to hide it. We spend about eight hours going in a big circle in the heat and dense jungle. The bugs are the size of a 747, or at least feel and sound that way. They are around us more than I have seen anywhere in this country before. The ground is wet and swampy making our steps tenuous on the spongy floor. Occasionally, we can hear the trickling of water somewhere in the undergrowth, which would sometimes form brackish pools of tepid water serving as breeding ponds for the next generation of mosquito larvae. The stagnant smell of damp soil, rotting compost, and sour sweat hangs in the air. The farther we go, the wetter and sloppier it is. Our only consolation is the knowledge that it will be slow going for Charlie also.

The point man, Dou comes back to report that we are within one click of the river, and about two clicks downstream from the crossing. Mike, Twan and I go to scout the riverbank leaving the rest to clean and ready their weapons. It is getting late and the blackness of night is closing in fast. We have no choice, but to settle in and wait out our last wet and miserable night in this mosquito-infested swamp.

The sun is just filling the sky with a blaze of color when we arrive at the river. All is still, almost too still. On the other side is a small boat, the kind the locals use to cross the river. Twan points out that there is one on this side just a short distance from us. No one is around so Twan and I take it and cross the river. Out in the middle of the river, we make a perfect target for anyone waiting to pick us off. (Man, I do not want to be out there)

Once on the other side, we work our way around to the far side of the clearing. In the very back of the clearing sit the two men that were left to hold the possession. We could have just slipped up behind them, put a knife to them and done away with them. Twan takes a small stone and pitches it into the trees on the other side of the clearing. The two men jump as if they have been shot, but nothing else moves. We call out as we approach them. They tell Twan that no one has been there. Thet, one of the men left to watch the crossing, says that they were starting to think we had forgotten them. We talk a little more then return to the river, and cross in the same boat we used to cross over. We put it back just like it was with one exception, that exception is a grenade is placed under it. The pin is pulled, and it is placed in such a way that if the boat is moved, the grenade will go off.

Veto and I talk about where to place the explosives, how to set them off, and what to do about the ten men with Twan that are still out. We are going to place four claymores on both sides of the trail, just at the bend before the river. We place charges at the base of two large trees just before the river, so they will fall back down onto the trail. All of these are setoff by remote detonation. The next part is the tricky part. We are to mine the riverbed on this side and on the other. If anyone works their way by this, we will place claymores on both sides of the clearing. Now, just to be positive that they go the way we want them to, we set up a field of fire with the two 60's that Twan's men have. One team set up on the left side, and the other on the right side of the clearing. Twan leaves two of his men behind to make contact with the ten men who will be coming along, hopefully before the N.V.A. John and Lep are on the radio to see if there is any N.V.A. radio traffic. Up to now, there is only the usual chatter. We scoop firing positions out of the sandy soil, and cradle our bodies in the shallow depressions, waiting for the enemy to attempt a river crossing. The jungle is still, even the local coalition of mosquitoes have temporarily withdrawn to regroup for the night assault. The silence and a soft sweet smelling breeze that has come up mesmerize me. However, the burning sting of insects digging into my flesh soon interrupts the quiet moment of reflection I have. We inadvertently position ourselves astride a foraging column of 3/4" long Marauder ants that have infiltrated our fatigues to attack the living obstacle blocking their path. They are similar to the African army ant in their ferociousness, and draw blood with their pincer- like mandibles. It takes all our willpower to keep from tearing our clothing off to kill the little monsters. But to do that would give our position away, so we are forced to quietly move back in hopes of moving out of their way and to pinch where they are on us in hopes of crushing the ones that move with us. I hope that we will be able to move out of here without making contact and not have to fight our way out.

As the shadows begin their movement across the jungle and the sky becomes a blaze of color, Veto signals that Twan's men are coming in. Shortly after they cross the river, all hell breaks lose on the other side. Veto sets off the first set of claymores, then the second set. Firing starts, but not in our direction. The N.V.R. is shooting as if we are still on the other side. One of Twan's men comes up to him laughing like mad. A company of N.V.R. followed Twan's men into the ambush while about 20 Viet Cong have picked up our trail, and approach from the other side. Now they are shooting at one another. When Veto set off the first set of claymores, the N.V.R. opened up on what they thought was our location, only it was the Cong. When Veto set off the second set, the Cong thought the N.V.R. were my men and dropped in a couple of mortar rounds. We sit back and watch the fireworks for about ten minutes. One of the Cong must have gone for the boat, for all at once he is flying through the air in what is left of the boat. The firefight goes on for about five more minutes, and then there is only silence.

They must have seen whom they are fighting, because now they are coming around the bend in the trail after us. Veto sets off the charges on the trees. One falls on about five of the Cong, and the other tree just clears about ten more. Some run into the jungle, to avoid the trees falling on them, the rest jump into the river. Veto pulls back up the hill as more and more leap into the river. With more then 20 of them in the river, the far side mines are set off. This sends body parts, blood, mud and water everywhere. A body makes it to our side of the river. They open fire on us, just as the sun melts behind the hill. If we can just hold them off on the other side for a 1/2 hour. They all come at us at once. About 15 make it to our shore when the near side mines go off, sending more bodies, blood, and junk into the air. The remaining Cong that have make it to our shore thinking they are safe, are cut down by the Yards with the 60s. The rest retreat back to the other side, and start to send incoming mail. We hold our fire for as long as we dare, hoping they will think we pulled out. We then open up with all we have for ten minutes only to quit firing with the hope they will try to come across again. It works, for they start to try to cross one more time. We keep very low and quiet; most of them are on our side when Veto sets off the first of five pairs of claymores. The Yards open fire again cutting a bunch more down. To this point, we have not lost a man. The enemy is not that lucky for the beach is spattered with their blood. The dead are pilled on top of one another. There are body parts all over, there is an arm hanging from a tree and the river is running red with their blood.

The time for us to move out is at hand. I do not want to go at this point, for this is a chance to get back at them for all they have done to us. A determination is made that Twan and Veto are to stay behind, and cover our rear as we move off to the west to our pick up point. The V.C. or whoever is left notice us moving out and start to cross again. The retreating Yards with the 60's also see them. They reset their weapons and open fire when most of the VC cross into the middle of the river cutting them to bits. Just as Twan and Veto are ready to pull back, they come again. Veto puts timers on the claymores, setting them to go off from the top of the hill down. This is done to chase them back down the hill.

We have nearly reached the top of the hill when we hear the muffled whacking sound of approaching choppers coming in from the south. The olive drab Hueys hover in under the relentless clamor of slapping blades as we break into the clearing. Crouching low, I run under the swirling rotor of the first chopper and tell the pilot to hold for five, we have two men coming in. He starts to say he can only give us three, when the concussion from the first two sets of claymores rip through the early night air, followed by the third, and fourth sets of claymores.

The pilot looks at me and then back at the jungle with a panicked expression that says, "Lets get the hell out of here!"

Mike takes hold of him and says, "We will not leave without

the two remaining men and we still have three minutes for them to reach us."

The jungle is growing silent as we load into the birds. The door gunner swivels his M-60 in the direction of the tree line where we came out. He flips off the safety, and anxiously scans the jungle. We hear a running gun battle that is drawing closer by the second. Suddenly, Veto breaks into the clearing on a dead run with Twan right on his heels. Both are firing shorts bursts over their shoulders at the pursuing V.C. that are only 30 meters behind them. The rotor blades are spinning faster as the pilots throttle down. The skids of the half-hovering choppers are nervously shifting from side to side in anticipation of lift off when Veto dives into the belly of the lead ship. With a final surge of power, our Huey tilts its nose forward and lunges upwards. Rounds slam into the hull as the pilot fights for altitude.

In the final, slow motion seconds waiting for Twan to make the second ship, I look up and say "Oh God, help us out of here. Please get us the hell out of here alive!"

The prop wash from the second bird is churning up swirls of dust and leaves as Twan grabs one of the skids. A swarm of V.C. and regulars pour out of the jungle as the second chopper gives a final shudder and lifts off. The door gunner's 60 is spitting a metallic stream of brass casing out into the air as he fires down at the enemy. Looking back, I see some of Twan's men struggling to pull him into the chopper but not before his body jerks from a parting round slamming into his back. As we bank over the jungle canopy, I can clearly see the red muzzle flashes from the enemy below. We have cut it close but miraculously; we make it out of this hellhole this time. I say this time for I know; somehow, we will be going back.

As we fly southward through the soft blackness, I feel a profound sense of sadness. We have just come within a hair's breath from that final nightflight, but that is no consolation. Dark thoughts of an aborted mission weigh heavily upon me. This sense of desperation is compounded further by feelings of guilt for Twan. His father Lok, entrusted him to my care, a trust I don't shoulder lightly. Now he is lying in the next chopper with a bullet in his back and because of our radio silence, I don't know if he is alive or dead. What am I to tell Lok? During the months we had lived with his tribe, I had grown to love that gnarly little old man and he had trusted me with the life of his eldest son. I fear that I have failed this as well. We have gotten out, but at what cost.

It seems that with each whack of the rotor, each pop of the exhaust, my inner turmoil grows and drives the hatred I feel for the North Vietnamese deeper into my heart.

Someone is knocking at my door. "Come" I yell.

It's Mike with a big cup of hot coffee. "You look like hell this morning Sir. Did you have a bad night?"

"I wish I could stop reliving our last mission. I dream about it every night. You know I can't find a single thing we did wrong. What time is it?"

"It is 0830, and you are wanted in OPS in ten minutes. A civilian chopper just touched down." Mike says.

This means either we will know what we did wrong, or we are going out on a good one. I dress and leave for the OPS tent.

Chapter 11

I feel like I have taken a step back in time, as I walk up to the OPS tent. There stands the same two MP's. They stop me and ask the same questions. Inside the tent are the same people as last time. Except this time, there is a high-ranking officer sitting in the second row of chairs. I am shown to a seat and told that there is coffee over on the table. I am to help myself if I want some. Colonel Lee comes over to me as I am getting a cup of coffee. I take coffee this time to help me wake-up.

The Colonel says that I am to give my full attention to the General when he comes in.

I ask, "Who is the man in the second row?"

"He is the Generals replacement and was ordered to be in on this briefing." My insides jump for joy with what the Colonel Lee just said. A briefing means we are going out again, and this is not to be a butt chewing.

"Sir, my second told me that a civilian chopper landed about 30 minutes ago."

The Colonel just looks at me with one of those looks you

receive when you ask a question that cannot be answered and walks away.

I look around for the guys in the typical spook suits. There is none in the room. I did see one as I was coming over to the OPS tent, but no spooks are here. The fans start their low moan to life, as I take my seat. The fans coming to life is a sign that the General is on his way into the tent. The General enters with two guys in suits and everyone stands to attention. Even the General seated in the second row. The General and his followers mount the platform. The order is given to take our seats.

"Captain Howard, front and center." I walk to the front with great hesitation for my jungle fatigues are in bad need of a pressing, they are clean but not pressed, my boots have not seen polish in months, and I need a shave. As I approach the platform, the General steps down. I stop in front of him and give a salute.

He returns the salute and says, "Stand at ease. You and your men did a fine job on Nightflight. (When he said that, you could have knocked me over with a feather) We have received reports that you and your men upset the N.V.A'S plans and put the N.V.A. and their friends on the run. We have some captured documents that state the North Vietnamese have put a price on your head and that of your men. How they found out who you are? We don't know, but we will find out. Would you be interested in going back there to destroy that camp?"

"Yes Sir, I would Sir!"

"Your records show that you are a pilot, and have been given the Distinguished Flying Cross for saving a team several months ago."

"Yes Sir!"

"This time you are to fly one of their birds out. They have

two ships sitting on a short strip two miles from the camp. Do you think you can do it?"

"Yes Sir, I can Sir."

"Here are your orders. Operation code name is "Hard Ball". Commit them to memory, and then destroy them. You and your men will be taken to a special camp. We have it set up to prepare you for this mission. You will eat only local food cooked by local people. The weapons you are to carry will be weapons we have taken from the V.C. This time you are to decide when to start. Just so long as it is not over two weeks before you embark on the mission. All of your men have been awarded the Bronze Star and you are to receive the Silver Star. I understand this will be your first Silver Star. It will go good with the two Bronze Stars and DFC you already have. Also orders have been cut for you to be made Major when you return. Good luck and good hunting."

I am so taken back by what is said and what is going on I totally forget to salute as the General leaves. Colonel Lee comes up to me and says something. I just look at him.

He then says, "What is wrong with you, Captain?" With that comment, I return to my senses. (I am surprised that the NVA have put a price on our heads. What did we do?)

"Captain, you and your men put a real big dent in their plans to mount a major offensive. The prisoners that came back with you have given intelligence so much information. They have told us of eight training camps, four supply depots, and a prisoner of war compound. The captured papers we have tell of great losses in men and material. The Chinese say you and your men killed so many men that it will take at least another year to be back up to strength. It was stated in one of their reports that you had NVA killing VC and VC killing Chinese and vice versa. They do not like you. Go hit a home run Captain, or should I say Major Howard." I am so stunned by what is said about Nightflight, that I totally miss the Major part again.

On the way back to the company area, I meet Mike. "Mike I have good news for all of us. Assemble the men in the mess tent in thirty minutes."

Mike stops to tell me that Phil had just received a visit from the Red Cross. They informed him that there had been an auto accident about a month ago; both of his parents were killed.

"Mike how is Phil taking it?" I ask.

Mike says, "He is taking it bad to say the least."

I then go into my hooch and take out my notebook and write down how I feel. I like to keep track of what is going on. It goes back to my college days and taking notes. I found that if I wrote down how I felt about what the Professor said, my recall was better. I take out the orders and start to go over them. After about twenty minutes of going over the orders and committing them to memory, I push back from the desk and go over to the mess tent, taking the orders with me.

The closer you are to the mess tent the more you understand why it is called a "mess tent." There is the smell of coffee brewing and breakfast being cooked on the stoves. If you have a good nose, you can pick out the smell of bacon and eggs frying. The toast is done, and some flapjacks are on the grill. Two big pots of orange juice sit by the door along with the coffeepots. The tent is full of tables and long benches. The square tables with chairs are for the officers. The long tables with benches are for the enlisted men. The benches are made from unfinished wood planking, and if you try to slide down them, you will have a butt full of slivers. The air not only has the smell of food cooking, but you get the odor of old canvas that has been soaked by the monsoon rains, and is now a collector of mold and mildew. The only people in the tent besides the cooks are my men. They are sitting around a long table in the middle of the tent. On the table are two pitchers, one of coffee and one of juice. They have taken one of the chairs from the officer tables and put it at the head of the long EM table. I take the seat at the head of the table and start by talking to Phil.

"Phil, I am so sorry to hear about your folks. Do you want me to put in a request for you to go home?"

Phil answers "NO; my place is here with my team, besides the Red Cross already asked me that and I told them no. My parents are already buried, and I have no other family there except Carol. I have no brothers or sisters. My only family now is Carol. I have a letter here from her. In it she tells me all about the funeral. She is very sad about my loss, and she has it all taken care of. Carol is a great woman and understands that I have to stay here." (In my mind, it just does not seem right, but who am I to tell him to go home. I just hope he is ok)

"Ok let's jump right to the meat of what was said in the briefing. We are going back to finish what we started. We have orders to return to the area of Nightflight; to destroy the base camp, and bring back any POWs that might be there. Operation is to be called HARDBALL. In addition, the North Vietnamese have put a price on our heads. It looks like we did a lot more damage then we thought. The General has read some captured North Vietnamese and Chinese papers that said we set them back about a year in the area. A recon team has placed the Chinese that were training the Cong out looking for us to the far to south of the base. What do you say we go kick their ass again?"

"YEAH, YEAH!" is their answer.

"Also all of you have been put in for the Bronze Star for Nightflight. We are to be on the flight line in three hours. See you all out on the line. Phil, if you need to talk to me, I would like to help."

"No sir, I will be all right. Once we are back in the boonies." I know what he means, when we are in the bush our mind, for the most part are working to keep us alive. Not that we don't daydream now and then but most of the daydreams are of good things and times. It is probably nature's way of keep of holding on to your sanity.

Back in my hooch, I try to nap. My mind is racing thinking about Phil and what had happened in his life. I do not know what I would do if it had been me getting that news. To try to clear my mind I slip back to a time, when my parents were living in Newport, RI. It was one of those times when my Dad had shore duty and the family lived with him. Newport is a small town on the southern coast of Rhode Island. It has many rich people in the summer and only the Navy in the winter, or so it looked to me. They had a house one block from the ocean. The house was built in 1792, and was in good shape. I do like old homes, and the history they hold. It was in this house that we became a family for the first time that I could remember. My Dad would take my middle brother and me to play little league ball in the park, and to Boy Scouts during my summer visits. (Man, I had a father) They lived there only a short time for about two years. But I learned what it was like to have a Dad. There were times later in my life that I wished he could have been around more, not only around for me but also for my middle brother who really needed him around. A Dad is important to a boy growing up. I only hope that when we return back to the world, I can spend time with my kids.

"Knock, Knock!"

"Come in." Mike walks in.

"Yes, Mike what is it?" I say half a sleep.

"Sir! There is some skuttle butt going around that you are to be made a Major, and have to move up to H&H. Is it true, Sir?" Mike asks.

"I know nothing about it." I answered.

"Thank you, Sir we don't want you to leave." Mike turns and goes out. I stand up and go to the OPS center. Once inside the office, I ask to talk to the Colonel. I am shown into his office.

"Sir, May I ask a question?"

"Yes. What is it?" answers the Colonel.

"Sir, Is it true that I am up for Major?"

With a stern look, the Colonel replies, while nodding his head in the affirmative, "Captain, Where was your mind in the briefing? I told you to pay attention to what he had to say."

" Yes Sir, Thank you Sir!" I say and turn to leave.

"Major!"

"Yes Sir." I say turning around.

"This will not remove you from this mission. Now go put you shit together. You and your men will be leaving soon."

I salute and say, "Thank-you sir," only to turn and leave.

Back in my hooch, I try to get some sleep until it is time to go out to the flight line. But my mind starts to think about life in "The Nam". Wrenched from the quiet cadence of life back home, most men never really acclimate to the harsh realities of the Nam. Sometimes you wait out another anxious night with Charlie stalking the blackness, the squeeze of a trigger finger between life and death. Sometimes damp and shivering in the cold highland nights or sweltering in the oppressive heat and humidity of the lowland days. This is an environment too hostile, too intolerable for the average American to adjust to. Prior to "Nam", the closest most men were to the chaos and carnage of war is the sanitized portrayals of John Wayne wading through squads of Jap soldiers on Iwo Jima. Vic Morrow fighting his way across France every Tuesday night on "Combat, but "The Nam" is for real, a real world of hurt just too painful and too traumatic for the sensitivities of all but a select few.

My experience is an exception not unique, but certainly an exception. Not that I was born to blood lust or inclined to violence, but I have been tempered by a past which blunts the normal shock and revulsion encountered by most men who are thrust against the brutal backdrop of war. For me it seems to come easy, almost natural, like second nature. It is not that I don't experience seasons of fear, even that cold, anonymous fear that knows no rank or age. But oddly enough, I seem to thrive on the sheer rush of danger, keeping one-step ahead of the enemy is a game I have grown to enjoy. I feel at home in the confines of the jungle. I enjoy pitting my instincts against someone else, whether I am hunted or hunter. To me life in The Nam is either kill or be killed. All my training, time in country, and my youth has done one thing for me and that is hardened me to it all.

Killing came early in my tour. It was on my first patrol out into the bush. We were following a trail that was recently cut by V.C. across a field of six-foot elephant grass when our pointman spotted a glint of metal up ahead. We each took cover in the thick undergrowth; concealing ourselves as best we could, and waited for the oncoming patrol to pass. It was a squad of V.C. fanned out in a "V" pattern. We could hear the swishing and rippling of the stiff blades of grass as they drew closer. Each of us was straining to lay as motionless as possible to avoid contact. Their pointman passed by without detecting our presence, followed in a staggered succession by the others. The rest of our team had managed to hide themselves in the tall grass safely outside of the pattern except me. As the wedge passed, I could tell by the sound of their rustling in their line of March that each soldier was growing closer. I suddenly realized that the last man in the sweep was heading straight for my position and would step on me in a matter of seconds. I had to act. Sweat was pouring from my body as I unsheathed my knife. I waited until the last possible second. My chest tightened, a deep breath caught in my throat, and then I sprung to my feet, grabbed the startled soldier by the mouth with one hand, pushing him to the ground. I then lunged the blade into him just below the ribcage with an upward move of such force my hand entered his chest. I then twisted the knife from side to side in hopes of cutting his heart.

His face was a portrait of wide-eyed terror. The AK-47 slid from his right hand to be lost in the tall grass. His left hand desperately grabbed at my right arm twisting my fatigue sleeve in agony. His eyes fluttered and darted from side to side in one final spasm of life; they then went to a blank stare as the light of life left him. There was a faint gurgling rasp in his throat, as the last breath gasped out. He loosened his grip of my arm. His body gave a final quiver, and then went limp in my arms as I removed my knife. It was so quick and not a sound was made to alert his comrades.

Most couldn't stomach the personal responsibility of taking a human life, even killing a faceless stranger at a distance in the anonymity of a night firefight. But to kill a man with your own hands, cold and impersonal, face to face, so close that you can look into his eyes, see the fear etched in his face, is a nightmare too unbearable for most to live with. But I do it with a detached proficiency. I have reached a place where I can kill without qualms. To stand over someone with his or her blood on your hands is difficult. Maybe what makes it easier, is that inner defense mechanism which helps me to turn off emotions in order to preserve my sanity.

Maybe, if I stay hard, and don't let down my guard, I will make it through it all in one piece. I'd done it before, and I am confident I can do it again. Besides, there has been only a relative difference between survival in "The Nam" and getting by in the concrete jungle of the Lower West Side of New York City. Not to mention the times spent hunting in the hills and woods of southeast Kentucky.

It is time for me to go to the flight line, so up and at it. I put all my things in my two-foot lockers. I put the keys in a bag, take them over to the security shed, and lock them up. We are to take nothing with us, so I feel naked, as I go to the flight line. All my team is here, so we board a chopper for our training camp. Once onboard the chopper the feeling of being naked goes away because I have all my men around me. I look around to see most of the men are catnapping. Phil is sitting away from everyone reading and rereading the letter from Carol.

The training camp is different this time. We are not the only show in town, and that makes it hard to work. We spend one week going over the lay of the land. Our training consists of zeroing in and rehearsing with the communist weapons we are to use, becoming familiar with the area, and putting a plan together on how to pull off the mission. We are given an objective, and a little outline of what is required of us on a mission like this. How we do it and the timetable for getting the job done is up to us. On this one, we are to decide when to go. I check with the weather people as to when the next new moon is. I am told it is in three weeks. I want to go on a night of a new moon. A new moon casts so little light we would be hard to see.

I enter the Como Tent and ask to put in a call to Colonel Lee. The Como Sergeant puts the call through, and hands me the phone as he leaves the tent. The Sergeant knows that when an Officer to an Officer places a call, it must be private. The phone rings, it is picked up. A voice on the other end says Scrambler 1-3. I turn the scrambler on and set it at 1-3. There is a pause and the person on the other end asks who I wish to speak to. My answer is "Colonel Lee." The Colonel comes on.

"Colonel Lee, Captain Howard here would you contact the General.

"We want to be inserted in the field on the night of a new moon. The next one is not for three weeks."

The Colonel answers, "You are aware of the Generals thinking on OPS like this one. Are you not? Also you do know how he feels about those (CIA Type) people don't you?"

"Yes Sir! I do Sir!"

"This one and Nightflight were both ordered by the same people."

"Yes, I know Sir, but it was the General that gave me the orders Sir." I stated hoping not to step on any toes.

The Colonel tells me that I will be called. It takes a long nerve racking three hours until I was called to the phone. The call is not from the General or anyone on his staff. The voice on the other end sounds very far away. He does not identify himself. All he wants to know is why three weeks before going out on the mission. I explain about the new moon and the cover total darkness will give. There is a long pause and then he gives the "OK". The next three weeks go by fast. It is like being back on the training field.

The time is 2000 hrs, and we are starting to load up the bird for our trip north. The plane is the same one we went out on last time, even the flight crew. No one stops us as we board the plane.

Mike looks around, turns to me and says, "Where is the search party? What are they going to trust us this time?"

"It looks that way." Is my come back. The crew boards and starts the motors. One thing I never received a straight answer was why is it the flight crew does not board until after we are on board.

A jeep followed by a deuce and a half roll up to the plane. The General followed by his replacement come on board. Four men take a large box out of the truck and put it in the plane. The General says "good luck and good hunting." His replacement says, "Men I, I mean we, will be expecting you back in four months." He then joins the General in his jeep. They speed off followed in a cloud of dust so thick you could not see the deuce and a half behind them. Lucky for us the slight breeze is blowing away from the runway and us. The plane starts to taxi as all eyes are on me.

"Sir, what is in the box?" Veto asks.

It is time to put myself at rest for a couple of hours. What is in the box? I ask myself as I drift off to a state of half sleep. The slow steady drone of the engines coupled with the mummer of voices around me gives me a feeling of comfort.

I start to think about a hunting trip I took with Moon and Bo. It was when we were in the eighth grade. We were looking for bear at the time. Moon went to the East Side of a small valley while Bo went to the west. I went down the middle walking in a creek that had dried up. About 10 minutes later, I see bear tracks coming out of a cave in the West Side of the valley. I can tell the tracks went to the creek and are going the same way I was. Just ahead, there was a bend in the valley to the left. As I walk closer to the bend, a lot of noise starts to reach my ears. I cross to the far right side of the dry creek bed; I walk to a point to see around the bend, there was a 400 lb. Bear. He must have caught a whiff of my scent for he stood-up on his hind legs and came at me. I dropped to one knee and lifted my muzzleloader to take a shot. Bang my rifle went off, and he dropped. My shot had hit him just below the chin and took off the top of his head. In a matter of seconds, Moon and Bo were there. Bo said he saw the bear from up on the hill and was just about to take a shot. When the bear stood up, he said he did not know what made it stand up. But in no time, it was clear, because he heard my rifle go off only to see the bear fall over backwards.

As we climb to altitude, the air becomes chilly in the belly of the plane. This snaps me back to the real world. There is the smell of gun oil, damp uniforms and men around me. Here at this time and place there is a feeling of peace. It sounds strange for someone who is about to put his life on the line for his country to say he feels at peace, but that is how it is for me now. You are very close to people you share life and death with, and we have done that repeatedly. We sit in this half-light, some thinking, some sleeping and some talking. Every so often a face is lit by the drag on a cigarette that should not be lit. The faces are all different, but strangely appear the same. Each face shows the lines of combat, the wrinkles of fear and the age of stress making them look much older then they are in years. You come in country a bright-eyed kid, some in their teens and others in their twenties. After a short time, your appearance takes on the look of a man in his thirties or forties. Stress, fear and boredom carve the face.

The speaker crackles to life above my head. It is the pilot speaking. He speaks in that all too common voice of someone, who will be going back to a hot meal, clean sheets and the O-club once we are out the door. He informs us 20 minutes until jump point. The black coveralls we wear are closed, the black chutes are put on, and the face black is applied. Our landing zone is a rice paddy about five to seven klicks from the NVA camp.

The Red light goes on. Standing in the door, I look down watching for the yellow flash of light. The yellow light is our signal to come on in. There it is. The pilot banks around and comes in at 1200 feet above the ground, out the door we go. We free fall for 550 feet then pull the D-ring. Pop, the shoot opens and you swing under it looking for the ground. The ground is hard to see for there is no moonlight. It is dark. About 20 feet off the ground there are sparkles coming up at me. It is a rice paddy full of water. Splash, I am down Ok. Then all around me, I hear splash, splash, and splash as the rest of the team comes in. Off to the east we run, just behind one of the dikes we form up.

I tell John, "Dig a hole and bury the jump gear. Who has that box the General put on the flight?" I ask.

Veto asks around and reports that no one saw it come down with us.

"Now then where is our contact?" Just to the north comes

click, click. Mike gives one click, which is followed by three clicks. That is signal that we have linked up with our local contact.

What a surprise it is to see Twan. The last time I saw him he was going into surgery to have a bullet removed from his back.

He says, "Say old man how you doing?"

"Who are you calling an old man?" I come back.

After greetings all around, Twan tells us that he has his men watching the camp. The NVA have one company in the camp and that the Chinese have moved the training camp about 20 klicks north. Most of the VC action is in the area just to the south of the DMZ, about 20 klicks from here. I ask about the airstrip. Twan tells us it has two platoons plus about 20 people to work on the three ships.

"Three ships? I was told that they have two." I say with a questioning tone.

"Yes three. They moved another one in last night."

"What types are on the ground now?"

Twan looks at me and says "I no not the names. One has two engines with wing on bottom. One is one engine with wing on top that turns. The other look like plane you call Puff. We talk more when we make it to my village OK!"

Chapter 12

It is sun up when we reach Twans village. The mist covers the hilltops. The grass is damp under foot and the air has that smell of spring about it. Twans wife, Dau, has breakfast for us when we arrive. Twan's wife is a small, attractive woman. She is dressed in a rap around skirt of bright colors and is bare breasted like all the women in the village. Her long black hair is down to just below her butt. She and Twan make a perfect couple. Twan himself is a small man that looks much like his father, just younger. His two small children also look like him. They are both little girls about two and three years old. She asks us to sit and brings the food to us. We sit on grass mats in the middle of the village. The breakfast is a large bowl of beef (or is it water buffalo) soup with a bowl of rice on the side. The soup is very good, but the rice has that world's worst smelling stuff on it.

After eating Doc and John busy themselves by giving medical help to the people of the village. Roy and Phil go check on the village water supply and sanitary system while Twan, Mike, Veto and I go into the long house. We sit down in a circle to talk about the mission. Twan has six of his best men around the outside of the hooch. Twan draws a map of the NVA camp pointing out the defensive positions. He points out the hoochs they bunk in, the supply buildings, the headquarters building and the building they take prisoners into for questioning. I ask if they have any prisoners now. Twan says that he does not know because they never see any prisoners leave the building. Mike asks if he has seen any people like us going in there.

Twan answers, "Yes just two days ago. A big truck goes in with one that was taken there."

We talk most of the day about how to penetrate into the place, do our job and escape back out. I have not told my men until now that after destroying this camp, we are to steal one of their birds and fly out with any POWs we find. As this fact comes out, there is a sense of loss in the men. I have never kept anything from them before.

"It was in my orders not to tell you any of this till we were in place." I say, hoping they understand. "We are to destroy the camp and while Charlie is looking for us there. We are to go north to the airfield and fly one of their planes out.

As the sun is about to drop behind the hill to our west, we set out for the NVA camp. The hills to the west are black shadows, while the hills to the east are alive with the color of the sunset. The colors here are more alive and vivid then back home in Kentucky. As we drop down into the cover of the trees, it becomes dark quick. We want to be in position by midnight the next day. With that in mind, we have a long way to go. We have decided to travel by night, because there is less chance of being spotted by Charlie. It is more difficult to move by night, but I have been blessed with better night vision than most. Even as a child when we went coon hunting at night, I was the one that could see the dogs running ahead of us. Once the coon was treed, I could see it without a flashlight.

Also the Gooks don't expect to see Americans moving by night. The night sounds help cover any noise we might make. Twan has two of his men on point. The Yards have eyes that can spot a trip wire or booby-trap a mile off. The farther we move into NVA country, the more signs of war we see. Not the land war scars you see in the South. But the scars that are left by the moving of equipment and our bombing of their supply lines going to the South. Every now and then, we see the remains of someone the N.V.A. has tortured and left as a sign to the natives not to help the enemies of the North. The Yards will leave the head of an enemy killed in battle on the top of a tall stake as a sign of warning. It is something to see. I can't forget the first time I saw one of them. Man, it is a sight to come around a bend in a trail and be face to face with a head stuck on a stick.

As the sun is starting to come up in the east, we take cover in an old tunnel system. The tunnels look like they have not been used in months. The jungle has taken over and is growing back in the places that were once cleared. Twan sets his men in groups of three in each of the observation points that Charlie has dug. The way this system is set up you have clear coverage for a full 360 degrees around you. It also has two exit tunnels in case someone over runs your position. There is one main bunker in the middle of the system where we set up our C.P. We have a commo net set up with each group of Twan's men. Every two hours all the LPs are to report in. With the day equivalent of an NDP in place, we have time to sleep. After moving all night, we are beat and need some sack time.

The day had been a peaceful one with few bugs, and time to sleep. Now the sun is going down. It is time to saddle up and move out. We have gone through everything to be positive we left no sign that we were here. The Yards take point and move out into the coming darkness of night. The first two to three hours go by with nothing happening. Then the lead man gives a down signal and we drop into the bush along the trail. Coming down the trail are three NVA with two Chinese officers. I am laying in about three inches of water that are alive with God only knows what. What do I do now? As the last one goes by Mike, he stands up and takes him out with a garret. A garret is made from a thin wire about two feet long with a wooden handle on each end. You cross your arms, put it over someone's head and uncross your arms fast. This will take the head off without making a sound. Then Veto puts a knife into the base of the skull of a Chinese officer. By putting the knife in at the point where the backbone and skull meet you sever the nerves and the person makes no noise. If you cut their throat like you see in the movies they make a gargling sound. John and Doc jump the next two and kill them. This still leaves one and he is the last Chinese. After turning around to see what is going on, he starts to run back down the trail. As he arrives at a point where he can see Doc, a shaft from a crossbow hits him in the left eye. He makes a grab at the shaft as I put him face down in the water. We then have to do something with the bodies. I take the ear off the one in the water, while the others do the same. Lip, one of Twans men, takes the head off the top ranking Chinese officer and puts it on a stake. We find a lot of papers on them, but nothing of any value to the guys in S-2. We place the dead in the water, position large stones on them to hold the corpses down. I ask Lip to place the head at the next cross trail to put Charley off the trail. Lip picks the stake up and asks if it's better to go back to cross trail?

"Lip, that is a very good idea. We cannot wait for you to return. Can you catch up?"

Lip just smiles and runs of back down the trail. With that done, we are off again.

Just ahead of us is the camp. The light from the camp lights up the night sky. We use it as beacon. The camp is asleep with only five men on guard. All around us is the jungle with its night sounds covering the little noise we make. The plan is to take out the guards without setting off an alarm. Twan is to send five of his men to kill the guards with their crossbows. The crossbow is a perfect assassination weapon. Then we are to plant charges under the barracks and the supply buildings. Then pull back to the headquarters building looking for all the info we can find. If anyone comes out of any of the buildings, we will blow the whole show in one felt swoop. Veto, John and Doc are to plant the charges on the supply buildings. With Mike, Phil, Roy and three of the Yards taking care of the barracks. That leaves Twan, two of his men and me to cover the headquarters building until the others are done. We will leave the rest of the Yards outside the camp to cover our rear. After all the charges are planted, we are to meet at the headquarters building and take a look-see for what we can find.

Mike asks "What about the prisoners?"

I tell Twan, "Twan, send three of your men to the jail to see if anyone is there, if so set them free. If any need help, aid them out of the camp. We will care for them later."

The camp is set in a horseshoe shape with the open end facing the river. The headquarters building is at the upper center.

The barracks buildings are to the right. The supply buildings are to the left. The headquarters building is a typical long house built on stilts about four feet off the ground. The three barracks buildings are also of the long house type with thatch roofs and screen walls. They are about three feet off the ground. The supply buildings are made of corrugated steel and look like our supply buildings sitting on the ground. Behind the headquarters building sits a square building also made of corrugated steel, but having no windows and a steel door. It is to this building that prisoners are taken, along side of it sits a shed with a generator running in it. The camp is circled by barbed wire. Inside that is a high fence with barbed wire on top. They have put lights up on the fence and a watchtower at each of corner of the compound. There is one guard in each tower and one at the gate. The fence runs down and into the river, so the only way in is through the gate. We could cut a hole through the fence, but that might cause an alarm.

Hai, one of Twan's men that had been watching the camp, tells us that the NVA change the guard every three hours and a change is due in 30 minutes. I think it would be best if we hit them halfway between guard changes. To hit them in the middle of a shift, we stand a better chance. The gooks not on guard should be asleep and the ones on guard should be getting tired. If we start any later, the next shift might be getting up. We sit back to wait the two hours. Knowing that will put us in the middle of the new guard shift. The air hangs heavy on us even with a slight breeze coming up from the river. The sound of night creatures abounds all around. Mosquitoes and other flying things start dive-bombing us at will. The creatures that creep on the ground are starting their attack on anyone that is sitting or lying down.

We watch the changing of the guards, only to see the new guards sit back and doze off. The hour passes slowly with the only attack coming from the infernal bugs. Finally, it is time to go to work.

"Twan, send your men out to take care of the guards. The signal to start will be one click on my cricket."

With all the plans and personnel now in position, we sit back to wait a half an hour to start the attack. It is now time for us to move out. I take my cricket and go click. We move out to the sound of the guards falling. The gate is open, and there is no one around. Twan's men take the uniforms off the dead guards, and put them on. They then take the places of the guards. It is real quiet in the camp, as we move with great stealth planting our charges. As Phil crawls under the barracks, one of the Gooks rolls over in his sleep causing Phil to freeze, but only for a second. The only noise in the barracks is that of men sleeping. There is snoring and the sound of sleeping people moving around, but no one is awake. Namg, in coming out from under one of the barracks comes face to face with someone sitting on the back step smoking a cigarette. As he reaches for his knife, the Gook turns to grab his pistol. Just as his hand grabs the pistol, a hand goes over his mouth and a knife is put into his brain. Namg looks up to see Doc lowering the gook to the ground. Doc had finished the supply buildings, and came over to see if he could help. Lucky for all of us he did.

The headquarters building is laid out with a large room running the length of it with the back half split up into three sections. The large room is probably a briefing room and classroom because the walls are covered with maps and charts of all types of equipment. The center section in the back is open with two tables set up as desks. This area looks like the Sergeant and XO would use it. The section to the right is the radio room and there is one man sleeping there. One of the Yards puts an arrow through his head just above his right ear. The radio room has all its equipment along the wall that separates it from the large room. Most of the radio equipment is old and well used except for the last radio on the table. That one came from the U.S.A., and is probably used to monitor our radio transmissions. Along the outside wall is a table full of papers and junk. The office on the left is the CO's office. It has a new desk and chair with three file cabinets on one wall. The other wall is one big window that overlooks the main gate.

In the CO's office, we find more maps and a lot of stuff the guys in S-2 would just love to obtain. I am going through all the papers looking for something on the base at the other end of the trail when Mike comes in.

"Eric, we have everything in place. Did you find anything on the other base yet?"

"No, not yet, it would help if I could read this stuff. Twan is reading the stuff I give him in case there is something in all this mess."

"LOOK!" Twan says. "I find a list of supplies that come here in the morning. It also says the place they come from. Look on map and see if something is marked 183-107."

"Yes, it's right here on the coast." John says as he looks at the map on the wall.

"If that is the other end of this supply line it's deep into the north. Don't these people use map location like us and most of the world?"

Roy answers John, "No they don't. They have a code they use in case we intercept any of their messages. We now have one of their maps which helps."

Mike turns to me and asks, "Do we set an ambush for the supply convoy or do we blow this place and run for it?"

"Let's think about it. What if we blow this place and leave? When the convoy arrives, they will know we have been here. If we wait for them we will have a fight on our hands. Now if we blow this place and call in any air strike on the convoy we are covered."

Wham! What was that? Looking in the direction of the sound, I see a truck blown skyward. One of Twan's men comes running over to me and informs me that the convoy has just arrived.

I am almost able to say, "I can see that."

Then all hell breaks loose. The explosion has awakened the camp. The sleeping NVA start to pour out of the barracks. Veto sets off the charges under the barracks sending a lot of them to meet their ancestors. He then blows the supply buildings. The explosions send dirt and wood into the night sky. The scene is one of people running for cover in the glow of the fires that the explosions have set. We duck back into the H.Q. to avoid being hit by God only know what falling out of the sky.

I say, "John set up the AN-109, and call in the Fast Movers to cover our being here."

The supply building must have had a store of ammo. Because after the charges we set went off, there is a second and third explosion too large to have been our demo packs. The night takes on a red glow from the fires in the camp. The explosions have taken care of most of the troops in the camp. The ones that make it out from the hell in the building are being cut down by heavy fire from the Yards that are set up on the porch of the H.Q. To my surprise the NVA are putting down their weapons and giving up.

Now what do I do with prisoners? The answer came swift and from the last place I would have expected it. The NVA Gunboat opens fire on us only to kill their troops. We now have a fight going on two sides. There is one battle with the people on the river. The other battle is with the convoy coming down the trail. Veto pulls out his mortar tube and drops a 60, which comes up short of the boat. He then adjusts and drops a second. This one hits smack amid ship and sends the boat straight to the bottom. We now only have one fight on our hands.

In all the excitement, I have forgotten about the men that I sent to see if anyone was in the prison cells.

"Doc, go see if they found anyone in the cages and report back to me."

I then turn my attention to getting us out of here.

Doc comes back and says, "The cells are empty, but the stench of death is heavy in them."

"What happened to the people we were told were in there?"

Doc answers, "That just behind the building on the blind side is a large pit with dismembered bodies in it." He then goes on to tell me that a book was found, and it has lists of names in it, and it looks like they have kept track of anyone that has been in that hell hole.

I ask, "Any American names in it?"

Doc answers and says, "At a quick look-see, it looks like they have not had any Americans for at least three months. It also shows that the ones they did have before were sent to the Hanoi Hilton. That's good news because if they were sent to Hanoi, there is a good chance of them still being alive.

The firefight that started along the road is now in full swing. I turn to Phil and ask if we have a way out of here that is quick, so as not to be spotted by the NVA.

He says, "Yes we can. We can go out through a hole in the fence caused by the barracks being blown." John comes over to inform me that the Fast Movers are on station and we better Didi-Mau. We cross the carnage of the camp, and make our way through the hole. It was not that far to the fence, but it takes what seems like forever to clear it. When the barracks went up they must have had about 50 men in them for there are bodies all over. The smell of burning flesh is strong. The hole in the fence is about five feet across and opens onto a trail leading in the direction of the airport. My men and I, along with about 20 of Twan's men go about one Klick down the trail and set up an ambush. Twan and the rest of his men go back down the road the convoy used. We are to wait for Twan and the rest of his men to come in. The sun is starting to rise, the light level is increasing and it will become very unsafe to stay around here too long. Hi, one of Twan's men, is sent back to look see if the rest are on their way. He is gone no more then two minutes when Lip comes in.

I ask Lip how he is and if all was well with him.

Lip tells me he is sad. I ask, "Why are you sad."

With a shit-eating grin, he says, "Because I miss out on all the fun. I see explosions over trees and know the fun started before I am back to join in. I did get to plant boob-trap on road that take out truck trying to backup out of fight. The other men are coming just behind us. They will be here in a couple minutes. They will click one to be ok."

The Fast Movers did a good job of sanitizing the area. The firing has stopped, and all is still. By the looks of the area of the camp there is not a living thing could have survived in that. Hi comes back and he has Tien with him. Tien informs me that

Twan is leading the people from a second convoy away from us. The NVA must have asked for a second convoy that we missed looking through the papers. We are to go on to the airport. Twan will meet at the western end of the runway just before sundown in seven days. If he is not there by 2300 hrs we are to go on without him.

Looking at the map is a downer at this point. It will take us one day to make the airstrip, going by the back route. With that, we have seven days that would leave six days of hiding from gook patrols. That is not safe.

I ask Roy and Mike to come over and look at the map with me. "If we go to the airstrip now we will be there for six days before Twan can meet us."

Roy chimes in and says, "if we were to travel west for one, maybe two days, we could be in Laos at Chi's village."

"What do you think?" I ask Mike.

"Roy has been in Chi's village before." Mike reminds me. "So he knows them and they know him."

Roy says that it would be good to get out of The Nam and that Chi can give us the supplies we need. Roy like Veto had been to Nam before. Roy's first tour in Nam was with the 101st Airborne Division. Roy had gone out with his old unit to set up a supply line in Laos.

I turn to Hi and tell him to take the 20 men that are with him and go on to the airport.

"We need you and your men to scout out the airport. We (us Americans) are going into Laos to restock on supplies. I want you to set up a watch on that airport. It is very important that you do not let them know you are watching them. Please log all that goes on. Find out where all the people are and where they go. We will meet you at the western end of the runway. The signal will be one click answered by three clicks with a one-click comeback. Understand it."

"Yes!"

"We will see you in seven days at 2000 hrs."

Chapter 13

It is an easy trip, for this part of the world, to Chi's village. It's taking us just over 30 hrs. We did not push ourselves, just kept to the open animal trails and watched out for contact. Once in Laos we are on the lookout for scouts from Chi's village. We know they are out there. It is the seventh sense that lets me know. (Almost like the ability to smell a cop when you run shine.) As we near a small stream, two men step out of the heavy undergrowth with their hands in the air. It turns out Chi has two of his best warriors meet us and lead us into the village. The village sits on a hill and has a good view all around. To the west is Thailand and to the north and east is Vietnam. To the south about 150 klicks is Cambodia. The people of the village are just getting back from the morning chores when we arrive.

Chi has us meet him in his hooch, where we are given a typical Lao lunch. Chi does not look like his Lao brothers. His appearance is different, because his father was a Chinese soldier and his mother was Laotian. Because of this mixed marriage he is taller, about 5'10, not as stocky as the typical Laotian, and has more of the Chinese features then the other people of the village. His hair is cut very short and it looks like one of those brushes you use to scrub the floor. When you first meet him, you have no problem picking him out from the other villagers. Chi is a very friendly person to people he likes, but is a ferocious enemy to those who try to take advantage of him. He has helped SF troops since 1960, and is a good friend to us, but hates both the North and South Vietnamese. The Vietnamese killed both of his parents' about ten years ago.

Over lunch, Chi asks why we are in this area. I cannot tell him the complete truth so I say. "We have to hide for three days.

Chi asks, "Why are you hiding."

"We hit an NVA camp over in Nam the other day, and need to put Charlie off our trail so we can go home." I tell him this in case someone in his camp is a supporter of the North Vietnamese. If it were to be relayed back to the gooks then they would start looking for us to go back by the southern route. When in reality, we are going back east to the airstrip.

The next three days are spent getting the things we need and getting the weapons cleaned and gear set. Chi has a direct link to the same supplier who is supplying the North Vietnamese. It is through China that the NVA receive most of their supplies. We stock up on explosives, ammo and food. We are also lucky in that we now have the newest pistols with silencers from Russia. It is during this time I learn that Roy has a lady that he is very interested in living here. It seems that during his last stop here he fell in love with a girl named AK. I would not have expected that from Roy. He had a girl back home by the name of Edith, but like so many of us received a "Dear John." The girl here is very small and good-looking. I think she is one of the prettiest women I have seen in this part of the world. She has the typical black hair that is long and straight. Her skin is smooth and has a light tan color. Her eyes are large and look like black marbles set in snow. Her figure is well rounded, but like most of these people she is lacking in chest development. (Too bad about those the small breasts) Her legs are long and muscular, as is the rest of her. She is maybe 4'7". Ak is also Chi's daughter. Roy wants to take her home with him at the end of this tour. (How do I tell him we will have a lot of trouble getting her out of here? Not with her people, but with our people). How do you explain a girl from a country you are not suppose to be in to the people down in Saigon. The people down in Saigon don't like us as it is and they will have a field day with this. I can just see some little E-4 typist sitting in an office screaming about this when he has the paperwork to type up. I sometimes think it would be a good idea to have everyone in this country spend at least half of their tour on the front lines. I have heard stories about people who come over to Nam spend one year and go back without seeing any action. It is not fair for some of us to spend all our time on the cutting edge. While others sit back in their safe offices in the south with their air conditioning, clean bedding, bowling, hot meals, and all the other comforts of home only to give us a hard time about everything.

It's 2200 hrs, time for us to move out. The sky is black and the cloud cover hides any light from the moon or stars. Some of Chi's men moved out to the east-southeast about one hour ago to pull any Dinks off. We move out to the north-northeast. The track back to the airbase is a long one, because we must cover our movement. The trip into Laos was easy, for if we were followed, it would not mess up the mission. Now if we were spotted we would blow the mission. Chi sent Wi his son and his best scouts with us to the border. But from then on, we are on our own. The hump back to Nam is easy and we have no problems until we cross the fence into Nam.

Phil is on point with Roy then me. Behind me, John followed by Doc with Veto behind him. That puts Mike walking tail. We are just into The Nam when Mike taps Veto and gives him the signal that there are NVA coming up behind us. Veto in turn passes it on until all of us are down in hiding. It is a group of ten NVA and by the looks of it they are heading in the direction of the camp we took out. The gooks are not even paying any attention to what is around them. They are laughing and kidding round with one another. Mike looks at me as to say "now what?" If we follow them, they might lead us around any traps they have set. To follow them could give us away. To take them out would not be easy, as there is ten of them and only seven of us. We have had worse odds. The NVA made the decision for us by stopping and almost sitting on Roy. With silencers on our pistols, we open up on them killing all, but two. Those two head back the way they came. Mike and Veto take off after them. Shortly there after, we are greeted by the retort of shots ringing out and then there is nothing. John asks how many shots I heard.

"Only four, how about you?" I say.

"Four also," John answers.

As we are disposing of the bodies, Mike comes back without Veto. Doc asks, "Where's Veto." There is a long silence and then Mike tells us that Veto has taken a round in the head.

"He went quick, I think he was dead before he hit the ground." is all that Mike is able to say. I can see that he is badly shaken.

I ask Doc to give Mike something to calm him down.

"Phil you and Roy go back and do something with Veto's

body."

Mike knows we cannot take Veto's body with us, and to put it in a marked grave would just give us away. Just as Phil starts out, sounds come from back down the trail. We jump for cover and wait for whoever it is. I say a short prayer, like everyone does over here when the shit hits the fan. I ask Mike if he hid the body. He did not answer. Because just then we surprised by the sight of a burning torch coming around the bend. If we aim just behind the torch and open up quick, we have a chance of getting out of this. But it would also give our mission a no win situation. It would be in our best interest to let them pass, and then take them out from behind.

As they go by us, I see that it is some of Chi's men. A signal is given to make contact without a shot fired. The lead man is Chi's son, Wi. He tells me that they started to head back to their village when they heard the shooting and came to see what happened.

"Lucky for you we did." Wi says. "If we had not come one would have gotten away. I kill him with arrow in back of head."

I tell him "Thanks Wi," and ask if he would take Veto's body back with him and turn it over to our people.

He says, "Yes" but wants to send two of his men with us. Wi tells me they will only stay with us till we arrive at the first camp, and then return home.

That sounds like a good idea to me. So I tell him, "Ok, only if they do not start a fight without my orders."

"They will follow your orders." Wi tells me.

"OK. Ok, let's move out." I tell everyone. I am pleased that Wi had followed us and is now going to take Veto's body back to our people. It would be hard to leave a friend buried in an unmarked grave somewhere, never to be found. As so are an innumerable number of men.

The rest of the hump back to the camp we hit several days ago goes fairly easy. I say fairly easy, but I cannot stop thinking about Veto and how he will be missed, worrying about Mike who was a lifetime buddy of Veto. Having gone to high school together stayed in touch until being back together on this team and all that carried with it. We stop just outside the remains of the base to say our good byes to our Laotian friends. We also want to check if there is any activity at the base. I send Phil and Doc ahead to scout the trail to the airbase, while Roy and I go into the base. Which leaves John to watch over Mike. To my total surprise the NVA have not come back, except to pick up their dead and what supplies are still usable. I do not think there was anything useful here. The smell of death hangs in the air like a heavy cloud. The ground still has the reddish tint of blood from the numerous bodies which layed here. Even if it was our enemy and it was a kill or be killed time, there is sadness about this place.

It looks like they have decided not to try to reopen this base. They have set a lot of booby traps, so we reset them to stop the Dinks when they come back. As we are about to leave, there is some action back up the trail. It is easy for Roy and I to work our way around to the back of the action. As we come upon it we found ten dead VC with WI's men taking off the heads of the dead. One of them tells me that they are going to put the heads of the killed on poles and place them in the base as a sign that the locals have been there. In a way, that was a good idea. Because then the NVA will think the locals and not Americans that have hit this base. I send Roy back with them so they do not trip any of the traps.

The hump to the airbase is hard, because we have to travel by day. If we make contact now, we will lose the advantage of surprise and possibly endanger the others. The jungle is very dense and hard to move through. About two hours out from the training camp, we come across an abandoned village. The ground around it is nothing but bomb craters and the area is without any trees or large bushes. Two of my men go ahead to check it out. They come back to say that it is empty now, but it looks like the NVA use it as a night defensive position. Oh Goodie! How many more of these do they have setup and where? We have to move out of here and not leave any sign we were here. Boy, did that info make the rest of the trip difficult. Behind every bush or tree, we start to see Charlie. It is not that we are scared, just careful. I want to booby trap every place Charlie could set up an NDP, but that would give us away. Charlie would be in place long before we hit the airfield. It is now getting dark and we still have a long way to the meeting point. I send John on ahead to make contact. Mike is starting to come out of it now, and asks what he can do. He is given an update, and asked if he is all right.

Mike tells us that he is sorry he flipped out back there. He goes on to say that he is ok now and that he wants to resume his duties as XO.

I ask, "What happened, if you can talk about it?" It has to go in my report, and the only way to find out is for Mike to tell me. The longer I wait the more details will be lost.

Mike starts by saying that it was not his fault. Veto was on point and Mike was looking back over his shoulder when the first shot was fired. He turned around to see the second round hit Veto just about in the middle of his nose. The back of his head then exploded and Veto fell dead. Mike then put one round into the chest of the first gook and then took a shot at the second one. The second one then took a shot at Mike that missed. By then he was around the bend in the trail. Mike then goes on to say "It was dark, I could not see, He could have been anywhere. I pulled Veto's body off the trail, and covered it as best I could. That is when I heard someone coming, so back I came. I did bring Veto's weapons with me, didn't I?"

"Yes you did, and the people you heard were Chi's men. They came to help when they heard the shots." Roy chimed in.

Mike smiles and says, "Let's move out." (It feels good to have Mike back working.)

John comes back with Twan, just as we clear the ridge and make sight of the airstrip. Twan was at the contact point last night his people are setup just as I had asked.

"How is the airstrip guarded and how many men does Charlie have?" I ask.

Twan says, "Hao has a map that we should look at."

Hao comes over with his map, and it looks like it came from some store or something. On it are all the buildings, the runway, the bunkers, the minefield and all the trails to the NDP's plus their positions. It even shows craters in the runway and how to miss them. The map also has the distance from one point to the next.

I look at Twan as much as to say, "How did he do this." Hao answers before I can ask. Hao had been a scout for a company of engineers and they showed him how to draw and to measure off distances for a map. He learned to measure from a distance by using sticks and string.

I say, "Thanks this is a real help. Now all we need is a time-table of what happens in that camp."

Hao hands me a timetable, and says it may be off by a minute or two. I thank him and tell him we with this information we now stand a good chance of getting out of here alive and completing our mission.

At 0100, the Dinks change the guard, and according to Hao the ones that come on fall asleep by 0230. That is the best news I have heard in a couple of weeks.

"When do they change the guard again?" Mike asks.

"Not till 0900, but they bring food out to the guards at 0600." Hao answers.

We sat back to wait until 0300, at which time we will move in. It is time for me to rest and reflect and what has happened. The night is alive with bugs of every known kind and then some. The ground is alive with black bugs that look something like spiders. They walk up to you touch you, with one of there feelers and then run away. It is good to see something in this country that runs away. Everything else wants to attack you. The other good thing is we have not seen any of those buggy whip leeches. The mosquitoes make up for that though.

At 0300, we move out. Twan has two men positioned to kill the people in the NDP's, but before we can takeoff, we must blow the radio room and any phone lines leading out. The map shows two Radio rooms, but no phone line.

"Hao, do they have phone line leaving this place?" I ask.

"No, they don't any longer. There was a line to the camp we cut before, but it is not there now."

"Good that makes it easier. Mike, you take this radio room while John takes this one. Set your timers to go off at 0330. Roy you and Phil take care of the Bunkers and hooch's of the off duty troops. Twan, can you send some men with Roy and Phil as back up?"

Twan points out several men and tells them to go with Phil. Doc and I will plant charges on the other planes. As we move out Twan and some of his men go to the building that has the supplies in it.

We will take the chopper that is sitting on the runway ready to go. The bird is a Russian made that will hold about 12 men along with their gear. After planting the charges on the other planes, I turn to see Twan and his men running across the airfield with boxes. They are to load some bombs and explosives onto our bird. It will be about a three-hour flight out of here, and with a little luck we maybe able to drop our load on a target of opportunity. If our luck holds, we should be able to make Laos, then south and be back in country in time for our R&R.

Twan comes over to me to say he found three RPG's and about ten boxes of explosives with detonators and they are all on the plane. I thank him, and ask if we can give him a lift somewhere. He says "no, but he will see us off." Twan and his men are to stay behind, and keep the dinks hopping until we have a chance to make it out of the area. Twan is then to make it look like the locals did the job and split for home. I do not envy Twan or his men for what they have to do. This is going to become one hot place when we fly out of here. Roy and Phil grab my arm as I move to cross the airfield.

"Eric, we must put a move on this."

There were three men sitting on the back steps of one of the hooches. We took them out with the pistols and silencers. We did not wake anyone, but there was movement in the hooch. I cannot believe our luck so far. Twan's men have silenced the NDP's. The only two people who came up went down without a sound.

Both radio rooms were empty of personnel. I do hope our luck holds.

As we enter the bird, I realize that all the switches, dials and gauges are in Russian with small tape tags in Vietnamese. With a sigh of relief, I am thankful I have learned Russian. It is time to bring this ugly bird to life. The rotors start to turn slowly, very so slowly at first, then start to speed-up. The noise is so loud it could wake the dead. The bird comes to life just as the explosions start. Wham! First, the two radio rooms explode, and then as we move off the pad the other planes go up in balls of fire and smoke. As we turn the Chopper to make a run for the sky. Tracers go off in all directions. Twan has his men firing into the buildings, and also at the guards that are now awake.

Just as we clear the outer perimeter, the supply buildings take on the look of Chicago after Mrs. O'Leary's cow kicked over the lamp.

We are up and on our way out of here. We fly just above the treetops, as not to be seen on any radarscope. If some hotshot Mig jockey wants to know who we are, we are sunk. At about 10 klicks out, I go down between two hills and follow a stream that will take us to the fence. At 20 klicks out, the radio comes to life. They want to know who we are. Where we are going and what is the call sign of the day. John keys on the radio and starts to talk into the mike. From what I can gather, he makes as if he cannot understand them. They are speaking two different tongues of Vietnamese. If John can keep this up for just couple of minutes more, we will be over the fence. But no way, we are that lucky. Out of the northern sky comes a Mig like it is a dog after a cat. My only hope is that down in this valley he cannot move around me as fast as he should. This will give us a chance to shoot him down. He comes in high and dives on us from behind. As he starts to pull up, Mike and Roy open up on him. Just as he is even with our nose, Doc leans out the door and hits him with an RPG. He tries to roll and fire at us again only to explode in a great ball of fire. A second Mig is now on his way, so I put our ship as close to the water as I dare. If I were any closer to this here river, we will need scuba gear. The river bends back and forth, which makes it almost impassable for us and there is no way the Mig can, make a straight run at us. We are just about at the fence as the second Mig comes back into our view. He went right over us as if he did not see us. He then turns around and does the same thing again.

"Boy this is spooky." Doc says, "If he does that again I think I can take a shot at him."

"Ok just don't miss, you may not have a second shot." Mike tells him as I start to pull up, so as to be able to drop our load on a truck convoy that is about to cross a bridge over the river. It is a crude bridge make of wood and large tree trunks. Doc fires as he comes around for the third time.

"I got him," Doc screams. Doc hit him all right, but not before, he shot us. We aren't hit badly. The Mig did punch a few holes here and there and one where it did not need to be. Most of the damage is confined to the tail boom. But that Mig did hit our fuel cell. Not real bad, just bad enough, so we are losing fuel. Luck was with us this time, as it did not cause an explosion. Our only hope is to lighten the ship, and try to make Laos. If we can keep going due west, we will be over the border in 20 minutes. To make things worse we are also losing hydraulics. Oh well here goes.

Doc comes up to tell me that Phil has been hit, and is losing a lot of blood.

"Will he make it?"

"Yes he will, but he will not be able to walk for sometime."

"I hope you don't plan on us having to land and go on the run. Phil could not make it." Doc says.

"No I plan on flying this crate out of here. How is everyone else?" I ask.

"Roy was nicked in the hand from some shrapnel, but it's nothing to worry about." Everyone else is doing just fine. How are you?" Doc said with a smile. There is this burning feeling in my right shin, but that is all.

Doc leans down to look at my leg only to turn quick, run to the back, and retrieve his bag. "You have a large cut with a small piece of metal sticking out in your leg. It has to come out." Doc says, as he cuts the leg of my pants.

"Who will fly this crate while you cut on my leg, Doc?"

"None of you can fly, and what if the gooks send in another Mig." John chimes in to say, "the gooks think we went down. When our load hit the ground, they thought it was our flight going down."

John then tells us he had taken six flying lessons in a small chopper back in Wyoming. Doc tells him to take over, so he can remove the shrapnel out of my leg.

With John climbing into the left seat. I yell, "Who is in charge."

Doc says, "If I don't remove this slug the answer to that question will be a mute point."

I tell John. "Hold the ship on a heading of due west, and to stay just off the tops of the trees". I then swing around to let Doc at my leg. I must have passed out, because the next thing I remember is Mike's voice saying "we must be over the border by now." I look up to see it is getting light out. The engine starts to sputter as it runs out of gas. Just in front of us and to the left is a rice paddy. John gives me the controls.

"We are going down." I say, as the ship banks to the left and begin a slow descent to the flooded rice paddy. We hit with a jolt, bounce once, twice and splash we are down.

We run for the trees, with Mike carrying Phil, before we can be spotted and take cover until we know where we are.

"Mike do you have the map? Does anyone have any idea where we are?" I say as I look back at the ship. "Hey that is no rice paddy that is a swamp. Give me the map."

If we went due west from the point where we were hit we would be here. But there is no swampland in this area. The nearest swampland is to the south. The DMZ is about 100 klicks to the south of where we were to have crossed the fence.

"How long was I out?" I ask.

Doc tells me that I was out for about an hour. I say, "Lets see that ship has an air speed of about 70. That would put us, just about here on the map. But that can't be right. There is no swampland anywhere around here."

"Mike go back to the ship, and look to see what direction the compass reads. Also bring the portable radio that's in under the right front seat. It may be Russian, but John may be able to tune it to one of our channels. If not, I may be able to send a message out in code using Russian. Our people try to monitor all radio traffic from the north. With luck they could on line and hear us."

Mike comes back and tells me that the compass is reading almost due west. My hand compass does not coincide with that reading. In shooting a reading, I find that the one in the bird is off by about 85 Degrees. Knowing that and the time we were airborne after being hit, it is not hard to find that we are just to the north and west of the DMZ. Roy points out that if that is true we will find a friendly village about five klicks to the southwest. There should be a fork in the river that feeds this swamp just over behind that tree line and then about two klicks up we will find a set of rapids. The fork is right were Roy said it was, and then the Rapids come into view. But someone is at the rapids.

We put Phil down, and send two men down to the right and two down to the left. I stay with Phil, because my leg is killing me. The land is sloping down to the river on both sides with the rapids being made by the two sides twisting the river over large rocks that have fallen into it. I can see what looks like a woman doing wash and two or three kids playing in the water. The hills on either side are steep and give a good view of the river both up and down stream for a long way. It takes forever before our two parties are in place. I can see Mike and John on one side, but only Doc on the other. There have been no shots fired, so where is Roy? I look back down at the woman only to see Roy walking up to her. They talk for some time, and it looks like Roy starts to laugh. He signals us to come on over to him. Mike and John come to carry Phil and me.

There is great happiness and fun when we all come together. The woman tells us that we are near the village of Lao Bao in South Vietnam. On the trek to their village, I learn there is a firebase about four klicks to the south. Once we reach the village, the village chief meets us and is tell us he is happy to see Roy again. It seems Roy was also here before. The chief name is Hi, and he has men working with the Americans. We are given something to eat and drink as he sends some of his men with a coded message I had given them to the firebase. I ask Roy if he can be trusted. Roy tells me yes he has worked with the Americans in this area for sometime and is a good man. After a short uneasy nap for me while Doc worked on Phil's foot. My leg is sore, and I am on edge in this village I have no intelligence on. One of Hi's men comes back to tell us a patrol from the base is on the way.

In short order the patrol comes in to the village. Lt. Anderson from 1st company 101st Airborne come up to me and introduces himself to me. He informs me that our people have been looking for us. Word had come down that we might have been shot-down. When my message reached the firebase, they notified Na Trang that we were found. A dust off was called in and we will be on lifted out shortly. To the hospital in their firebase, where Phil will have his foot taken care of.

At the firebase, Mike tells me "Eric, the doctor here is sending Phil to Na Trang.

"They do not have the right people here to take care of him." John tells me.

Before any Doctor can put any of us to sleep, they have to have someone from SOG Headquarters present. They cannot work on us without a SOG member present, unless it is a matter of our life or death. This is done, because of what we know, and what we do. The people back in the States don't want anything to leak out about what we do so a censor has to be there to cover in the event someone says something. I hear tell that once a guy said just a little too much, and that all the Doctors and Nurses had to sign a long statement that they would say nothing to anyone under penalty of jail time if they did. I have been told that at one time it was so bad that a doctor could not give you aspirin without first calling the group Commander for approval. We have a team of our Doctors in Na Trang and Japan to work on us, and in this way, they don't have to worry about what we might say.

"What about the wound I have to my leg?" I ask.

"Eric they are sending all of us on to Na Trang." Mike answers.

As we lift off from the firebase, I tell Lt. Anderson "Thanks for all your help and good luck."

Chapter 14

I do not like this food. Why is the food in a hospital the worst stuff ever? Even in the most remote, inaccessible, godforsaken firebase, the food is better. I do not understand how someone can cook eggs and have them turn out green and slimy. Cook bacon so it looks and tastes like old tires and toast that is as limp as a wet noodle. You would think hospital food, and preparation of it, should be of a quality to help the wounded recover. Not make them feel worse. Let's not talk about these tin plates with the small compartments that do not keep the things on it apart.

You would think the food would be the same in all units over here. But no, the number one place to find good chow is in the Officers Club in Saigon, and then only because "The General" eats there. Second, would be the Officers Mess in main supply area because they have first choice. Third, the main base camp for any large unit commanded by a Lt. Colonel or above. Fourth, smaller base camps and remote firebases. Fifth, anywhere C-rats are served. And then, last but not least come the hospitals.

"Sorry Mike for rambling on like that. What have you heard

about Phil?" I say to Mike as I try to become comfortable on one of those lumpy cots. (You know the kind that no matter how you lay on them something is sticking you or pushing on you in such a way as to inflict a majority of pain.) "How is Phil doing?" I ask.

"The doc's here have done all they can. He is being transferred to Japan for an Orthopedist to look at him." Mike tells me.

I ask. "Will Phil be back?"

"No, they are going to just patch him up and then send him on to the Fort Benning, Ga. That way he can be close to Carol and his parents. He may lose all use of his lower body. A metal fragment hit him in the middle of his back and a 50-caliber slug hit his foot. It was his right foot that was bleeding so badly."

"Doc did not even know about the back laceration till we had to move him out to the bird in Hi's village. With all the blood from Phil's foot and us carrying him. Doc did not even look for a back wound. Besides Phil never said his back hurt till we put Phil on the litter."

"You know what an Old Mother Hen Doc is about us. Man, does he feel bad about not looking him over before we left the village. The Chief Surgeon here told Doc it would not have made any difference. How is Doc doing?"

"The Chief Surgeon gave him something to sleep and he is in the bed across from Phil. He will be out for sometime I am told. He really needed it. I don't think Doc had much sleep since we came in." said Mike.

"How is Phil doing?" I ask.

"Phil thinks he will be all right. But it doesn't look good. Just any hour ago, he said his right foot felt like it was asleep. The doctors here cut that foot off last night to save his leg. Infection had set in real bad. It was already turning green. Phil is just over in the next tent. Want to go over?"

"Yeah, I can walk over."

Mike tells me he has been with our men since we arrived two days ago.

"Two days. That long. I did not think I was out that long." I said.

I started to think about Phil, and all the things he was going to do when he returned back to the world. I can't help thinking about what that sweet little girl is going to think when she is told. He was an active guy. Phil played first base for a softball team that won a couple of tournaments. He liked to go camping and all types of other outdoor stuff. Bass fishing was one of his many loves. Now he would have to put that all behind him.

"Let's go see him before they ship him out. What does he know about his wounds?" I ask.

"He knows his back is messed up but thinks it will be all right. He does not know about the foot." Mike tells me as we cross the area between the tents.

The smell of death hangs heavy around this place. Everywhere you look, you can see people who face death in a different way, then the men up on the line. Up there death is something that happens. It is more often than not swift. If you are not next to the guy that is hit, you can just turn the other way. But these people must face it straight on. They put their hands on it every day and every night. You look in the faces of the Doctors and Nurses and can tell they are tired. I would not want their jobs.

When I see death, it is for the most part my enemy. These people work to keep people alive, both the enemy and our guys. I have been to this kind of place before and every time it is worse. It is worse because death in a hospital unit like this is personal where death in the field is impersonal. Impersonal even when I must use my hands to take a life. In the field, we work to stay alive by killing, before we are killed. While the people that work here are trying to save lives. I thank them for it, especially when it is one of my men.

"Hi Phil, how you doing?" I ask.

"Just fine Sir. They tell me I am going home. I guess I have one of those million dollar wounds you hear about. I am sorry that I have to leave you and the rest of team. Please let me know when y'all are back in the states. Carol and I want y'all to feel like our home is your home. Y'all do know our address in Atlanta, don't you? Just drop in any time. It will be all right. Sir, May I ask you to send me one of these jackets with the Nam map on the back? Just put the price in with it and I will send you the money. Also, in my footlocker is a letter to Carol, please send it. Thanks." And with that Phil falls asleep. He was asleep before I could tell him that he would probably be home before the letter arrived. All outgoing mail is opened and checked to make sure nothing is being leaked to the world. (This is S.O.G. you know.) We talk for sometime before the Doctor comes in, gives Phil a look see, gives him a shot and tells us that he will sleep for sometime now. So Mike and I go to the Mess Hall for coffee. In the mess hall sits Roy with this look of total loss on his face.

"Say Roy what is wrong with you." Mike asks.

"OH, just Veto's gone and now Phil is going home. The team is breaking up round me and it does not feel good." Mike and I both concur. "Here I sat drinking coffee and thinking about all the things we have been through. This team has had the lowest loss rate in the group. We have been in the field for more than 21 months without losing a single man. Now with in one week this team is down two men. Oh we have lost some of the Yards that work with us but none of our people till now. It is getting close to the time for all of us to go home. I just pray that we, the five of us that are left, can walk out of this country. Or at least not be carried out on a litter like Phil, or worse yet in a body bag."

"What are you two going to do now? You know they are going to give us an R&R." I say. "Mike wants to go to Thailand and Roy wants to bring his girl, the one in Chi's village, down south to be married. For me I just want to eat one of the steaks we have in the mess hall, have a big slug of Kentucky white lighting and then sleep without having to keep one eye open."

One of the family traditions I had to learn as a kid was the art of making the best moonshine west of the Appalachians. The corn came from our fields and was lovingly cared for. The still was over 150 years old, but kept in great shape. We are proud of our shine. It has the kick of a mule but leaves no bad after taste. I also learned the art of running shine to Tennessee. Them dam revenuers would not let a poor hillbilly make an honest days livin. We ain't never caused no pain to no one.

Doc comes into tell us the medics are going to be moving Phil out to the flight line soon. As we head over to see Phil. I have Roy find John. The four of us meet in front of the hospital, and together we enter and go to Phil's side. We want to tell him, if he is awake, that the team will meet in back in the states. He is awake, but very groggy.

"Phil we just want you to know we will miss your jokes and funny way of looking at things. We will set up a get together when we are all back in the States." The medics come in to put Phil on his flight to Japan, and then he's headed home to Carol.

We say a very sad good-by to Phil as he looks up at us and

says. "Man I wish we were all going home now not just me. You guys take care and don't forget to come by the house when y'all return back to the world." Phil tells us as the medics carry him out.

At the flight line, we watch as Phil is loaded into the bird. The aircraft comes to life and taxies out to the end of the runway. As we watch we can see the bird straining for altitude.

That pilot is in some kind of a rush to fly out of here. "What does he know that we don't know?" I ask.

One week later the rest of us are on our way back to our base camp for a reassignment. After we are settled in, I walk over to the OPS tent to report in. The walk over to OPS seems longer than before. All around me are the sounds of men getting ready for the upcoming night. The LPs are going out to their holes. While the rest of the men in camp are getting into place for the harassment that comes with each night.

We are placed right on the middle of what was once Charlie's main line of supplies to the south. This camp was built here to try to slow if not stop some of the supplies. Charlie does not like us here and has hit this camp with harassment fire every night since we opened it up. We send out patrols every night. Only to have Charlie drop five rounds from one spot. Move to another spot and drop some more. It was like he knew where our guys were for every time he moved he would move away from our people. The incoming would start about one hour after dark and stop about three hours later. They never seemed to hit anything important. It was like they just wanted to keep everyone awake. Then just when you were to the point of being able to sleep through it they would hit something important. More often then not it was either the mess hall or the latrine. For the life of me,

I can't figure out why the mess hall and the latrines are the two targets they hit most. Every so often, they would hit the supply dump not doing much damage as it was well dug in. But not as often as the other two places.

The camp is set up with the arsenal, communication bunker and OPS shed in the middle. Around these are five long buildings set in the shape of a pentagon with the short sides pointing at each other. Between the ends of each long building sits a latrine. One long building houses the mess hall, the kitchen and the shower room. Our bunkrooms are in one. The other two are for the other two teams we share this little bit of home with. The last is for visitors or others people traveling through.

A trench is lined with punji stakes then it circles these five buildings. Outside this circle is the grouping of tents for the local troops. Only to be followed by a five pointed star shaped outer defensive perimeter. In each of the points of the outer star is a mortar pit. Plus there are mortar pits at each of the points on the inner pentagon.

Outside the outer defensive perimeter are several strands of concertina wire and a minefield. Special Forces and Mike Force people occupy the inner defensive positions. The outer defensive positions are manned by the CIDG troops. CIDG troops are the Civilian Irregular Defense Group. These are the people of the local villages who have received training and are now working to free their villages from the VC and NVA. They are good fighters and willing people. My Mike Team is made up of Montagnard's who have more training and been with us longer than the CIDG's.

It is to this place we look forward to returning after a little walk in the woods. Here we can have a hot shower and some hot food. The air is not the cleanest, because every day they burn the stuff that people leave behind in the latrines. What you do is put diesel fuel or kerosene on the stuff and incinerate it. This leaves a foul smell hanging in the air over the camp.

As I walk over to the OP Center to report in. I cannot stop thinking about Veto and Phil both are going home. Veto to be buried with his brother looking on and thinking how he may have put the seed in Veto's mind about the service. Phil on his way state side to see his wife and to spend the rest of his life in a wheelchair. To be one of the people he would say, "Were not living only existing." How he has to exist.

I look up and say, "If you do exist and you hear me. Don't make Phil spend his days sitting around. Let him walk and live a normal life somehow."

At the OPS office, I am told we are to have a short R&R, and that the replacement personnel will be in Na Trang in ten to 15 days. After the R&R, we are to go to Na Trang to bring the new people up to speed. The next and last mission for us as a team will start in 30 days. In my mind I ask "Why did we come back here only to return to Na Trang for R&R." Then I remember all our personal effects and clothing are here. I ask if the new men are cherries, or if they have been in country before.

Col. Lee tells me that they were part of a team that was down to three men, and like us, they only have 60 days till DEROS.

That is good and bad to know. Old troopers are set in their ways having worked within a small team setup. All teams have their own personality. We are all trained the same, just each team leader has his own ways about him. This makes each team different in small ways and it is small things that will get you killed.

I ask, "Who leads the team." I am told it was a guy by the name of Johnson. I did not know him, so I dropped that line of inquiry. I then tell the Col. that I do not want to go on R&R.

Col. Lee looks at me like I am crazy, then he says he wants to know why.

"Because I am too short, and if I let down now, I may not be sharp for our last mission." I tell him

He then says. "A team to our north just lost both their CO. and XO. They need someone to fill in for 15 days, till their replacements would be in camp."

"If you are offering it to me, I will take it, but only if any of my men that want to, can also come along." I interject.

Col. Lee says, "No, but I could take my XO."

Mike, who had come in behind me said "yes that he would like to."

"It is set, your orders will be typed, and you will fly out tomorrow at 1100 hrs along with the supplies for the camp."

The orders were typed in 10 minutes, and read that we are to return to our team at Na Trang in 15 days. With that I go to my hooch, pick up my soap, clean jungles, and a jug from home. Then I head for the shower; I must have stood in that shower for an hour or more. After the shower, I head for the mess hall. The cook puts two of the thickest steaks on the grill he has set up when I walk in the mess tent. I sit alone at one of the tables by the food line and eat the steaks, some fried potatoes, and bread. Until I'm ready to explode. After eating and sipping on the jug till I am full and have a nice glow on. It's now off to the rack for some sack time.

Lying on my rack, my mind starts to think about what it would be like to be back in the world. No more little walks in the woods. None of our Yard friends to help and none of their good food. Was I ready to go back to the rat race of life in the world? I have a fitful sleep between thinking about home, Veto, Phil and the mortars being fired both in and out of here. At 0400, I am up and go over to the mess hall. With a cup of coffee in hand, and my grits and eggs on the way, I return to contemplate life and what to do.

I would only be back with my wife and children for a year before being sent on a return trip to The Nam. It works like this in SF; you spend two years in country, return home for one year only to come back to this place for another two. Debbie will understand if I tell her how I feel about it. Why go back to the world, lose your edge only to come back, and have a better chance of being killed. More troops are killed in the first two months in country, just after going on R.R., or returning after being out of country then at any other time.

After sitting and thinking for about two hours I leave for the OPS Center. On my way to OPS, John and Roy came up and asked, "What's up."

I told them about the temporary duty that Mike and I have been assigned. I also let them know about the new men and the next mission.

"What are you going to do now?" I ask.

"I am on my way to reup for another tour." John says.

Roy chimes in and says he wants to go home if Ak is with him. If she is not with him, he wants to stay.

"That is real funny; I'm going to stay also" came out of my mouth.

Roy then looks around and asks what about Doc and Mike. "Do you think they will reup also? "

As we arrive at the OP's office door, Doc comes out with a smile on his face.

"What is so funny, Doc?" Roy asks.

"That is so funny you ask. Well let's see. It could be that the three of you are here to do the same thing I just did, and what Mike is doing right now. Could be. What a bunch of nuts we are. Man do you think they will keep us together."

"I don't know, but I will ask when I when I am in there." I say.

Inside the OPS office, Mike is just about to leave when I take hold of his arm. "Mike what are you doing here?" I ask.

"I reuped for one more tour. What are you here for?"

"To do the same." I say. "John and Roy are on the way to reup also."

"If it is possible, let's keep the team together." John says from behind me.

"Mike and I will go to the Old Man and ask him. We will let the rest of you know what he has to say later." I say as we go over to his office and ask to see him. Mike and I are shown into the Colonel Lee's office.

"Sir! What is left of our team, have all signed on for another tour. Is it possible to stay together as a team? Sir!"

"Captain, you and your men have done more than your share. Why do you want to stay in country?"

"Sir, we feel that there is more to be done, a lot more. Why should we leave now? Why should we leave before the job is done? Sir, we as a team want to stay and do our part."

"Captain it is time for you and your men to go home. If any of you do not want to go home, then you will all be assigned to other teams. This is done, so as to give them the help that comes with age and having been here. Do you understand?"

"YES SIR!" Mike and I give him a salute and go out of his office.

Once we are outside the old man comes out. "Captain Howard" he calls. I turn around to face him. "Captain I will hold your request till later this morning. The dispatch run leaves here at 1000 hrs, you have until then. Think it over. If you or any of your men still want to stay by then I will submit your requests. If not, I will destroy the requests and it will just be forgotten. Also the base you are going to was hit again. They lost three more of their team. For that reason, you may take three more of your men with you."

"Thank-you Sir," We say.

As Mike and I go to the mess hall for a cold drink he asks, "Do you think they will reup?"

In response I answer, "I don't know. I just hope they really think about it. Doc should be able to be accepted into medical school by now. Not to say anything about his soon to be wife, Ellen. She writes to him all the time, and has the connections to help him. Roy has his GI bill to pay for him to complete his masters. Mike you have a wife, and by now there must be enough in that bank of yours for that gold mine in South America."

"Say did you see the stack of letters Doc received. Man, he had a mailbag of his own. Now not to change the subject Eric. What are you going to do? How are things at home?"

"Mike, I am going to stay. I have spent a lot of time thinking about it. I put in a request for a Mars call home and will hear back soon. I really want to talk with Debbie first, but yes I am going to stay. What about you are you going to stay?"

Mike answered with "It may sound sick, but to get even for Veto."

"Man we already killed the gook that did Veto. What more can be done? Besides when you go out with revenge on your mind, you are not as sharp as you should be, and that could get you and every one with you killed. Do you want that?"

"No, I don't. Eric, I guess I don't know what I want." Mike answered.

"Ok! Let's call the men together and decide who will be going with us." Mike goes to find John, Roy and Doc as I go to the mess hall.

As we sit at one of the tables, I start by telling them about the A-Camp that Mike and I are going too. I also tell them that we can take them with us. The team there is down to a two-man. I finish by telling them that they do not have to go. In no time at all, they volunteer.

"Ok! Lets go have your orders cut so you can leave with us." I go to the commanding officers office and ask to see him. I am shown in.

"Sir, my men would like you to destroy their requests to stay. I will be staying. Also the other men in my team would like to join Lieutenant Danville and myself as replacements at the camp."

One hour before I am to leave for the new camp the Mars operator comes in to the mess hall for me. He has my wife on line. The Mars system is a one-way radio like a ham operator has. You talk to the other person until you finish then say over and then they talk to you saying over at the end so you can talk back to them. Debbie tells me she would like me home. But would rather have me home in good shape, one piece, alive and not to have to worrying about me returning here.

Later that morning, Mike and I are on our way to a camp in the central highlands. John, Roy and Doc will follow in about two hours, as they will be coming on a later flight that is bringing more supplies. This camp has been over run twice in the last five months. It will be our first priority to reinforce the defenses. On board our chopper is six 60s and four 81s with enough ammo for two weeks. We also have a second bird coming in behind us with more ammo and rations. A ground unit is bringing in a pair of 105s for the camp. The 105 will be in camp in two days. A CH-47 is to our right with concertina wire, claymores, two cases of C-4, some communications equipment and some PSP. I do not like being in a hot base so I am bringing as much stuff as possible to keep my backside cool. Not hot temperature wises, but hot Charlie wise. As I said, this place has been overrun twice already and I don't want to be in the third. Both the CO and XO were killed two days ago and three of the others last night. I may not want to return to the world now, but by the same token, I don't want to buy it here either.

As we come in over the camp, we can see where Charlie as made it easy for himself. To the north is a river that is shallow. To the west and south are open fields with little cover or so it looks from the sky. To the east is a dense jungle. There is less then a 200-yard kill zone before the trees. As we come around to the west, the land looks different. It now looks like a washboard. There are several small ridges running parallel to the outer defensive perimeter. They start at about 50 yards out and are spaced at several yard intervals. It looks like they are about three feet in high. To the south, it looks even worse. The ridges continue around to this side but are higher. They must be five feet high and spaced at 6 foot intervals. Someone could be standing in one of the valleys and not be seen. Looking close you can see where slits are dug, so as to be able to go from one valley to the next.

"Mike look at this. Do you see what I see?"

"Yes, Eric it is easy for the Dinks to sneak up on this camp.

What do we do to put a stop to them?"

"Mike, the only thing I can think of now is to call in an air strike. Although that would put it right on top of us. But it could destroy the excess Charley had made for himself."

Mike answers, "Eric, we could put several drums of foo gas on remote detonators for the time being."

"Mike let me think about that." I tell him.

"Eric, could we move the camp over to the other side of the river? See that spot just to the south of the river and around that hill."

"Say, give me your radio would you?" I ask the pilot. I put in a call to the OPS center. OPS this is Captain Howard, Code name, Eagle. I want to move camp A-937. Grid locations to follow. Good, will follow up then we land. Over and out. Mike, once we land call OPS with the new location. Then OPS will be sending conformation in the A.M. We will know then.

"That is if we make it through the night, Eric. Remember Charlie likes to hit a camp right after some new people come in and we are new to them."

"Mike, did you pack a deck of cards?"

"Yes, Sir, I did."

"Good, give them to me." I ask the pilot to fly us around this camp once about in the middle of that second valley. As we go around, I throw the cards out, one at a time. The cards have our team logo on them and are all the ace of spades. That will give Charlie something to think about. As they are known as death cards to the V.C. We do not have the chance to do this often, but now is the perfect time to. The cards are not to scare Charlie off. They are to slow him down, which they sometimes do.

It will take sometime to build a new camp but it will be the safest thing to do. It could buy us sometime as they try to find out who we are.

Right now, the camp is in the worst possible place from a defense standpoint. I do not know why the camp was placed where it is. I just know it is not the best place to fortify.

Chapter 15

Once on the ground, we meet the remaining members of the team Sergeant First Class Gary McCoy, Sergeant Edward Norwood, Tomas Dillingham and their LLDB'S and CIDG Troops. This was at one time a company of 1400, but now there are only about 800. My counterpart is a man named Cung. Cung is one of those typical leaders you find in this part of the country. Typical in that he knows what he is doing. Not like the people down in the south that only are promoted because they are someone's brothers, sleeping with someone's sister or something like that. He kind of reminds me of a Vietnamese Sid Caesar. He has been in this camp from the beginning, and has told everyone it is in the wrong place. Now he has someone who agrees with him. The most senior A-team member is a Gary McCoy. He is the light weapons, and Demo Sergeant. This is his second tour in country, and at the rank of E-7, he is the one in command of the team that is left. Gary tells me he is glad we made it. He did not want another night to go by without help and someone to take over.

After we do the normal meet and greet, we head to Ops. Placed on a large table is a map of how the base is laid out. Cung, Gary and I go over the map as to placement of the ordinance and personnel. After some discussion, we decide on our plan of attack.

The first thing that must be done is repositioning the mortar tubes in such a way as to provide better cover around the perimeter of camp. They need to be strategically placed in such a way as to cover the east, west and south. We can cover the river to the north with rifle fire. We must then build a place to coordinate the mortars from. Then we place the 60s in a circle just inside the second strand of wire at 60 degrees apart. We put an 81 in place just behind the 60 at due south then put two at 90 degrees off from that. That would leave one as a spare. I also find out from Gary that there is a bulldozer in the area, and it can be airlifted in. They had used it when they first came here.

"Ok Gary, give Mike the contact information, and let's start moving the heavy weapons. As for the troops, Gary you know whom you and Cung have. For tonight, why don't you two move your people around to fill the needed positions? I have three more of my men on the way in. They will be here shortly. You can use them. We will go over personnel and jobs in the morning. Mike, call the engineers and have that bulldozer here ASAP."

"Ok Sir. Should I also ask if they have anything else we can use?" Mike asks.

"Yes, do it." I say as I turn and walk over to the team bunker.

I now have the time to think about my past and future. To remember what has happened to make me what I am today. The time spent in the hills of Kentucky, on the streets of New York City and all the training I have been given by the military. I am a pilot, a member of Special Forces, an expert in light and heavy weapons and demolitions.

I can parachute, and scuba dive. I speak three languages and read two. They are Russian, Swedish, and Montagnard. Montagnard was the hardest to learn, as I learned it second hand. It was just after we came into country. John had learned Vietnamese, and Phil and Doc had French. The French had ruled this country for years, and they had tried to make French the official language. So most of the locals speak some French. When we learned we would be working and living with the Montagnard people, I asked for someone that could speak their language. We were assigned an interpreter that spoke Vietnamese and Montagnard. It was through her, I learned an adequate amount of Montagnard to start. After living with Lok and his people, I learned a lot more of their language.

In just over one hour, the dozer can be seen coming in hanging from a CH-57 follow by two CH-47 choppers. Once on the ground Lieutenant Smith the officer in charge comes over and asks what we need done and where he is to put his men up.

"Put your men up in the team bunker. Mike will show where it is. This is Lieutenant Mike Danville, my X.O." I say as we walk to an area in the center of the camp. "After they are setup we need a hill right here about five feet high. Then start to knock down those trees to the east. Can you give me a clear killing zone about 400 yards out?"

"Yes Sir. No problem Sir. We will get started right away. Can you give us some protection Sir?" Lieutenant Smith asks.

Cung was with us, so I ask him to assign his best men to keep an eye out for any enemy movement and to take care of the engineers.

"Yes sir I will."

As work starts, the chopper with John, Roy and Doc lands, followed by another one with more supplies. I inform John, Roy and Doc of the situation and ask them to help for now. I go on to tell them that there will be a meeting in the morning to go over the plans and assignments.

Night falls on a camp of people who are wide-awake. We have put out all our NDP's and LP's. It is now time to sit and hope Charlie does not come tonight. I have my net up around me in the hope it will keep the bugs off. If you look off to the west, you can see the mosquitoes forming up for the attack. It will be nice if the only attack that comes tonight is from those little pests.

As the night drags on, Mike comes over and asks if I smell something. The air does have an odor in it.

"Oh, I know what that is, that smell is coming from the engineers."

"What do you mean Eric?" Mike asks.

"Mike, the engineers eat C-rats don't they. What you smell is the C-rats."

"Eric you know, I forgot all about that. Thanks, I was worried about it, but now I remember. What time do we change the guard?"

"Mike it would be in our best interest if we keep this camp on full alert all night. Then let half the men sleep in the morning, and the other half in the afternoon. The Lieutenant and his men are asleep now, but if we need them they will be up. If not they will guard the camp, and do their work most of the day. The Lieutenant said he would take over for us at 0500. Then we can sleep. The Lieutenant and I went over where we want to move the camp. He also has a drawing of the layout, so as to be able to lay it out as planned.

"Eric, we do not have permission to move the camp."

"I know but when did anything like permission stop me before. Besides, we know if the camp is left here it will be overrun again and again, right."

"Yes, Sir, you are right. I just hope the brass sees it the same way."

BOOM !!! Off to the left, by the river there is an explosion that is followed by another and another.

"Cung is on the horn for you Sir." One of the members of the camp team tells me.

"Yes Cung, what is it?"

"Captain Sir, Charlie tries to sneak in by the river. We have minefield in river, he step on one, no more Charlie."

"Can you tell how many there are?"

"Yes, it looks like about 100 come across river."

I immediately get on the horn to one of the mortar pits. I say, "Drop one PH round at the river crossing." Wham, the first round hit. "In ten, left five and drop a HE. " Wham. "Five to the left and fire when ready." Six HE rounds slammed home.

After the smoke clears, Cung is on the horn again. "Cung what can you see." I ask taking the phone from Tom. Tom is one of the A-Team that was in camp when I came in. He is a southern boy like me. I can tell by his accent.

Cung answered and tells me that all we did was kick up lot of dirt. Charlie had headed for the hills, when the second round hit.

"That is good now they know we have some firepower and may think twice about coming back soon." Tom chimed in

Mike looks at him and says, "No now they will hit us harder.

With more men, and they may step up their mortar attacks on us."

"Do you have any VC in your group?" When you work with these people, you learn quickly that there is VC, in every Vietnamese Company.

"Yes, I have two." Cung answered. "I know who they are. Need I get rid of them?"

"Cung, have they left camp since we set the tubes up?"

"No, they still in camp. I no let them make contact with any outsider. Ok?

"Yes, that is good, let's put them in position next to the two tubs at the south side of the perimeter." I tell Cung. I then settle down again thinking about Veto and Phil. In my mind, I know I am going to stay in country and know the rest of the team will go home. Here I am in a hole in the ground, in a camp that is not safe; my feelings turn to sadness. I am sad, because of the loss of life. When you put yourself in a known camp in the middle of Charlie country, it is hard to hide. Hide like we do when we are in the bush. Hide and the Dinks do not know we are there. Now we are the known target waiting to be hit, and that is not a good feeling. The rest of the night is still, except for the bugs. So in my down mood, I fall into a half sleep.

I start to dream about the time when the guys in Kentucky wanted to have some fun. The next town north of home had a mayor that was a real jerk. (Yes he was a relative of mine, but a jerk anyway) He had this Horse-drawn carriage; he would ride in for special occasions. He loved it and spent a lot of the town's money on it, saying it was good for the town's image. It was decided we would take the wagon apart one night. Then put it back together on the top of the town water tower. It took some planning but we pulled it off on a night of the new moon. It took six of us most of the night. As the first rays of the morning sun were coming over the mountain to the east, we were done. What a beautiful thing it was to see. This highly polished black Surrey sitting on top of the 50-foot water tower. It just gleamed it the morning sun. Lonnie the Mayor was just returning to home from Frankfort, KY. Frankfort is the state capital of Kentucky. As he came over the hill and down into town he caught sight of his pride and joy. High a top his towns water tower. I am told he cried. No one in town could figure out how to bring it down without breaking something. Everyone just looked at it and shook their head. I think they knew who was responsible, but would not say anything. In the end, a helicopter and some state highway engineers from Frankfort came down and removed it. From then on, the buggy was locked up in the Sheriffs Department Garage.

The sun is coming up as I start to come back to the world of the living. "Mike, is everything Ok? Why did you let me sleep so long?"

"Yes, everything is ok. You needed the sleep. We even have a Dink that tried to slip in last night. Cung is talking to him now. Let's go, they are in the Communications tent." In the tent is the Prisoner, sitting in a chair with his elbows tied behind the chair. His ankles are tied to the chair too. Cung is sitting on a chair in front of him. The prisoner looks like he just went 15 rounds with Sonny Liston and lost, but he is talking to Cung. We stand in the back of the tent, and watch what is going on.

Mike asks, "How far do we let Cung go in his interrogation?"

"Mike, we have been told to let them handle it. That tells me to stay out."

Cung turns and asks if we can obtain a chopper to take this man down to Saigon.

"Ed another member of the base team is working the radio. Ed, will you put a call in to see if we can arrange a flight for this prisoner?"

"Sir, no need we are getting company from Saigon in about two hours. They are coming up to see about the changes in camp location.

"Ok, Ed put in a call and informs them about the prisoner."

"Yes, Sir. Will we be moving the base? I do hope so, as this is on hellhole of a place." I answer, "I will try my best to have it moved."

The engineers are moving across the river when we come out of the tent. As they go into the river, you can see that the bottom is hard enough to take the dozer without it becoming stuck. By the time I was next to the Lieutenant, he had his men cutting the outer perimeter.

"Lieutenant Smith! Say Lieutenant Smith, if we can have the outer perimeter in place and the mortar pits in by nightfall, we can move some of the LLDB over tonight. That will give us cover on both sides of the river. Then tomorrow we should put in the arsenal and communications bunkers. In that way we can move the main team over in two days. "

"Yes, Captain we can do it. That is if we do not receive any harassment, the inner and outer trenches will be in by nightfall. Do you want us to use the dirt from the trenches to build a hill in the center of the area?'

"No Lieutenant, but we will need to cover the arsenal and com-mo bunker. Then a couple of towers, so we will be able to see to the other side of the river. Say by the way, where are you from?"

"I am from Trenton, New Jersey Sir. Why do you ask?"

"It is the accent. Before entering the Army, I would spend part of my summers just outside Philadelphia."

Lt. Smith smiled and said, "I have a cousin just outside Philadelphia. She lives in a town call Souderton.

"Man that is just up the road from where I was. What is her name?"

"Judy Alders now, it was Benton before she was married."

"Did she work in the Highway Diner nights?"

"Yes, she still does. Do you know her?"

"Yes, I would stop on my way home for a bite to eat now and then."

"Say, what is your first name anyway?"

"It's Pete, what is yours?"

"Eric, Eric Howard. I think I have heard Judy talk about you Pete. Isn't this a small world?"

"Yeah it is. If you want this camp done, I better check on work."

As the Lt. walks over to his men. I turn to Mike and say. "You should have seen that Judy. She had the biggest pair of knockers. She had at least a double D, if not more by the age of 16. The rest of her was good to look at also. She was a bit on the dumb side, but a nice conversationalist."

The chopper has landed over by the new camp. Two full Colonels and a Lieutenant Colonel jump out as I am arriving there to meet them. A little ways behind me is Cung with his prisoner. The Colonels and I start to talk about the moving of the camp. I hear Cung ask the Lieutenant Colonel. "Sir" he says to the Lieutenant Coronel, "Where do you want me to put this prisoner?" The Lieutenant Colonel looks at him and then looks at me as much as to say why do I want him.

The pilot then leans out of the ship and says, "Sir we have a request from Na Trang to bring the prisoner back with us."

The Lieutenant Colonel turns to the pilot and says, "We don't want some smell old Gook in the ship with us.

At this Cung turns and yells, "This man has information that may help save the lives of some of our men and yours. NOW where do I put him?"

The pilot comes out and takes the prisoner. He then says, "This is my ship. I have orders from my HQ to bring him back and that is just what I am going to do. Sir."

One of the Colonels asks, "Captain Howard, Why do you want to move this camp?"

"If we don't move it we will continue to lose a lot of men Sir."

The Lieutenant Coronel comes over to where I am pointing out the factors involved with why we need to move the camp, and waits for a break in what I am saying. As soon as he had a chance, he speaks up "Colonel Coleman, Sir. Did you know we were to return with a prisoner?"

"Yes I did, is there a problem with that Lieutenant Colonel Bates?"

Lieutenant Colonel Bates answers very sheepishly, "No Sir I was just not aware of that fact Sir." If looks could kill, Bates would have been dead from the look he received from Colonel Coleman. Colonel Coleman then tells me to go on.

I go on to explain the reasons. We then go up in the chopper, and I point out all the problems with the old camp. I then show the brass the good points in moving across the river. After about 30 minutes of talking it over, they say it is a good idea to move.

As we land, Charlie hits us with some early mail. The brass wants out and out quick. So quickly, I never found out who the other Colonel was.

Mike, Cung and I jump for cover as the bird fights for air and climbs out. When they are about thirty feet up, the co-pilot opens his door and drops a large bag. At first, we do not know what to do. Tom runs out and picks it up.

Tom then yells at us. "It's the mail." As Tom is giving out the mail, he comes up to me and hands me one large brown envelope and one small envelope. The large brown one is from HQ, and is just the everyday BS that goes on in a permanent firebase. In the small one, I find out that the orders have been changed. With that news, I open the orders to see if it is true. In the envelope with the common stuff are orders. The orders read that we are to stay here until DEROS. (I do not like this one bit, not one little bit, went through my mind like a shot)

Camp construction is going nicely, but not as fast as I would like. The days are hot and sticky. The nights are boring, except for the mortar attacks from over in the tree line. They will fire one round; we will watch to see where it comes from. Then they will fire a second and move quickly. We will drop one round where they were. After the first night of this, we tried to drop one on each side of where the last one of theirs came from. Once we were lucky. We know we are lucky, because after our round hit there are several explosions. The rest of that night is quiet.

The bugs seem like they are becoming tired of us. The numbers that will fly, crawl, or slither up to us is getting smaller by the night. I am not complaining, just stating fact. When night comes, patrols go out. I do not want to send any of the men from the other team out. I know they can do it but they are to step down in three days.

"Cung, Can your men go out without any of our men with them to night." I ask.

"Yes, them welcome chance to show you what they can do." answered Cung.

"Good that way we can put the team on positions to strengthen the defenses. My men will start going out with you tomorrow night."

Construction goes quickly and in two days all is just about ready. Life has settled into a day-by-day routine. We will send patrols out by day. Then sent ambushes out by night.

We made contact with the local chief, and he moved his people into camp after one night when the VC came and raided his village. The VC came to his village one night just before nightfall. The VC leader screamed at chief that he was a puppet for the Americans. They then took all the rice the village had put up. They killed the two water buffaloes. Put all the chickens into empty rice sacks. They killed and cooked one of the pigs. All this time, the people of the village were tied to trees in the village. After eating the pig they killed, and downing all rice the villagers had fixed for their dinner. Then VC took a young girl 14 years old out in to the woods. Then they came back, grabbed another girl about 12 years old, and took her out in to the woods. The VC that were in the village while the gang rape was going on in the woods took one of the young men and asked him to join them. He said "no" and spit on them. This made them mad. They then tied him up. Put his head on one of the tree stumps and tied it so he could not move. They then put a long nail in his right ear and tapped it with a pistol butt. They then would ask him another question. If his answers were not what they wanted, they would tap the nail in a little more. The village chief tells us it took 3 hours for the boy die. After the boy was dead, they took the boy's mother and tied her spread eagle on the ground. They then took out what looked like pliers. Using them to break every bone in her fingers. They then asked her another question. If they did not like her answer, they broke another bone in her finger. After all her fingers were broke, they moved to the toes. After all the bones in her hands and feet were broke in a way they took a club and started with her legs and arms. They then went to the body. Somewhere in all this, she died. During that night, 15 of the villagers were tortured to death. The only thing that stopped them was one of our patrols.

As the patrol made up of 20 CIDG troops and two of my men came upon the village, the VC ran for the hills. Chief Phog was so happy, he wanted to move his people into the camp right then. He put all the men in his village into our training program, to help clear the area of VC. Life in this camp would not have been bad, if it weren't for the shelling just about every night.

Mike, John, Doc, Roy and I sat at the mess table after dinner, and talked about what is going on. We also discussed what we planned to do. I told them I had decided to stay one more tour, while the rest are going home in 45 days. We talk about all going to Saigon for a going away party before they leave for home. It will be hard to obtain an ok, but it is worth a try.

Doc had written to his girl about coming home. She has looked into him going to Med. School, and sent him some college junk on it. He spends every free minute looking it over. We kid him that he will have it worn out by the time he is on the plane for home. He has a letter from one Medical School that tells him by being a Special Forces Medic, and having been in Viet Nam for two years. They will wave the normal requirements, and he can start with the next class.

Doc just smiles and says, "That's ok, Ellen has more for me at home."

Mike has it planned that the first place he will go will be to see Veto's family. He wanted to let them know what a great guy Veto was. Veto's folks knew Mike from when he was Veto's guide in Jr. High. I think they will like to see him. Mike has been receiving letters from Veto's Mom and Dad since we have been here. Veto's Dad asks us all to come over for the first Fourth of July, whenever we are all in the states. Mike will take Linda and move wherever the Army wants him. He has decided to make the Army his life. He has written to Linda to tell her this, and to all our surprise, she said, "That was ok with her."

Roy is the one I all worry about because he tells us he will not leave without Ak. I sent the paperwork in for him to be able to get married almost two weeks ago, and we have had no reply to date.

That makes Roy want to go back to Chi's village now. He wants to bring her down here, but he has to stay in camp for at least 40 days. That will only leave 5 days for him to return to Chi's village deep in Laos, pickup Ak, and make it back to Saigon, before he had to fly out to the world. Roy tells us that if she is not with him when it is time to go home. He will go AWOL, and split for Laos. I know that is only talk. Roy would not do anything that stupid. He loves the U.S. too much to lose everything for one girl.

"Sir! I have a radio message for you." One of the Yards comes in with a coded message for me.

"Thank-you I will decode it and see if I need reply." I say as I stand up to go to the HQ for the codebook. "Mike, will you come along with me?"

"Yes Sir! May I bring my coffee?"

"Yeah Mike, and grab me a cup on the way." Inside the HQ, I open the safe and take out the codebook. The room is dark and cool. We had it built underground with about six feet of dirt on top. The HQ is in the same building as the commo room but you cannot move from one to the other without going out and around. That is one of the things we are going to fix, before we leave in 40 days. The light from the lamp makes it hard to read. "Who is in the radio room, Mike?"

"Tom is on duty. Why?"

"Oh Yeah. Well, someone had better teach that kid to spell. When do we expect to have that radio totally up and running?" I ask.

Mike tells me that the next two choppers will have the rest of their gear, and the Signal Corp men to run it. Then in two days, they will have it all together.

"You know Mike, I don't know if I like having some line company radio team here. Well anyway let's see what this is all about."

Howard, Eric C.: Captain.

You and 12 men from your LLDB Team are to report to camp A-876. We will send a UH-1H for you in 10 days. This will be for a short training mission of   10 to 15 days. You are to tell no one where you are going or when you will return. Danville, Mike, Lt. will be in command of your team in your absence. You may let him know. Radio confirmation sig. Alpha, Alpha.

"What is this all about Eric?" Mike asks.

"I don't know, but here is your chance to command a team. Do take care of them. If you don't, I may just have to kick you ass all the way back to Nah Trang. Mike you are the only one who knows about this. Let's keep it that way for now."

"OK, Eric." Mike says.

"What 12 men are you going to take?" I answer.

Mike says, "I don't know. Who are the best in your opinion?"

"Let's ask Cung who he would send. Do that Mike while I find out where this camp is." I search the maps looking everywhere, and I cannot find it. I search from the DMZ to the Gulf of Thailand, from the South China Sea to Cambodia and Laos.

Cung comes into the room, and takes a seat by the table. "Yes, Sir what can I do for you?" Cung asks.

"Cung, I need 12 of your best men for a special mission. Sorry I can't tell you more. Can you pick them for me and have them here in the morning?" With a total look of surprise on his face, he looks for words, but has trouble coming up with the right ones.

"Sir? Sir how long will they be gone?"

"Sorry I can't tell you that."

"Then Sir, where are you going?"

"Sorry I can't tell you that either."

"What can you tell me?"

"I can tell you I have orders to take 12 of the LLDB men to a point unknown to me. A chopper will pick us up in about 10 days. That is all I can tell you, because I don't know any more, and I have orders not to say more even if I knew more."

"Thank you for telling me the truth. Sir. I will have my best men by the entrance to the bunker at 0800 tomorrow."

"Thank you, Cung. I am sorry I cannot tell you more. See you in the morning."

I meet the men that are going to be going with me at 0800,

and have nothing to say to them. Except that I want to talk with each and every one of them one at a time, starting after breakfast. That is fine with them. They like to sit down and talk to us, but do not have much of a chance to. They take pride in their story, and each one has a story. A story about their family, or about their village and what the communists did to them. The next nine days go by just doing the normal things. I also try to become familiar with men that are going with me, so I can better understand why they are doing it.

Sun Tzu once said, "Keep your friends close and your enemies' closer." (I think that should also go for your potential enemies)

Chapter 16

As the morning sun rises, it is covered with a heavy haze. A sunrise looks like we may be in for some rain. I sense that something is about to go wrong. I seem to be able to tell when something is going to go very wrong, never specifically what, just something.

"Mike, you take care of the team, and don't you let anything happen to them. If you do, I will haunt you the rest of your life."

"Eric, if you don't make it back till after Roy, Doc and I will have rotated out, have a safe second tour. I will write and let you know where Linda and I are living. Please promise to come spend some time with us."

"Ok Mike, I promise. But don't let her tie you up in her apron strings."

"You know I would never let that happen. Not to change the subject, but we received word late last night that Roy and Ak can be married in 90 days."

"Mike that is 60 days after Roy is to rotate out of the Nam."

"I know Eric, but HQ has extended Roy's tour for 65 days and assigned him to Embassy duty in Saigon. By doing that, he can get married and take Ak back to the states as his wife. The U.S. Ambassador pulled some strings for Roy, and has it all set up. Roy is very happy, and almost impossible to live with. He not only had a short timers calendar going, but also a second one that tells him how long till he is assigned to the Embassy in Saigon."

"Mike, Is he a danger to himself and the others out on patrol?"

"Eric, I think he is. It would be in the best interest of the whole team if we could get him to stand down now instead of later."

"Mike I have an idea. Let's cut some orders to send him to Nah Trang for thirty days of testing before the promotions board. That would get him out of the field before he can get himself and others killed. Roy is a good trooper, one of the best. But his head is not into being out in the bush. I think he has been out in the bush too long and is ready to stand down. Get John in here please."

"John, I am going to send Roy down to Nah Trang for testing for promotion. I am doing this to get him out of the bush. You know about the Embassy thing don't you?"

"Yes I do Eric, and I think it is the best thing for him and the rest of us. We all have been trying to keep him out of trouble. All he seems to think about is that skirt he wants. The rest of the team has asked me to talk to you about getting him out of here."

"Good so the others will not think I am playing favorites. John, place a call to Nah Trang. I want to speak to the promotion board."

John tells me. "Eric I have a Captain Halley on the horn" and hands me the phone.

"Captain Howard here. Captain Halley I would like to send one of my men down to you for some testing. No, there is no problem with him. I would like it done because he has been in the field for 23 months. Central command has extended him for 90 days in country, and he is going to be on Embassy duty in thirty days. He then will be married, and rotate state side in 60 days. The Ambassador pulled some strings to get him extended, to be able to marry this girl. What we need is a safe place to put him for the next 30 days. Can you help? Yes, I know you do not have any test that takes 30 days. Captain Halley, do you remember a night 13 months ago? It was a night when you and your team were pinned down on the other side of the fence. Do you remember being told it was too hot to send an extraction team to get you out? You do. Good! Now do you also remember the Sergeant that called you when he was five klicks out from your location? You do. Good! That Sergeant was Sergeant Roy Forestin the same one I now want to send to you and the team that was with him was my team. We volunteered to come get you guys out. Good! Yes, I can have him there first time in the morning. Thank-you Captain Halley, It was nice doing business with you. Thanks again." With that, I hand the phone back to shocked John who just sits and looks at me. "Good, now that is out of the way. Now how do I get him down there? How do I explain it to him?"

"John, get on the horn and get us a flight for tomorrow morning." After several minutes, John tells me that there is nothing available.

There is a knock on the door, just as John tells me there is nothing available until tomorrow night.

"Who is it?" I say. "It is Cung Sir. May I come in? I have word for you."

"Yes come in" I answer.

Cung comes in with a look of worry on his face. He begins by telling me one of the men that are to go with me was shot in last night's firefight. He also tells me all the other men are looking forward to our little outing in the bush.

"Was he hit bad?" I ask.

"No sir, it is a small shoulder wound but he can not use his arm so good now. Should I find another man to go with you Sir?"

"No Cung, I don't have the time to get to know him. I like to know how each and every man thinks, and I do not have the time for that now. Let me ask you something. The VC you have in your company, you know who they are right?"

"Yes Sir! I do Sir."

"Good bring me two of them."

"Why Sir?"

"Cung, I need two prisoners to send to Nah Trang for questioning."

"Sir! I was also going to tell you that we have three people we find sneaking in to camp last night. Why not send them?"

"Good Cung, but why did you not tell me this before?"

"Sir! I was more worried about you and the men who are to go with you. That is why I did not start with the prisoners. Sir!"

"Cung where are these people now? Are they still able to talk?"

"The people are in the interrogation room. They want to talk a lot; we did not do anything to them so far Sir!"

I tell John pull the plug on trying to get a lift for Roy, and get on to HQ. "Tell them we have three prisoners we want picked up. I will put Roy in charge of prisoners and send him with them. That way he will be in Nah Trang."

"Mike, Go get Roy for me. Do you have HQ on the line John? Good tell them Roy is coming down with the prisoners and will be staying for a promotion board testing. Thanks."

The answer is "Ok and they will call back with an arrival time." Roy comes in while I am typing up his orders. He looks like hell. I do not say anything about the way he looks but go on finishing his orders.

"Sir! You sent for me. Sir!"

"Yes I did. Here are orders for you to take three prisoners down to Nah Trang and then stay for promotion testing. That way you will go on to Saigon from there."

"Sir! Yes Sir!" And with that, he turns to leave. But stops and turns back to face me. "Eric why are you doing this? Is it because I love a girl from Laos, a gook, as you would put it?"

"Roy it was a hard choice to make. I have to look out for the team and each man in it. You must admit even to yourself that since you received the word about what the Ambassador did for you. You have not been yourself. Do you know who it was that contacted the Ambassador on your behalf? "IT WAS ME THAT DID THAT". As a matter of fact I also put you in for a promotion and a letter of accommodation is in your file from me."

"Roy what you do with your life after you leave here is your affair. You will always be a good friend. You, and the rest of this team and been through too much not to have a very special feeling for one another. Please do not think I did this out of prejudice or anger, for I did not. I did it out of love. Love for you and the rest of the team. You must know that we have something, as a team that can never ever be replaced. I feel this way because we have shared life and death so often together, we are more then team mates. For me, you and every other member of this team will always have a special place in my heart that no one will ever replace. Roy go home, have a good life and raise many little Roy's and Ak's. We will stay in touch, and after this is all over, we will meet again. Now get out of here, and get ready to go. We will meet in the mess tent is two hours."

"John, do we have a chopper on the way in?"

"Yes Sir! It will be in a 0430 tomorrow. I also have received a confirmation on the promotion testing for Roy."

"Good give it to him."

The mess tent is set up for a party. It looks like someone has attempted at putting some color into an otherwise dull drab world. In the center of the tent is a table with several types of food and sweets. Mike and John are sitting in one corner with a case of beer on ice.

"Mike, where the hell did you come up with ice?" I ask

"Since when did you start asking where something came from? Sir! You are the one who once told me never to tell you where I obtained anything. You said if you did not know you would not have to lie when asked, Right?" Mike says

"Yes Mike I did. But ice out here?"

John comes over to me puts his arm around my neck and looks me straight in the eye. He then tells me that he is not going to reup. He then hands me a letter, and says to read it.

The letter is from his Mom. In the letter, she tells John that Sue has been over to the house a lot in the last couple of months. Sue is no longer with the other guy, and would like to make it all up with John. She is very sorry, and wants to be forgiven.

"That is good news John. But when did you know Sue was screwing around on you? How did you find out? When did this come about? I am confused. You have been keeping something from me, not to mention the team. Or was I the only one not to know? Do you think you could forgive her and give it another try?"

John puts his hand up as if to say stop. "Sir! I just did not tell you or anyone in the team. It was just after the mission that Phil was hit on. With the death of Veto, and Phil being injured, you and the team had a lot on your mind. I did not want to burden you with anything more. Yes, I do Eric. I really want to try to put it back together. This war has done so much to a lot of people, I think I have to try." (Boy am I glad. I never told him, or did not remember to tell him, I had told the Colonel to destroy their requests. All good things work out in the end or so they say)

Roy comes into the tent dressed in nothing but a towel and yells, "Here I am, and throws the towel up in the air to reveal he has a Lao type thong on." Well we now know that the old Roy is back, and with that, I get a smile on my face. Mike comes over to me with a beer in his hand. He tries to hand it to me. I have to say "no thanks" because I am going to have to be leaving anytime now on my mission. We party for a little as a group. I then excuse myself to get some sleep. I get a good sleep until one of the locals sticks his head in and yells incoming chopper.

I go outside to see who it is for. I can tell right away it the bird is for the LLDB team and me. She is coming in low and out of the south. It is a UH-1H that has no markings on it. It is a new ship, not like the drab dirty green ones the Army flies. This ship is a dull very dark green. The doors on both sides are open and out of each of them stick a mini-gun. Under the ship are two

55-gallon drums of napalm pinned to the skids. Just below the two front doors are small wings. They look like steps except each has a round rocket pod attached. Under the nose of the ship, like a double chin is a grenade launcher. This bird looks like it is ready for anything. The tumult brings the rest of the team out to the pad.

Once on the ground a crewmember gets out. He is not in any standard uniform. His uniform is black coveralls with a black flight helmet. I walk over to him and introduce myself. He says nothing. He just hands me a package. He then tells me to go change my uniform. In my tent, I open the package to find a black fatigue shirt and black cargo pants to match. There is also a pair of boots. Not standard boots, but boots that look like my mountain climbing boots. I dress and head out for the bird only to be stopped by my team.

Roy will be in Nah Trang by the time I am due back. If this takes longer then planned, the rest of the team will be headed home. That is if they are not all ready home. This is a very sad time for all of us. We have grown to really care for one another. With a tear in my eye, I say my good-byes and board the chopper. With me is the 11-man team of LLDB. We are one short but that is OK.

As we lift off, I feel like I am losing something. I sit on the deck of the bird with my feet resting on the left side skid. Along side me, sitting on the floor is one of the LLDB team. I do not want to look back at my team as we lift off. I don't for that would cause too much pain. It is now time for the ominous plain envelope to be opened. The crew chief hands it to me and I start to open it. Just out of the corner of my eye, I can see two other birds just like the one I am flying in. Then I become aware that I had not seen the two other choppers land with this one. Where were they? What were they doing as we loaded on this one?

About one Klick out from the camp, and about 25 feet off the ground I start to open the orders when all hell brakes loose. One of the men sitting on the right side of the bird yells "In coming." There is an RPG coming up at us. The pilot in a vain effort to miss being hit banks hard over to the left. Causing me grab hold of the doorframe to brace myself.

The next thing I know there is one horrific explosion, and that I am flying through the air without being in the helicopter. I realized I had been ejected out the door like a rag doll and that there is a lot of noise and heat behind me. I must have traveled 10 to 15 feet straight out from the bird. Now everything seems to be taking place in slow motion. I look to see what is beneath me and how far it is until I hit what ever it is. Below me is a flooded rice paddy or what looks like a rice paddy. The two ships that were with us are now firing everything they have at who ever it was that fired that RPG at us. In looking back, I feel lucky for having been blown out. Lucky because there is nothing left to be seen, but a ball of fire and twisted metal. You would be hard pressed to tell that mess was ever a helicopter. The incoming rocket must have hit the napalm tank on the right side. This explosion must have set off the ammo for the mini-gun and the rocket pod on the right side. That impact had thrown me clear of the bird. The explosions on the right then touched off all the fuel for the bird, which then caused everything to explode.

As I am falling, I can see the little guy that had sat on the floor next to me falling just in front of me. He is missing his left leg and he is on fire. I now become aware that I to am on fire too. You know when you are falling like this the mind does strange things. First it seems to take forever and you see things. Like I see Larry's face in front of me. His face had that same expression as it did when he saw the rat under the pier all those years ago and again and the last time I saw him.

The last time I saw Larry was two days before I shipped out for the Nam. It was Christmas and I wanted to say my good-byes. My Mom and Dad also wanted to see Debbie and the grand-children. We had a little going away get-together at the Swedish American Club in New York. Larry, Sonny, and the old gang from New York were there also. Larry had that same look then. His number in the draft was real low, and he could be called up at any time.

As Larry's face fades away, it strikes me that this could be my time to die. Then fear comes in because I might not die, only be very badly hurt. There is a lot of noise all around me. It is from the ship I had been in being ripped apart. Ripped apart by all the explosives she carried, also from the two other choppers going after the VC that shot us down.

As I hit the water in the rice paddy, I realize this is not so bad, or so I thought. The water and knowing how to fall kind of made it not as hard a landing I had expected. I look around me to see where I am and how bad it is. The water is muddy and sick smelling so all I can think of is to get to one of the dikes and get out of this shit. There is one hell of a pain in my legs and stomach and I think one of my arms is broke. As I try to crawl for the nearest dike, I find the guy that fell in front of me. He is not moving, but is alive. I can see the flames from the fuel spilt on the water are getting close to us. We are no longer burning as the muddy water has put out the flames. I grab him with my good (or what I think is my good) arm and try to get us both out of the spot we are in. I can now see a regular Army chopper overhead, and some idiots are jumping in the paddy. As they get closer, I can tell it is Doc and Mike. I try to crawl to them, but my hands do not seem to work so well. There is great pain in both my legs and my left arm. The fire on me is out, but I still fell like I am on fire. To my relief Doc and Mike are at hand to help. I look up at Doc only to see he has tears in his eyes. I try to talk but nothing comes out.

Doc yells. "Hey guys it the Captain!"

Roy yells back. "Who?"

Doc then yells "Eric our Captain." With that everyone is in the paddy to get me out of the shit.

John chimes in with, "See I told you that that was Eric's ship that took that hit. I knew it! I knew it! Is he going to make it?"

Doc looks up at him and half whispers. "I don't know it looks bad."

There is a call for the litters. Doc tells every one to be careful for there are several broken bones. He then leans down to me and says, "You may have saved that mans life and I hope you can hear me. I know you are still with us."

I try to say something but nothing comes out of my mouth. I then try to move something, but again nothing happens. What a strange feeling I have. It is like being in a body that does not belong to me. I can see and hear, but have no control over this body. As they lift me on to the litter, there is no question as to whose body it is. The pain is unbearable, and in every part of this body. Doc tells the men lifting me to go easy for my left leg is broken, and so is my left arm. The right leg may also be broken. He also tells them that my right arm is burned and may have a fracture in the upper arm.

Roy asks. "Doc, how did he get over to where we found him? Not only himself, but to drag the other guy with him. Look at those drag marks. That must be 20 to 30 feet."

"Roy I do not know, I have heard stories about people doing thing like that but I can not tell you how they do it."

'Doc are you going to fly in with him?"

"Yes. I am. Get on the horn to Nah Trang and inform them as to what happened and that we are coming in? Also have a surgical team standing by when we land." Doc looks to see if I have my dog tags on. I don't, because I was told not to have them on. Doc goes on to say, "Have them pull his medical records and have them at hand, as he will need whole blood and a lot of it."

I can hear all of what is going on around me, but cannot get anything out for them to hear. I try again but now we are on the chopper heading out and the noise level is high too high to be understood. "Hey! Look at me," there are words coming out of my mouth, but I cannot make them loud enough to be heard. As Doc starts to cut the burned clothing off me, he looks at my face. To his surprise, he sees my mouth move. He leans over close to hear me.

"Doc, do not lie to me. How bad am I?"

He sits up straight with a startled look and says. "You are too mean of a SOB to die. It would take a lot more then this to put you under." This is all said with a tear in his eye.

They now start an IV running into me, and Doc gives me a shot of morphine. Everything starts to go black, as I find the strength to reach up with my right arm, and grab hold of Doc's shirt. "Don't let me die, not here, don't let me die. I do not want to give those bastards that. Do not let me dieeeee."

The next thing I perceive is that it is very cold. I am so cold that I am shaking. Is this heaven? Is heaven cold? I am told hell is hot. So that is not where I am. My eyes open to see the inside of a tent with tables lined up side by side. There is a huge light over each table and a series of trays by each. There is no one in the room but Doc and me. He comes over and says. "Welcome back to the world of the living. We are about to try to put you back together, somewhat." I look over at the door to see this figure walking in dressed in this god-awful color green suit. He also had on a cap, mask, and shoe covers to match.

"Doc, who is this guy I ask? He looks like he is here to rob a bank." Doc tells me that Nah Trang had him flown in from Japan to help put me back in one piece. The doctor looks at me, and then asks Doc if I am always this funny.

"No sometimes he is worse. I cannot remember the last truly funny thing he said. However, he has kept our team safe and together for almost two years. He does mean a lot to me and our team."

"Ok, let's get to work. Captain, we are going to patch you up as well as we can here. You will then be sent to Japan for additional surgeries. From there, you will be sent state side for the final work and physical therapy. It will take sometime, but we think you will be fine when it is all over. This man, pointing to Doc will be here to help if needed. You may feel safe here; you are in Nah Trang. Now try to relax, breath deep." With that the gas passer, who I did not see come in, put a mask on my face and the doctor puts a shot in to the IV. With that, I fade to blank.

With great fear, I try to open my eyes. What is the first thing I see, but Doc, John, Roy and Mike sitting around my bed? Doc comes over close and looks into my eyes, and takes my pulse. "GOOD MORNING!" he says, "How do you feel?"

"Fine I think. I knew I was not in heaven, because you guys

were here. I was a little worried about hell, but Nah. How long was I out? How did you all get here? Where am I?" Doc just looks at me and then tells the other guy, it is ok to come over close. As all I can do is whisper.

Mike answers first things first. "How do you feel?"

"Fine I think? Well to tell the truth, I feel like I was run over by a train. Cooked by a bad chief, and kissed by that butt ugly girl at Fort Benning. Now please answer my questions."

Doc tells me I was out for 36 hours. I am then told that I am in the medical unit at Nah Trang. Mike and John had contacted HQ for permission to come down to see me. Permission was given, as the replacement team is ready to take over. Roy was all ready here, and received the ok to come over to the M.A.S.H. unit. "Any more questions?"

"Yes one or two more. First how are the people that were on the bird with me?"

They all look at one another then back at me. It took some-time before anyone answered.

Then Doc tells me. "You and the LLDB guy you pulled to safety were the only two that made it out. The ship disintegrated killing everyone other then you two."

John then spoke up and added. "There were parts of that ship covering a half-mile area. We looked all over and could only find one boot with a foot still in it. It was the co-pilots right foot. One of his dog tags was in the boot. There was nothing else but parts, real small parts."

Mike hits him upside the head and tells him he should not tell me that.

I ask, "How is he. That LLDB guy. Say what is his name? Will he make it?"

"He is ok and they think he will make it. He is missing a leg but our people will fit him with a new leg. Just like the ones, they do for our troops. His name is Loku. He has a wife and two children. We had her flown into be with him. She tells us she wants to thank you for saving his life, and is going to name their next child after you.

"My last question for now is what were you all doing flying out there?" I ask.

"Just as you lifted off the helicopter for Roy landed. The pilot on landing told John, Doc and I to get in." He was ordered to take us one Klick out to meet a village chief that wanted to come into the camp and that he had several wounded US soldiers. Also, our people had confirmed this. We were just making our turn to head to the village, when the pilot spotted the explosion. So what could we do but come to investigate." To a man the group said, and we are glad we did.

As I start to fall off to sleep again, we all say good-by and promise to meet in the states in about two months. Doc tells us that I will be in Valley Forge General Army Hospital. It is just outside Philadelphia. We should try to meet there just after the New Year.

"OK!" I say. "It is set on the second of January. Ok!" Everyone agrees. It is set, and with that I drift off to sleep again.

It is a fitful sleep filled with a nightmare. In the nightmare, there is fire everywhere. There are bodies falling. One of them is mine, but I am not in my body, for I am standing on a hill watching. There are also parts of other people falling past me. I can see heads with their mouths open in a scream that dose not come out. Arms with their hands grabbing for something that is not there. Legs that look like they are trying to run but get nowhere. All of this is going on around me, and I am helpless to do anything. My body that is floating now tries to help but can do nothing. All is falling into a pit of fire and being burned but not consumed. I reach for my body only to pull in a boot with a foot in it. It is hot and yet I feel cold, that icy cold feel of death. I try to scream but nothing comes out of my mouth. Or so I think for a nurse is awaking me. She looks at my chart and takes my pulse and blood pressure. Offers me a drink of water, gives me a shot and tells me to try to sleep. The shot really worked. Because the next thing I knew, they were serving breakfast.

It must be at least two or three days since my last meal. But how do I eat? I have my left arm in a cast from my shoulder to my wrist. My right arm from shoulder to elbow is broken and is burned from elbow to wrist. There it sits. That tray of food only inches from me, and I can do nothing. It is so close the smell is making me hungry. Even for hospital food, it smells good. At last, one of the Corpsmen comes over and says "Sir I am Corpsman Stone. May I help you?"

"Yes please do." I answer.

"Sir your buddies left your beret. Where would you like me to put it?"

"In my bag over here by my right hand, please." After I am finished breakfast, I ask how does one go to the latrine around here.

"We will put you on a bedpan if you need to Sir." With great embarrassment I say, "Yes please."

I have a cast also around my hips and on both of my legs. That makes it impossible for me to move myself anywhere. What is even worse is that I have to ask someone to help me do any-thing. I have to ask to be fed, to be put on the pan to take a shit, to shave, and to brush my teeth. I hope they take some of this off soon.

Somewhere, somehow, there is someone worse off then me, I keep telling myself. As I lay here, I cannot stop thinking about my lovely wife Debbie. She has written to me, and I have not written back. Not in sometime and now I cannot write for myself. I have to dictate a letter to her, and tell her I am coming home, in one piece. In her last letter, she could not wait until I was home. I wonder if she would still want to see me after all of this. I have not seen myself but would bet I look like death warmed over. What do I have to lose?

As the corpsman, Corpsman Stone walks by me, I say. "Say Stone will you write a note for me. It's to my wife."

"Sir, we do not have time now. We are moving you. You will be on a plane to Japan in about 30 minutes. I have a friend who works those flights. Her name is Judy Knighten, and I know she will be more then happy to do it for you. I will ask her to stop by, and do it for you."

The move to the plane was no fun at all. First, they wheeled me to a chopper for a short hop to the flight line at Cameron Bay. Then by truck to the plane, and finally up the ramp and onto the C-130 for my flight to Japan. All this happens with much bouncing around and no air-conditioning. With every bump, I feel like there are 99 knifes digging into me.

There must be forty pounds of plaster around me and plaster casts do not, I mean do not, let in any cool breezes, let alone any air. (Now I know how a lobster must feel when you put him into a pot of boiling water to cook)

The inside of the plane looks much like the ones we jumped from. Except instead of seats along the sides, there were lines of bunks staked two high. Once we were up and the medications were given out, this cute little nurse comes over and tells me her name is Judy Knighten. She also asks if I still want that note written.

I say, "Yes please. If you do not mind, and it does not take you away from you duties." Judy replies that she likes to help and it gives her pleasure to see young lovers staying in touch through hard times. She also tells me that some of the guys going home this way did not even want their ladies to know they are coming home at all.

I tell her that I had not written to my wife Debbie in some-time and now that I am going home, I do not know what to say. "Do I tell her about what has happened? What do I say? How do I tell her?"

"Why don't you just tell her what hospital you are going to and that you would like to see her? What is her full name? I know just about what to say, and will tell her I am writing for you be-cause you can not write."

I give Judy the address and Debbie's full name. "Why don't you also give Debbie my parents phone number, and ask her call them to fill them in on the details?" I gave Judy the phone num-ber. I ask for a shot to take the edge off the pain, and help me sleep.

While Judy goes to get my shot, I look around at the other men on the flight. Across from me is a black man. The only way to tell he is black is by his left hand that is hanging over the side of his bunk. The rest of him is all wrapped up in bandages. The bunk above his, I can see a kid of about 19. He has no legs. There is someone in the bunk below me. I cannot tell much about him. All I can see is that he is receiving some blood and has IVs running in to him. My bunk is the first on the left after the flight deck. There are six rows of two bunks. There is one up and one down on each side of the center walkway. That makes 24 bunks in all. We have 12 medics on the flight, so there is one medic for every two bunks. The last row is empty, which means there are only 20 bunks in use. The men in the bunks are in different stages of being rapped up like mummies. I look more like an ad for Plaster of Paris, then I do a mummy. Judy brings my shot, and tells me this flight is all Special Forces and not to worry about that secrets act, as we are all in this together. This time the shot is put in the IV stream, and then Judy asks me to count backwards from 100. I start 100,99,98,97,96, 95,------.

Chapter 17

I awake to being moved from the plane to a truck. The pain in my lower stomach is unbearable. I look up to see the medic preparing to give me another shot. "Can you tell me how bad it is down there, in my groin area? Please." I ask. As I wince in agony. The suffering is intolerable. It is worse then being kicked in the nuts by a mule.

"Well Sir," he answers looking at my chart, "you have a piece of shrapnel where your right leg and body meet. It is not very large but in a place where when you try to move your leg, it pulls on the stitches. It is more in the lower stomach then leg. Do you understand where I am saying?"

"Yes I do. But did it hit any of those other parts down there?"

"No Sir, No you still have the most of the main equipment, you were born with." He tells me.

"Hey! What do you mean by most of the equipment?"

"Well Sir, you still have the big guy."

"Oh! Good I was scared there for a minute." With that said,

he gives me the shot and I fall asleep again.

Most of the time I spend in Japan is a blur. Not even a chance to see a Geisha Girl or try some rice wine. I remember some things but not much. One thing I do remember quite well is a Doctor telling a Nurse, not knowing I was awake, that he did not think I would be able to walk again, because of my hip socket being broken. Broken right where one piece of metal is still located holding the joint together. I tell myself that he is full of shit. As long as I have both my legs, I will walk. I am not going to be one of those gimps. I have children to play with and a wife to love. I am doped up most of the time. Although every so often, I am awake to a point. When this happens between injections, it lets me know where I am, and what is going on. I am still in casts on both arms and legs. I also have a cast around my hips that cover part of the way up my back. There is an IV tube in my left hand. I am hooked up to a machine that goes beep, beep. There is a tube up my penis, and a bag on my rectum. Thankfully, I am an officer, and I have a private room.

After being in Japan for one week, they tell me that they will be doing do two operations on me in the next two weeks. One operation is on my upper left arm, which allows me movement from the shoulder to elbow. The cast now only goes from elbow to wrist. The second operation is on my lower left leg to set the bones. This means I now have a cast from just below my left knee to my foot and I am able to move my leg at the hip on the left side. One week later, I am packed up for shipment state side.

There is a long trip by ambulance to the air base. Once at the air base, I am carried onto a plane. I cannot see the plane, as it is raining and they have me covered so as not to become wet. This plane is much nicer the one from the Nam to Japan. The inside of this plane has both seats and places for the litters. The walls and ceiling are covered with an off-white paneling. The floor is tile and has a small blue and white design in it. I am in the front part of the plane with the other officers. Second on the left is my litter. We are placed one by one on each side of an aisle, and separated by a blue drape. It is as if you have a private room with soft walls. If I turn my head there is a small window to see the world go by. Not like the other men and women on the plane in stacks of two, like I had on the way to Japan. The trip is a long one, so I sleep most of the way.

Our first stop is in California where about 75 of the wounded are taken off or walk off. It is then onto our next stop. We land at Andrews Airforce base outside Washington D.C. I am then, along with two others, taken by Helicopter to Valley Forge, Pa. On the flight to Valley Forge, I can see out a window. Looking down on my home country is a culture shock. When I left Viet Nam, the air was hot and humid. Looking out here, I can see beautiful white snow covering the ground. The air has a nip to it, and it does not try to suck the life out of you, like the air in Nam.

In Valley Forge, I am put in a private room just across from the nurse's station. The hospital here is a whole bunch of two story buildings connected by enclosed walkways. The building is like the old two story barrack you would find on most training bases. They are all painted white, and made of wood. Each ward is a wing of this system and is laid out the same. As you come onto the ward, you pass between a group of rooms. The first room on the right is the nurse's station followed by the rest room and shower room. On the left side is a group of three private rooms, these are for the officers. You then go into a large room that is the open ward. This is where the Em's are located. This room is laid out with four groups of beds on each side of a large aisle down the center. Each of these groups has four beds in them. They are placed with the bottom of each pointing to a small aisle running from the main aisle to the windows. Two beds pointing at the entrance the other two pointing the dayroom. There is then a short wall and then the next set of four placed in the same manor. At the opposite end of the central aisle from the entrance is a room as wide as the ward and about 12 feet deep. This room had windows on three sides and is called the dayroom or sunroom depending on whom you ask. The floors are polished each day and have a high shine to them. The men in the wards that can do some work, sweep the floors and help with other things. As for me, I am in the first private room on the left. It is a small room with a nightstand, a bed table and one chair. There is a TV on the wall, just below the ceiling beside the door. The window is just to the right of the head of my bed. It is in this room that my life takes another turn.

Here I lay, broken and down in spirit. I cannot help but to think. Think about what my life will be like now. It is like all my wishes and desires have been taken from me in an instant. I wish someone would come and cheer me up. I can cry, I cannot laugh and most of all I cannot move much. The only things I can move are my eyes, fingers, toes, left upper arm, left upper leg and my bowels.

I open my eyes and look up, and see Sonny standing in the door. Tears fill my eyes as he says. "Man you look like hell. What couldn't you take care of yourself without us?"

Here is a guy that has had to fight for everything he has, but he came all the way down from New York, on a weekday, to see me. With him are his wife Ellen and Larry. Boy, talk about being hit with a brick shit house. Sonny had never been outside the city before in his life, but he came to see me. We talk and joke about the old days. But mostly about that day the cops lost a car through the pier. Sonny wants to know when I will be out of the Plaster of Paris suit.

I say, "They tell me in about three to four months, but it could be sooner because I am healing quickly. Say Ellen, would you please light me a smoke. You will have to stay till I am done, for as you can see I can't do anything for myself now."

"What do you do for fun around this place?" Larry asks.

"Well every night they take me out for a walk and use me as the goal posts in a game of football." I am saying that because I am laying here with both my feet up in the air in traction.

The gang stays for about two hours, until the nurse comes in and tells them they have to leave. As they are leaving, Larry turns and tells me he will be back next week and wants to see the football game.

I tell him, "Ok and bring a camera." With tears in my eyes, we say good-by. Sonny and the gang were my first visitors.

My parents have called, but will not be down until the weekend. Later that night, the second night in V.F.A.H., Debbie comes in just as I am being taken off the bedpan. She looks in to see what is going on, turn's red and goes out. The corpsman on his way out tells her it is safe to go in now. She comes up to me, and gives me a big kiss and tells me welcome home. I am so happy to see her. We talk and talk about many things. I tell Debbie that I have signed up with the continuing education officer. I am going to take classes to obtain my Masters in Astrophysics. The University of Texas has an extension, correspondence class I can do while I am here. If I work it correctly, it will take less then two years. But mostly we talk about the children, what she is doing and how her internship is going. Her grandfather left a large trust fund to pay for her education and to live on. She is from a well to do family, and has a live in Nanny given to us by her parents. They love their grandchildren, and think the world of me.

At about 11:30, Nurse Jefferson comes in and asks Debbie to go, because it is time for me to be cleaned up and given my shots. Debbie leans over me, and gives me a big kiss and tells me she will be back tomorrow. I spend the next two days being poked, prodded and x-rayed. The evenings are spent with my wife.

Early Friday a nurse dressed all in light blue comes in to my room. She looks at the chart and then at the nametag on my wrist. She then tells two guys dressed the same way to come in. They bring a gurney in with them. I am put on this cold thing. (Why do they keep the gurneys in an icebox? I think to myself) then down the hall we go. I am on my back looking at the ceiling. It is just like you see in the movies. Whiz goes a light then another and another and another. Then bang through a set of swinging doors and down another long hall with more lights. Whiz goes a light then another and another and another. Then through another set of swinging doors, down another long hall. . Whiz goes a light then another and another and another. It seemed like they wheeled me for miles before we turned through a door with a sign over it. Operating Room 17, once inside the room, it is cold and I mean really cold. It feels like you could hang meat in here. They take the blanket off me and cover me with a white sheet. Doctor Larkin come up to me and tells me. "We are going the reposition your hip joint to the proper place and put on a smaller cast. It may be small enough for you to be able to sit up."

Then the room is filled with a sound like a big dentist drill.

"OUCH!" "Say man are you trying to cut my leg off." I snap at the guy cutting my cast off.

"No I'm not Sir." He then looks at where he was cutting, looking back at me he says. "I did not know that you still have a piece of shrapnel sticking out of your skin."

"What did you say?" Doctor Larkin asks.

"I said there is a piece of shrapnel sticking out of him and into the cast. I did not see it until the patent winced in pain. I then looked to see what the cutter hit. There is a piece of shrapnel under the cast. They were supposed to have taken all that out back in Japan."

Doctor Larkin then tells the corpsman, "Let me see what you have there, Corpsman." The doctor moved into take a look. The doctor bends over to look under my cast were the corpsman stopped his cutting. He then turns red in the face and yells at one of the nurses. "Go tell the Chief Surgeon, please, that I would like to see him in here on the double." The doctor then takes the saw and very carefully cuts around the shrapnel. When he is done, there is this hunk of metal sticking out of my hip with plaster stuck to the top. Which gives it the appearance of a strange mushroom? Doctor Larkin is an Orthopedic Surgeon, and holds the rank of Lieutenant Colonel in the Army.

"Yes Doctor Larkin. What is so important that I had to come down here and scrub in?" the Chief Surgeon asks as he enters. Doctor Michael Howell is the Chief Surgeon, and holds the Rank of Colonel in the Army.

"Sir, I want to ask you about this patient, and what to do about him. His chart shows he had three operations in Japan. Two operations to set bones. One operation to remove the shrapnel from his hip. It also states the patient is ready for reconstructive surgery of the right hip. As my corpsman was cutting the cast off patient, he screamed in pain. I looked to see what was going on, and I find this large piece of metal sticking out of his hip near the groin. The people in Japan even went so far as to reinforce the cast where it made contact with the shrapnel. No wonder whenever we would move this man, he would be in great agony. See Sir here is the piece in question." He points to the strange mushroom I have growing out of my hip near to my private parts. Doctor Howell then calls for an X-ray machine to come take some pictures of this. He asks one of the nurses to find a camera, and take some shots of my mushroom.

"Pisst! Say before you start taking pictures would you please cover you know what." I ask the corpsman standing by my head. He looks at me and then looks down at the mushroom then back up at me.

With a smile, he tells me he will put a lead sheet over the little general. "Don't want to lose the use of it. Sir!" The corpsman tells me.

"Sir!" I say to the Doctors around me. "The people in Japan only did two operations on me. One was on my upper left arm and one on my lower left leg. There was talk of another, but it was never done."

"Thank you for telling us." Dr. Howell replied.

Doctor Larkin asks Doctor Howell to look at the X-rays. "Doctor, See here, this is why that piece is still in him. If they would have removed it, he may have had no chance of ever using that leg again. Yes and there is also a small piece over there. Look you can see it better in this picture."

"Yes I see it. What do you propose to do?" Dr. Larkin asks Dr. Howell.

"I think we can take out the large piece and put in a pin. If we put the pin in like this he will have a chance."

Dr. Larkin then states. "That sounds good, but what about this small one over here? I think it is in a place where if we take it out there is no way of telling if we will have movement in his joint."

Dr. Howell takes a closer look and says. "I say clean it up and leave it in for now. We can then see how he does and remove it later if needed."

"Ok" Dr. Larkin agreed.

I am lying here taking in all of this, and they talk as if I am nothing more then a machine that is broke. The Chief Surgeon comes over to me, and tells me they are going to take out the large piece of shrapnel and replace it with a pin.

When he is all done I ask. "Well what about the little piece of shrapnel. Are you are going to leave in me?"

He looks at me with surprise. He then looks at Dr. Larkin, and then back at me. "Well son we think it is best left where it is for now. We will smooth it up and clean the area so it will be less painful." At that the corpsman puts a shot in to the IV, and tells me to start counting backwards. I only reach 99 and I am out.

Several hours later there is someone trying to wake me. In a half sleep, I hear someone saying, "Try to move you left leg." Why do they want me to move my left leg? When it is my right leg they worked on? About an hour later, and with a lot of pain, from trying to move my left leg. It moves. It moves up and down.

The return trip goes quicker, more than likely because I am half-asleep. Upon entering my room, I see Debbie sitting by my bed. Her last rotation of the day is over at 4:00 P.M. that puts her here by 5:00. She looks like she had been crying. After I am lifted into bed, and we are alone, I ask what is her problem. She tells me that she is worried about me. All she wants is for me to be all right. If I could have moved, I would have jumped for joy. But even trying to move is impossible in forty lbs. of plaster.

"Debbie, the Doc tells me he is going to work on my arms tomorrow and I might have use of both of them."

Debbie just smiled and said then that means we can hug then. She then asked if my parents had been called. I tell her that I had the corpsman call. I talked with them and they are coming in on the weekend.

As we sit, at least she sits while I am prone on the bed, and talk. We talk about what to do in the summer. It comes out that her father has this big summer home on some private lake, and we can have the house to ourselves for the month of August, while her folks are on a trip. That is if I am out of this place. Debbie is real good with people and she makes me feel real good too. My days are spent between the operating room, and the PT room, and then back to bed. The time drags by until Debbie comes in to see me.

After two more operations, I can finally sit up. I can feed myself and I am able to move around in a wheelchair. It is nice be able to move around. I have a motorized wheelchair that takes me where I want to go. But I am still moved by gurney for visits to the exam rooms and surgery.

It is Christmas Eve day, and the ward is all done up for the holiday. Debbie asks if I have a Christmas gift for my nurses and corpsman.

"No I don't." I tell her.

Debbie became a little incensed with me for that. "Now am I to go shopping? The only place to buy anything is at the PX and they do not have anything that could be considered worth as while gift."

I hand her a key ring. "Here is the key to my safety box. It is over in the Nurses office. Take some money, and go buy something for them. That is if you do not mind."

"What do you want me to buy and how many?" Debbie asks.

"There are four corpsmen that have taken care of me, and three nurses so one each?" I tell her.

"Ok but are they, men or women." She then asks.

"The corpsmen are all men. One of the nurses is also a man. I would say what ever you think is appropriate." I tell Debbie.

She says, "Ok" and leaves saying "good by, be back soon." Debbie stops at the nurse's station and talks with the corpsman. After a short time, she looks in on me and tells me she will be back in about three hours. It being Christmas Eve, Debbie has the day off, so she was here in the morning.

I look back at the clock as she leaves and it is just 0930. Well she said she should be back by 1300, so I lay down. Sleep came on me, and then and at 1330 I awoke, and still no Debbie. The guy in the next room (Lieutenant Paul Thomas) and I wheel ourselves over to the Officers Club for lunch and returned to still no Debbie. Lt. Thomas lost both legs at the knees to a VC booby trap. Just before 1800, she returns with several large bags. In them are small gifts for all the staff that is all except Doctor Larkin. He is the surgeon that has done most the cutting on me.

Debbie tells me to give out what is in the bags and she will be back shortly. I ring for the Nurse Jefferson to give me a hand. Everyone is so happy, and all 32 gifts are given out before Debbie returns. In her arms are two large boxes. I look at her, and say

"What the hell." One is for Doctor Larkin and the other one is for me.

"Doctor Larkin will not be in till the morning" I tell her. She now helps me open my gift. In the box is a heavy white robe. You know the kind that is in your room at those five star hotels. Debbie says I need it "because it is colder the all hell in the hospital." Debbie being Debbie has another surprise for me, and the other nine guys out of the 35 that are normally on the ward that are not home on holiday leave. Nurse Jefferson is in on her little secret as are the other two corpsmen. She closes the door to my room and tells me she wants to be alone for a little bit. I have this shy grin on my face, and she looks at me and said "No not that. There will be time for that later."

There is a lot of noise out in the hall. I look at her and say, "What the hell is going on out there?" Shortly after that said the door opens. The corpsman comes in to wheel me out of my room, and into the dayroom part of the ward. The dayroom is all setup for Christmas. The likes of which I have never seen before. Debbie and some of the other families visiting the guys stuck here for the holidays have set up a party. There is food and gifts, and all sorts of stuff. The hospital lets us party even after the normal time for lights out. This is one of the nicest Christmases I have had in a long time. The only thing that could have made it better was if my parents and children could have been here. I find it is just a shame the hospital will not allow young children on the wards. My Mom and Dad are not here because they and my two brothers are down in Kentucky with all of that side of the family.

Chapter 18

The New Year 1970 / 1971 comes in with a whimper not a bang. Debbie is out of town visiting her parents. The old gang from New York is in the city partying. So here I lay alone with the other lonely forgotten War Veterans of an unpopular war. Wounded for the freedom the people of this country so enjoy. These men would have laid down their lives for freedom. Freedom is something the ass holes in our country now take for granted. Damn this time of love and peace. Freedom is earned, and for the most part, the Liberals take it for granted. That reminds me of something I once read in Viet Nam. It was on a wall in a bombed out French Chapel. Written there many years ago by a Frenchman Legionnaire while under assault by the Vietnamese of Ho Chi Minh. It was later translated into English by a Marine Corpsman that was also under attack in the same Chapel. What it had to say has sticks with me. It read.

**"For those who fought for it, Freedom
has a sweet flavor the protected will never know."**

I do have something to look forward to. I look forward to the fact that my old team from Nam will there to visit me in two days. We will have our New Years celebration then.

On the second of January at 1300, the ward erupts in noise. I have my team with me. Mike and Linda come in from Fort Benning, John and Sue traveled from Germany, Doc and Ellen came from Boston, and Roy came in from Fort Dix NJ. Mike tells me Phil is coming in from Monte Carlo.

I ask, "Why Monte Carlo?" John tells me to ask Phil. You should hear it from him. About an hour later, Phil walks in. It is really good to see Phil walking. "Phil, that is one of the best things I could see. To see you walking is just wonderful." "Why Monte Carlo, and where is Carol?"

He tells me that when he returned home, he found out that Carol had sold their home and everything that could be sold. "She had also taken all of the money that they had in savings, and checking and moved out of town. She had not been seen since. This all took place about a month after my parents were killed in the car crash."

"Why did you not look for her?" I ask.

"Well Eric, I did. I checked with all the people we know, and no one would say anything. It was as if the town had a bad case of amnesia. That was until one night at the local bar. I was sitting at the bar alone when the people behind me said. "Say isn't that Phillip Hess over there? Yes it is, and isn't it a shame about his wife Carol taking up with that Darkie (southern slang for blacks) and running off. I hear she sold everything, took their savings and moved out in the middle of the night."

"After I heard what they had to say, it did not make a difference anymore. My parents are dead; I have no other family but you guys. The people of this country hate us Nam Vets. I decided to split and start a new life. I took every penny I had, and went to the South of France. There I met this old Greek fellow that wanted someone to work in his arms business. So I talked to him about it, because of my training in S.F. He put me on his payroll in an instant. I now have a very good paying job, a house in the south of France. A real nice car to drive, and I am learning to fly fixed wing aircraft. I am now partying with the rich and famous. It is a good life, and it helps to take my mind off what happened. How do you like my new foot? It works just great."

To lighten things up, Roy chimes in "Nothing to worry about. Ak is just at home, not feeling too good. She is going to have a baby, and it is difficult for her."

"Hey, let's start this party. I have reserved the dayroom for the night." I told the team. I received permission to use the dayroom, as long as we were not too loud. "Let's move there so as not to disturb those who have not gone home for the holidays. Most of the ward has been empty since just before Christmas." We party into the night with no interruptions from the hospital staff. It is great having the team back together. We have a picture of Veto on the table so he is here in spirit. It's getting late, and I start to feel ill. "I think its time for me to return to my room." Doc looks at me, and tells me I look like shit and need some sleep. On the way back to my room, we decide to have a get-together every New Year Eve.

Phil chimes in. "I have lots of room, and when Eric is out of the hospital you all should come to Monte Carlo to see me." Everyone says, "Ok" and that it that.

At my room, everyone says his or her good nights and good-byes, with the exception of Phil and Debbie. After everyone is gone Phil says, "This is probably my last trip to the states. As an arms dealer I am status non-gratis in this country. My job has cost me my citizenship, and I could give a damn about it."

I do not question him on his choice, because I know he has been put through hell since he has been back and before. As he leaves, Debbie just looks at me with a question in her eyes. I tell her about the time we found out his parents were killed by a drunk driver, long after it had happened. "We were out on a mission and when we returned the Red Cross came and told him about it. It was far too late for him to go home to bury them. It bothered him that he could not be there to see that that it was done right. However, he did have Carol; he thought Carol would take care of everything. I did ask the Red Cross people, after he had walked away, about the funeral, and who was there. I was told that it was a Military Funeral, and that they were buried in a National Cemetery near Atlanta. The Special Forces people out of Fort Benning took care of most everything along with help from his wife."

Debbie then tells me "that it is sad."

"The people in this country will never understand all we went through over there." I give her a big kiss, and ask her to send the medic for me on her way out. As Debbie turns to leave, there are tears in her eyes.

Nurse Jefferson comes in and gives me a shot. I go to sleep. I dream of the green landscape in Nam. It is so vivid that it shimmers as if a living thing. The breezes blowing down the valley moved the foliage so they swayed back and forth. As if trying to move in unison to manufacture better cooling breezes. It could have been a beautiful place to spend time. If it were not for the fact, that every living thing was out to cut, stab, and shoot or kill you.

It had been about 11 months now, and I am walking on my own with a walker, but still use a wheelchair if I have far to go. I told those doctors I would walk in a year and I did it. Now I need to work on running. The physical therapists tell me that I will be an outpatient after the first of the year.

This time when Christmas comes again, I have been to a shopping center and have a Christmas gift for everyone on staff in the ward. Debbie is now Doctor Deborah Howard, and is in the last part of her specialty internship. She comes to V.F.G.A.H. right after her last hospital rounds are over. There is a small party in the dayroom for all the people on the ward and their families. Debbie's parents are in Paris for the holiday, and mine are in Kentucky as usual. After the festivities on the ward, we go to the O-Club for a late dinner. Just before dessert is served, the waiter comes to our table, and tells Debbie she needs to call her service. She excuses herself and goes to the phone at the front desk. Two minutes later, she comes back to the table, sits down, leans in and whispers to me. "A pregnant woman that is in hard labor and I must go."

"Ok! Talk to you later, I love you." I tell her as she stands up to leave. Debbie comes over to me, and gives me a kiss, tells me. "I am a love." As she goes out the door, she turns and gives a wave good-by.

The next day Nurse Jefferson comes into my room and tells me I have a phone call at the nurse's station. We do not have phones in our rooms. The only general use phone is a payphone mounted on wheel. It is rolled to the patient for their use. "Yes" I said payphone. I wheel myself over to the phone in the nurse's station. "Hello who is this?" "It is your wife." My response is "Oh Hi! How is everything? I love you."

With a very downhearted sound to her voice, I hear. "I am ok it is just we could not save the mother, but both baby girls will make it. I am sorry I had to run out on you last night. Can you forgive me? Please!"

"Of course, I can forgive you, I love you. However, there is no need to apologize. I am sorry for the loss."

"Will you be here for New Years? Mike and Roy will be. Phil is not coming, and you are aware of why. Doc is in Harvard Medical School, and cannot make it. The Army has sent John to South America. Therefore, he also will not be here. Ok. Looking forward to it. We will be in the O-Club about 1900. I have reserved the back room. Miss you. Love you. See you then."

"Thank-you for letting me use your phone, Leroy." Leroy Jefferson is a Lieutenant in the Medical Corp. and has been my nurse for the past 13 months. He is also one great guy, and a Nam Vet. Leroy is about 6'6" tall and looks like he should be a linebacker for the Pittsburgh Steelers football team and not a nurse. I learned his great-great grandparents were slaves in Alabama. "Say Leroy, what are you doing New Years Eve?"

"Nothing Sir," he answers. "Then please stop by the O-club and have a drink with me." I ask. Leroy tells me he will think about it.

At 1900 on New Years Eve 1971 / 1972, I wheel myself to the O-Club and have a drink at the front bar waiting for someone, anyone to show up. I am just about done with my first Bourbon and Water, when Mike and Roy come in. Behind Mike and Roy stands Ak and Linda. A while later, in comes Debbie. "Ok let's go to our room and start this party. The bar is all setup and there are plenty of snacks." The party starts up slow. We are all standing at the bar when Roy tells us. "Ak lost the baby in June." He and Ak are over it, and doing fine.

The girls are sitting at one of the table, just talking girl talk. The guys are at the bar telling jokes and swapping war stories. At about 2300, one of the people that work the front desk opens the door and shows Leroy in. Mike, Roy and I go over to him. I give him my hand and tell him "Welcome, come in and join us. You know everyone, don't you? Oh, no you don't, come with me." I wheel myself over to where the ladies are playing cards. "Ladies I would like to introduce the best nurse in this hospital and maybe the Army to you. Linda this is Leroy. Ak this is Leroy. And of course, you know my wife Debbie. Leroy what would you like from the bar?"

"Do you have Gin, Sir?"

Yes we have gin, and while we are here, let's drop the Sir shit Ok?"

"Ok I would like a gin and tonic." Almost before he had finished talking, Mike handed Leroy a tall gin and tonic.

"Thank you siii. Ok I caught myself." Leroy said with a big smile.

"Let's turn the TV on, and watch the ball drop in New York. We are all just standing around." (All but me that is) Talking and waiting for the count down as the ball drop starts. "10,9,8,7,6,5,4,3,2,1 Happy New Years." Champagne corks pop. Everyone cheers and hugs all around. We drink Champagne and sing Auld Lang Syne.

At about 0015, Leroy comes over to me and says. "Thank you for inviting me. It was real nice of you and your friends to have me."

I say, "Leroy you have been very good to me since I have been here, and you are now one of my friends." With what could have been a tear in his eye, he looks down at me, and tells he has never been treated so well by an Officer patient, in all his 12 years in the Army. As he turns to leave, he waves, and tells everyone "thank-you" and "good-by" as he goes out the door. By 0130, everyone is on the way out the door saying "good-by" and "see you again."

Debbie wheels me back to my room, and tells me goodnight and she will be back to see me the day after tomorrow as she will be on call till then.

In the morning, (or should I say late morning) Leroy comes into my room. "Excuse me Sir. I just wanted to tell you thanks for last night. Also please tell your friends thanks." He turns to leave.

"Leroy! I say in a commanding voice." He turns around. "Leroy look I told you last night that you are a friend to me. Please do not forget it."

"Yes Sir I will not forget. You have been the nicest officer patient I have had on my ward."

"Say Leroy, May I please have an ice pack for my head. An aspirin or two would also help."

As he turns to leave, he says, "Ok Sir, I will be right back with that!"

The next two months were spent in boredom. I am now living in the BOQ. It is a nice little place. It has a living room, bedroom and kitchen. The only thing I have to do, besides going to PT, and having my stitches removed, is read and watch TV. Debbie comes to see me every night, but still I feel like there is something missing.

My life holds no challenge; it is boring after the high intensity life of Nam. I do not look forward to a life of boredom. If this is all life has to offer? Then what is the use? Larry comes to visit about once a week, and it is fun hearing about what he is in to. I also have Sandy, who comes to see me about once a week, he bring me some magazines like Soldier of Fortune and others like that. I am looking for a way to have added some adventure in my life. I have stopped having the nightmares, and am sleeping better now.

I am up walking around, but not as well as I would like. The physical therapists tell me I am doing very well. They tell me that I am due to be discharged from the hospital in about two months

Now the time has come for me to make a decision. Do I stay in the Army? On the other hand, do I take the disability retirement and leave the Army? If I do retire, what will and can I do in civilian life? Well the Army had been my life up to now. Why change? I decide to stay. To keep me occupied I am put in charge of the drug room here in Valley Forge. I think this was done, because no one around the hospital would mess with a Beret. Not that I could do much. I have a lot of free time now that the operations are over, the casts are removed and stitches are out. Now I can walk, talk and chew gum at the same time.

It is during this time that I learn Larry and the old gang from New York is riding with an outlaw bike club. They have asked me to come along. When the weather is good, I say. "I have to think about it." I do need to think about. I try to feel Debbie out as to what she thinks of bikers. Her opinion is that they are sleazy bums, and should grow up, and put their life together. After she tells me that, I do not want her to know that I am thinking about going for a ride with them.

Two months later, the hospital is now ready to ship me out. All my friends, except Phil come to see me on my last day in

Valley Forge General Hospital. There is a small ceremony at which General T. Bolderson, the Head of the hospital gives me my oak leafs. I am now a Major in the U.S.Army. He then presents me with my third Purple Heart and the discharge forms from the hospital. I am given orders that give me a 30-day rest and recuperative leave. I now have a chance to move in with Debbie and my three children. Debbie has set-up a home for us just outside Philadelphia. It is about half way between where she is finishing her Medical Residency and Army Medical Center.

After my 30-day R and R leave is over, the Army assigns me to temporary duty. This is temporary duty, so I can build up my strength and to show I am ready to return to full time duty. I must be able to perform all my duties, before I can return to active service. I am assigned to an Ivy League College in Boston as the interim head of the R.O.T.C. department. It is a sheltered assignment, as most of the students are taking part in anti-war protests. There are many hard feelings between the general population of students and the R.O.T.C. Department. Being that I am in the R.O.T.C department, I have to be in my uniform on campus, which draws a lot of negative action from the peace nicks. Oh well it is just until I am ready to return to action. I will soon receive my masters in Astrophysics. I do not know what it will do for me, but I might as well finish it. Now with this college, they have a policy that I can take class here for little to no cost. I am thinking about signing up to obtain a master's degree in Clinical Psychology. Thinking it may help in understanding how and why people think the way they do. So why can't I do it? I spend my time between classes and taking PT classes. I have also looked up Doc, but he will be in classes all week. With no time for a break, so he has invited me to his home on Sunday for lunch.

At lunch on Sunday, we talk about all that has happened in our lives. He is working hard to finish as he is now in his second year in Medical School. Doc does find it a little hard to follow the things that are being taught. He is very pleased I am doing so well after all my injuries. He finally admits that he did not think I would be able to walk, let alone be able to do all I am doing. After lunch, we sit on his back porch, have coffee, talk, and smoke cigars until the sun goes down. At about 8:00 p.m. I tell him I have to return to work. I have to prepare Monday's training schedule, and it must be up on the board before 10:00. We will meet up again real soon."

Ed shows up on the weekend two weeks later. "Say Ed, how did you find me?" I ask. Ed is Sonny's brother and one of the old gang. He is a tall skinny guy with long dark hair and a full beard. He is one of a few guys that ran with the gang that was kicked out of school before graduation. He tells me that he had gone to Valley Forge Army Hospital to see me and was told I had been discharged. As Ed was leaving he met Leroy in the parking lot. He had met Leroy several times when visiting me in the hospital. Ed stopped Leroy, and asked him where I was. Leroy knowing who Ed was, told him, so here he is. "We now have some good riding weather and you look like you need to get out on a skoot."

"Ed I don't have a bike. How can I go?" Ed then tells me they have a member doing time and his old lady said I could use the bike.

I asked. "Don't you guys' hate it when someone touches your bike? Let alone ride it?" Ed tells me this guy is not going to be out for sometime, if ever. I don't know how he knows that. "Ok, I will go in two weeks. That way I have time to make an excuse, to be out for the weekend."

It is Saturday morning two weeks later. The day is bright and sunny. There is just the slightest cool breeze blowing. I have gone to the state and obtained a permit to ride bike. Here we are with about 50 bikers. Some look like they just crawled out from under a rock. Others look somewhat clean, and others looked like a bank VP out for a Sunday spin. It was a very different group of people then what I expected. Well any way we started off. The hard-core bikers were in front followed by the average people and then the bankers. All of this was followed by two pickup trucks both pulling trailers for bikes that may break down. I am just behind the hard-core bikers with Ed along side. All of the front group are on Harleys, then follow some Harleys and some British bikes and in the back is the Jap bikes. Ed tells me that a Jap bike is called a rice burner and no self-respecting biker would be found dead on Jap shit. We ride for about 20 miles out into the country. At about the 20-mile point the Bankers turn around and head back. As they leave, a cheer goes up from the front of the group. About five miles later most of the group behind us take a cutoff to the right and leave the rest of us. Another cheer goes up as we pull off into an open field. I must say it feels good to be off and turn the motor off. I am riding a 1956 Harley that has an 1100 motor and open pipes. The ride is stiff and noisy, but it is fun. I walk around to loosen my legs and stretch.

Ed comes up to me and says, "Give me two bucks, for the beer and dogs."

I look back to see two guys taking a keg of beer out of one of the pickups. Someone else is digging a pit to cook over. There is one of the hard-core standing out by the road as if he is looking for someone.

Off in the distance can be heard what sounds like thunder,

but this did not stop. It keeps getting louder and louder. The source of the sound becomes close you could feel the ground shake. Off in the distance, you could see a cloud of dust being kicked up. It kind of looks like those scenes in the movies. Where you see the dust from the Indians coming to attack the fort. As they clear the last hill before getting to us, you could see what looks like about 100 bikers coming in full tilt. Man what a sight.

I turn to Ed and ask. "Who are these guys?"

"They are Angels from up the coast." Ed tells me.

Now I know why the others turned off before we entered this place. Now what do I do? Before I could answer myself, they were coming into the field. The second guy in the bunch is someone I know. It's Larry! This is a time of great conflict with in me. Part of me wants to run; the other part wants to take part. You know you hear all the stories about the Angels and what they do.

Larry walks up to me and says. "Eric, what the hell are you doing here?"

"Well Larry it's like this. I felt bored. Like nothing was going on in my life. So when Ed here, Ed, Ed where are you? Well anyway Ed asked me to come along for the ride and I did."

Larry and I sat down to drink and eat. We talked about Nam and more. Larry tells me how when he returned from The Nam he to had trouble fitting in. How he had an experience at an airport and how people who saw him in uniform would spit at him calling him a baby killer. "Eric, why do all the jack shits in this country look at us Nam Veterans like that?"

"I don't know Larry. They just do." I answer.

It is during this time span I also have been thinking about returning to racing sports cars. As the income picks up, and with

Debbie's help, I reach a point where there is cash to buy parts for my Austin Healey, that I had delivered from Kentucky. After getting my license to race and winning several races. I am pleased to have received a sponsor, then two sponsors which helps pay for a truck and crew. I am having a great time living two lives. This just puts some of that excitement of living on the edge of death back in to my life. I am only happy when I could die at any moment. If life holds no challenge, it is no fun. Not to mention that from time to time, I slip out to ride with the gang from New York.

Life now has a completely new meaning. I am an officer in the U.S. Army by day and a sports car racer on the weekend, not to mention being a biker on the side. Debbie comes to the races on the weekend and brings our children. We have made many friends in the racing community, and the weekends are becoming like a family reunion. The year goes by fast. I have had only one other chance to ride with the gang from New York.

I remember that run. It took us up into the hills of Vermont to some small town. As we traveled up the back roads, we picked up about three other groups along the way, so there must have been about 40 to 50 of us when we came into the town. We rolled right down the main street stopping at a local bar to wash the dust out of our mouths. The bar is on the only paved street in town. The local fuzz must have called the state for help, because as we sat around the bar a whole mess of state police came in. We were told we were not wanted in the town.

Pete, one of the leaders, said "Man we have every right to be here. We ain't done no wrong." The cop told us to leave town. Pete again asked by what law he could do that." The cop said "all right. We could stay so long as we stayed out of trouble." The trouble that was to come was not from us. As the day went on, the town's people grew madder and madder with us, and we were not doing a thing wrong. Well, except maybe the fact that some of the women, married and unmarried, came to party with us. We had left the bar, and were in a campground about two miles out of town by then. The women would come up to the grounds with cases of beer and food. They were looking to find out what it is like to bed down with a biker. This was to be the weekend I was to receive my colors. The colors are the patches you have on your rag to show who you are riding with. I had shown I could hold my own in a fight, and this was to be my weekend. It was just after midnight, that the first shot was heard. My first reaction was to find my weapon and jump into the firefight. As I sat up, it hit me that this is not Nam. As the second shot rang out. I ran for the cover of the trees only to trip over my boots that I did not pull on in all the excitement. Larry was right behind me followed by four other guys.

Larry turned to me and said "Eric you commanded an A-team in Nam. Get us out of here."

By now, we had about ten guys and the same number of women ranging in age from 18 to 40. Some of the people who came late were not even dressed. What a unit I have now. In looking back at the fire, we could see a whole lot of town's people looking around. They wanted to see what was up because there were cop cars coming from everywhere. I told the guys and gals to split into three groups. The ones that had all their clothes on were to go over to the fire and talk to the cops. The group that had no clothes were told to head for the lake. The ones that had some clothes on were to go move the bikes down to the lake without starting them. I went with the group that met with the cops.

"Officer, we have a problem. These people came up here and

started to shoot at us. Man they could have killed us. I want them put in jail. Man, I am a Nam vet and I have been shot at by the best, but these people scare me. Arrest them. Take them out of here."

The cop thought for a minute, and then told the towns people to leave. One of the town's people then told the cops that we have his wife. I said, "Look around. Do you see any woman tied to the trees or held down anywhere? If there are women up here. It's because they came up of their own volition, and could leave anytime they want." I looked around to see who was behind me, only to see the other leaders of the gangs that came along with us. The cops then told the towns people to leave. He turned to us and said that we were to leave in the morning for our own good. He would leave two cars down at the entrance to the park to see that there was no more trouble.

I told him. "Thank you for your help and understanding."

The rest of that night was quiet as far as the village people were concerned. We partied all night drinking and some did dope, which I did not do, and had the women dance and whatever all night. Because of what happened I was not able to receive my colors, but that was ok since there will be a next time. In the morning, with great pain in our heads, we packed up and headed out. The only way back was to go through the town. So with a cop car in front and one in back we headed to town. Several of the women had no way to return back to town, so some of us gave them rides on our bikes. The worst part of that trip was going through town. We stopped in front of the church, and let the woman off to some obscene words from the natives about what they had done with us. We told them we would be back to do it again real soon. The cops took us all the way to the highway, before they left us to finish our ride home.

I rode with the gang back to New York City, because I had left my car there. Once in the city, I am back a day early, so instead of returning to Boston, I head home to see my wife and children. Once home, I shower and have a nice dinner with the family. I tell Debbie that most of the physical examinations I need to pass to return to active duty are done. I let her know that I have passed then all with flying colors.

Debbie asks me if I really want to go back to being shot at. She also tells me that I do not need to do that if I am worried about the family income. We do not need my income, and that she is very worried about me being killed or wounded again. I tell her it is not the income; it is that I love what I was doing. Our country needed me to help defend the freedoms we do so dearly love. Early Monday morning, I have breakfast with the family and then leave for Boston.

It is New Years Eve 1972 / 1973 and Doctor Debbie and I are off to the south of France to see the team. We have received airline tickets from Phil and are just beside ourselves with anticipation. John and Sue, Doc and Ellen, Roy and Ak are with us. Mike can not make it, as he is somewhere doing his duty for our government. Little did I know at the time that this was to be the start of an annual thing? We have a great time, and all is well with everyone. We have Dinner at the Grand Casino. I learn to play Baccarat, and spend time siting on the beach watching all the half-naked people.

Chapter 19

It is now late fall and I have passed the entire medical battery of tests the Army has given me. The other entire list of things I had to prove I could except two. One is a flight exam with an instructor to show proficiency. The second is a series of parachute jumps. When these two things are finished I will be back on active duty. Back doing what I love to do. Classes for me at the college are small. We have a lot of trouble recruiting for the R.O.T.C. program due to the Anti-War feeling sweeping the country. If only those people could only understand the need to defend our freedoms. If we do not stand up to defend ourselves from our enemies who will. The quote I once saw on a bumper sticker is so true. " If we outlaw guns only outlaws will have guns."

As winter sets in I am home for winter break. We have moved to New York City. Debbie is now in private practice on Park Avenue with two older doctors. The two doctors she works with are family friends of her parents. It is nice to be home with the family just relaxing. We are now with child again. We talk about the fact that she has started her practice, and how being pregnant will effect her new job. She asks me what I think she should do. I am not one to tell her what to do. I ask if she thinks it will be too difficult.

She is worried about working as a pregnant Doctor. Worried about what harm it may do to the baby. What the women seeing her may think? I confide to her.

"First off, the women you are taking care of are pregnant. Are they not? It is not as if you are single. Second, you could not be in a better place, if a problem does come up. Third, if it does become too hard for you near the due date. Could you not take a maternity leave? Fourth, but not last, you and staff will be monitoring your pregnancy very closely, wont you? That is what you office is all about, is it not?"

Debbie tells me she had not thought about it that way, and will talk with her partners to see what they have to say. My wife was at the top of her class in her medical school and at the top of the list on her internship. She served her residency in one of the best hospitals on the East Coast. There were several hospitals that wanted her on staff. She had many offers to choose from, but wanted to be in New York with at the clinic she is with. Not that a Park Avenue Practice is all that bad.

The children are in bed fast asleep, as we sit by the fire in silence for several hours. Then Debbie moves away and turns to me "Eric, if you really want to go back on active duty, I understand. It has always been in you and your family to serve our country, and that is one of the things, I love about you. Your duty to God, Country and Family is unwavering and commendable. Let's go to bed."

It is now 1:00 AM, and the phone ringing wakes me. I sit up in bed and grab for the phone. I say "Hello" with anger in my voice.

It is Sue and she is crying and trying to talk. I calm down, and talk to her in a soft soothing voice to calm her down. "Sue, what is it? Is something wrong? Are you and the kids ok?"

Sue stops crying long enough to tell me that John was thrown from his horse and fell braking his neck. He is in the hospital now, and the doctors do not think he will make it. She has called Mike. Linda answered the phone and told Sue, Mike is out of the country on some mission. Doc is on his way, and will be in Cheyenne, Wyoming in the morning. She does not know how to reach Roy or Phil and asks me to. She tells me that she is sorry for not calling me first. As she did not have our new phone number. Doc gave her the number in New York for me.

I say "OK! I will find them and I will be there as soon as I can." My first call is to Phil. I find out he is in England, when I reach him. I tell him what had happened, and that I am leaving for Cheyenne, Wyoming as soon as I can. Phil is out of breath, and tells me he will call back soon. My next call is to Roy. Ak answers the phone, and she tells me he is at the base and gives me the number. I call the base operations office and tell them I need to speak to Sergeant Roy Mannly. The Desk Sergeant tells me he can not put the call through. I become pissed and say. "This is Major Eric C. Howard, and I need to speak to him A.S.A.P. If you do not put me through to him now, I want to speak to you night commander."

There is a set of clicks on the phone and a voice comes on. "This Captain Richard Zahll, how may I help you?"

"Hello this is Major Howard, and I need to talk to Sergeant Roy Mannly. He was part of my A-Team in Nam, and I need to inform him that another member of the team was in an accident and is not expected to live."

"Sir! I remember you. I was with A-team 456, when you were hit in Nam. I will send a runner for Sergeant Mannly now, hold the line."

I hear the Captain yell at the Desk Sergeant to find Roy, "NOW". He comes back on the line and asks if there is anything more he can do.

"Can you have him in Cheyenne, Wyoming in the morning?" I ask. To my surprise, he says he will have him on a MATS flight within the hour.

Roy walks into the office, as the Captain said that. He salutes, and when the salute is returned. Roy asks, "Sir, what is going on? Who is going somewhere?"

"Sergeant the phone is for you. It is a Major Eric Howard. Take it here, I will be in the other room."

"Hello Eric, what is up? Why are you calling me here? Has something happened, is Ak ok?"

"Calm down Roy. Your wife is fine. It is John that is not all right. I just was on the horn with Sue, and she tells me John was thrown from his horse. The fall broke his neck. The doctors do not think he will make it. Your Captain is making arrangements for you to fly to Cheyenne, Wyoming on a MATS flight tonight. Doc is on his way, and I will see you there. Have to go now, Bye."

I no sooner hang up the phone, and then it rings. It is Phil, he tells me to go the private side of LaGuardia Airport. There is a private flight center just to the south of the entrance to the private flight line. "Tell no one and I will be there in 10 hours."

I wake Debbie, and tell her what has happened while I pack a bag. "Do you want to come along?" I ask. Hoping she tell me "no."

Debbie tells me "No this is a private thing between you and your old team." She tells me she is sorry to hear what has happened, and thinks I need to go alone. If I wanted her to come out later, she would be more then happy to. The next nine hours are spent packing, making calls and thinking about all that happened since meeting John all those years ago at S.F. training. His love of life, and way he was. One hour before Phil is due to arrive; the doorman calls me to inform me that my cab is out front. With a heavy heart, I kiss Debbie good-by and go downstairs. The ride out to the airport seems to take forever.

I take the cab to the private side of the airport, and leave the cab just outside the gate. I walk about one block, and enter the flight center waiting room. There is no one around, so I take a seat. About 10 minutes later, a man comes out, and asks if he can help me. I say "No someone is picking me up soon." He asks if I would like some coffee.

"Yes please."

He then tells me, there is a pot just through the door marked crew. I can help myself. With a cup of coffee in hand, I take a seat. About 20 minutes later, Phil comes into the sitting room to find me sitting looking like I had just lost my best friend. He grabs me by my arm, and says to come along. Out onto the tarmac we go. I look around for a plane, and all that is there is this all black four-engine jet with Swiss marking. He heads straight for it. Up the ramp he goes with me right behind him. Come to find out, this is his plane, and he is flying it. We fly to Cheyenne, Wyoming by an around about route in just over three hours. I rent a car. Ask directions to the hospital, and off we go again.

Doc and Roy are at the hospital sitting in a small room looking like death warmed over. "What is happened? Is John going to make it?" I ask.

Doc comes over to me, puts his arm around me, and says. "No he will not. His top two vertebrae are crushed and he had a concussion. The concussion caused a severe trauma to the brain. John is not able to stay alive without help. Sue wants him to stay on life support, but that will not help. There is no chance of him ever coming out of the deep coma he is in. Even if John was able to recover from the trauma to his brain, he could not live without life support."

"So what I hear you saying is that there is no hope, and it would be best to let John go in peace. Is that right?" I know by asking Doc, I will receive a straight answer. Doc is not one to let life slip away easily.

"That is just what I am saying. Now how do we convince Sue that this is the right thing to do?"

"Doc, you talk to her. Of all of us here, you are the best one to do that. Please you handle it."

Sue comes into the room we are in and sits down. "You guys were John's best friends. He would often say that you guys meant more to him then anyone else. I know, and respect his feelings about you guys. With that said. Do you all feel the same as Doc about John chances of coming out of this?"

In unison, we nod yes. She then tells us, with tears in her eyes, "John wanted to be an organ donor. After that is taken care of, what do we do? He wanted a military funeral." She turns to Doc, and asks, "Would you go talk to his doctor, and let them know what we decided?"

Doc tells her "Yes."

I say. "Doc, may I talk with you first?"

"Ok, what is up?"

"Let's go out of the room. Sue, I will be right back."

Outside the room, I ask Doc "I do not remember. But did John contract malaria like I did."

"No, Eric he did not. You were infected when you were blown out of the helicopter. It came from being in that muddy water."

"Ok," I answer. Doc goes to find John's doctor. I return to the room.

I tell Sue, "Doc has gone to inform the staff about the decision. Now let me take care of the funeral. When and where do we want to have it?"

Doc comes in with John's doctor. The doctor goes up to Sue, and asks if what Doc has told him are her wishes. Sue nods yes. "Do you still want to honor his wishes about organ donation?" Sue again nods yes. The Doctor hands me some papers, and asks me to help her fill them out and sign them.

Phil asks the doctor to step out in the hall. Out in the hall, Phil asks, "How long will he last off life support?" The doctor tells Phil "John has already expired. The life support system could not keep him alive. His brain activity stopped just minutes ago. Now with the wife's permission, we only are waiting for the Surgeons to come and retrieve the organs for transplant. The police have come and gone. There is no question that it was an accident. I would say his body would be available tomorrow sometime after the harvesting of the organs."

Phil sticks his head in the door and waves for me to come out. I exit the room to see what he wants. In the hall, Phil tells me "John is already dead. The police have come and gone. They are convinced it was an accident. So all that is taken care of. The surgeons will harvest the organs as soon as they arrive. John's body will be ready to go to a funeral home tomorrow afternoon. Now let's go tell Sue. Do you think we should take Sue for out lunch? Look at the time. It is three p.m., and we all have been on the go for who knows how long."

"That is a good idea. We can then talk about the arrangements for John's funeral." I answer.

As I walk in the door, I go straight to Sue. I put my arm around her. "Sue, John is gone. He passed away very peacefully. Would you like us to come with you while you say good-by to him?" We all walk down the hall in silence. At the door to his room we stop, and Sue goes in, she walks up to the bed bends over and gives him a kiss. With tears running down her cheeks, she tells him she loves him and will forever. We come over to the bed also with tears in our eyes and say our good-byes. I take Sue by the arm and we leave the room in darkness. As we walk back down the hall I turn and say. "All right, who want to go have a really good lunch? Sue would you please join us? We need to sit down and talk about what John would have us do for him. Does anyone know a good place to eat around here?"

Sue looks at Phil and Doc standing over by the door and starts to cry. Doc comes over to her and says. "It was for the best, he would never been able to walk or feed himself again. Besides the head injury, his neck was broken at the second vertebrate. The nerves that pass through there were nearly cut through. This would have left him paralyzed from the neck down. Do you think John would have wanted to live like that?"

"No." Sue answered.

"Neither do I, so it was for the best. Now tell me where you want to go for lunch."

Sue takes Doc by the hand, and starts to walk out of the hospital. She stops and turns to me, and hands me the paper work and asks, "Would you please take care of this for me?"

"Yes I will."

Doc turns to us and tells us "Just across the street is a diner. One of those diners where you know the food is good by the look of it."

"Say, the coffee is good."

We order lunch and talk about the funeral for John. Sue tells us he wanted to be buried in Arlington National Cemetery, with full military honors.

I excuse myself from the table to use the phone. Ten minutes later, I am back at the table. "The funeral will be at Arlington National Cemetery. The body will be flown to Bethesda, Maryland as soon as it is released to the funeral home. An honor guard from Benning will be here today about 1700 to escort John to Bethesda. The service at Arlington will be held on Saturday at 1300 hrs. I know that is five days away, but the graveside teams from Benning, Brag, and Germany cannot make it until then. In addition, "Yes Mike will be there. Any questions?"

Everyone just looks at me with a look of question and amazement. Sue with a question in her voice asks. "How did you do that? We were told that there was no space at Arlington, and to bury Special Forces personnel was next to impossible. What else do you have planned? Please don't think I am not appreciative of what you have done, but how? No, I do not want to know."

"The only other thing I did was to arrange a fly over by a flight of helicopters and have a second bag piper."

"Do we stay here? Or do we find some rooms in town. I am ready for some sleep?" I ask.

Sue invites us all out to the ranch. There is lots of space. The drive to the ranch takes about an hour and a half. Along the way, we see very few houses, but lots horses, cows and open land. At the ranch, John had built a large log home. There were several out buildings and a huge barn. The house had that feel of the old west. Just to the right of the house was a long building. It looked like one of those motels you would see along some country road that at one time was the main highway. There were nine separate doors in the front wall. Which lead into bedroom. Each room had a bathroom of it own. Sue calls this building the bunkhouse. They had help that came in each fall to bring the livestock in from the fields.

After a nap and some dinner, we all sit around the living room and talk about old times. The times we have shared and the times we will remember. As we leave the living room for a nights sleep, Phil turns and states he will fly us to D.C., but he cannot stay. We all know why and feel bad for him, but what can you do?

I go to my room in the bunkhouse, and think on my feelings about Arlington. I would not be going there, if it were not for John's wishes to be buried in Arlington. To me, Arlington is a place I would not, and do not want to be. I am that way, because Arlington was the home of Robert E. Lee and the Union stole it from him and his family. His wife, Mary Anna Custis Washington (the great-granddaughter of Martha Washington and step-great-granddaughter of George Washington) was removed from her home by Union Troops as well. She was never allowed to return.

Just before falling asleep, I call Debbie and tell her all about what happened, and to let her know the arrangements had been made. She tells me it was for the best that Sue let him go. He would not have known any kind of a life after the injury had happened. If what he was facing could be called a life. With that much brain damage, he probably would not have even known who Sue and his children were.

Debbie and the children meet me in Washington D.C. We have dinner with all the team from Nam except Phil and their families. It is a big group of people, but the mood is very morose. There is little conversation, and what we do talk about is just anything insubstantial.

Saturday is a clear day with the sun shining, and there is a cold wind blowing. The service is downhearted, but wonderful. There must be at least 300 Green Berets at the graveside. Every rank from Sergeant E-5 up to full bird Colonels and a General.

With the service over, Sue goes home to Wyoming. To raise the three boys, John Jr., Eric, and Michael the way John would have. She will not be alone. For each of us tells her if she ever needs any help, just call and we will be there.

My trip home with Debbie and the children is a sad one, for I have lost a friend. A very dear friend. He was the first of my team to die since leaving Viet Nam. How can you live through all those years of combat around the world, only to die in your own back yard? The irony of ironies.

After John's funeral, I spend a lot of time thinking about all that has happened. My mind wonders what life has to bring for my family and I.

As New Years 1973 / 1974 approaches, Phil sends airline tickets to everyone. Phil, in his infinite wisdom has invited not only the team members and their wives, but also their children that are old enough. He has also invited Sue and John's children. As I think of John and his death, I know this New Year would not be the same. All of the remaining team members and their families are in a very somber mood. The New Years dinner was a very nice one. It was good to see Sue laughing at some of the stories about the past. All of us are on the same train to Paris and then on the flight back to New York. I will be driving up to Boston the next day, so I have asked Doc and Ellen to come home with us. It is a sad good- by to Mike, Linda, Roy and Ak who are going back home. The seven of us drive to our home for dinner and conversation. The Nanny takes the three children, and feeds them, while the four adults have a drink. Doc asks Debbie many questions about how it was for her in medical school. While Ellen and I talk about the children. It is at this time, I learn Ellen is pregnant, but has not told Doc yet.

I ask her "Why?"

Ellen tells me that she is only one month late, but knows she is pregnant. She wants to wait one more month before telling Doc. I tell her, I will keep her secret. In the morning, we leave for Boston. The drives is a quiet one, as both Doc and Ellen fall asleep just north of New York, and do not wake until I stop in front of their house. We say our good-byes.

Back at the college, nothing has changed. The students are still protesting the war. The professors are still teaching their liberal claptrap. It seems to me that if they would take their heads out of their asses they could see the truth. We in the R.O.T.C. Department tell the truth about why we are in Viet Nam, and not the liberal or should I say communist spin. That is because of an origination known as SEATO. SEATO is like NATO except for the area of Southeast Asia. As a signer of the agreement, we required to answer the call for help from the other signatory parties.

On the following Monday morning, I receive a message that I am to call the office of General P. L. Lee at Fort Benning. When I finally find the phone number for the base and the call is made. The base operator puts me through to the General's office. The General's Aid Captain Wasnoski tells me, I am to report on Thursday at 1400 hours for jump evaluation and then on Saturday, I am to have my flight with the chief instructor. He also tells me, my replacement will be on site Tuesday morning to replace me, and I am to turn over to him the command of the ROTC unit.

This means I will be back on full duty soon, I hope. I know that I will be all right. It is just another hoop to jump through. I can do it.

I put in a call the travel office at Benning for travel information. After sometime spent on the phone with Trish Trales in travel office, and trying several different itineraries. We find out that there is a flight from JFK to Atlanta at 0600 arriving at 0930 on Thursday. With it only about a two-hour drive that would give me plenty of time.

"Let's book that one and a rent for me a car, please." Trish asks if I have a secretary. "Yes I do."

"Then I will call them with the reservations for both the car and flight within the hour."

I tell her "Thanks a lot. It was a pleasure doing business with you" and hang-up.

I then call Debbie to tell her, I will be on my way home tomorrow. But can only leave her a message. The only message I leave is. "I Love You". On Tuesday, when Debbie arrives home, I'm sitting in the front parlor with a bourbon and water in one hand, and flowers for her in the other. After seeing me, she runs over and jumps in my lap, almost spilling my drink and sitting on the flowers, we kiss. We are both so happy we could just die. I love this woman. After we have dinner and are relaxing in the parlor. I show Debbie my itinerary, and ask if she would take me to the airport the day after tomorrow.

With great speed, Debbie leaves the room. In about ten minutes, she is back. "Eric, I have taken tomorrow off. The receptionist will reschedule my appointments." We spent Wednesday just relaxing and being with each other. Thursday morning comes and I have my dress greens on early. Sleep did not come easy for me that night, for every nerve I had, was a little on edge.

At 0430, Debbie drives me to the airport. This is one of those mixed emotion days for me. I am dejected that I am leaving my wife and family again, but ecstatic that I can now prove I am ready to return to the service of my country. It is sad to stand and watch the love of your life drive off into the hustle and commotion of traffic on her way to work.

On the flight to Atlanta, I upgraded to first class, which made the trip that much better. More leg and elbow room. Sitting in the seat next to me is a man from DC. He works for a senator that is one that thinks the Military should have better pay and equipment. We talk about what he does and what I do. I tell him as much as I can. When we land, I go to the rental car counter and pick-up the keys to my car. I have one small bag with me, and put it in the trunk. I only have one small bag, because I am going to be issued new uniforms, a flight suit and helmet to use. All I am carrying is my personal bath kit and two changes of civilian clothes, plus two changes of BDU. The drive is a nice drive one, once you are on the outside of the loop of highway that circles Atlanta. I cannot help but think it was somewhere on this loop that some drunk killed Phil's parents.

Fort Benning is just like I remember. At the front gate, I am stopped for the normal checks. I am directed to park my rental car, and go into the office for my temporary car pass. The Desk Sergeant stands and gives me a salute, which I return. He then asks me for my orders. I show him my ID card, and tell him I am here by orders given to me by phone. Second Lieutenant Douglas Nelson comes out from the back office salutes and asks my name.

"Major Eric C. Howard" is my answer to him. He asks me to wait a minute. He returns to the office he came out of. In just a short time, the Lieutenant returns with a large brown envelope. He hands it to me telling me he was informed that I would be coming in. My orders, billeting information, and a map of the base are in the envelope. The Second Lieutenant then hands me my base pass and a sticker for the car. He salutes me and tells me to have a nice stay. As I head for the S.F. section of the base there are trainees marching, running, and being loaded in truck going every which way. The main drill field has several groups of men marching back and forth. With each group of men there are several Drill Sergeants yelling at them to get in step. Boy! Does that bring back a boatload of memories? Most of which are not the best of memories. As I enter the jump school area my mind slips back to when I was here. The same old barracks the same mess hall.

As enter the S.F. section I am stopped by an M.P. He walks up to my rental car, looks in only to step back and give me a salute. The M.P. then comes back and asks for my ID and wants to know where I am going. I show him my ID and a copy of my order. He looks at them and then he hands them back to me. He then steps back giving me directions to the BOQ, salutes and tells me to have a nice day. Have a nice day?? What are they trying to tell me?

The BOQ is a nice new brick building. The grass is cut to perfection. The white rocks that line the walkway look like they were just painted. This is S.F. country, all spit and polished. The room I am assigned is on the first floor about half way down the hall. I have a sitting room, bathroom and bedroom. The place is as clean as any I have been in. There are fresh towels in the bathroom and clean sheets on the bed. The TV is turned onto the base channel. This channel gives you the base weather and the schedule of events for today and tomorrow.

I shower and change in to my BDU. It is now time for me to report in to the Jump Master office. In his office I come face to face with Jose Manterley. Jose is now a Major and heads the jump school.

"Hey how are you, good to see you finally out of the hospital." He says as he grabs my hand. "How long was it 14,15 months they kept you locked up in there?"

"You are doing ok?" I answer.

"I am doing real Good." Jose says. "Let's do this paperwork and go to the O-club for an early dinner and some drinks. I would like you to up to date on what has been going on."

"When do I make my jumps?" I ask.

"We will make the jump tomorrow at 1400."

With a question mark in my tone, I say "the jump? Aren't there three jumps required?"

"Yes but for someone with your background, we will be doing only one HALO. If you survive that we are done."

"What do you mean by we?" Jose turns to the wall and points to a jump schedule.

"Tomorrow 12 men from the eighth training group will be jumping. You and I will be jumping with them. They are in their

35th week of training and will be jumping into an unknown location. This is to be a full combat style jump. Don't you think you can do it?"

"Jose, I am ready for anything. When am I going to be fitted with the equipment?"

"I will pick you up at 0630 tomorrow. Do you want to pack your own shoots?"

"No your people can handle it."

"If they don't work I will just look up the man that packed them and kick him so hard in the ass he will have to open his mouth to shit."

We then sit down at his deck and I fill out the paperwork. Here I am again signing my life away. That done I tell Jose I will meet him at 1700 in the O-Club.

Back at the BOQ, I call Debbie to tell her I love her and the kids, and all is well her in B-town. I do not tell her about the HALO, because she knows what that is, and would worry. She asks me if I have met anyone I know.

"Yes I have, Jose Manterley. Do you remember me telling you about the time that I stole a chopper to pull him and his team out of VERY HOT SPOT? You do not? Remind me when I return home and I will tell you all about it. I am meeting him for dinner at the O-Club. So I must run, will call tomorrow night. Bye Love" and I hang-up. Into the shower I go, jumping into a pair of black slacks, western style shirt, and my cowboy boots. Light a cigarette and out the door I go.

The O-Club is an old building that was probably built as an Officer Club for the officers that fought in World War I. It has a large dining room and two smaller bars. Banners and flags from every unit in every base here hang on the walls and from the ceiling. In a corner of each of the two bar rooms' stands an old wood burning stove that still works. There is the stale smell of cigarette, cigar and pipe smoke hanging in the air. Just the kind of a place a real man could feel at home. No elegant décor, no frilly doodads or anything like that. The food is excellent, the drinks are not watered down, and the people working here give you respect. Once in the club I ask for Major Manterley and am shown to his table. The server come to the table and asks what I would like. I have blackened catfish, fried potatoes, and a side of greens. For the after dinner fair, I go with the local choice of peaches in cream with brandy sauce.

After we have finished dinner, we adjourn to one of the bars, to have a few drinks and exchange war stories. The heat from fire in the wood stove feels good, as it is cool in late January, even in Georgia. We sit near the stove and talk about all that has happened to both of us.

He tells me. "Thanks for flying in to Death Valley to pull my team out. The way the helicopter looked after it landed. I think it was a miracle, we made it."

I learned that all but one, a Sergeant Littleton, was killed or badly wounded about seven months after I flew into pull them out. I tell him that all but one of my team made it home safe. He had never met my team, as they did not go with me on that trip. He tells me he has gotten to know Mike Danville.

"Mike is out on a mission now but will be back soon."

I learn Mike has told him all about what happened to me and how we lost John. "It is sad when you lose people like that." Jose asks how John's wife and kids are.

"Fine last time I talked with her. In Special Forces we are all one family."

Chapter 20

Major Jose Manterley is out front of the BOQ at 0630 on the dot. We are off to the supply room for my jump suit; oxygen equipment, helmet and the new style jump boots. Then on to the rigger hut, where the parachutes are packed, and labeled for the days jumps. Every shoot has two tags. One tells you the date it was packed and the person that packed it. I am handed two parachutes, one is the T-10 main shoot and the other is a reserve blossom type. On one tag is dated just three days ago and the name of the Rigger, Master Sergeant Thomas Daters. A second tag has my name and the date of my jump.

I look at Jose and ask him, "Why were these shoots packed for me? Do I need to worry?"

With a look, Jose tells me, "They are brand new shoots and will be given to you after the jump today. But you were not to know. So do not say anything. It was on the orders of Sergeant Major Ivers McCoy." With that said Jose walks out of the hut and takes a seat in the Jeep. I follow and do not ask any questions. I have a feeling there is no way Jose will tell me anything more.

We arrive just as the briefing is about to end. The M.P. at the door stops us to check our ID's. He asks us to go to the front of the room where we will be introduced to the class. On the stage, giving the briefing is a tall well-built man, who looks to be about 40 years old. As we arrive at the front of the room, he yells "Attention officers on desk."

The class stands to attention. The man on the stage, Sergeant Major Ivers McCoy, introduces Major Jose Manterley and then turns his attention to me.

"Gentleman it gives me great pleasure to introduce Major Eric C. Howard. The Major is here to make a qualifying jump. The Major must requalify, to return to active duty. He spent over a year in the Hospital recovering from severe wounds he received in Viet Nam. While in Viet Nam, he was awarded three Purple Hearts, two Bronze Stars, One Silver Star and the Distinguished Flying Cross. Gentleman Major Eric C. Howard." Everyone in the room stands and gives a cheer. "Ok be seated. The Majors will be jumping with you to day. They will go out after you and are not part your 10-day survival trial period. You will be jumping into the Okefenokee Wilderness Reserve. You each have a map and each is marked with the pickup points. Only one man to a point. Anything other then that is a failure. The letter at each point designates your pick up point for the end of your survival trial period. I do hope each one of you knows your letter designator. The only difference is the Majors will be picked up one hour after they land. Captain I have your maps and call signs. I will give them to you after the briefing. Your take-off time will be in 30 minutes. We will have Lieutenant Johnson and Sergeant Stevens on the flight to over see the jump. Are there any questions?"

"No."

"Ok, Dismissed."

After the trainees are all out of the room, Sergeant Major Ivers McCoy leaves the stage and walks over to us. He gives a salute and puts his hand out to me. I return the salute, and take his hand.

"Major Howard" he starts, "I want to thank-you for what you did for my brother, Gary. Gary was assigned to the base you had moved just before you where hit so badly. When he returned two months later, he had nothing but high words of praise about you and what you did and the way you handled the situation. As he tells it in his own words and the words of the others two men that based with him. You saved their lives and the lives of the men that followed them into that base. Thank-you Sir for what you have done."

I reply saying; "I did my job, nothing more."

The Sergeant Major shakes my hand again, gives a salute and turns to leave.

"Say what was that all about?" I ask Jose. He tells me to follow him. In a corner office of the building is an office with the Sergeant Majors name on the door. Inside on the wall is a photo taken two days before I left the base. The photo is of his brother Gary, Ed Norwood, Tom Dillingham and I. Below the photo is a plaque. The plaque is engraved with these words. Captain Eric Howard and the men whose lives he saved. "I did nothing more then what was expected of me. Shoot it was my job." I say with a sigh.

Out on the flight line sits a C-130. (Boy this is like old home week) This C-130 is just like the ones we jumped from in Viet Nam and the aircraft used to take me to Japan. The sight and smells take me back. It was not easy to walk up the rear ramp because I so vividly remember pain and how I felt when leaving my men. The inside of the bird looks just like it did then except there a seat along both side instead of litters. The smell of death is not here, just the faint smell of fear left by the men that have made their first jumps from this bird.

Jose and I take the first two seats on the left side of the aircraft. Then the 12 trainees file in. They position themselves six on a side. The Lieutenant and Sergeant come on board looking to see where we are. The Lieutenant walks forward and asks Jose if he would please move to the other side. Jose hands me a map and a piece of paper with the call sign and other notes on it, as he moves to the left side of the aircraft. The ramp in the back comes up and closes with on ominous bang. The engines revs-up and we start to roll.

I now have mixed emotions. (You know the kind emotions you feel when watching your worst enemy drive your new Corvette off a 500-foot cliff) One is of worry because I have not made a jump in a long time and the other is of relief knowing I am not jumping into a hostile area. We make a slow arch turning to the southeast, level off and start our climb to 1400 ft. It is now time for me to study the notes and map. On the notes are the radio frequencies to be used, the altitude we jump from, the grid co-ordinates for our landing and the pickup point. Looking at the map it will be three-quarters of a mile hike from landing point to pickup area. Not bad as long as the lay of the land is good. For the most part the Okefenokee is swamp or wetland. There is dry place for us to land and make our way out. Luckily, our landing zone is close to the edge of the reserve and is mostly dry.

The red light starts to flash. The Lieutenant comes on the horn and tells everyone to standup, check their equipment and their buddies. I stand check my straps to see that they are tight and all my equipment is in place and ready. Jose come over and checks me, I in turn check him. All is ok. The red light is goes on steady and the ramp starts down bringing in a stiff breeze and a lot of noise. The green light flashes and the order to move to the ramp is given. The two lines of men move toward the ramp, forming up behind the Lieutenant and Sergeant. The green light goes steady and the Lieutenant and Sergeant step aside and tap each man in turn on the back to jump. Two by two, they walk down the ramp and fall out into the wild blue yonder. As Jose and I approach them, they signal us to stop, as the green changes to red. The plane banks around ever so slowly, as we ready for another pass. We are to jump about one half mile northeast of the other jumpers. The light goes green and with an ok signal and a pat on the back, we take that walk down the ramp and jump into the abyss.

As I am falling, I check my altimeter. It reads 13,000 ft. Looking to my left, I see Jose, and give him the thumbs up and the ok sign. He returns the signal. I look around at the beauty of it all. Blue sky above and green earth with open water here and there below. Looking back at the altimeter it reads 11,500 ft, and then 10,700 ft. looking to the east I think I can see the ocean. My attention is drawn back to the altimeter, which now reads 7,000 ft. The orders are to open at 900 ft instead of the normal 550 ft., so I have some time to enjoy the ride. This is nice not to have to worry about who will be on the ground. No need to look for the flash of someone shooting at me or wondering if the area is safe to land in. I look back at the altimeter as it beeps at me. The first alarm was set for 1,100 ft, and it works perfectly. With a glance at Jose and a point at the altimeter, it is now time to pop the shoot.

At exactly 900 ft, the parachute opens to a full wing. Where is Jose? He is not in my sight. Pulling on the steering cords to make a turn, I find him about 30 ft to the west, and above me by about the same distance. Looking at the ground to find our LZ, I find it is about 50 yards northeast of where I am. The T-10 is easy to steer by pulling on the steering cords. With a slight pull to the right, I am on target. Just before landing, you pull on the backset of cords to flare the wing. This puts you on the ground softly and by walking ahead as you land there is no falling down. With my parachute rig now off, I look for Jose. He is coming down from the south, and looks good on his approach. As his feet touch the ground, he stumbles over a small ridge in the ground falling forward.

I go over to him and ask, "Are you ok?"

Jose sits up and starts to chuckle. He looks up at me and says. "It was you I was worried about. And now who looks the fool, who is sitting in the mud."

As we pick up our parachutes, and start out to the pickup point there is a lot of splashing and noise coming from behind us. After all that time in combat, I start for the tree line and cover, pulling Jose with me. At the tree line, we stop and look back in the direction the noise is coming from. "Look there, on the south side if the clearing, someone is coming out of the tree line." I say. As they move closer, we can tell it is three of the trainees. Two of them are carrying a homemade litter. On the litter is one of their comrades.

We go over to them to see what is going on. The tall, well built one, a Sergeant E-6, by the name of Newhouse, informs us that during the jump Sergeant E-5 Felman hit a tree and landed hard. He has a broken leg, and is unresponsive.

"Sergeant don't you know you could do more harm by moving him?"

"Yes Sir, I do Sir. I am a medic, and I checked him over before moving him. We called in and were told to meet up with you."

His neck is braced, and he is immobilized. I then give a quick check on Felman. Jose gives a call into HQ, as we head out to our pick up point. The going is easy, as we do not have any water in our way. As we approach the area, I can see it is a parking lot of some sort, and there is a helicopter on the ground. It is sitting with its rotor on idle. As soon as two of the flight crew sees us, they run over and take the litter. They load Sergeant Felman into the bird and strap him down. The rest of us board and we lift off quickly. Once airborne the second officer hands me a headset. It is given to me, as he was under orders too. I find this a little strange, as Major Manterley is the one in charge of our jump. The pilot informs me that we are heading to Hunter-Stewart as that is the nearest base with a hospital that we can use.

As we approach the LZ, you can see there is an ambulance and several cars waiting for us. Once on the ground the medics come running over to remove Sergeant Felman, and load him into the ambulance. Just as quickly, they are gone. A Major walks over to us, hands me an envelope and informs the pilot that we are to return to Benning ASAP. The pilot asks to be refueled, and with it done, we are up and on our way.

I open the envelope. The first page tells us once in Benning, the two trainees are to report to their commanding officer with no stops or diversions.

I tell them and they both salute and reply, "Yes Sir, Will Do Sir."

The second page tells me that Major Manterley and I are

expected in the flight line briefing center upon our return. It has been cleared for us to sit down in front of the briefing room. In looking at Jose I know he or someone else had something planned. I do not know what, just something. I tap him on the shoulder, and say, "if it were not for the rental car and my gear I could have stayed at Hunter. That is where I am going next for my flight evaluation." He gives me a strange look, and turns to look out the window in silence. Now I know something is going on. The rest of the flight is quiet with only the noise of the engine and rotor cutting the engine exhaust.

The return time at Benning is a little later then originally scheduled due to our detour to Hunter-Stewart with the injured trooper. As we land in front of the briefing room, there are people everywhere. But the biggest surprise comes as I walk in the door. There to greet me is Mike and Roy. Mike is now a Captain and Roy is an E-7. Both are stationed here, and have been hiding from me until now.

Mike gives me a hug, and tells me that Sergeant Major McCoy has planned this whole thing. "When word came down you were coming here. It was hard not to hear about it. The word went around faster then wildfire."

"The Second Lieutenant you met at the gate was under orders to inform the Sergeant Major the minute you arrived. Do you remember when he excused himself and returned to his office?"

"Yes I do why?" I asked Mike.

"He was also ordered that the minute you came on the base he was to warn me and hold you there till everyone but Major Jose Manterley was out of sight. Your little trip to the O-Club put a real big damper on the evening for a whole lot of guys. It was to have been a poker tournament night. Oh well you may have saved me some money."

"Let's go find the Sergeant Major. You know he requested to be in charge of your briefing and did not leave the communication center, until you were on your way back to Benning. He almost had a bird when the word came down about the incident with the Trainee. He wanted the flight to return straight to Benning. It took a Full Bird Colonel from the Medical Unit to divert your flight to Hunter-Stewart. If the Wing Commander here had not been in on this you would have spent the night out there. Do you remember Major Thomas Sanborn?"

"No I do not, should I?"

"I would think so; you stole a helicopter from him. He wanted you court-martialed. Until you came in with all the wounded men. He was still mad about his bird, but glad it worked out and you returned with everyone alive. He is the Wing Commander here."

"I hope he is not still mad about that, is he?" I ask.

"Eric you are here now, aren't you?"

"Ok I understand."

As we enter the room, I can see that the stage is set with two long tables. There is a rostrum in the middle between the tables. The tables have four chairs to either side. At each place is a card with a name on it. To the left of the rostrum the first card has my name on it, then Mike's name followed Roy and Doc. The chair for Doc is leaned forward to show he would not be present, but remembered. To the right the first name is just a title, The General, next is Sergeant Major Ivers McCoy, then Command Sergeant Major T.L.Littleton and then Colonel Sanborn.

"Mike where have I heard the name Littleton?"

"Eric don't you remember the First Sergeant you, in your

stunt with the stolen chopper, pulled out of what became known as Death Valley."

"Ok so what is going on here? Is this some kind of roast? Am I to be the butt of some jokes?"

"No Sir, not at all Sir. Everyone at the head table, you either saved their life or the life of someone close to them. The front two rows of tables are also people that have the same type of story. This is our way to say thank-you for a job well done."

"Mike you make it sound as if I am about to die and this is a pre death eulogy."

"Eric that is not the way we mean it. This is the first time we could show how we all feel and want you to know that."

"Ok, Ok, I understand it. Now who is The General?" I ask.

Mike tells me, "Phillip L. Lee is who he is, but I did not tell you. It was to be a surprise."

"It will be a surprise, I don't know him."

"Yes you do. Let's take our seats as every one is waiting for you." Roy tells us.

The food is excellent. The wine is French; the bourbon is from Kentucky. Then comes the part of the night I am dreading. First Mike and Roy take the rostrum, they start with a joke about me in my casts at Valley Forge Army Hospital being put on a bed pan by a little 5' 4"blond, big breasted female RN and how she almost dropped me on the floor. Mike then introduces Sergeant Major Ivers McCoy. The Sergeant Major presented me with the Parachutes, I used to requalify saying, "I was now back in the fold and I was to jump with pride." He then went on to tell about what I did for his brother and the men with him. He in turn introduces Command Sergeant Major T.L.Littleton. He hands me a flight helmet saying that I was, and will always be one of the best chopper pilots. He then goes on to tell his story about that day in what was now called Death Valley. How I came and pulled him and 11 other men with him out of that hellhole. He goes on to tell the audience that the helicopter had so many holes it looked like a sieve. I keep looking at the General on the other side of the table not knowing who he was.

As Command Sergeant Major T.L.Littleton was finishing he says, "Gentleman it gives me pleasure to introduce Major Thomas Sanborn. Major Sanborn was in charge of the Air Wing that Captain Eric Howard procured the helicopter from to save our lives with."

Major Sanborn stands up and comes over to me, shakes my hand. Then goes to the podium and starts. "When I was informed that one of my helicopters was stolen, I was very mad. So mad, I wanted it shot down. But when the message came in that the helicopter was returning to base and asking medical staff to be at the pad. I asked why. I was told Captain Howard was now returning with 12 men and most of them are wounded. I was told that Captain Howard, by himself, had flown six klicks up river under heavy enemy fire to save a trapped A-Team. There was no one in my command that would go, so when he heard about what was going on he took it upon himself to go. The helicopter he used had to be scraped after the flight, as there was very little of it could be used. I was still mad but also proud of him for what he did." The Major turns, gives me a salute and takes his seat.

After the Major sits down, Sergeant Major Ivers McCoy stands up and walks to the rostrum. "Let us all now stand for General Phillip L. Lee."

The General stands up and moves to the rostrum. As he arrives at the rostrum, he stops looks straight at me, and gives me a salute. Once at the rostrum he starts with, "This man Major Eric C. Howard is one of the bravest and most committed men I have ever met. I can tell he is not comfortable with all this hoopla by the look on his face. I can also tell he does not remember me, and for the most part, probably not most of you. That does not mean he does not care, just to him it was just in a day's work. I know he looks at what he has had done as only his job. He has told me that several times."

Turning to me he asks, "Do you remember me now?"

I shake my head "no" with a puzzled look on my face. Facing the audience again, the General states. "See what I mean."

The projector comes to life and on the screen behind him are photos taken in our base camp. The one we were sent out from time and time again. The one we shared with two other teams. The first slides show a Colonel pinning on an award. As I look closer, I can tell it is the General and I in the next slide. You see him and my men getting medals. There are two more slides show-ing the base and some of the things that went on. Now I know who he is.

He turns to me and asks, "Now do you remember?"

I stand walk over to him and shake his hand. "Yes Sir, I do sir."

The General then hands me a small case. He tells me to open it, inside is the Vietnamese Medal of Honor. "Major Howard I was to have given this to you when you returned to camp back in Viet Nam. You never did return. Instead, you wound up in the Army Hospital at Valley Forge. It took over a year for you to be discharged. The Medical Staff did not think you would walk again, but here you are. Ready to return to full duty. We thank-you for your service to our country. I am sorry it took so long, but it now gives me great pleasure to give this to you. On behalf of the Government of the Republic of South Viet Nam, I here by present you with the Vietnamese Medal of Honor. Your country and Viet Nam government want to thank-you for your service in the course of freedom. Keep up the good work and welcome back." He hands me the gavel and takes his seat.

It is my turn to say something. "What do I say?" I adjust the microphone to have time to think. I fiddle with the gavel. I look up and say. "Oh well lets make it short and sweet. I wish to thank Sergeant Major Ivers McCoy and all of you that are here tonight for this gathering. I now invite all of you, Enlisted and Officer alike, to the Officers-Club for one drink on me. Thank-you and good night".

The General comes over to me, and asks me to ride with him in his staff car. Once in his car and on our way to the O-club, the conversation turns to Washington D.C. and my thinking of being posted to the Pentagon with my next promotion. "General, thank-you for the offer that is if that is an offer, but I must say no at this time. I do so want to go back into the field. But when my next promotion comes through, I will consider a move like that."

He answers me by telling me that with my next promotion, I will not have the flexibility to go into a hostile area that often, and if I turn down a posting to the Pentagon, it would look bad on my record. Refusing a posting like that is not the way to win friends and influence people in high places, especially those people outside of Special Forces. The General then goes on to tell me that the promotion boards for Lieutenant Colonel and above are heavily weighted by regular army officers, most of whom do not look kindly upon Special Forces promotions. I thank him for his interest and express to him that I will keep that in mind when and if the time comes.

At the O-Club, the General and I both have one drink. I then take a ride with the General back to the BOQ. Once in my room, I take a long hot shower. As hot as I can take it, without burning my scarred skin. Once in bed and asleep, I start to dream.

I dream I am back in Viet Nam at a firebase, one of the most forward of them high in the central highlands. The LP's are out and in place for the night. The hills are alive with the sounds of birds, monkeys, lizards and all kinds of exotic jungle wildlife. The oddest one to me is the fuck-you bird. (Which by the way is not a bird at all?) It is a lizard. You would swear someone is out in front of you yelling fuck-you, but no it is just a lizard.

Then you have the rock apes. This animal will sit just outside your NDP or LP and throw this and that at you. I remember on one dark almost moonless night a message comes into the OPS room.

"HQ come in please, LP 1 calling HQ, come in Please, I have incoming, over"

I return the call saying, "This is HQ, and I hear nothing at this location, over".

LP 1 comes back with, "HQ I have incoming, over".

I return "LP 1 this is HQ, we do not hear a thing at this location please explain, over".

The radio then comes alive with "HQ this LP 1, and I have this rock ape out to my front and he is throwing shit at this position. I mean real shit and does it stink! Over"

There is a knock on my door that snaps me back to reality. I am so glad I have today off. My head aches and my stomach is queasy. I really did not have a lot to drink. It had to be because of the HALO of yesterday. High altitude and low oxygen can do that to you.

Chapter 21

"Who is it?" I ask.

"Mike and Roy" I receive. "We are here to see what you are up to and ask you to have breakfast with our wives and us."

"Come in, but be quiet."

Mike comes in followed by Roy. Mike asks me if I am all right.

"Yes I am, just a little slow this morning, probably from the high altitude jump yesterday."

"Yeah right, those HALOS can do that to you now and then." Roy says with a sarcastic grin.

Mike then asks, "What time do you need to leave for Hunter-Stewart?"

"If I pull out of here by 1600 that will give me plenty of time." I reply.

Mike asks, "What is your report time?"

I reach for my brief case saying, "Let me look. I am due to report at the H and H Company office at 0930 tomorrow. Why?"

"Eric, why don't you take the morning shuttle flight that leaves at 0530. I can arrange it. We can have you to the flight line in plenty of time. That way you can come over to the house and see Linda and not have to drive."

Roy chimes in with, "Ak wants to see you again too. Her English is improving and we have an extra bedroom. No kids you know. Well not yet anyway." I have a very puzzled look on my face. "You did know we lost the baby in third month. Didn't you?"

"Yes I did and I was so sorry to hear that."

"That's ok we are working on having a child. We really want a child, and the Doctors tell us it is ok to try again. You can leave the rental car at my place. So pack up and let's go. Linda is cooking breakfast and it will be done soon."

"Man you don't give a guy a chance do you? Ok, I am packed let's go."

I put my bag in the back seat and the parachute in the trunk. The new helmet needs a bag so I put that in the passenger seat. Roy rode over with Mike. As we are preparing to leave, Roy runs over to my car and knocks on the passenger side door. I unlock the door and he starts to enter.

"Oops, I almost sat on your helmet."

Mike said, "I should ride with you so we can stop and pickup Ak. Is that ok with you?"

"Sure just as long as Linda does not burn the breakfast. I only like burnt toast."

"Do not worry Linda is a whiz in the Kitchen." Roy tells me. "She has been teaching Ak to cook since we have been in base. Ak can now cook on a stove. Everyone on base is calling her Sunny because they have trouble saying her name. She likes being called Sunny and introduces herself that way now."

I say, "Ok, so where am I going."

"Oh right, you don't know. At the corner turn left, go to the stoplight and turn right."

"ROY STOP! All I need is the name of the street and house number." He gives me the street name, and the house number, and off we go.

As we are driving along I ask, "Is there some place on base to buy a bag for that helmet you are holding?"

"I do not know, but Mike may. He is trying to be accepted to the flight program. That's why he knows about the shuttle to Hunter-Stewart. He has gone over about three times taking test and being prodded by a flight surgeon. Do not tell him I told you that please."

"Ok, I will not tell him you blabbed to me." We stop in front of Roy's EM housing. As I comment to Roy "This is much nicer then I was thinking it would be, not bad at all." Roy runs into the house literally "ran into the house not looking where he was going".

I run out to see if he is all right. But before I could reach him, he is up and in the house.

"Knock, Knock is anyone there?" I say. Ak, I mean Sunny comes to see who it is. As soon as she sees me, she screams and runs to give me a hug.

"Come in please, Roy washing his face now as he received a bloody nose running in to the building. He be right out." Roy enters the living room sheepishly.

"Sorry, let's go, Linda will wonder where we all are."

I go out first to put my bag, and helmet in the trunk to make room for all of us. I am driving a Ford Mustang. (This was not my first choice, but all they had were Fords. So what the hell, I have AAA for when it breaks down) we are ready to drive off, I ask for Mike's address, with that in my head off we go. You know looking around now, I do see many people I know and others I know I have seen before. I am bad with names, but rarely forget a face.

We pull up into Mike's driveway, only to avoid bikes and other toys. As we enter the house through the kitchen door, Linda drops a bowl she is stirring and comes to give me a hug and kiss on the cheek. Mike enters from the living room, dining room area holding a child about a 1 year old followed by a 3-year-old boy.

"What was that crash, is everyone ok?" Mike asks. Looking down he sees the broken bowl. "Roy, you and Eric better come on into the living room. Let us leave the girls to fix breakfast. When Linda learned you were going to be on base she set out to learn to make biscuits and gravy. I have been having them every morning for three days now. Sunny has been learning to make grits, so they have it covered. Roy here started to acquire a southern accent from all the grits she has been feeding him. Yes, I know we are in the south. The people around here sure don't let you forget it."

I speak up saying. "Did you forget I am a Southerner and proud of it? I stand when Dixie is played."

"Ok, OK" I GET IT." Mike tells me.

"How old are the children and what are their names?" I ask. "The boy is three and his name is Eric. This is Patricia and she is 11 months. "Eric, come say "hello to Uncle Eric." He comes over to me, as I kneel down and very shyly and give me a hug.

Linda asks from the kitchen, "Does anyone want orange juice?" Roy and I both say "yes."

In about 15 minutes, we are seated at the dining room table eating and talking. Linda asks about Debbie and my three children. I tell them that Debbie is in private practice in New York and that Debbie is due to have our next child in July.

"You know sex?" Sunny asks me.

"Of course that is how Debbie is pregnant." I joke.

With that said, Sunny looks at me with this strange look on her face. Roy jumps in and tells her it is a joke.

"Sorry. Yes it is a boy, and we will name him Eric Frances. My daughter is the oldest. Her name is Ingrid Lynn, then two boys, Eric Charles the VI, and Eric Frances the III." Linda looks at me and asks "Two Eric's?"

"Yes Eric Charles is in Kentucky growing up just like I did, while Eric Frances will be with his mom."

Mike says to Linda. "I will explain later."

After breakfast while the ladies are cleaning up the kitchen, Mike, Roy and I step outside for a smoke. While we are outside, I ask Mike about where I could find a bag for the helmet I received last night.

"There is a store off base that would be the best place to buy one. They carry the same ones as on base, and they are 20 to 30 percent less in town. Would you like to go?"

"Yes I would as long as it is "ok with the ladies." Linda sticks her head out the door and asks what is going on out here?

Mike looks at her and asks, "What do you mean? We are just having a smoke."

"Oh, OK, Sunny and I were going to go over to the Wives Club for some Bridge, is it ok?"

"That is just peachy. Eric and I are going to go into town for a Helmet bag for his new brain bucket."

Linda tells Mike she will take the kids. "They like the daycare room there."

Mike tells her "Ok just don't lose too much money. You do know Linda, we have the kids to feed."

"Ha, Ha very funny Mike. Be back in time for dinner, it will be ready about 7:00 p.m."

"Ok, we will see you then."

"Say Mike, I was going to take everyone to the O-Club for dinner."

"Eric we could not go. Linda and I do not have a babysitter. Roy and Sunny are not doing the best financially. That is why Sunny is here so much. She just does not know how to handle money and has put them in a deep hole. Linda is helping her learn what money is and how to save. Remember when Roy came in from Fort Dix. Well Sunny signed a lease on a furnished apartment costing about half his pay. She also applied for a credit card and received it. On that credit card, she charged a TV, and a bunch of clothes. The card was over the limit in two weeks. When the bills started coming in, Roy asked her about it and she told him it was ok. The Card Company said she could pay over time and she had saved $4.50 to pay them. Roy is still trying to have the Jag look into it. He said Ak did not know enough English to understand what was being told her."

"Can I help?" I ask.

"No Eric, we can handle it. The Jag had the lease broken so that is out of the way. It is just the damn credit card. The credit card people have been notified that under an Act of Congress, they cannot force payment. They were also notified that the way they scammed Ak, the Jag filed a court action. However, the bill collector scabs still continue to call and send letters that look like court orders. Every time Roy is away, and Sunny receives a letter or call, she sends money to them, which makes it harder for the Jag and not to mention the loss of money they cannot afford to lose. Say lets go to town and find you that bag. On our way out of the base, Roy wants to stop and pick up the mail. Is it ok with you Eric? Mike asks.

"Sure, why not?" I answer.

The town is a typical post town, lots of bars, adult bookstores, and the usual pawnshops. As we turn down one of the side streets to cut over to the store Mike told me about.

Roy says, "Over there is the best whorehouse in town. Or so I am told."

Both Mike and I have to turn to look at him, "What did you say?" I ask.

Roy turned a vivid shade red and says very sheepishly "Several of the men I work with tell me that is the place to go to here in town. But I have never gone there."

I look at him and say "Oh really."

As we approach the Surplus Store, Mike tells us to look for a parking spot; we find one about half the way down the parking lot, right between an Army Jeep and a Deuce and a half from the post.

I ask Mike, "What are they doing here? He tells me that the supply sergeant at one of the leg companies comes here at the start of every training cycle to pick up some of the equipment they use that is not supplied by the Defense Department. In the store, I find a very nice hard-sided case for my helmet.

We then head to a local Burger Shack for some lunch and a couple of beers. This is one of those places every guy on the base likes to come to for a meal that is not Army chow. I have a ¾ lb.

Burger with cheese and bacon, but forgo the beer in favor of a sweet iced tea. (Only in the south can you have a real sweet tea. I do not know why they cannot make them as good up North)

After we eat and talk for about two hours Mike asks me "if I would like to see the house he and Linda are looking to buy."

"Yes I would, but why are you thinking of moving off base?"

"Eric the housing on base is not big enough for our family now that and Linda is pregnant again."

"So what are you trying to do keep up with Debbie and me?" I ask.

"Eric, don't tell me you two are going to have another child." Roy says with a bit of a question in voice.

"Yes we are. But where were you?" I told Linda that over breakfast, I tell him.

Roy looks confused and says, "I don't know, must have been in the bathroom at that time."

The town has faded behind us as we turn down a small country lane and over a small hill. We stop in what looks like a farming area.

"That is the house off to the left, back in those trees over there" Mike points out.

"Can we go up and see it?" I ask.

"No not today, as I have not called the agent that has it listed and the gate on to the place is locked. The people that used to live here have horses, and will move them when the place sells. We made an offer last week, but the owner is in California till Monday."

"Ok, so who is taking care of the horses?" I ask.

Mike tells me the owner's son lives just over there and comes over several times a day to let them out and to feed them. He puts them back in their stable every night.

"So why is the place up for sale?"

Mike tells me the owner has moved to California and the son will be moving as soon as the place sells.

"I have a question for you. Mike. You and Linda are both city kids. The two of you grew up in inter-city Philadelphia. Why are you thinking of moving to the country? And have you really thought about what country life is like? Are you both ready for all the work it takes? Also what about when you are sent out on a mission. Do you and Linda think she can handle it alone? Remember I grow up in the country, and it is not an easy life."

Mike looks at me and answers me with, "Yes, We have been thinking about this type of move for sometime. When Linda became pregnant this time, we decided it was time to make our move. The two of us wanted to talk with you about your youth and what it was like to be a farm kid."

"Mike, first off I will be glad to talk about it. Second, I was not a farm kid. I grew up on a large Plantation with a lot of people doing most of the work. Yes I had my chores but not much to do with the fieldwork, but after dinner, we will talk about it.

On the drive back to the base, I think about what my life was like growing up and how much fun it was being in the hills of Kentucky. All about having horses to ride, a creek to swim in, and room to run around to play. I did not have to think about cars in the street or gangs to worry about. I think it would be a good idea for me to stay in the BOQ again tonight, since Roy and Ak are having the problems they have. I have not checked out, so I still have my room to go to, but how do I tell Roy without making him feel bad.

As we go through town, on the way back to the post Mike stops at an ice-cream parlor saying "Linda asked me to pickup so ice cream and this place makes the best ice cream in town."

We all go in and look at the different flavors they have. My eyes light up when I see they have coffee ice cream. Mike buys a half-gallon of pecan and heads for the door.

"Mike is that all you are getting?" I ask.

"Yes, why do you think we will need more? Or do you want something else?"

"Yes I would like a different flavor, and do you really think one half-gallon will be adequate?" I say. Mike looks at me and then at the bucket he is holding.

"You might be right, we might need more. What other flavor would you like?"

"Coffee would be nice" I answer.

"So, let me have a half-gallon of coffee, please." I say to the young guy behind the counter.

Mike walks up behind, in a very deep voice he tells me "This is mine and I will pay for it." We take the ice cream and go back to the car.

As we are driving, I turn to Roy saying, "Roy, I have been thinking and it has nothing to do with you, but I think I should go back to the BOQ for the night. I have a lot of reading to do, to be prepared for tomorrow. I want to be on top of everything, so I can be back on flight status. I hope you understand. He looks at me with dejected eyes and says he understands. He just hopes Sunny will understand.

It is about three hours until dinner and the girls are not back yet. I tell Mike and Roy that I am going back to the BOQ for a shower, and call Debbie, as she should be home now. I also need to stop at the Sergeant Majors office to pick up the new inserts on Halo's. I tell them I will be back in two and half-hours. In reality I want sometime to think, to think about all that was said today and time to think about Roy and Sunny and all their problems, time to contemplate Mike and Linda buying a house in the country. Not mention taking a short nap.

At the BOQ, I call Debbie and fill her in on what is going on. She asks if there is anything that she can do to help Roy and Ak. She tells me she likes Ak new name, it fits her. Debbie and Sunny had a good time last New Year in Monte Carlo and became good friends. Debbie asks how I am doing. I tell her good, but I just do not know what to say to Mike and Linda about the move they are contemplating. Debbie tells me to tell them what it was like for me growing up, and not to sugar coat it or make it worse then it was. "You turned out pretty good did you not?"

We talk for sometime more and end with," I love you and miss you." I take a shower and stand under the hot water for sometime thinking about what to say to Mike. What Debbie said about just "tell it like it was, is the best way, so that is what I will do." After drying off, I lie down and drift off to sleep. The alarm I had set starts to ring, which wakes me up. Oh well, lets start moving, I tell myself.

Back at Mike's house, everyone is out in the back yard. The adults are sitting on deck chairs and the children are playing in the grass. The grill is hot and a picnic table is set. As I walk around the house, everyone looks at me and asks, "If I am ok?"

I say, "Sure why?"

"You look like you have a problem" Roy tells me.

"No I just woke up from a nap. Getting old you know, and the lack of activity sitting around in class for the last two years. Let's eat I am starving."

Mike goes to the grill lifts the top and pokes a couple of thick steaks. "Eric, how do you want your steak?"

"If I stick my fork in it and it goes MOOO that is just the way I like it." I answer.

Roy turns to Sunny and tells her that I used to drive the cooks in Nam crazy eating my steaks that way. Army cooks are taught to burn or boil meat, undercook veggies and make everything taste the same. Now the cooks that cooked for the Officers on big bases and places like that were very good cooks. Not like the ones that prepared the meals for the enlisted men.

Mike chimes in with that "Roy is exaggerating; it is not that bad at all."

Roy zings back with, "Yes, well you are an "OFFICER", how would you know."

Everyone has a laugh out of the exchange. Mike says, "Ok! Everyone have a seat at the table. Linda, would you see to it that the children are seated while I set the rest of this on the table."

Linda takes Patricia and puts her in the highchair beside her. Roy helps her by putting Eric in a booster seat between himself and Sunny. I stand and watch what is going on until, Linda tells me to sit at the end of the table between Mike and Roy. The dinner consists of T-bone steaks, twice baked potatoes and creamed corn that Linda had put up last summer.

"Linda I did not know you knew how to can things?"

"Yes Eric, I have been learning to do a lot of things like that since Mike returned from Viet Nam. We started talking about moving to the country shortly after his return."

"What made you guys think that way?" I ask.

"Well Eric, it was all the things you guys talked about while in Viet Nam. Mike would tell me stories about what you had said about your life in Kentucky, and how much fun it sounded. So over the last couple of years we have looked into moving, and what it would entail. Especially, how much work it would be, and if I could handle it when Mike is away."

"Boy you people have done a lot of thinking about it." I say. "Mike showed me the place you were looking at and asked if I would talk with you about what living in the country was like. But, by the sounds of it, you have done a lot of thinking and learning already. What more can I say."

Mike speaks up," What we would like to know is what it was like for you. Was it hard on you or did you have fun."

"Let me think about it while we finish dinner. We will talk over coffee later. Just not too late, as I have to go over to Hunter-Stewart early in the morning."

After dinner and ice cream, Roy and Sunny excuse themselves to leave for home. As they get ready to go, Roy tells me he will see me in the morning and leaves.

"Mike is everything all right with them?" I ask.

"Everything is fine. When the girls returned home, Roy told Sunny about what you wanted to do and she was fine with it. You know they are trying to have a child, and I think it worked this time because Sunny tires out easily and is not feeling all that well in the morning, if you know what I am saying."

Mike and I retire to the deck chairs with a cup of coffee while Linda puts Patricia to bed. Eric is in his room playing with his toys. After a while, Linda, from the backdoor, asks if we would like anything. "No, thank-you." She comes out with a small dish of coffee ice cream and sits down with us.

"What was it like for you growing up? Did you have chores to do? Did you have fun?" Linda asks.

"I think I had a very good time as a youth. It was not always easy but it was a lot of fun. Yes, I had chores to do but still had time to just be a kid. Would I do it the same if I had a choice? Yes I would and I would have no worries about raising a child that way, for the most part my oldest son is now living with his great grandfather in Kentucky, just like I did." I then start explain to them about our family history, and how the eldest male has grown up this way, since the family first came to this country.

Linda stops me to tell me, "Mike has already told me that part."

"Well as I was saying it was a good life and I would not have changed any part of it. I had a lot of fun playing in the woods and going swimming in the creek. No, it was a good life. I tell them some of the things I was into but not all of it. Some of the fun times, I had with friends. I also told them about some of the things that weren't so much fun, but still not that bad to make my childhood a "bummer." After we talked for about an hour, I said, "I think I better go. I need to read something's for tomorrow and put in some sack time. Mike, will I see you then?"

"Yes Eric I will pick you up at 0500. It is only a 10-minute ride from the BOQ to your flight and they know you are on the flight out. See you then."

"Good night." I reply.

Once I am back in my room, I call Debbie to see how she is and how the children are doing. I tell her all about my day with Mike, Roy and all their families. I let her know that Linda is pregnant again, and she has been learning to be a farm wife. She has learned to can, put up preserves and has read many books on how to live in the country. And that Mike, Linda and I spent a few hours talking about what it is like to live out in the country. After we say our good-byes, I take a long hot shower and go to bed.

As I drift off to sleep, I start to dream about some of the things I did as a kid growing up. Living in a small town there was not much we could do as far as organized activities. We had to make our own fun so to say. We had to have a good imagination. I remember we would tie a rope to a tree so we could swing out over the creek to fall in with a big splash. We'd have pick up football games in someone's field. We would play Yankees and Rebels. We did not play cowboys and Indians, as we did not see the Indians as an enemy. Going camping in the woods was fun too. Making our own fun was a way to learn. Some people might question whether I was testing the limits, which might be seen as wrong, but not illegal. Like the time we put the horse drawn carriage on the water tower, or the times as an older teenager, I would run "moonshine to Tennessee."

I remember the time when I was in grade school, when I put Limburger Cheese in the heating system at school to have sometime off. There was to be a Rodeo Meet on a Saturday and this was a Thursday. I thought I needed some practice and wanted Thursday and Friday off. In the coatroom at school placed between the two classrooms there was a large wood burning furnace. It had a heat vent pipe that went from the back of it into the two classrooms. I was deliberately late for class that day, so I could be the last one into class. If the teacher saw you ride up to school before the bell rang. She would not count you as late because you had to stable your horse and put out food and water. I made sure she saw me riding into school that day. Once in the coatroom I slipped out a large chunk of Limburger Cheese I had obtained from Jeb the day before. Jeb was a friend of mine that had graduated the year before and was working in a grocery store about 20 miles from home. Jeb's real name was John Edward Bloomfield. We called him Jeb because he was a good horseman and he reminded us of the Confederate General know as J.E.B.Stuart. I then place the cheese on top of the heat pipe behind the furnace and went into class. About an hour or two, the entire school reeked. It was so bad some of the kids were starting to feel sick. My teacher's desk was in the front of the room. The vent into the room pointed right at her desk. As she told us to leave the building, her eyes were watering. Once outside you could almost see a cloud coming out the door behind us. They had to close the school for almost a week and a half. When we were finally able to go back to class there was still a very slight odor in the air. To my great surprise, I was never in trouble for that. I did not know if they knew who did it, until I returned to Kentucky for our 5-year class reunion.

Chapter 22

It is 0400 and I am up and sitting at the desk in my room. There is a knock at my door.

"Who is it? I ask.

"It is Sergeant Major McCoy. Sir, may I come in? Sir"

"Yes please do," I answer.

McCoy enters the room and apologizes for the early hour. He proceeds to tell me that he was informed by flight OPS I was to fly out this morning. In addition, he needed to see me before I took off. We stopped by yesterday, but you were not here. We checked with the BOQ people and they told us you had gone out with your two buddies. I was told you were expected back. I am glad you did return. Under one arm, I see he is carrying a large box. He gives me the obligatory salute. I respond in kind and tell him to have a seat. Before he takes a seat on the couch, he hands me the box. As it's placed in my hands, he starts with telling me about what happened the other night.

"Major Howard, after the ceremony several of us, thirty to be exact, had a meeting and decided you probably did not still have your flight suit. Do you?"

"No, I do not Sarge. It went by the wayside somewhere"

"Good, that is what we thought. It was decided that we should give your something." As he is talking, I open the box to find a new flight suit with my name, rank and wings already stitched on. The unit patch for 5th Special Forces is on one shoulder, which was the last assigned combat unit side, but the assigned unit side is empty. There is also a new pair of Nomex gloves in the box. "We did not know what unit you would be assigned, so we did not put a unit patch on for you. Do you need a ride to the flight line?"

"No Sir, but thank you for asking. Mike is coming to give me a ride."

"That is ok. When you return from your flight evaluation, please come over to my office. You are going to return to Benning are you not?"

"Yes I am. I have a rental car to return, and will most definitely need to thank everyone for all their generosity and this wonderful gift you have given me. I am touched by all your kindness" with a suggestion of overwhelming gratitude in my voice.

Sergeant Major McCoy tells me "There are no thanks needed, because you have done too much for all of us involved with this gift. It is our way of saying thank you. It is our pleasure for having known you, and for all what you have done for us."

As the Sergeant Major Mc.Coy is about to leave there is another knock at my door. "Come in" I yell.

It is Mike and Roy. The Sergeant Major gives Mike a salute, and excuses himself, closing the door behind as he leaves.

Mike asks, "if I am ready to go." I tell him "yes but I need to pack my new flight suit before we go."

Roy steps over and takes the flight suit from me holding it up for all to see. "What did the Sergeant Major give you this?"

"Yes, him and about thirty other men. I do not have my old one any longer. Nice gesture on their part, don't you think." I say.

Mike takes it from Roy looks it over and says "Man this is one of the new type, where did they get it? These were just approved. All you need now is a new flight bag." He goes out to Roy's car, and comes back with a new flight bag. Mike tells me "Here you need this. Let's put a move on there is people to meet and things to do."

As we drive over to flight OPS, Roy asks if I am ready.

"I think so. As ready as I ever will be, I think. Say Mike, thank you for the flight bag, but won't you need it? Because I hear through the grapevine you want to take flight training. Is that true?" Roy is driving, so Mike turns towards the back seat and just looks at me.

"What? I ask.

Mike looks back at Roy and then back at me saying "Did Roy tell you THAT?"

I answer, "Mike, you know how things are around here. Do you really think you could keep it from getting out? We all know now Em's talk. Sorry Roy, present company excluded. So answer the question, is it true you are trying to do that?"

"Yes it is Eric. I am. Linda and I could use the additional pay it would give us. Besides after I leave the Army, it would be a useful skill to have looking for employment in the civilian world. Not a lot of jobs are looking for someone with weapons training now, not a legal job anyway. Are they?"

"No, I would say not, but are you really thinking about getting out?"

"No, not just yet, but you do have to plan ahead. Don't You?"

"Yes I guess so. Would you like me to see what I can do to help?"

"No Eric, I want to be able to know I did it on my own." Mike answers as we roll to a stop outside OPS. After Mike and I get out of the car, Roy drives away. I look at Mike and ask, "What is going on? I don't think I can take any more surprises right now."

"No new surprises Eric, I am going to talk to the recruiter about availability of space in the next flight class that is all."

"Ok, let's go. I answer.

Seated at a desk inside the OPS room is an overweight female E-6 in a badly fitting uniform. As we approach the desk, she asks, "What do you want?"

"My name is Major Eric Howard. First off, aren't you taught to stand to attention and salute an officer? Second, what is your name and who is your commanding officer? Is he here?"

With that said she stands to a very lackadaisical attention and gives us a very reluctant salute.

"My name is Lovette, Karen Lovette. My commanding office is Captain Drown and his office is just to your right and down the hall."

"Sergeant Lovette, where is the "sir" that belongs with that." Neither Mike nor I return her half-assed salute. I turn to Mike and tell him to obtain our passes to board from the soon to be PFC, and let them know I will be back. With that, I turn right and head straight down the hall. I locate the door with Captain Drown's name on it and walk in. Behind the desk is a PFC. He stands to attention and salutes me asking if he can help me.

"Yes you can. I want to have a word with the Captain" I say.

"Yes sir, may I tell him who wants to see him, Sir?" The PFC asks.

"I am Major Eric Howard."

"Yes Sir, I will tell him." The PFC turns to the door behind him and knocks. "Yes" what is it can be heard from the other side of the door. The PFC opens the door and tells the Captain "Sir A Major Eric Howard wishes to speak with you." The Captain tells the PFC to show me in.

As I enter the interoffice, the Captain stands and asks, "What can I do for you, Sir?"

"Captain Drown, your Desk Sergeant, Sergeant Lovette, has no military protocol. She is rude and lacks the proper respect due an Officer or anyone else. When Captain Danville and I approached the check-in desk, she remained seated, did not stand to attention, or give a salute or any greeting other then "What do you want." After I asked her name, and who her commanding officer was. She did stand but not to attention and the salute she gave was strained and not proper. I want her written up and busted down to PFC. Will you do it or do I need to write her up myself?"

Captain Drown tells me, "Major, I apologize for the way my staff has acted. I will take care of it right away. The Sergeant will be disciplined."

I turn to leave, but stop and turn to him "Captain I will be returning from Hunter-Stewart in three days. Upon my return, I will come and see you. I would like to have a copy of the disciplinary action report that will be placed in the sergeant's file along with any other reports or actions about the Sergeant. I will be speaking to General Lee about this matter." I then turn and leave this office. As I start to close the outer office door, I hear the Captain yell, "PFC get in here now." On my way back down the hall, I can hear yelling.

I enter the main part of the building to find Mike. Out of the corner of my eye, I see the PFC talking to Sergeant Lovette. She stands up, throws her pen down on the desk and half runs towards the Captain office. I turn to Mike, and tell him I think it would be a good idea if we boarded the flight now.

Once on the plane, Mike turns to me and asks, "What happened back there?" I tell Mike what I said to the Captain and what I expected him to do.

"What do you expect from line troops, Eric? They do not have the same discipline and Espy De Corp we have."

"I know that but military discipline is military discipline and all should live up to it. From the bottom to the top and all sections of the service should know and conform to all regulation. I know we do not always conform to the regulations, but that is in combat or on exercises where they can get in the way or have someone killed."

"Eric you can be so hard nosed sometimes. Mike says as the plane fills up with people.

The ramp closes and the engines start. We start to move but stop and the ramp goes back down. Up the ramp comes a nurse with a man on a litter. They take their place and the ramp closes again. We roll out to the runway and stop for what seems like an eternity. Finally we are airborne. Once we reach our cruising altitude, I turn to Mike and ask him what he thinks his chances of getting into flight school are. He tells me he has a very good chance, as he has letters of recommendation from many of the staff in Benning and from Hunter-Stewart.

With a look of sadness in my eyes, I ask "How come you did

not ask me for a recommendation?"

"Eric, I did not ask you because you have done so much for me and our team. I wanted to do this on my own."

"Ok, I will stay out of it for now, but if you need help, I am here for you. You know that I hope."

"Yes Eric I do and I appreciate it. As you have learned since returning here, there are many people from General on down that think the world of you and what you have done. It would not be right to use that influence to help me."

"OK" I answer (but in my mind I think for now that is)

As we enter our final approach, I sit back and think about what it was like for me what I first started the process of getting into flight training, all the training and studying. I wonder if Mike can make it with a wife and children to take care of. It takes a lot of studying, and time to learn to fly a chopper. It is not like fixed wing. In a helicopter, you have to constantly be on the controls and thinking. Not to mention that you have to fly with both hands and feet at all times.

The controls to fly a Helicopter are for the most part the same as a fixed wing aircraft. You have a joystick to control your climb, dive and bank. Bank is the rotation around the horizontal center point. You have two pedals for your feet, which control the yaw. The yaw is the turning of the aircraft around it vertical center point. The one big difference in a helicopter is that in your left hand is a control called the collective. The collective is a shaft with a rotating handle at one end. This handle is like the throttle on a motorcycle. You rotate it to increases or decrease the amount of fuel to the engine. The shaft is hinged at the end opposite the handle and connected to floor on the left of your seat. By lifting up on the collective, you change the pitch of the main rotor. This is what gives you the vertical lift to go up. By pushing the collective down you descend.

As we land and taxi to the terminal, it is back to what I have to do. Having been the first on, we are the last ones to deplane. At the bottom of the ramp is a Lieutenant to meet me.

As I come down the ramp, he gives me a smart salute, and introduces himself. "Sir, I am First Lieutenant John Laspino. I have been assigned as your aide for the time you are with us. May I take your bag sir? I will take you to your quarters Sir and then over to the Commanders Officers office for orientation."

I turn to Mike and ask him if we could offer him a ride.

"No Sir, I am only going over to that building, Sir." With that he gives me a salute, turns and heads over to a build about 100 yards away marked Intake Services.

I climb into the Jeep and wonder why Mike was being so formal, because the Lieutenant was standing with us, or because of what happened back at Benning with that Sergeant.

As we start off, I turn to Lieutenant Laspino and ask him "May I just call you John, when it is just the two of us?"

"Yes Sir if you like Sir" he tells me.

"Ok! Now there is another thing please drop the Sir also at those times. My name is Eric, OK?"

"Yes Sir, I will try to remember Sir."

"Ok so where are we going?"

"The first stop will be at your quarters. Then you are to meet with the Commanding Officer of the Flight program. He will go over the training schedule with you. We only call it a training schedule, not that he thinks you will need any training. We, all of us in the training command were informed of your background and are looking forward to having you with us. The Colonel knows you and has only the highest regards for you."

We have pulled to a stop in what looks like a housing development. "Where are we?" I ask.

"This will be your billet for the time you are with us."

I turn to look at a house. I turn back to the Lt. and say, "This is not the BOQ."

"No it is not. The Colonel told the base-housing officer to put you up here. The BOQ is next to the flight line and the Colonel had you housed here because it is quieter. I will take your bags in and be back for you in two hours Sir."

I remind John, "What did I ask you about the sir thing?"

"I am sorry, I will try to remember."

Once inside the house I look around as the Lt. places my bags in the large bedroom. When he returns he informs me the kitchen is fully stocked and to feel free to take advantage of the amenities.

As the Lt. leaves, I go to the phone and call home to leave the phone number and a message that all is well. Then it is time to hit the books until the Lt. comes back for me. (Boy do I have a headache) This is a lot to take in. All the new regulations and flight technology changes, since I was last up in an active duty unit.

The doorbell rings and I go to the door, I open the door to find Mike. "Hey Mike, what are you doing here? How did you find me?"

"Eric after I was finished at the recruiter, I went over to the BOQ to talk to you. I was informed you were not there. I asked them when you were expected, and was told you did not have a reservation. I was told to check with the base housing office. I call the housing office, and was told you would be here. What is going on Eric?"

"Mike, the Colonel in charge of the wing had the housing office put me up here. I was told the BOQ is near the flight line and this would be less noisy here."

"Eric, that is true. The BOQ can become noisy sometimes. I have stayed there and could not sleep a wink. This is much better. May I stay with you tonight? I have a meeting in the morning, and don't have time to go back to Benning and return tomorrow."

"Mike, you are welcome to. Take the second bedroom on the left." I return to the books. I am sitting in a chair with manuals on my lap; Mike is in the kitchen making coffee when ding-dong the doorbell rings.

"Mike would you answer the door, please?"

"I will" Mike tells me as he heads to the door and opens it.

The Lieutenant stands in the door dumb founded realizing he is face to face with a Captain and snaps to attention and salutes. "Sorry Sir, I must have the wrong address."

I can see who is at the door so I yell, "It's all right Lieutenant, come in.

"With a Sir, yes Sir." He enters. I put my manuals in the flight bag and go to the door.

"First Lieutenant John Laspino. This is Captain Mike Danville. Mike was my XO in Nam. Mike do you remember the Lt. from when we landed here."

"Yes I do Eric" Mike puts out his hand to shake the Lt.'s hand. Say, would you like a cup of coffee."

"No thank-you Sir. The Major and I must leave for the Colonel's office." The Lt. Turns to me reaches for my bag saying, "Sir we need to go now. It is about a 15-minute ride to the office."

"Ok let's hit the road," I say as I go out the door. I turn and tell Mike to make himself at home.

The ride to the Colonel's Office is not a smooth one. Once we arrive, I am more then happy to be out of the Jeep and make sure I am still in one piece. I grab my bag out of the back of the Jeep; happy to see it is still there. Up the four steps and into the building I go.

The Lt. comes running up after me "Sir let me have that bag and follow me" he says.

"I will carry my bag. You lead the way," I tell him and off we go.

Down the hall and turn right through a walkway connecting the two structures then turn left and continue for a short way. Both of the buildings we have walked through look the same, except the first is painted a pale green inside and the second is a light blue. They both have a central hallway with room on both sides. The walkway between the buildings has windows on both sides. The only other difference between the buildings besides color is this building has a large room at one end. We walk through this large room only to exit out a door into a second walkway between buildings; this one also has window on both sides, but the bottom half is painted over.

At the end of this walkway, we enter a large room with desks lining both sides of the room. Behind each of the desks there is a Sergeant typing away. Sitting in back of the Sergeants is file cabinet after file cabinet. In front of each desk are two chairs most of which are empty. On each of the three walls is a door. The door to the right has First Sergeant painted on the frosted glass. The one to the left has Executive Officer painted on the glass in the door.

The office straight in front of me has Commanding Officer

1st Special Forces Aviation painted on it. I look at the Lt. and ask, "Are you S.F.?"

He answers, "No Sir, I am normally assigned to the base commander. I am on a temporary assignment to you for your stay with us. Most of the Special Forces people are off doing other things that I am not privy to."

We walk up to the E-8 siting at the desk in front of the Commanding Officer door. As I approach the desk, he stands up and gives me a salute. He tells me the Colonel has been waiting for me and I should go in. I step to the door and knock. A voice from inside says, "Come in." As I enter the room, I am surprised to see Phillip Hunley. Phillip Hunley was my instructor in primary flight training. He comes around his desk with his hand out, as he takes my hand and tells me how glad he is to see me again. The Colonel tells me to take a seat. He picks up his phone and tells the Master Sergeant he wants no interruptions, and to bring in a pot of coffee some cream and sugar. The Master Sergeant brings in the coffee and leaves.

Colonel Hunley starts with "So I see. You did not take my advice about Special Forces. You did it anyway."

I answer, "Yes sir I did, and I am glad I did."

The Colonel says, "So are we, your record speaks for itself." We spend about two hours just shooting the breeze. He has my file on his desk and every so often opens it up and writes something on a slip of paper.

There is a knock at the door, "Yes what is it," the Coronel asks. The Master Sergeant opens the door and tells him Chief Warrant Officer Jackson is here.

"Ok tell him we will be with him shortly." The Colonel then turns his attention to me and says, "Major, CWO Jackson will be doing the ground testing part of your evaluation today. It will take about two hours. Then tomorrow at 0630, the actual flight-testing will commence. We will meet at 0500 to prepare; I will be your evaluator. When CWO Jackson is finished with you today, you are to report back to my office."

"Yes Sir. I will Sir," I say standing.

The Colonel picks up his phone, and tells the Master Sergeant to show the CWO in. The door opens and a tall black man in an impeccably pressed pair of BDU's enters. He gives a salute and stands at attention.

"Jackson, this is Major Eric C. Howard. You are to give him the ground school testing. When he is finished and PASSED the entire test, bring him back to my office. Do you understand Mister Jackson?"

"Yes Sir, I do. Sir, I will follow your orders to the letter, Sir" CWO Jackson answers. With that said he turns to me and asks me to follow him.

Sitting outside the office is First Lieutenant John Laspino. I turn to him and ask, "Have you been here all this time?"

"No sir, I came back about 30 minutes ago. The Master Sergeant told me you would be in with the CO till about now."

"Ok just so long, you did not have to wait here for me all that time" I say. I turn to CWO Jackson and tell him "This is my aide First Lieutenant Laspino." "Lieutenant, this is CWO Jackson. "With that done the Lt. picks up my bag and leads the way out.

"Mister Jackson, where are we going?" First Lieutenant Laspino asks.

"Lieutenant, we are going to the building # 43772. Building # 43772 is one of the classroom buildings behind Hanger 77. Do you know the way?" Jackson asks him.

"Yes I do" the Lt. answers.

"Lieutenant when we arrive I will be in taking some tests for about two hours. You are dismissed after we arrive, but be back in time so I may return to the CO's office." I tell the Lt.

"Yes Sir, I will Sir" the LT. answers.

As CWO Jackson and I enter the building, I hear the Jeep drive away on the gravel road. This brings on a feeling of despair. Despair in so much as here I am left with no way out. I have no idea of how to return to the house I am assigned or the phone number there to call Mike for a ride. What if I totally blow the exams? This is a very unusual emotion for me and I do not like it. I try to push the emotion out of my mind and concentrate on the task.

The building we enter is made of wood. The structure was probably built for WWII. It is one big room with three smaller rooms in the back. Twelve long wooden tables that seat eight men per table, arranged in two rows of six with an aisle on both sides and down the middle. At the front is a raised platform about two feet off the floor. On the platform is a table with three chairs behind it. On the wall behind this table are two clocks. One shows the time of day and the other looks like a stopwatch. We walk to the front of the room and stop. On the first table to the right, there is a folder, four books and a cup with several pencils in it.

CWO Jackson asks me to take a seat where the materials are located. As I take my place, he goes around to the front of the table. After I am seated, he points out the materials on the table.

"This is the examination Sir." pointing to the folder. "The books next to it may be used while taking the test. You may also use anything you have with you. I cannot answer any question other then those that do not relate to the material in the exam."

He turns and points to the clock that looks like a stopwatch. "That is your count downtime. When I tell you to start, I will set one hour on the clock. At the end of one hour, we will stop and take a break. If you smoke, have to use the latrine, or want to have a drink that is the time to take care of it. Any questions Sir?"

"No I do not" I answer.

Jackson mounts the platform, and reaches for a small control box. "Are you ready to start Sir?" he asks me.

"Yes I am, let's get this over with" I answer.

"Sir, take your time. There is more then enough time for you to complete the exam. You may start now" with that the clock starts its countdown.

The exam starts with weather, then navigation and on to map questions. I work along not looking at the clock until I have completed the entire folder. I glance up at the clock and see I have 25 minutes left. With that I close the folder and put my pencil in the cup and sit back.

CWO Jackson looks down at me and asks, "Are you finished with part one Sir?"

"Yes I am, and what do you mean part one?" I ask.

"I am sorry, Sir I forgot to tell you this is a two-part exam. The break is needed, so I may setup for part two. Do you want to take a 15-minute break, or continue on to part two when it is ready Sir?" CWO Jackson tells me.

"I think I need a smoke now. A bourbon and water would also help" I tell the CWO.

"Sir if you go just out the front door and to the left there is a bench. I would not recommend having a bourbon and water at this time. I will set up part two and when you are ready please come back in. The second part of this set of exams will take about the same amount of time. I will need to call your Aide if you do the next part as fast as you did the first part. You should be done earlier then scheduled."

I tell Jackson that I have no idea of how to make contact with of the Lieutenant. Jackson answers with that he has a number to call.

"Thank you" I say and turn to leave. Once I am outside and seated on a bench. I start to wonder how I did on part one. Did I go to fast and miss something? Should I have reread the exam, or could that have caused me to change an answer that was correct. Oh well, that is all water over the dam now.

As I finish my second cigarette, CWO Jackson comes over to me "Sir do you mind if I join you?" He asks.

"No, not at all" I answer.

"Sir I corrected part one of the exam, and you did not have a single question wrong. In all my years as an instructor here, absolutely no one has ever done that before. Colonel Hunley told me that you were an exceptional student when you were in his class. He also informed me of your flight record Sir, and that you were awarded the Distinguish Flying Cross in Viet Nam. Sir, if I may I would like to shake your hand and say thank you."

"You do not need to thank me; I was only doing what any other pilot would have done. But you are very welcome for the gesture." We shake hands, have a smoke and return to the building.

As we enter the building, I see the table now has a large chart and other materials on it. As I take my seat, Jackson tells me my Aide will be here shortly and we should start. This part is not timed, so I do not have to rush to be done before time runs out.

As he takes his seat on the platform, he tells me to go ahead and start. This part of the exam is on the two helicopters I will be flying. The regulations that govern the two helicopters flight, and the regulations that govern military flight in general. I start in on the exam with a renewed feeling that I can do this.

About one half-hour into the exam, I need to take a latrine brake. I stand and ask if I may go the latrine. CWO Jackson says, "Yes, let's take a 15-minute break" I stand and ask where the latrine is located. "The building to the left of this building is the latrine," Jackson answers.

As I go out the front door a Jeep pulls up and stops. It is First Lieutenant John Laspino. He comes up to me and asks if I am done already.

"No I am not, just had to take a latrine break. Go in and have a seat I will be back and complete the exam. It will not take long, as I am over half finished" I tell him. The latrine is typical of the ones you find state side. It has six stalls along the wall to the right as you enter. There are six wall-mounted urinals on the back wall and six sinks on the left wall. It also has the smell that its being used a lot. I use one of the urinals, wash my hands, and head back to finish the exam.

As I exit the latrine, I see there is now two staff cars parked in front of the exam building. Upon entering the exam room, I am met by Colonel Phillip Hunley, his First Sergeant Douglas Daliety and the Base Commander General Wesley Shefler.

Chief Warrant Officer Jackson comes up to me and says, "Major Eric Howard, I would like to introduce General Wesley Shefler the Base Commander."

"General Sir, this is Major Eric Howard." We exchange salutes, he puts out his hand, and we shake hands. Colonel Hunley introduces his First Sergeant Douglas Bailey we continue with salutes and hand shakes.

The General then turns to CWO Jackson and asks, "What does the Major have left to do to complete the exam?"

Jackson answers the General with "Sir the Major has completed the exams, and I have no problem with saying he has passed."

Trying to hide a stunned look on my face, I just smile, knowing I have not finished. Jackson then goes on to tell the General that I passed the entire exam without making a single mistake.

"Good then we can go. We will meet in my office in one hour" the General states as he turns and leaves. The Colonel and First Sergeant start to leave when the Colonel stops and says, "We will see you there, Major."

After they have all gone I say to CWO Jackson, "What was that all about? I did not finish part two. What is going on here?"

"Major Howard, Colonel Hunley came in while you were in the latrine and told me the Base Commander was due at anytime, and we needed to be done when he arrived. The Colonel then said, CWO Jackson if you feel the Major is ready you are to pass him. That is if you, in good faith and you are comfortable with telling the General, the Major is finished. I was, you are the first student to have done as well as you did and to do it in so short a time." With that said, he takes my hand, and shakes it saying "Sir it was a pleasure meeting you and good luck in your career."

"Thank you Jackson, I would like to say it was a pleasure and good luck to you also. But aren't you coming with us to the CO office?"

"No Sir, I have to write up my report and turn in the paperwork by 0500. Also I was not invited."

"Well I am inviting you," I say.

"Sir, thank you, but no thanks."

"I will see you in the morning" he says.

"Ok then but how are you going to return to wherever you are going?" I ask. Jackson tells me he has his car parked behind the building and he will be fine.

"See you at 0530 then and thank you" I say as I leave with the Lieutenant leading the way.

Once in General Wesley Shefler's office and the Lieutenant is excused for the day the door is locked. There is only the General, Colonel Hunley, another Colonel and myself in the room. "Major Howard let me introduce Coronel Tate. Coronel Tate is here from Washington and wants to talk with you." We shake hands and then directed to a couple of chairs that are in front of the Generals desk.

As we sit down Coronel Hunley asks if anyone would like a drink. Having just finished an exam that I worried over, I was the first to say, "Yes if it is ok with the General." The General speaks up and tells me it is ok, and he has a bottle of Makers Mark put in his liqueur cabinet for just that reason. He goes on to say, "What else would a man from Kentucky drink?" After the drinks are served, and I have taken a long pull on mine, and make a second drink.

Coronel Tate starts to talk "Gentlemen as you are all well aware. The action in Viet Nam is not going well. We have several teams out that have not been heard from in sometime. We need help in that area. I have been sent here today to talk with you, Major Howard. If you were agreeable, we would like you, after your in-flight exams tomorrow and when we can obtain a replacement for you, as it was to be your next assignment. You are needed in Washington to help locate the three teams we have lost contact with. We cannot order you to do this, as it would be a volunteer mission only. I will be leaving shortly to return to Langley. You may reach me here" as he hands me a piece of paper with a phone number on it. "Please think it over as we could use your help and experience." With that said, he arises from the chair, salutes the General and says "Thank you gentleman," turns and leaves the room. Colonel Hunley locks the door and returns to his seat for what seamed like hours no one spoke.

After sometime, the General says, "Coronel Hunley, what do you have planned for the in-flight exams?"

"Sir, we will be in the UH-1D first thing in the morning. First Major Howard will have to show proficiency in knowing where and what all the switches, fuses, instruments and controls are for and how to use them. We will then be in the air for about a two-hour flight. The Major will have to show me he can handle the aircraft. There is also a navigation evaluation during this time that he must pass. Upon returning to base he will have to do an auto rotate to show he proficient in emergency landings. We will then take a short lunch break. After lunch, we will do the same thing again in the AH-1 with an added exam on the use of and proficiency on the use of the weapons system. We have a live fire set up for the south range. When we return from the live fire there will be a debriefing and then we are done."

The General tells the Coronel that sounds good. He then turns to me and asks if I am ready?

"Yes Sir I am Sir. I have been working for this for a long time. I want to be back in the field Sir." I say.

"Good man, we need more like you. The General stands, comes around from the back of his desk and puts out his hand.

I take it. We shake hands as he says, "Major good luck tomorrow, we will meet after you are finished and talk more. Till then sleep well and good flying." I salute and leave the room.

Outside the room, the Lieutenant stands and asks, "Sir, are you ready to go?"

"Yes I am, take me back to my quarters and you are then dismissed."

On the way to my quarters I ask the Lieutenant how do I reach him if need be. He hands me a card with three numbers on it. One is the office he works in; the next is his home number and last is the radio room. The radio room can contact him on the radio he carries at all times. At my quarters, I go straight to my bedroom. As I walk through the living room, I tell Mike I will talk with him later. I have a headache and want to lie down for a short time.

About two hours later I am up and hungry enough to eat a horse. I take a shower, dress in tan slacks, a white shirt and my cowboy boots. In the living room, Mike reading one of my books on flight. As I enter the room, he looks up and asks, "Are you all right." I say "yes but hungry enough to eat a horse."

Mike answers with "Give me two minutes and we can go over to the club for dinner."

"Ok I will call my Aide. Mike tells me not to as he has a car. We have a nice dinner, and Mike asks about the training and what it takes to fly a helicopter. I know he has been reading my books on flight, weather, and the mechanics of the birds. He has been asking many good questions. I have observed him just standing, staring at the helicopter on the ground and in flight several times. It is now obvious to me he wants to learn to fly.

When we return to my billet, I go to my bedroom and try

to think of a way to help him without him finding out. When I meet with General Shefler tomorrow, should I talk with him about Mike? If I do, what do I say? How would it look for me to say anything to the General about Mike? Should I tell Mike why I went to Special Forces after Flight School? I have a million questions but no answers. I know I will talk with my best friend, the person that has given me the some of best advice. I pick up the phone, and call my wife. I am in luck Debbie is at home.

"Debbie I love you. I could use some of that level headed advice you give me"

"Ok Eric what did you do now? What kind of trouble did you cause now?" She asks. (She knows me, doesn't she? Sometimes she knows me to well to say the least)

"No! No! I have not caused nor am I in any trouble except I do not know what to do about Mike. He wants to be admitted into the flight program and he has told me not to help him. But you know me; I want to help him. But how do I do it without him finding out?"

"Eric, I think you will know when the time and place are correct to drop a hint in the proper ear. You are very good at that. Do not worry over what to say or who to say it to. When the time is right, it will fall into place on its own."

"Thanks Debbie, you always seem to know just what to say. I will be home in a couple days. I love you. Will talk with you tomorrow. Good bye." I put my mind in park and I am off to bed and a good nights sleep.

Chapter 23

The alarm starts to ring at 0400, and I hit the snooze button. Now it is five minutes later, and again the alarm sounds off. Oh! Shit I have to remove myself from this bed. This is going to be the day of days. The restart of my active duty career. I could have used about two more hours of sleep. Why do they want to start so early? The normal start time of activities is 0630 after breakfast. Oh well I need to start my day. I dress in my BDU's and boots. pack my flight bag with my flight suit, helmet, the books and charts I will need for today's activities. The doorbell rings at 0445. It is Lieutenant Laspino, but he is not alone.

"CWO Jackson what are you doing here?" I ask.

"Sir we are here to pick you up and take you to breakfast with the Colonel. After breakfast, we will go to the flight line for our first flight of the day Jackson tells me.

"What do you mean we?" I ask.

"I will be the crew chief on the UH-1D flight this morning," he answers.

"Since when do we have a crew chief on evaluation flights?" I ask.

"Sir the only bird available for this morning's flight is one that just went through its annual overhaul and I am going along as part of the flight evaluation on the helicopter. The General approved it. He will be having breakfast with us. So we better be on the stick" Jackson tells me. Now I have something else to worry about. What if the bird has a problem? Will it fly and can it fly safely? Oh well I have flown choppers with a lot of holes in them, losing fuel, hydraulic fluid and the power going out. So what else is new?

We pull up to a stop in front of the Mess Hall. The hall is empty except for General Shefler, Colonel Hunley and a man in civilian clothing. The cooks have been cooking and it smells good. The three of us walk up to the table, and General Shefler stands and tells us to sit down "We have to be out of here by 0630, so the troops can have their breakfast."

As we take our seats, the food placed on the table. Just like down home, there is a big plate of bacon, another of ham and one of fried potatoes. The cooks bring out two large bowls, one with grits and the other with gravy. They also place two large baskets of biscuits, three pitchers of orange juice, three pitchers of whole milk and a pot of coffee on the table. One of the cooks starts with the General, and asks how he wants his eggs cooked. I am too hungry too just sit and talk, so I start the plates, bowls, and pitchers going around the table. The conversation is just normal stuff, until we are just about finished eating.

The General starts with introducing the guy in civilian attire. "Gentleman I would like to introduce Mr. Stanley Coats. Mr. Coats is down here with us today to observe how we do our training." The General then introduces everyone at the table to Mr. Coats by rank and name. After the introductions are finished, the General tells Mr. Coats that he will be spending the day on base with First Sergeant Bailey. He then turns to me and says, "Good luck and good hunting today, Major Howard. The rest of you are dismissed."

As we file out of the building, CWO Jackson taps me on the arm, and signals for me to follow him. As I turn to follow Jackson, the General stops Lt. Laspino to tell him he is to return to his regular duties until notified otherwise.

Behind the Mess Hall, there is a small building; this is where CWO Jackson is headed. It's a briefing room used for special briefings. The walls covered with maps and charts. There is a large table in the center of the room with ten chairs around it. CWO Jackson and I sit down and wait for the Colonel. The Coronel enters followed by two men with MP armbands and side arms. (What is going on now goes through my mind?) The Colonel takes a seat and the MP's take up a position on either side of the door.

"Major Howard" the Coronel starts, "we are to preparing this as fast as possible. The flight manifest for today has not changed other then the helicopter we will be flying is morning has been modified with some equipment that is of the most sensitive nature. We are not to talk about what we see, or how the equipment works or what it does. Major you will be instructed by Mr. Coats how to the use of the equipment. This will not only be an evaluation flight for you but also the equipment. Do you understand?"

"Yes Sir, I do Sir," I answer.

The Colonel goes on to say, "CWO Jackson has already been instructed on the equipment. (That is why he is going with us goes through my mind.)

"Major, are you agreeable to this?"

With a question in my voice I ask, "Sir, will this have or could this have a negative effect on my evaluation?"

"No Major, it will have no effect on your evaluation other than you will be one of only five pilots with the ability to use the equipment. Are you willing to go ahead with the flight?"

"Yes Sir, I am. I answer. He answers me with "good" and turns to the MP's. He tells them to bring in Mr. Coats.

Mr. Coats enters the room along with two other armed MP's carrying a black box about two feet square. One side has dials, knobs and switches on it. The opposite side has three armored cables about a foot long hanging out. One of the cables had a standard wall plug on the end. The other two have a black plastic bag covering the end. He puts the box on the table, and plugs the cable into an extension cord. The dials light up and there is a slight humming noise coming from the box. Mr. Coats then takes three manuals from the briefcase he was carrying, and hands one to each of us.

"Gentlemen, please open the manual…please open the manual I just gave you to page three and follow along, he starts. One and one half-hours later Mr. Coats tells us "Gentleman that is the TLTK 140 and how it's used. Do you have any questions?" I learned a long time ago that in situations like this the fewer questions the better, so I do not ask any. I could tell by the way the briefing went, the others had gone through this before, and I could ask them my questions later.

Colonel Hunley stands up, and thanks Mr. Coats for his time and we will meet after the flight. With that, Mr. Coats leaves the room followed by the MP's that came in with him.

"Major Howard, are you ready to start?" the Colonel asks.

I state, "No Sir, I am not. I have a few questions to ask you."

"Ok Major, what are they."

"Sir, what is this all about? Why am I doing this? Will it have any effect on me being placed back on active duty?"

"Major first it will only have positive effect on your future. You were chosen because of your record and the accomplishments you have shown. We all know you will have no trouble with the evaluation flights. Your flight work with the unit in Boston shows that. You have nothing to worry about. The service needs men like you. Are you ready now?"

"Sir you said, you need men like me correct? Well I may be out of line but so what I think…. Colonel this is just between the three of us. Ok?"

"Yes Major, what is it?"

"Colonel, my XO from Viet Nam has applied for flight training. He is a good man and learns quickly. In my estimation, he would be a very good candidate for the program. The only thing is I told him I would not interfere."

"Major, if you think he is a good candidate. I will look into it for him and I will not say anything about our conversation about this. Is that what you would like?" the Colonel states.

"Yes Sir, I would not like Captain Michael Danville to know I had any part in this, and thank you Sir for your understanding" I say.

"Major I told you before, that you were the best student I ever had and I greatly admire your friendship. Now let's get this day over with so we can relax and have a drink."

As we leave the building, Mr. Coats and the two MP's enter and retrieve the TLTK 140 and the manuals. The trip to the hanger takes about ten minutes and there is dead silence all the way.

In the hanger we pass four Armed MP's, and proceed to enter the hanger. There in front of me is probably the most beautiful sight (second only to my wife) my tired old eyes have seen. The helicopter has a new paint job, and is so clean you could eat lunch off it. The Colonel and I enter the hanger dressing room to put our flight suits on. Once back at the helicopter, the Colonel tells me to take the left seat. The left seat is for the pilot in command. He takes the right seat, while CWO Jackson takes his place in the back. The bird is rolled out of the hanger, and I go through the start up process without even thinking. I go down the checklist verbally without looking at it. The Colonel with a puzzled look in total disbelief sits with his copy of the checklist in hand and watches me. The engine comes to life, and the rotors start to turn ever so slowly at first. Colonel Hunley starts the checklist for the TLTK 140 telling Jackson which switch to turn on and the dial setting. The Colonel takes the radio and calls the tower for clearance to takeoff. The tower comes back with, "Flight 1007 you are cleared for a straight out departure. At one half mile out and at 1000 feet altitude turn right to a heading of 47 degrees. Have a good flight Sir, tower over and out."

I look at the Colonel and ask, "Are there any other flights in the area?"

His answer is, "No Major, all other flights will be grounded till we are 20 klicks out.

"Ok here we go." I pull the collective up while twisting the throttle. Five feet off the ground, I nose down slightly and climb as we move forward. At 1000 feet, I rotate the bird to a heading of 47 degrees, in what seemed at no time at all, we are 20 klicks out from the base. It is fun to be up flying. The first flight of the day goes without incident, and I do all that is required of me. About 30 klicks out from the base, Colonel Hunley calls for clearance to land. The tower tells us to hold for 10, so I put the bird on a slow circular pattern. It is still cold out. (So there is no bikini-clad woman sunning herself. I have never cheated on my wife, but it does not mean I cannot look, does it?)

The radio comes to life and informs us to approach on a heading of 146 degrees holding and altitude of 1000 feet. We are then told, at two clicks from the base to descend to 500 feet for a straight in approach at 60 knots. We are then clear to land at Hanger 77. As we come in over the outer marker, I can see there is no flight activity in the area at all. I make my approach straight down the middle just three feet off the deck. As I come to the turn point for our hanger, I slow to a hover. I then rotate the bird, to be in place pointing at the hanger door. With a small amount of throttle and the nose slightly down, I move into position over the X. I pull the nose up to level and decrease throttle until I very softly settle to the ground.

The Colonel deplanes and looks to see how close to center I am on the pad, as I shut the engine down. He comes back to his door and tells me I am off my mark. He then gives a chuckle and tells me I am off by about one half inch. I remove my helmet and unbuckle myself getting out. The ground crew is already starting to move the helicopter back into the hanger as we walk away.

CWO Jackson stops me and says, "Sir I will be staying here for sometime checking on the equipment. I do wish to thank you for a very nice flight and would fly with you at anytime."

I thank him and ask if I would see him later. The CWO tells me he will see me later when I fly the Cobra. We shake hands and go our separate ways.

The Colonel's driver meets us as we leave the hanger, after we had removed our flight suits. The driver hands the Colonel a note. The Colonel turns to me, and tells me he has to go to his office, but he will take me to the Officers Club on his way to his office.

As I walk into the club, I see Mike sitting at a table. I walk over to him and ask if I can join him.

"Yes, please have a seat" Mike says.

I ask how his morning went.

"It was ok. I will know later if I made it in or not."

"Mike, how long will you be here? I ask.

"They tell me I will know by the end of the day."

"So how did your first flight of the day go?" Mike asks.

"It was good; it is so nice to be up flying around, especially when no one is trying to shoot you down. I did once or twice, look to see if anything was coming up at us, but it went well. Sorry I am rambling on."

"How do you think it look for you? Will you still be here for dinner?" I ask.

"Eric that depends on what they have to say, but I will let you know as soon as I know Ok?"

"Now let's eat," I say. Mike and I spend about an hour in the club. I play dumb about his chance of getting into flight school. I know with the conversation I had with the Colonel about him. He will be admitted to flight school. Now can he live up to it or I will be the fool. Just before we leave, a Second Lieutenant comes in and looks around the room.

Mike leans in and says, "That's the recruiter for flight school.

The Lieutenant sees Mike and walks over to our table. As he

approaches close to us, he says to me. "Excuse me sir for the interruption, but I need to speak to Captain Danville"

I say, "That's ok" and stand up to leave.

"Major Howard, would you please wait for me? I need to finish what we were talking about" Mike asks.

I say, "Yes I need to call for a ride. I will be at the front desk." I really do need a ride so I go to call the First Sergeant. The phone is in use, so I stand off to one side and wait. The person on the phone is about to finish their call, as Mike walks up to me. There many people around me.

Mike says, "Major Howard, Sir. Do you know where to find First Sergeant Bailey?"

"Yes I believe I do, Captain Danville. Do you have a car?" I ask.

"Yes I do Sir," Mike answers.

"Well let's step outside and I can help you."

Once we are outside, and in the parking lot. I say to Mike "Ok! What's up?"

"Eric, I have been accepted into the program, and I need to report to First Sergeant Bailey, as soon as possible."

"That is just great news. I am happy for you. Now do you think you can make it through program?" I ask.

"Yes I do. Now where is the First Sergeant Office?" Mike asks again all nervous and excited.

"Where is your car?" I ask.

"Follow me" Mike says. At Mike's rental car, I tell him I will show him the way if he takes me to the Commanding Officer of 1st Special Forces Aviation.

Mike asks, "Is that far out of the way from where I need to be?"

"No Mike, they are next door to each other."

"Ok let's go." I show Mike the way, as best as I remember it. We only had to back track once. When we enter the parking lot, Mike asks me which building it is, I tell him to follow me.

We go up the stairs into the building, down the hall and turn right through a walkway connecting the two buildings. We turn left and continue. The next building is the one with a large room at one end. We walk through this large room only to exit out the back door into a second walkway between buildings. At the end of this walkway, we enter into the large room with desks lining both sides of the room. On each of the three walls is a door. The door to the right has First Sergeant painted on the frosted glass.

"We are here." I tell Mike. "The door over to your right is the First Sergeant. I am going straight ahead. Let me know what happens. OK?"

Mike says, "So…you have been here before."

"Yes Mike I have. The Commanding Officer, Colonel Hunley, is the person I have to prove I can still pilot a chopper. We had our first flight this morning, and now will be doing my second and last test flight, I hope."

"Did you know the Colonel before?" Mike asks.

"Yes I did, he was my flight instructor back when I was taking flight training."

"Do you know the First Sergeant?" Mike asks with a strange look on his face.

"I was introduced to the First Sergeant, but we did not talk with one another. Why do you ask?" I tell Mike.

"I was just wondering if you had anything to do with me being sent over to talk with him." Mike says as he looks at me with an inquisitive expression.

"Mike, I only said glad to meet you First Sergeant, nothing more. Now I must go and prepare for my flight. Talk with you later." I pat Mike on the back and head for the Colonel's office. If all goes well, he will never know I said anything about his desire to enter into the flight program, I think to myself.

As I approach close to the Master Sergeant standing in front of the Colonel's office, he stands and gives me a salute. "Sir the Colonel has left for the pad. I was told to have Lt. Laspino drive you over to meet him." He picks up his phone, and says something into it. He then asks me to have a seat. A short time later, Lt. Laspino comes in, and leads me out a back door in the Colonel's office. Once outside we jump into a Jeep, and we are off to the pad.

In about ten minutes, we arrive at the helopad in front of Hanger 79. Another beautiful sight comes into view. It is a well-maintained Ah-1, Cobra helicopter, fully loaded with its armaments. On its chin turret is a 7.62mm multi-barrel minigun and a 40mm grenade launcher. On each of the stub wings, located one either side of the aircraft, is mounted a M200 rocket launcher. (This is really like old home week. If I had only one choice of helicopters to fly this is it.) The Cobra is fast, maneuverable, well armed and hard to shoot down. The maximum speed is 220 mph range is 350 miles. It can climb to just over 11,000 feet, and has a climb rate 0f 1,230 ft/min.

As I walking around the bird, the Colonel walks up to me and says. "She is beautiful, isn't she?"

"Yes Sir she is" I answer.

"Let's suit up and go for our flight," the Colonel tells me. Once in the dressing room, we put on our flight suits and walk out to the bird. We climb in and take our places. The Colonel tells me to go ahead and start her up. With a flick of a switch here and there, the engine comes to life. The rotor starts to turn slowly at first causing a slight rocking motion, and then faster and faster as the engine builds up speed. The headset comes to life with the Colonel telling me to hover out to the launch pad 11 North; with the skids just off the ground, we leave the hanger area. At the launch pad, the Colonel tells me to exit the field due east and climb to 9,000 feet. Rotating the bird due east heading and with a lift and a twist of my left hand, we are on our way. The radio crackles and I hear the Colonel telling me there is a speed limit until we clear the outer marker. So I twist in fewer throttles to reduce our speed. Once beyond the outer marker, I twist in more throttle and continue to climb. In no time at all, we cross the coast and are headed out over the Atlantic. The radio hisses as the Colonel tells me to turn and head to test fire range Bravo. I bank to the right, and the Colonel then tells me to follow the in-structions, and head in that direction. As we near the coast, I am told to cut the forward speed to less than 150 mph for the flight in. About four klicks out my speed is down to just 60 mph and I feel like I am crawling. The Range Sergeant gives the instructions on Channel 2. I switch my radio over and ask for instructions. A voice comes back telling me to "drop to 80 feet, and approach the range on a heading 300 degrees. Just after crossing over the red building, my targets are a truck with a red star, a small group of tents and a tank. All will be stationary, hit as many as you can." I am to make my first run using only the minigun. After my first run, I am to make a second run on the truck using the 40mm grenade launcher. If I am in a position to use the M200 rocket launchers, I am to take out both tank and truck, if not I am to make a third run on the tank.

I quickly switch to the intercom on the bird and ask the Colonel "if it would be all right if I did all three on one run." He tells me "No."

Back to the range channel. I tell the Range Sergeant, I am commencing my run. The Range Sergeant tells me I have a clear range and to commence my run.

As I cross over the red building, I can see the targets set up in a large field. The first target is the group of tents just to my left about 150 yards in front of me. Then the tank slightly to the left and 50 yards down range of the tents, and finally the truck off to the right at about 30 degrees and 50 yards down range of the tank. That would put the distance between the truck and tank at about 80 to 90 yards. A tight shot but I know I could hit all three in one run. Ok I will do as I am ordered. On the first run, I hit all targets dead on. I bank out hard to the right and turn so I am lined up to make my second run.

If I time this just right, I will not have to make a third run. First, I arm the grenades as primary system and rockets as secondary. The distance to the truck is closing fast. I pull the trigger and switch to rockets and grenades just in time to pull the trigger again. I then pull up and rotate on my vertical axis to see how I did. I did it both targets are hit. The radio crackles and I hear the Range Sergeant say "good shooting sir. You are now clear to leave the range no third run needed."

I tell the Range Sergeant, "thank you" and head for the barn. I switch back to channel one, and ask the Colonel if there is any further testing needed. I hear him say the only thing left is to do an auto-rotate, with that said; I head to the Emergency Landing Range area for an auto-rotate.

As we approach the area, we see several students doing their testing. The radio comes to life and the Colonel says "Major would you just circle the area for now?"

"Yes Sir I will." After sometime, the Colonels next question startles me.

"Major, do you remember how to do an auto-rotate?"

"Yes Sir, I do Sir," I answer.

"Good then let's fly out of here before anything happens. The students using the area at this time are not S.F., and I do not trust them." With a smile on my face, we head for the barn.

Once on the ground with the engine shut down, we climb out. The Colonel comes over to me, and shakes my hand. He then tells me that I did him proud, I had not lost a bit of my edge and was still a very good pilot. He asked me "if I had ever done any thinking on becoming an instructor." I told him "no I had not." His answer was "good because I was too good of a pilot to be just teaching men to fly, but as an attack instructor, I would be one of the best." The test firing I had just finished was superb. I was only the third pilot to make it in just two runs. Most try but miss the second target. The Colonel then goes onto say "Lets take off of these flight suits, and go have a drink."

Lt. Laspino is parked out behind the hanger as we leave. Colonel Hunley tells him to take me to my quarters and wait for me to clean up. We are to meet at the Officers Club in two hours.

"Sir" I say. "Were we not to meet with General Shefler when I was finished today?"

"Yes Major, we are to meet with the General. We will have time with him after dinner. You went through the evaluation much faster then planned. See you in two hours.

Back at my quarters, Mike is packing and getting ready to

leave as I come in. He has a large canvas bag in his hand. I know this; he did not have it when we came over from Benning.

I ask, "Mike, are you leaving and what is in the bag?"

He answers with the biggest smile I have ever seen on his face, "Eric, I am in. I must now go home to Linda, and tell her I will be starting flight school in 10 days. I did it, I did it." Mike says with a bit of a smirk in his voice. 'I did it on my own. I need to run to make the flight back to Benning. Will I see you there?'

'Yes Mike, I will see you there and congratulations on getting into flight school." I tell him as he runs out the door to his rental car. As I watch him drive off, I feel a weight lifted off by back. I am sure he has no idea I said anything, I just hope he will make it through the training.

I go to the bathroom and shower. After about 20 minutes under the shower, I go to my room and try to decide what to wear. Do I put on a clean uniform or dress in civilian clothes? All my BDU's are dirty and I only have one clean shirt to wear with my uniform. If I wear that tonight, I will not have a clean one to return to Benning. What can they do to me if I wear my civvies? So I put on a pair of black slacks, a light blue shirt and my black cowboy boots. I also have picked up a black leather suit coat. I am ready I think.

The doorbell rings and Lieutenant Laspino comes in as I open the door. The Lt. asks if I am ready. "Yes Lieutenant I am as ready as I ever will be. Do you think it will be ok if I am in civvies?"

The LT. answers, "Yes Sir, I do sir as I just saw the Colonel entering the Officers Club in civilian clothes."

"Good, ok let's go" I say. As we drive over to the officers club, I think aloud "I wonder what the General has up his sleeve.

Why do I need to see him tonight?"

The Lt. looks over at me and asks, "Did you say something?"

I tell him "no I was just thinking out loud." I ask the Lt. if he will be staying around while the Colonel and I have dinner.

"No Sir I was told I would be called after your meeting with the General."

"Ok that is good. Just between you and me. Do you know what the General wants to talk with me about with me, do you?" I ask. The Lt. tells me that he does not know anything other then the General as a set of orders for me. "

"Oh great" I say.

The parking lot at the Officers Club is filled with cars, Jeeps and motorcycles. That means the dining room will be full and a waiting list will be in place. I tell the Lt. I will see him later and enter the club. The place is full of people, and I do not see Colonel Hunley. As I pass the first bar entrance, someone behind me calls out my name. I turn to see who it is, as I do not recognize the voice. It is Major Sanborn from Benning.

"Major Howard, Will you please follow me?" he asks.

"Right behind you." I say. We walk through the dining room to a small room just off to one side. As I enter the room I see General Shefler, Colonel Hunley, and Chief Warrant Office Jackson seated at a large round table, each of them dressed in civvies with drinks in front of them.

The General says as I enter the room, "Come sit down. This is just an informal get together. What would you like to drink? No don't answer that, I know what you drink." He turns to the waiter and tells him to bring a tall bourbon and water and use Makers Mark.

As the waiter leaves, Colonel Hunley asks, "Well are we going to eat or just sit here and have drink?" When the waiter returns with my drink, he asks if we are ready to order. Everyone says, "Yes we are." With the orders taken, the waiter leaves the room.

The General stands and says, "Gentleman I would like to toast Major Howard on his return to active duty. With a here, here from all gathered, we drink. During the meal and with coffee and cigars, the conversation is General is upbeat. After everyone is finished, General Shefler asks Colonel Hunley and me to stay while the rest are to go to the bar. He tells those that are leaving, we will be along shortly.

Once everyone is out of the room, he starts by taking a large brown envelope from a case he had by his seat. He hands the envelope to me and tells me. "Do not open the envelope till you are back at Benning, and then only in the presence of General Lee. You are to fly a Uh-1H back to Benning at 0930 in the morning. Major Sanborn, CWO Jackson, Mr. Coats and two MP's will be going along. CWO Jackson will be your co-pilot. You are to tell no one. Once at Benning you will be meeting up with Captain Smeeds. Major Sanborn knows who he is and will identify the Captain. Captain Smeeds will then take Major Sanborn, CWO Jackson and Mr. Coats by truck to an undisclosed location. You and Major Howard are to report to General Lee. Is this understood?"

"Yes Sir, I will do as you order Sir." I answer.

"Major Howard, Lieutenant Laspino is waiting for you in front of the club. He will be staying with you until you leave in the morning. If you like you may give him the envelope now, and join the rest of us in the bar."

I say, "Yes sir I think I need a drink." I start to stand up.

"Major, here take this case and put the envelope in it, until you are in General Lee's office. He will return it to me later." I take the case and place the envelope inside. I look to find the Lt. Lieutenant Laspino parked in a slot marked Base Commander just to the right of the door going out.

He sees me and comes over to me. "Sir, are we going now?"

"No Lieutenant, not right now. But I would like you to take this case and keep it safe. I will be back out shortly. The only reason I am going back in is to say my good-byes and have one quick drink, I will be back soon."

I am back inside the Jeep in ten minutes, on the way to my quarters. As we drive up to the house, I see every light in the place is on. I know they were not on, when I left. The Lt. notices the look on my face and tells me, "It's nothing to worry about. The cleaning crew has been here to check your quarters." I tell him "good night," take the case and go into the house followed by the Lt., then straight into my room. I tell the Lt. to use the small bedroom for a good night's sleep. I feel safe and have one of the best sleeps I have had in a long time.

Chapter 24

The sun shining in through my window wakes me up. Even in January, the sun has warmth to it. A warm shower changing to cool and a hot cup of coffee prepare me for the coming day. To make things easier for me today, I dress in my flight suit. I still have two hours until I meet Major Sanborn, CWO Jackson, and Mr. Coats, and I am very hungry. I hear the only place to have a good breakfast is at the base coffee shop. Now where is it located? The base phone book has no listing for an on base taxi service. There is bus service on base but the closest stop to me is four blocks away and then it would be over three blocks to walk to the coffee shop. Not to mention I now have a suitcase, flight bag, helmet bag in addition to what I left New York with.

Then I remember what Lt. Laspino told me the day I arrived here. The house is fully stocked. Take advantage of it. In the kitchen are dishes, pots & pans, glasses and silverware. In the icebox, I find bacon, eggs, whole milk, butter, orange juice and a lot more. The stove works. So it is bacon, fried eggs and some spuds that were in the lader. There are three pans going on the stove, a coffeepot perking away. The smell is heavenly. The only thing missing was the lard to fry the eggs, but bacon grease is almost as good. After looking for sometime to find the bread, it is now in the toaster. With plates of food on the table, I sit down to eat. It had been a long time since I have fixed myself a meal on an Army base. This is good. After I am finished eating, I put the dishes in the sink and have a new cup of coffee in hand I light a cigarette.

I think back to being in Boston. How Doc and Ellen had insisted I stay with them. It was after the second month being in Boston, I finally submitted to their request. Debbie was on my case to stay with them. She did not think it was a good idea for me to be alone. She was worried that I might be pushing myself too hard to be in shape. Doc and I would share driving to the college. I drove most of the time because I had a parking spot and he had to find a parking space, and had to pay for it. Why am I thinking this now? I know because of the breakfast I just cooked. I would cook breakfast for the three of us back then. I look up to see Lieutenant Laspino standing looking in through the back-door window. I am now back in reality with the door now open. I ask, "Lieutenant Laspino, what are you doing there?" The Lt. answers with, "I have been ringing you doorbell for ten minutes. The front door was locked, so I came around back to see if all was ok. I saw you sitting here, and knocked on the backdoor. Let's grab your bags and go," the Lt. says.

"I need to clean up this kitchen"

"Sir, you do not, the housing people will do it once we are gone. Have you not noticed the bed is made every morning? There are all new towels everyday and a clean coffeepot."

"You know, come to think of it, you are correct. Ok, let's go."

At the flight line, two armed MP's are loading a large crate into the UH-1H. Major Sanborn, CWO Jackson, and Mr. Coats are standing to one side watching what is going on. As I am getting out of the Jeep with the orders case in hand, Lieutenant Laspino takes my bags and hands them to an MP that has come over to us.

"Sir this is where I must leave you. It had been a pleasure to know you and I hope to meet you again Sir."

We shake hands; Lt. Laspino goes back to the Jeep and drives away. I start to walk over to the Helicopter, but I am stopped by another MP carrying a rifle, without a salute or bye your leave. The MP pulls the rifle up and tells me that no one is to go near the helicopter.

In a very gruff voice, I tell him "I am to fly this bird, and need to do a preflight. So get the hell out of my way."

The MP replies with, "Sir my orders are to let no one near that helicopter."

"Sergeant, or should I say soon to be Private step aside."

"No Sir, you are not to be allowed near the Helicopter."

I then ask him "Who gave you those orders? The MP informs me it was a Captain Henderson.

"Well I think my oak leafs out rank a pair of railroad tracks, so step aside."

"Sir I cannot do that" the MP says.

"Ok you want to play it that way." I say as I head for the phone in the hanger followed by the MP. As we enter the hanger watched by all present, General Shefler and Captain Henderson come out of the office, I am heading to. The General asks me if there is a problem.

I put the case down and salute the General saying, "Sir. Yes

Sir, there is a problem and it is right behind me."

I am now pointing at the two MP's, "These people have harassed and hindered me in the performance of my duties. They have <u>NO</u> military protocol or respect for an officer." "This one" pointing at the E-5 with the rifle, "was threatening, aggressive and disrespectful in his manor. I demand a General Court Martial for him. He should be busted down to a Private, and an action put in his jacket. No one should be threatened like he threatened me. He is just lucky I did not take the rifle from him, and shove it up his ass. I will be glad to sign the complaint and appear at his trial at anytime."

The Captain then tells me the Sergeant was only following his orders.

I looked at him and say, "Now I can see where his disrespect comes from. Do you not salute a senior officer?"

The Captain snaps to attention and gives me a very good salute. "Sir I am sorry Sir."

The General is having a hard time keeping in a bit of a giggle. "Major Howard, these men are not Special Forces. I will take care of this. Why don't you go do your preflight while I talk with these two men?"

"Yes Sir, I will Sir. General I was not kidding about having the Sergeant busted. I do want it done. Will you please see to it for me?" I ask the General.

"Yes Major, I will see to it. He will be disciplined."

"Thank You Sir." I give a salute to the General, and then turn to grab my bags from the MP that is carrying them. He looks at me, as if I am some hard ass. After I have my bags, he gives me a proper salute and turns to face his Captain. As I am approaching the front door of the hanger, I hear the General tell the Captain to write up the paperwork on the Sergeant and that he wants it on his desk in three hours. The General then adds that the Sergeant may not be the only one facing Court Martial.

With a smile on my face, I walk out of the hanger. CWO Jackson walks up to me and tells me "Thanks."

I ask him, "Thanks for what?"

"Major we have been here for over an hour, and had to endure the same type of harassment from the MP's.

I put my helmet on the left seat, and tell CWO Jackson, to come with me. We head back into the hanger. The General and his Aide are starting to leave, so I say "General, May we please have a word with you?"

He turns back, and answers, "Yes you may."

Both CWO Jackson and I walk over to him, give a salute and I state, "General Shefler, are you aware the MP's have also been harassing the other people that are to fly out with me today?" He looks at me then CWO Jackson. He turns and tells the Captain to stay put. The General then turns back to us and asks CWO Jackson to explain. CWO Jackson tells the General all that was done, and how they were made to stand in the sun, with no shade for over an hour. "After repeated attempts to talk with the MP's. We were told to shut up and be still, or we would be taken to the brig."

General Shefler, red faced turns to the Captain and tells him. "Captain, you and your detail are dismissed as soon as the Helicopter is off the ground. I want no further action taken involving the men the Major is with. Do you understand Captain Henderson? After you are dismissed, I want you and all the men assigned to this detail, in full dress uniform, in my office. You have one hour to comply. Do you understand Captain Henderson?"

The Captain answers. "Yes Sir I do Sir."

With that said, the General leads the way back to the flight line. Once there he asks Major Sanborn and Mr. Coats to gather around. When we are all together, he asks Major Sanborn and Mr. Coats to tell him what went on. Both men tell him that from the minute they arrived the MP's were very hard on them. Yelling at them to stay back, and not say a word.

Major Sanborn then tells the General, "Sir I did not receive a salute or even a good morning Sir. Just told to halt with a weapon pointed at us. The MP's would not even let the refuelers near the helicopter. We tried to tell them who we were, but to no avail."

With what I just heard about the refueling, I head to the helicopter. After turning on the power to check the fuel load, I return to the General. "Sir!" I say. "There is inadequate fuel in the bird. It is so empty it could not move ten feet from where she sits." I then signal the ground crew that is standing just inside the hanger to come over. With the arrival of the ground crew, the General asks them if they had a problem with the MP's guarding the helicopter.

The Master Sergeant in charge salutes the General and answers, "Sir, we have not been able to get near that helicopter since yesterday when the MPs first showed up. They have been standing around the bird, with the rifles at the ready, since 1600 yesterday. The only person that could get close was that man" pointing at Mr. Coats, "and that was yesterday at about 1700."

"Mr. Coats, is that true?" the General asks.

"Yes it is. I was told to check if there was room for the box and to make sure it would be safe." At this point, the General tells the ground crew to ready the helicopter for flight.

The Master Sergeant salutes and says, "Yes Sir it will be done.

The ground crew then leaves to refuel and check over the bird.

The General then asks Mr. Coats if the box contained the TLTK 140. Mr. Coats tells him "yes it does." The General asks Mr. Coats what he told the MP unit. His answer is, "General all I told the Captain in charge was to protect the box and to allow no one access to the box. I did not say anything about the helicopter. I also told him who was going on the flights and when we were to leave."

"So the Captain knew the names of people that would be going on the flight with you, and you gave no other instruction to the Captain other then to guard the box?" The General asks.

"Yes General, the Captain knew the names of everyone going on the flight and no I did not give an instruction other then to guard the box."

The General then asked, "The box where was it stored overnight?"

Mr. Coats answers, "The box was stored in the MP's office, until it was delivered here by truck just before we arrived. It stayed in the truck until about 15 minutes ago."

The General then asks, "So the box was not on the helicopter, the entire time you were here?"

"General they only put the box on the helicopter when Major Howard arrived. It was like they were waiting for him to arrive."

"Did you see them stop the Major?" the General asks.

"Yes, we all did. The MP acted like the Major was going to destroy the box."

"Thank you Mr. Coats and the rest of you. I will be here until you takeoff to make sure that is no more problems. Have a safe flight." General Shefler tells us. We all salute, except Mr. Coats and go to the helicopter. CWO Jackson and I do the walk around and board the bird.

CWO Jackson as my co-pilot starts to read off the items on checklist as I start the engine. With the engine running, the rotors turning and everyone buckled in, CWO Jackson calls the tower for clearance to takeoff. The tower comes back with "You are cleared for a straight out departure heading 270 degrees. Your departure altitude is to be 500 feet for two klicks. You are then cleared to 6000 feet. Contact Benning flight control 20 klicks out. All air traffic is grounded till you are 15 klicks out."

"Thank you, Tower Flight 002 out."

With that all taken care of, I throttle up, and pull up on the collective. At three feet off the ground I look at Jackson and say, "here we go." At two klicks out, I start to climb and increase our speed heading to the first waypoint. The flight goes smooth, and at 20 klicks out from Benning Jackson calls the tower at Benning. We are told to approach the field from the south and to land at Pad 1. Pad 1 is the first helopad on the right, as we come in. Just like when we crossed the outer marker at Hunter-Stewart, there is no air traffic at all. The pad is now insight, it has two trucks, three Jeeps, and a staff car parked behind it. As we land, I rotate the helicopter so the right side door is facing the trucks. When everyone in the back gets out, four MP's come and take the box, and put it in the lead truck. Mr. Coats pulls himself up into the second truck. One of the Jeeps leads off with two MP's. The truck with the box follows it, then the second truck with Mr. Coats on board follow by a second Jeep with two MP's. With everyone away from the bird, I lift off and rotate it so the nose is pointing at the center runway.

We shut down the engine and turn the systems off. CWO Jackson deplanes and comes around to my side.

"Major Howard, I would like to thank you for the nice ride over and want to wish you good luck."

I answer him with, "Mr. Jackson, it was my pleasure meeting you. Say, how are you to return to your base?" Jackson tells me he is going back shortly with a Captain that has to retake his weapons class.

With that said, we shake hands and I walk over to collect my bags. General Lee comes up to me with Captain Patrick Norton. CWO Jackson comes up behind me, and salutes the General.

"CWO Jackson, this is Captain Norton."

"Captain Norton, this is CWO Jackson. He will be flying to Hunter-Stewart with you."

"Do you have orders, Captain Norton?" CWO Jackson asks. I just stand there and watch this going on around me. "Captain Norton, have you met Major Howard?" Jackson asks.

"No I have not."

"Major Howard, this is Captain Norton meet Major Howard." CWO Jackson says. We shake hands.

The General speaks up saying, "Major we must leave now. I have my car just over here." the General and I enter his car and drive off.

As we are driving to General Lee's office, he looks at me and asks, "Did you really tell General Shefler you were ready to shove a rifle up an MP's ass?"

I look at him in shock, "Sir how, when did you hear that."

"General Lee called me shortly after you took off. I needed to know when to expect Mr. Coats and his box. Wesley had a hard time keeping from laughing. He told me to tell you that the Captain and every man that pointed a rifle at you or anyone with you were going to have a General Court-Martial. The JAG office will be contacting Major Sanborn, CWO Jackson and Mr. Coats and you for sworn statements."

"Sir I am scheduled to leave for home tomorrow." I say.

"Major I take it you have not opened the orders you are carrying."

"No General, I was told only to open them in your office."

"Good" the General says. "When we arrive at my office there will be Colonels Bates, Stone, and Coleman waiting for us to give you a heads up you may open the orders now."

With that said, the General tells his driver "to take it slow and not to arrive at his office till told to do so." I open the case and take out the envelope. I open the envelope, and take out three pieces of paper. The first is a letter from the Director of Counterintelligence, CIA. The second is a copy of orders transferring me to the CIA. The third is a form for me to sign if I accept the orders on page two.

I turn to General Lee and ask him to stop the car. General Lee looks at me and asks "Why?"

I tell him "I need to think and walk. I need fresh air. I need a cigarette." Stop the car the General tells his driver. The car stops and I exit the car, and start to walk down the block. At the end of the block, I turn around and walk back to the car only to turn around again to walk away again. I do this several times before opening the car door and enter.

I say to the General, "General Lee, and thank-you for allowing me to see the orders before being in the presence of the Colonels. Are they in your office now?"

"Yes they are there waiting for us. Why do you ask?"

"Because Sir, I need sometime to think this over."

"Major, you do not have to give an answer now. We know it is a lot to ask of you, especially with the fact you just coming back on active duty. I can give you three days to think it over. All you have to do now is hear what they have to say. Look at some maps and then think about what is said. "OK" General Lee tells me.

"Yes Sir I will listen."

Once at the Generals office, I am introduced to Colonel Erin Bates, Colonel Adam Stone, and Colonel Tim Coleman. After introductions, we sit around a large table that is covered with maps. Colonel Bates starts, "Major as you are probably aware the government has ordered a pull out of our troops from South Vietnam. You are also aware we promised to help the Montagnard people in their struggles. We have had no contact in ten months with the villages of Ba-Choa, Ba-Ngu or the village of Lao Bao. I do believe these are three of the villages you spent time in."

I answer "yes and no. Ba-Choa is the village of Lok and yes, we spent several months there. Ba-Ngu is the village of Twan the son of Lok and yes, we spent sometime there. Lao Bao is the village of Hi and we were there only one day if that. Now Sergeant Roy Forestin of my Nam team had spent time there on his first tour. He was the 101st Airborne. If you can make contact with Dou Van Tran, he can help. Dou was our Kit Carson Scout and he may know where those tribes may be located. You do know that the Montagnard people are semi-nomadic people. They may not be where they were when we lived with them but could find out for you."

Colonel Stone stops me and informs me that Dou was killed about two months ago trying to help clear the way for an A-Team that was down to three men and under heavy fire. Dou and a CIDG group of 30 all lost their lives but saved the three men from the team members. Dou and the last eight CIDG died either in the dust-off chopper or at the hospital very soon after arrival.

"Do you have any idea on how we could contact these villages? Did you have and preset code or spot for message transfer?" I tell them "yes we did but they changed with each full moon. After I was wounded, my XO Michael Danville had all our information and I believe he turned it over to you General Lee. Did he not, Sir?"

"Yes, he did Major Howard. We have tried to use them but have had no response.

Colonel Coleman then takes over talking. "Major Howard, what we are here for is to ask you if you would please help us find and relocate the people of these villages."

"That is if they want to relocate that is" I reply.

"Yes, of course relocate only if that is their wish." Colonel Coleman answers.

I then tell all that are gathered, that I need sometime to think about it and will give them an answer in three days. General Lee stands up and says, "Gentleman if there is nothing further to discuss, lets adjourn. Major Howard, it is up to you. We cannot order you to do this. Think it over and let me know your decision with in three days. I will have my driver will take you to the BOQ."

"General Lee, May I ask a few questions before we go Sir?" I ask.

"Yes Major Howard you may" the General answers.

"First will or could my help involve me returning to Vietnam? Second How would we relocate the people and where would they be relocated too?"

Colonel Bates tells me, "Major Howard if we can contact the tribes without sending someone in we will. If no contact can be made, we might need someone on the ground. That could be you or someone other then you. Next, if the people want to relocate they would first go to Thailand and then possibly come here to the U.S. or anywhere of their choice."

I answer, "Ok now I need to think. General, May I talk with you after we dismiss?"

"Yes Major, please stay seated. And Colonel Erin Bates, Colonel Adam Stone, and Colonel Tim Coleman, you are dismissed. We will talk in the morning." Colonel Erin Bates, Colonel Adam Stone, and Colonel Tim Coleman salute and leave the room.

After the door is closed. General Lee asks me what I want to talk about.

"General Lee, Sir I do have to think about this and to tell you the truth, I am not happy about the way it was put to me. I am a blood brother to two of those tribes and those men know that. They know the bond we feel for they have been there also. I may be back on active duty. But am I ready to go back in to the jungles of Vietnam? Physically yes, I may be, but am I ready for the emotional part of that. I am still having nightmares every now and then about the Nam."

"Major Howard I am going to send you back to Hunter-Stewart in the morning to talk with the Flight Psychologist. Doctor Eric Jung is the best Psychologist in the Army for dealing with Special Forces personnel. He had been there and has seen it for himself. He had 19 months in The Nam. This is just between you and I, it will not be on your record," the General tells me.

"Thank you sir, I appreciate this and I will leave on the first flight in the morning." I tell General Lee.

"Ok! Now get out of here," the General says as he stands and gives me his hand.

Outside the building, the General's car is sitting waiting for me. As I come down the stairs, the driver opens the back door for me. I think it has its rewards to be a General. He drives me right up to the door of the BOQ, exits the car and opens my door. My bags have been in the trunk of the car since I landed so as I start to walk around the car. The driver opens the trunk and hands me my bags. I go in to the BOQ and obtain my room key. Once in my room I unpack, put my dirty clothes in a ditibag, and return to the front desk and ask if there is a laundry close by. The Sergeant stationed at the desk says, "Sir I can take that and have it back here in three hours. The laundry picks up and delivers for no extra charge." I tell the Sergeant "good here you go."

"Yes Sir I will take care of it for you. I will call your room when they come back"

I go back to my room and try to rest. It is about 1300, and time for lunch. With that idea going through my head, I remember I have a rental car parked in the lot. I need to call Trish in the travel office, and extend the rental. But for how long? Let's say four days. I call Trish only to find out she is at lunch. There it goes again, that grumble in my stomach. I leave her a message to extend my rental car four days.

After my call to Trish, I change into civvies, drive to the burger joint in town, for something to eat. That is if I can remember the way there. I do remember the way to the burger place. I make it there without making one wrong turn. The parking is not bad, and I find a place about three parking spots from the front door. After I order a bacon cheeseburger with no vegetables, fries and a sweet tea, I find a seat in a corner. Out of habit, I have to sit with my back to a wall. It feels so much safer that way as no one can come at you from behind. About half way through my lunch, a guy comes in, looks at me like he knows he, goes to place his order and when he has his lunch he walks over to my table.

When he is at my table, he asks, "Say, you are Captain Eric Howard aren't you?"

I answer "Yes I was. Do I know you?"

He answers. "I am Anders Andersen. I was XO in the A-Team that shared the base camp with you and your team in The Nam. It was Lieutenant Andersen then. Remember Colonel Lee, the base Commander. He is now General Lee and the base commander here at Benning now. After a few seconds, I did remember him. I remember he was full of himself and had a problem with us over the latrine. I tell him to take a seat.

He asks, "What are you doing here, I heard you were badly wounded and shipped state side. I have seen your OX from Nam but not talked with him." (In my mind I find this a bit strange as in SF we are all family) "Are you here for a visit?"

"No I'm not here just to visit. I have just returned to active duty, and I am here for my next assignment. I am now a Major." I tell him.

"Congratulations, that is good news. I made Captain two months ago." Andersen tells me.

"That is good to hear," I tell him, while in my mind I wonder what took him so long to be promoted. "Where are you assigned now?" I say. He tells me he is in supply, and has been for the last year and a half. (This raises another red flag in my mind. I ask myself why would someone with combat experience spend that long in supply state side with all that is going on all over the world. We have men in Central America, South America, Africa, Europe and Asia but here he sits.) I say nothing more just general conversation, finish my lunch and excuse myself saying, "I have to return to base." As I stand up to leave Anders tells me." See you on base."

As I am driving back to the base, I decide to call Mike and or Roy to see what they might know about Captain Anders Andersen. As I enter the BOQ, the Sergeant hands me my laundry and tells me it was $7.56. I pay him $7.60, as I did not have the correct change, and ask for a receipt. On the way to my room, I think that was cheap.

Once in my room I call Linda to see if Mike is around. Linda answers the phone with "Hello Danville residence."

I say, "Linda is Mike there?"

Linda asks, "Who is this?"

"Linda it is Eric, don't you recognize my voice?"

"Oh sorry, no I did not recognize it. I will get Mike; he is out in the back yard reading." Before I could stop her to ask if I could just come over she was gone.

After sometime, Mike picks up the phone and says, "Eric how are you? Did all go well?"

"Mike, may I come over and talk with you. Is Roy around?"

Mike answers, "Roy will be off at 1800, but you can come over at anytime.

"Mike, I have a couple of things to do. I will be over about 1900 if that is ok?" I say.

Mike asks, "Why don't you come for dinner? Linda is ok with that. Actually, she is here telling me to ask you to dinner. We will eat at 1900. Will you be here?"

"Yes Mike, I will see you then," I say and hang-up.

My next call is to Debbie's office. I am told, she is at the hospital. The secretary takes my message with the phone number I can be reached at and that I will be at the number after 9:00 PM.

(When talking with Debbie or anyone not in the Military, I use the 12-hour day so they can understand). With that out of the way, I lay down on the bed, turn on the TV, and try to think about what was said in the meeting this morning. I must have fallen asleep, because a knock on my door snaps out of a dream about Lok and his son Twan.

As I open the door, the Sergeant from the front desk hands me four cents. He says, "Sir here is your change. I thank him, and close the door. I should have known he would do that. We are not allowed take tips. After looking at the clock and seeing I still have two hours until I leave for Mikes my mind goes back to my dream.

Now awake sitting in a chair, it is hard not to remember the days I spent with Lok and Twan. They are both people you could not help but like and become close too. There was the time, we were made blood brothers of the tribe, and given our bracelets. What a day and night that was. Drinking their homemade wine and getting drunk. Dancing and have a good time. We ate till we were ready to burst, danced till we dropped, but never lost sight of where we were, or the dangers that were all around us, out in the jungle. Charley left us alone that night and most did not wake until late morning. Now how can I forget all of that, and not think about the people we left behind. What has and is happening to them? Where are they and are they all right? I am torn, because I do not want to go back there out of a feeling I theorize as pain. Pain for what I have been through, since being wounded; pain from being blown out of the helicopter. Pain from what I saw and felt.

But then I want to go back to help save Loc, Twan and their people from the horrors the Communist North will inflict on them. I have seen what the NVA and their followers do to people that work with or helped our allies and us. What am I to do? Maybe I won't need to go back. Maybe just helping to locate them from what I know so someone other then myself can go. I need to talk with my wife. She always helps me see things clearly. I turn the TV on to watch the news, only to turn it back off. Because all the news has on is how wrong we are being in Vietnam. The time is getting close for me to be at Mike's so I clean up a little and head out.

Chapter 25

At Mike's house, everyone is in the backyard except Roy. Roy will be along later. There is Mike starting the grill, Linda setting the table, and Sunny playing with Eric and Patricia on a blanket on the ground. Linda after seeing me goes into the house and brings me a tall glass of sweet tea with ice.

"Thank you. How are you doing with Mike going off to flight school?" I ask her.

"Eric I think it is a good thing, except for the fact that his primary flight training is at Fort Walters in Texas. Do you know anything about the place?" Linda asks.

"Yes Linda I do. That is where I took my primary flight training. Fort Walters is just outside the town of Mineral Wells. It is a real small town about one and one half-hours west of Dallas. There is nothing there but scrub pine, cactus, and sand. It is very hot in summer. The living quarters for a student's family are a bunch of trailer homes. They do not have air-conditioning to keep them cool just swamp-fans. There are snakes and scorpions everywhere you go."

Linda asks, "What is a swamp-fan."

I tell her "A swamp-fan is this tower that is built in front of an open window. The tower runs water over a screen that is set at an angle in front of the window. Then a fan blows air through the screen and into the house. Everything becomes damp, but it is cooler then not having it. I make it sound bad, don't I. Sorry but you asked. If you were to ask me, I would suggest you stay here while Mike takes his Primary Flight. Also as a side note, he will be kept very busy in the classroom, in the hanger and learning to fly both day and night. So busy he might not have time to spend with you and the children that much."

"Thank you for your honesty." Linda tells me, with Mike standing beside her. She turns to Mike and tells him. "See Mike, I told you every wife I talk to that has been to Mineral Wells, Texas tells me the same thing. I am not moving there. We will stay right here."

Mike looks at me then back at her and says. "Ok dear you stay here I will go without you."

To be funny I say, "Linda you do not have to worry about Mike. Most of the females that live there are so ugly the farmers lock up their sheep at night." Mike hits me in the arm and tells me to stop that it is bad enough.

As Linda walks away I ask Mike if there is a problem. "Well yes there is." Mike answers. "Linda thought primary flight was at Hunter-Stewart. I never considered that she did not know it was at Walters, to be honest I did not think of it either. Now I have been accepted, and leave in a few days what do I do?"

"Ok Mike, I will talk to her. Let me handle this. OK?" I say.

"Yes why don't you, Eric." Mike tells me as he heads to the grill.

Mike has two grills going, one grill has burgers and hot dogs cooking. The other grill has potatoes wrapped in foil, a pot of beans and some sauerkraut cooking. I go to Linda and ask her for some more sweet tea. She takes my glass and goes into the kitchen with me right behind her.

Once in the kitchen I say, "Linda it is only 16 weeks that Mike will be away, and he has been gone longer. At least no one will be shooting at him there. Besides, you have Sunny and Roy here to help you with Eric and Patricia. You would not know anyone in Texas, and it is so far from anywhere. You could become lost. Say, aren't both you and Sunny pregnant?"

Linda puts her head down and looks to be thinking for some-time. She looks up goes to the icebox and fills my class, hands it to me and goes out the door. I follow to see Linda walk over to Mike. She takes his arm and turns him around to face her. She then puts her arms around him and kisses his cheek. (It also looks like she is patting him on the ass) Linda then walks over to where Sunny is sitting on the ground playing with the children and sits down with them. Mike watches Linda walk away with a look of what just happened and his face. He then turns to me and puts both hands out in front of himself, palms up and what could be described as one huge question mark on his face. I shrug my shoulders and walk over to the table for some chips.

Roy comes into the back yard with a keg of beer on his shoulder, "Ok lets start this party" started he yells. "We have to celebrate. Mike is off to learn to fly, God help us all. Eric is back in the fold, God did help us all and I was promoted to E-8. I hope no one here has to be anywhere tomorrow. I know I don't."

Mike put his tongs down, and takes the keg from Roy, pats him on the back and says "way to go." I shake Roy's hand, and ask if there is any ice. Roy tells me the tub and ice is in his car, as Sunny and Linda run over to him. Sunny almost knocked him to the ground. I go pick up the tub and ice, and bring it around to the back yard. I put it next to the house out of the sun. After having a couple of hot dogs with sauerkraut, more beers then I should have I realized something. I am drinking more then ever before. Do I have a drinking problem?

Mike, Roy and I sit and talk about the future.

"Mike do you think we could find Lok and his people?" I ask.

Mike tells me he does not know, it could be hard to do as they move when times are bad and from what he has heard time are bad for the Montagnard people. Both the North and Communists do not like them.

Roy then asks, "What about Dou Van Tran, our Kit Carson Scout, he probably would know more then anyone."

"I just had a meeting with some people that told he was killed about 2 months ago." I say.

Both Mike and Roy tell me, "That is too bad, as he was a great guy." Then Roy asks, "What is this all about?"

"Guys I can not say more then our people want to help the Yards and they have had no contact with them in sometime. I was asked if I knew anything that could help" I say.

"If I think of anything I will let you know Eric," both guys say.

Mike then tells me if he could be of any help, just ask. Roy says "Ditto." I am starting to feel a little tipsy, so I excuse myself and head for the BOQ.

Once back in my room my mind wanders to a time spent with the Yards, it was the Christmas shortly after Twan was wounded.

I remember it as clear as a bell. We were sitting in the back of a skid just at tree top level watching the jungle flash by. The greens were so alive; it looked like they could just stand up and walk. The sun was just starting to climb into the sky. The date is December 24th, and we are on a toy run to Lok's village. It is hard to finding toys that the kids will like for they are not like the kids in the states. The kids of this village have never had toys made in the US before. The only ones they have had are things their folks have made for them. The little girls have dolls made from rice stalks and old material scraps. The boys usually have a toy cart or a wooden airplane that looks something like the ones that fly over the village. Both boys and girls might have a small boat made from bamboo to play with in the river. But this Christmas, we have two toys for each of the kids between the age of one and 13. The kids over thirteen consider them self-grown. A boy of fourteen is out fighting in the war, or taking care of his family if his father was killed. The girls are usually taking care of the old people, or having a family of her own. For each of the girls we have a doll with two sets of clothes and either a doll bed or a large piece of cloth to make something from. For the boys we have trucks, cars, planes and building blocks. Each child has a package with two things inside.

It was not easy to procure a bird to fly us up here but with a little horse-trading and the help of a friend who could be away for about three hours, we are on our way. I feel like something good is happening. I have special gifts for Twans two little girls. The trip to the village takes about one hour that meant we would only have one hour before we would have to head back. As we approached the village, the kids heard us coming and set up a ring around the place cleared for us to land. As soon as we were on the ground, forty kids came running up to us. They did not know we were bringing gifts; they were just looking for candy. As Dou deplaned, he told them all to go sit down in a circle over by the campfire. They saw the big bags we had with us. They all ran real fast to find a good place to seat. Roy and Dou started calling out the names of the kids one by one starting with the youngest. I have never seen kids so happy before in my life and come to think of since. I call Twan's two girls over to me. They came but kept looking back so as not to lose their place in the circle. They came up to me and from behind by back I pulled out two big, (larger then the ones being given out), packages and give them to them. Ne the youngest starts to cry and then the other starts. I started to cry with them as their mother came over. She told them to say "thank-you and to go play." Dau spoke to me for about 20 minutes without asking about Twan. It had only been 11 days since we returned, and I knew nothing about how he was doing. I ask her how she was doing being alone. Dau told me she was fine and the people of the village were helping her out. Time went so fast. It is now time for us to go. I say as I stand up without having to say anything about Twan. All the kids are to preoccupied with their new toys to see us go, but their parents say good-by and thanks. We have seen the kids of Lok's village have a full and happy Christmas. Oh, I almost forgot. We also took some food and candy for all the people of the village.

I now know I have to help find and save those people. Sleep comes easy and after a full 9 hours, I wake to see the sun just coming up. My room faces the east, so the sunrise in just out my window. Dressed in BDU's I head for my flight to Hunter-Stewart.

At the check-in desk sits E-4 Lovette. (Yes she was busted

down to an E-4.) As I walk up to the desk, she snaps to attention, salutes and greets me with a cheerful "Good Morning Sir, May I help you Sir." What a difference from last time I was here.

"Yes Corporal you may. I am on the flight to H-S this morning."

"Yes Sir, here is your pass sir. Have a nice day." then with a salute she hands me my pass. I salute back and turn to the hanger door to leave. As I approach the door, Captain Drown comes in the door and salutes me, and asks, "If all went well this time?"

"Yes Captain, it did I am happy to say. Captain, May I ask why you ask?"

"Major, it is because after your experience here last time, I did some checking and found out you were not the only one that had problems at check in. You were the only one that was willing to say anything to me. After asking several other officers that take the trip to Hunter-Stewart often, I found that this has been an ongoing problem for some time. I have told Corporal Lovette that I will be checking with people coming through here as to her actions.

I tell the Captain. "That is good now; let's just hope she keeps up the good work and thank you for your help." We salute and I board my flight.

After we are airborne, I think about myself. (Do I have a problem with drinking? Do I use it as a crutch to help me sleep? When I see the Doctor today, I will ask him if we can keep it off my medical report. I wonder if my nightmares are coming back. I hope not)

As I deplane, there is Second Lieutenant John Laspino. I walk over to him and say "Hi."

"Major Howard, I was looking for you. General Shefler would

like a word with you the Lt. tells me."

"Ok Lieutenant, but do I have time to see him and make my appointment with the Flight Psychologist, Doctor Eric Jung" I ask.

"Yes Sir, you do Sir. The Doctor will be seeing you at 1100 hrs."

"Ok then let's go see what the General wants." As were driving, Lt. Laspino asks me how long I will be staying.

"I am scheduled to return to Benning tonight." I tell him.

"That is good. I have been assigned as your driver for the time you are with us" He answers. The trip to the General's office is the same as before. Once in General Shefler's office, he tells me to take a seat.

General Shefler starts, "Major Howard, General Lee called me this morning and told me you were coming here today to see Doctor Jung off the record. Everything we say will also be off the record. It is very important that you are ready to carry out all your duties, especially at this time. We need your expertise, and talents. The war is winding down, not by our choice but by the choice of those in Congress. They are afraid of public opinion and ready to give in at all cost. If there is anything I can do to help you please just ask."

"Thank-you Sir." I say.

The General then goes on to say, "Major that problem you and the others had with the MP have brought to light a bigger problem. We over here in the Special Forces Area have been having an ongoing problem with the Base MP's that I was unaware of. As you know S.F. does not have a police force made up of our people here. I have sent a letter to Washington outlining this inadequacy. What I need from you first is a full written report on the incident that you had with the MP's. I have already requested this report from the others involved. Lt. Laspino is at your disposal to help in writing the report. He is a good and fast typist. Second, can you think of someone to help me if I receive the ok to have our own MP's?"

"I will sit down with the Lieutenant, and try to put it writing today Sir. I am scheduled to return to Benning tonight Sir." I answer.

"Major I have been given permission to keep you here till tomorrow night," I am told. "

Sir, I did not bring a change of uniform."

"Major that and your housing will be taken care of."

"Thank-you Sir" I answer.

"Sir as for the person to help you with setting up an MP force made up of SF. The only person I can think of is a Captain Nathan Forrest. He had an A-team in Vietnam and was a good leader. Prior to entering Special Forces and Vietnam, he was an MP at Fort Gordon. If he were still around, I would think he could be a good choice. Besides he is from an old southern family." I answer.

With a laugh in his voice, the General says, "Major some of us from the North are also good people. Anyway I will have the First Sergeant look up his record and thank-you for the information."

"Thank-you for asking me" I answer. "Now lets get started on that report." We stand and go out of the office.

"Lieutenant Laspino, take the Major over to the office we set up for him and help him work on that report we talked about."

"Yes Sir, the Lieutenant answers, "And Lieutenant I am counting on you to remember to take the Major to his appointment on time. General Shefler then turns to me and says, "Major you will be having dinner with me to night at my house."

"Yes Sir" I answer, the General then returns to his office, and

I follow the Lieutenant into the next building. One of the doors is open, and we go in. The office is typical of any office you would see on any base. There are gray metal desks in the center of the room with its chair sitting with its back to the window. In front of the desk are two more chairs. One side of the room is full of gray metal filing cabinets. The other side has an overstuffed chair and a sofa. The desk has an old typewriter on it along with a stack of paper and some pencils. The Lieutenant goes behind the desk, sits down and picks up a pencil. I look around and sit down in the overstuffed chair. As we start, there is a knock on the door and a Sergeant comes in carrying a tray with a coffeepot, two cups, cream and sugar. As he sets the tray down, he tells us "the General thought you might need this." He then turns and leaves, closing the door behind him.

After sometime of me telling the Lt. what happened that day at the hanger he looks at the clock above the door and tells me "We have to go now, Sir. The Doctors office is on the other side of the base, and it will take sometime to drive there."

As we drive through the base, I cannot help but note that there are very few people on this base lower then an E-6, but most people are officers. There are a lot of Warrant Officers, but few Enlisted Men. As we stop in front of the Medical Unit, I ask the Lt. "Do you know where Dr. Jung office is located?"

'Yes Sir, if you go in that door and turn left go down the hall till you the second hall to the right then he is about five doors down on the left."

"Thank-you, and where will I meet you when I am done?" I ask.

The Lt. answers, "Sir, have his Nurse call me in the cafeteria, and I will meet you right back here. Do you know how long you will be Sir?"

"I have no idea how long, maybe an hour or so." I answer, as I step out of the Jeep. The Lieutenants directions are nearly perfect, except Doctor Jung's office is the seventh door on the right. Once in his outer office, his nurse asks me if I am Major Howard.

I tell her "I am." She tells me to follow her. We go down the hallway and back two doors across the hall when she knocks on the door. From behind the door, a voice says, "Come In." The room is bright and airy with a half circle of overstuffed chairs set around a round table. On the table is a pitcher of ice water and several glasses. Doctor Eric Jung is seated at a very small table, just to the right of the door. He stands and tells me to come in and take a seat anywhere. I choose the one that has its back closest to a wall.

Doctor Eric Jung is a man in his late 40, about 6'1" tall with graying hair and a little on the heavy side. He has on civilian clothes and looks to be friendly. He takes a seat directly across the table from me, opens a notebook he has in his hand, and takes a pen out of his shirt pocket.

It seemed like an after thought, he stands back up and puts his hand out to me saying, "Excuse me for not introducing myself. I am Eric Jung." We shake hands as I say, "I am Eric Howard." We sit back down, and he starts by saying "So what brings you here to see me."

"To start with I am still having nightmares, not as bad as when I was in Valley Forge General Army Hospital, but still bad enough to worry me and cause me to not sleep as well as I would like. Then as of late I have started to drink more then I ever did, especially in the evening. I have an idea it may be to try to help me sleep. I would not call myself an alcoholic because I do not have to drink or feel like I have to drink every night. And now they want me to go back to Vietnam and help locate and extract the people of a Montagnard tribe I lived with."

"Major Howard; May I call you Eric?" Doctor Jung asks me.

"Yes, sure it is ok with me." I answer.

"Eric, why does going back to Vietnam bother you?"

"Doctor Jung I am not sure why. Maybe it is because I do not know if I will be able to find them, and if I do will I be able to extract them out safely. Maybe because I was injured so badly. I don't know?"

"Eric did this start after you found out about the possibility of returning to Vietnam or before?"

"It started before being told about the Yards. It probably started while I was still in the hospital." I answer.

"Eric then let's look at the two problems as one. Do you drink so as not to remember? Or do you drink because you remember? If you drink to not remember, this is a self-protection reaction and easily corrected. If you want to that is. By admitting you have a problem, or what you perceive as a problem, you have taken the first step to obtaining a handle on it. I have seen many men returning from Vietnam turn to alcoholic beverage to cover their pain. Before you leave my office, I will give you something to read that may help explain it to you. Do you have the nightmares more then four times a week?"

"No Doctor I don't. It is more like once or twice every two weeks and if it twice they follow each other within a day or two. There have been times they have come more often, and at other times I can go for a month or two without any nightmares."

We continue to talk for about an hour about my drinking, and my nightmares and what happens in them. Finally, the doctor asks if by talking about the nightmares does it help or make them worse.

I tell him, "Come to think about it they are more often then not to go away when I talk about them."

Doctor Jung says, "Good that is good. What you need is someone to talk with about the nightmares after you have one. Will your wife talk with you about the nightmares? I see by your records she that is a MD."

"Yes my wife Debbie is a MD. She has asked me several times to talk with her about the nightmares, but I do not want to scare her."

Doctor Jung asks, "If she was having the nightmares, would you not want to help her?"

"Yes I would Doc, but I am a man."

"Yes you are, but she your wife, and doesn't she have the right to know what is bothering you. You should not hide this or anything from her. You would probably be surprised at how much help she could be. Think about it."

I say, "Ok I will think about it."

"It could help to write about Vietnam too. The more you bring those buried thoughts out the easier they are to life with. Eric I think we are done here for now. If you feel a need to talk with me again we can. Anything we talk about is off the record."

I stand and tell him "Thank you, I do think this has helped."

As I turn to leave, he hands me a paper sack with some booklets in it. He gives me his hand and tells me to take it one day at a time and not to think negatively. I shake his hand and leave.

I did not remember to have someone call the Lieutenant, so I look for him in the cafeteria. It takes sometime to find the cafeteria, but I was able to locate it, and Lieutenant Laspino is sitting talking with a very cute red headed nurse in the far corner of the room. He has his back to me as I walk over to them. The nurse sees me coming their way and stands up. She asks if she can be of any help.

Lieutenant Laspino looks over his shoulder and stands saying "Sir, I did not hear them page me to the phone. I am sorry."

"That is ok Lieutenant, I wanted a walk." I tell the Lt.

"Sir let me introduce Nurse Marcy Rogers."

"Marcy this is Major Eric Howard." We shake hands.

Marcy says, "Major, John has told me about you. It is a pleasure to meet you."

"Thank you Marcy, all good I hope." I answer.

"Yes Sir, John has nothing but admiration for you. He is even talking about trying to be accepted into Special Forces."

I say, "Lieutenant is that true?"

The Lt. says, "Yes Sir, I have seen how tight your units are and how you lookout for each other. We do not have that same Aspire De Corp in our units."

"Well Lieutenant it is not an easy thing to do. It takes time, hard work and a lot of training."

Lieutenant Laspino tells me he has been looking into making the change, and thinks he can do it.

"Good for you I wish you the best of luck son." I say. "Now shall we move out?" I ask.

"Yes Sir, I will take you to your quarters, or do you want to go someplace other then there?"

"No my quarters will be fine. The Lt. says goodbye to Marcy and we walk away. Once in the Jeep I ask him. "Lieutenant, is Marcy the lady in your life?"

"Yes Sir, we have been dating for about 15 months." I tell him she looks and acts like a very nice gal.

"Thank you Sir, I think so too."

I am quartered in a different house this time, just down the street about five houses from the last time I was here. As we stop in front of the house, Lieutenant Laspino asks, "Will there be anything else until you are due at the General's home for dinner?"

"No I do not think so. Are the number you gave me still good to reach you if need be?"

"Yes Sir they are." the Lt. answers.

"Ok I will see you at what time?" I ask.

"Sir the General would like you at his home at 1900. Is that all right with you?"

"Yes that will be fine." I answer as I step out of the Jeep.

"Sir, Here are the keys to your quarters" the Lieutenant says and drives off.

Once in the house, I see a package sitting on the coffee table in the front parlor, inside is a change of clothes. (Say these are some of my civvies I left back at Benning. How did my clothes arrive here?) After making a pot of coffee and fixing a cup I turn the TV on and sit down to look at the stuff Doctor Jung gave me, after about an hour the phone rings.

"Hello this is Major Howard, How may I help you."

The voice on the other end says, "Major Howard, this is Captain Wasnoski, General Lee's aide. Sir I just wanted to make sure your clothes arrived and to tell you General Lee will be joining you for dinner at General Sheller's tonight."

"Thank you Captain for the change of clothes."

"You are welcome Sir. Have a nice day." He hangs up, and I have that feeling again. That feeling of now what is up?

Chapter 26

At about 1730, there is someone knocking at my door, looking out the window I can tell it is Lieutenant John Laspino. He has a staff car parked in front of the house with the lights on and the motor running.

After opening the door, I see he has Marcy with him. "Come in, I am glad I had clothes on. You did not tell me you were bringing a date."

Marcy tells me, "Oh no we are not going to the Generals. John has the use of the car for the night.

The Lt. speaks up, "Sir I am to drive you to the Generals house and then pick you up after the dinner. No one knows Marcy is with me. Can you keep it a secret?"

"Lieutenant, what is in it for me?" I ask trying not to laugh.

Marcy speaks up with "Well we could invite you to our wedding."

As Marcy says that, John looks at her "like what."

John tells her, "Marcy I thought we were not going to tell anyone just yet."

"John I think we can trust the Major, can't we?" Marcy replies.

"Sir I am so sorry to have sprang this on you. I did not think she would say anything. Can we trust you not to say anything?"

" Yes, your secret is safe with me, but if you want into Special Forces I would not say anything about this to anyone. It would be best if you were not married until after you make it through the training. That is if you are accepted, and make it through the training." I tell the two of them.

"I will make sure we do not tell anyone else." Marcy tells me.

In my mind, I see who wears the pants in this couple, and I wonder if John has the balls to make S.F.

We leave my quarters and drive to the Generals home. The Generals house is set apart from Officer's Row. Officer's Row is an area on the base set aside for the base officers and is separate from the general base housing. This area has its own park for the children to play in, a swimming pool, tennis courts and basket-ball court. The Generals home is the last house on the dead-end street. It is a large house made of brick. There is a garage in back and the yard is well maintained.

We pull up in the driveway and Lieutenant Laspino comes around to open my door, I have been riding in the back seat on the passenger side. Just like a high-ranking officer would ride.

I ask, "How will you know when to come and drive me back to my quarters?"

The Lt. answers, "the General's aide will call me on the car two way radio.

"Ok, see you then." I walk up to the front door only to be greeted by Captain Wasnoski, before I can ring the doorbell.

"Major, the General is waiting for you in the den. Please come this way."

As I enter the den, I cannot help but think, so this is how a General lives. General Lee comes to meet me at the door with a bourbon and water.

"Major I am glad you could make it. Did you have any problems today?" He asks me.

"No Sir, I did not. Everything went well. Thank you for asking." I say as I take a seat in a chair with its back to the wall. There are five chairs set in a half circle around a coffee table in front of the fireplace. The fire is warm and inviting. General Lee takes a seat across the table from me, and tells me General Shefler will be down in a few minutes. As I sit and sip my drink looking at the fire, I cannot help but think of all the friends I made with the Yards in Nam. The fire reminds me of the close friendships I made around the campfires with Lok and his family and tribe.

As I am off in my reflection of those times, two men enter the room. I did not hear them enter, but General Lee pulls me back to reality saying, "Major I would like to introduce you to Colonel Ted Wallace and Lieutenant Colonel Neil Marshall."

He then turns to the two men and says "Gentleman this is Major Eric Howard."

I stand and shake their hands. As we continue with our greetings, General Sheeler and his wife enter the room. We all turn our attention to General Shefler as he says, "Gentleman I would like to introduce my wife Marilyn."

After all the introductions are complete, we sit down and just talk about nothing in particular. After the second round of drinks, a man in a dark suit enters the room to inform us dinner is served. General Shefler arises and takes his wife's arm. We follow them to the dining room.

The dining room is a large room with a set of French doors

at the far end. There are two sideboards on either side of the room and a large beautiful wooden hutch to the left of the door we entered through. The table will seat eight but set for seven people. There are place cards at each setting with our names on them. At the head of the table with his back to the French Doors is General Shefler. His wife seated to his right, and next to her are Colonel Ted Wallace and Lieutenant Colonel Neil Marshall. The first seat to his left is General Lee and then I. The seat next to me is set for someone, but there is no nametag. As I find my spot, I notice the well-placed centerpieces and candles.

After we have found our places, waiting for the Generals wife to be seated, we sit down, General Shefler tells us "Gentlemen General Rogers from the Pentagon was to have joined us tonight, but he was unable to attend due to a situation we will discuss later. Now let us enjoy the fine dinner, my wife Marilyn as prepared for us. With that, he picks up a small bell and rings it.

In front of me, I find a place setting of a large china dinner plate with a fine cloth napkin folded on it. Above the dinner plate and to the right are two cut crystal glasses, to the left and above the dinner plate is a china bread and butter plate with silver butter knife. To the left of the dinner plate is a dessert fork, a dinner fork and a salad fork. To the right is a dinner knife, a teaspoon and soupspoon all made of fine silver. Through a swinging door in the left wall as you are looking out through the French Doors comes the same man in the dark suit carrying a tray with a bowl of New England Clam Chowder, which he sets down on the sideboard by the door he entered through. Following him is a woman dressed in a neat black dress carrying a tray of china soup bowls. The man ladles soup into a bowl and offers it to the General Shefler's wife. He returns to the sideboard where the woman has prepared a second bowl, which he offers to the General. This continues until all that want soup are served. After a few minutes, the couple comes back. He takes the soup bowl, as she serves the salad. I like my salad after the main course like in Europe, but I take it now. After the salad is finished and the plates taken away, the woman serves the twice-baked potatoes and peas from a serving cart. I do not take the peas, as I do not like them. Behind her comes the man with the meat. The meat course is a standing rib roast, which was done to perfection. The man stops behind each of us and asks if we would like a thick or thin cut. After cutting the meat, he places it on our plate and offers some juice for the meat. During the meal, there is little conversation.

After the dinner plates removed, the General thanks his wife for an excellent meal and asks "Now what special surprise that I had to stay out of the kitchen because of, do you have planned for dessert?"

Marilyn answers him with, "You will see."

Before the dessert is served, we are each asked if we would like coffee. Everyone one but Marilyn has coffee. After the coffee is served, the man and woman come back in to the room pushing a cart with large Baked Alaska on it. General Lee whispers to me that Shefler loves Baked Alaska but his wife is trying to help him lose weight. So this is special.

After we have finished a very good meal and thanked our hostess, we adjourn back to the den for more coffee or drinks. I have coffee because I have a feeling I will need to keep my wits about me. Of which I am not wrong.

General Lee starts "Gentleman we have a need to discuss. As of yesterday, we had a second runner from the Ba-Choa village contact our people in Na Trang requesting help. This is the village Major Howard was in for sometime. The team that re-placed the Major did not spend any or very little time with this tribe, as they never requested it. We have a team of five men in place to move these people further south but need an Officer to take charge. The only two officers we have at this time that have any extended time spent with this tribe are Major Howard and Captain Danville. Captain Danville has just entered flight train-ing, so we cannot ask him. I am not, at this time going to ask the Major to go, as he has just returned to active duty. What I am here to ask is if he would recommend Master Sergeant Roy Forestin for a battlefield promotion. I know it is a little unusual to do this. Or should I say very unusual? We do need an officer that knows the people of this tribe, and is well known to them. Lok, the chief of this tribe and his people have been a big asset to the war effort even after the Major and his team returned state-side. We need to help them. We have two Generals, a Colonel, a Lieutenant Colonel and a Major present. If we decide this is our best move we have the authority to promote the Master Sergeant to Second Lieutenant by orders from the Pentagon. Gentleman what are your thoughts on the promotion?"

Everyone looks in my direction; I look to see if someone has entered the room behind me. No one has. I then realize they are looking at me so I start with "I would first like to know who the two gentlemen are that joined us tonight, and what part they play in this."

General Shefler answers with, "Sorry that is my fault. Major. They are Colonel Ted Wallace and Lieutenant Colonel Neil Marshall from General Rogers' staff. General Peter Rogers heads the indigenous people's assistance group in the Pentagon, and answers directly to the Joint Chief of Staff. As I said earlier he intended to be here but due to what is going on over there he could not make it tonight. When we come to a decision, I am to call him."

"Thank-you Sir, will they be coordinating this mission?" I ask.

Colonel Wallace answers, "To a point yes we will be coordinating this mission, Major. We are here to ask you to come to Washington as team director for the relocation of this village."

" Well, Well" I say. "Ok lets start with first things first. Yes, I do think Master Sergeant Forestin would make a good officer, and is the right choice for this mission. He speaks their language, and is well known to them. I only ask that he not be told; I had a hand in his promotion."

General Lee tells me, "That request isn't possible. His present commanding officer Captain Kiel Hicks, you and the members of this board must present the recommendation for promotion.

"Oh well, I will sign it. I know he can do the job." I say. "Now if I may ask about this assignment for me in Washington. Is it voluntary or under orders?"

General Lee stops me and asks, "Gentleman is there any other comments or questions about the promotion before we go on?

Colonel Wallace asks, "Major, has Master Sergeant Forestin ever to your knowledge expressed an interest in promotion to becoming an officer? Has he ever discussed his intention on staying in the service?"

"Colonel, I would say like any good serviceman he looks forward to moving up in the ranks. And yes he has often said that the Army is his life. I would say he feels like I do in that there is no higher calling then to serve your country." I tell the Colonel with tongue in cheek.

"Thank-you Major. Then I would say, I see no problem with the promotion." Coronel Wallace tells General Lee.

General Lee then asks Captain Wasnoski to call General Rogers. He then turns to us and says, "Gentleman would anyone like a fresh drink?" I take bourbon and water this time.

With drink in hand I ask, "Ok, what is this about me going to Washington?"

General Lee tells me, "That will be talked about after the call to General Rogers." My attention turns to the fire in the fireplace. (In my mind I think. Ok I am back on active duty and now they want me to become a desk jockey. NO WAY! It may be time for me to pull back from this if that is all there is left for me) There is little talking going on until Captain Wasnoski brings the phone in and places it on the coffee table in front General Lee.

The General picks up the phone and says "General Lee here." After a few words, General Lee asks General Rogers if he may put him on speakerphone. The answer must have been yes for General Lee pushes the speakerphone button. "General Rogers, let me introduce the men here, First General Wesley Shefler, Colonel Ted Wallace, Lieutenant Colonel Neil Marshall and Major Eric Howard." After every one has said their good evenings, General Lee tells General Rogers that it is unanimous to promote Master Sergeant Roy Forestin to Second Lieutenant and assign him to the relocation of the village of Ba-Choa.

General Rogers says, "Good I will have the order cut and they will be in your office at Benning day after tomorrow. Now has the Major accepted the assignment in Washington?"

General Lee answers, "No he has not."

General Rogers says, "General Lee, take the phone off speaker and give it to the Major please."

General Lee says, "Ok" and pushes the button while handing me the phone.

He than stands up gives a signal for the rest of the men present to follow him. (I am left alone in the room with the phone in my hand and a General in the Pentagon on the other end. Talk about being railroaded…)

"Sir, this is Major Howard," I say with a slight quiver in my voice.

"Major Howard we need you here in Washington to help co-ordinate the relocation of the Montagnard people. Your name keeps coming up when ever we have contact with any of the Montagnard people. I cannot order you to take this assignment at this time, due to you just returning to active duty. So what would it take to for you to decide to come here?" General Rogers tells me.

"Sir, I do not know. I would like to help the Montagnard's. May I be frank with you Sir?" I ask.

"Yes, Major you may." He answers.

"General I have had little to no time spent behind a desk. I have no desire to be a desk jockey. I am the type of person that needs to be out in the field with my men." (Then in the back of my mind I remember what was told me in the staff car after the party)." General if my lack of administrative duties is not a draw back, and the rest of my time in the service of our country is not spent behind a desk, yes I will take the job. When do you want me there?"

General Rogers answers me with "Major, I have read your record and someone like you would be a waste sitting in an office. Your talents are needed both in the office and in the field. I promise you that you will have a lot of time in the field. With that said, I would have liked you here yesterday. But I know you still have a couple of thing there to take care of. I will have my staff make the arrangements. They will contact you at Benning later in the week. Major, thank you for your decision to join us. I am looking forward to meeting you, Major. Now is General Lee there I need to speak with him."

I say, "Yes Sir he is. I will find him for you." I put the phone on hold and go looking for General Lee. I find him in the dining room eating Baked Alaska.

"General Lee, General Rogers would like to talk with you." He stands up, wipes his face and tells me "thank-you."

General Shefler's wife asks me if I would like some cake. "Yes I would." I answer.

As we sit at the dining room table, General Shefler asks me if I have finished the report on the MP's.

I answer, "No Sir. I think it may take an hour or two until it is finished."

General Lee returns to the dining room and tells us our work is finished for tonight. He then turns to me and says, "Major, We will be returning to Benning tomorrow at 1500 hrs. Will that give you the time you need to finish up what you need to do here?"

"Yes Sir, I can have the report finished by 1500, Sir." I answer.

"Good then I must say goodnight." General Lee says as he turns to leave. Colonel Ted Wallace and Lieutenant Colonel Neil Marshall rise say goodnight and follow General Lee out. That leaves General Shefler, his wife Marilyn and me eating Baked Alaska. General Shefler picks up the bell and rings it. The man in the black suit comes in. General Shefler tells him to find Captain McClain.

"Captain McClain is my aide and I will have him contact Lieutenant Laspino to drive you back to your quarters, Eric."(Calling me Eric surprises me) He goes on to say. "I have followed your career since you were in training here all those year ago. You do not remember me but I was in command of the training here at the time you went through. I must say at that time I was disappointed you decided to go Special Forces instead of staying in aviation. I am no longer disappointed. You have made a good officer and your country is proud of you. If I may ask why did you go the way you did?"

I tell him "Sir, it was an article in the Army Times that caused me to go S.F. The article was about life expectancy in Vietnam. A helicopter pilot had a much shorter life expectancy then the others, while a person in the S.F. unit had the longest life expectancy. I wanted to live to see my children grow up.

"That is what I thought." General Shefler answers.

Captain McClain enters the room and informs us that the Lieutenant is here. I stand and tell the General and his wife "thank-you, the meal was excellent."

General Shefler and his wife say, "You are welcome, and Major you are welcome to come back anytime." He then goes on to say "Major if you would like a transfer to my unit, please feel free. I would like to have someone of your caliber working with me."

I answer "Sir I will definitely keep that in mind. Thank you again." I leave to find Lieutenant Laspino waiting beside the car, holding the back door open for me.

We do not talk on the way back to my quarters. Once at the house the Lt. opens my door telling me he will pick me up at 0800 to finish the report. I say "thank you" and go into the house. It is late, so I just go to bed.

Unfortunately, 0700 comes too early for me; I did not have a good nights sleep. My mind could not let go of several things. I kept thinking about my problem with drinking, Loc and his people, and if I was ready to move on with staying in the Army. I had never thought about leaving the Army until now, and I was not sure why I was now. I fix some coffee and breakfast only to just nibble at the food and drink four cups of coffee. At exactly 0800, there is the doorbell. I was in the uniform I had on when I came here and it does not feel right.

The Lieutenant and I go to the same office we were in yesterday and finish the report. After giving the report to General Shefler and a quick review of the report with him. The General asks me to have lunch with him and General Lee before we leave for Benning. As we leave his office he tells Lieutenant Laspino he is dismissed and to return to his regular duties.

Lieutenant Laspino walks over to me with his hand out saying "Sir, thank-you for our talk yesterday and I hope to meet you again real soon."

I shake his hand and tell him, "You are welcome and I wish you the best of luck, both in your career in the Army and with that lovely lady of yours. I do hope I'm invited to the wedding."

Lieutenant Laspino answers "Thank you and if we do marry you will definitely be invited." The General gives us both a questioning look, but says nothing. Outside the back door of the Generals office, Captain McClain is waiting.

As we drive over to General Shefler's house, he asks, "What was that all about back at the office?"

"Sir the Lieutenant introduced me to his lady friend yesterday at the medical center. She is nurse, and they have been dating for sometime." I tell him.

"Major you know more about my people then I do, but I do not find that surprising. I have known for sometime you have a way with people. That is obvious from your record." I thank the General for his comments.

At General Shefler's house, we find General Lee and his Aide waiting for us. After lunch, Generals Lee and Shefler move to the den with me in tow. General Lee tells me I will be flying him and his Aide back to Benning in a reworked Uh-1.

The flight back to Benning goes smooth. At Benning, I am taken to General Lee's office and given my orders to report to the Pentagon in three days. General Lee tells me it is a TDY assignment and will remain attached to his command at Benning. For certain reasons of command structure I will hold the temporary rank of full Colonel while assigned to the Pentagon.

With that, General Lee hands me a pair of Eagles for my uniform telling me "Major these are the first pair of eagles I had. I hope they bring you as much luck as I have had. I know this is a temporary promotion, but it will not be long before you make it permanent. Major takeoff your coat and I will pin them on for you." He goes onto say "Colonel Howard I have had my First Sergeant call Miss Trales in the travel office and here is your travel pass. You will leave here tomorrow for New York, and then travel to Washington on Monday. Lieutenant John Hood will be your Aide while in Benning. Come with me and I will introduce you."

"Sir, I do not know what to say or how to thank-you. I do not think I deserve this." I say.

"Colonel there is no one that deserves this more then you. You have been an example to all of us. Now shut-up and let's go." General Lee tells me with just the slightest hint of emotion.

Just outside his office, Lieutenant John Hood snaps to

attention and gives us a salute.

"Colonel Howard, this is Lieutenant Hood. He will be your Aide."

"Lieutenant this is Colonel Howard."

The Lieutenant salutes me again and says 'Sir it is a pleasure to meet you." I turn and put out my hand to General Lee. He takes it and tells me to be in his office at 0900 in the morning.

I say, "Yes Sir. I will be Sir."

Along side the building, there is a Jeep parked. Once in the Jeep, the Lieutenant says "Sir do you have anything at the BOQ?

"Yes I do."

"Sir we will go there first and then on to you permanent quarters here at Benning." I look at him with a questing look.

"Sir the General has had permanent quarters assigned for you. After you are in your quarter's Sir, will there be anything I can do for you?"

"Yes Lieutenant there is a rental car around here somewhere I need to retrieve. After I have the car that will be all. That is until tomorrow morning."

The lieutenant answers me with, "Sir the car has been moved to your quarters." (Ok, I have the keys in my pocket. Now did they move it? I am not going to ask. It is better not to know)

I am now in my quarters and still wondering what the heck is going on. This house is just like the one I had at Hunter-Stewart but bigger. I unpack and wander around in a daze. Without even thinking about changing my clothes, I drive the rental car to Mike's house.

It's about 1800 hours, so I find Mike and his family at home. Mike answers the door with a shocked look on his face.

"Sir, what is this, pointing to the Birds on my uniform jacket.

"May I come in?" I ask.

"Yes of course. Come in, Roy and Sonny are here too." I walk into the living room where everyone is seated. Roy snaps to a standing position, and gives me a silly salute.

"Ok enough of the jerking around it is still just me you guy's." I say. Mike tells me to take a seat "Eric so much as happened since you were last here. We just do not know what to think. First I am accepted into flight school, then Roy is order to report to General Lee's office at 0900 tomorrow and now you walk in a Bird Colonel. What is this Army coming too?"

"Mike, I can only think the Army has come to its senses. I am a Colonel only temporarily. I have been asked to join a team of people in the Pentagon working to help the Yards in Vietnam. I will be stationed here at Benning when that job is done as a Major. As for your flight school thing, I have no idea how that happened and I would think we have to wait till tomorrow to find out why the General wants to see Roy. Speaking of flight school Mike when do you start."

"Eric, I start on Monday. I have to be there at 0700. I will be going in on Sunday night. Linda will stay here, and when I have time off I will come and spend time with them. I know in the first six-weeks, I will have no time off. So why should we move? Mike answers.

"What are you going to do when and if you receive your wings?" I ask Mike.

"I will probably come back here. I think we will have the house by then. If we are turned down for the house, we will have to think about where the family will live. As you know the families do not always live where we are stationed. By the way how are Debbie and your children?"

"They are fine. Debbie and the children are living in a penthouse apartment close to Grand Central Station on New York City. It is close to her office on Park Ave. Well are we going to have dinner or have you already eaten?" I say.

Linda says, "Oh my I totally spaced out about dinner."

That is ok, let me take you all to dinner at the Officers Club. Mike and Roy are both in civvies, so no problem there. Linda goes to the phone, and calls the people next door. The people next door have a daughter who is 17 that watches the children now and then Mike tells me.

Linda comes back and tells us that Melinda will be here in 10 minutes. "I need to have the kids ready, Mike could you help me, then we can go." I call the O-Club to reserve a table with no problems at all.

At the O-club, we have a nice dinner and drinks. Roy keeps looking around as if he is expecting something.

"Roy, what is your problem?' I ask.

"Eric, I am not an officer and always wondered how the other half lived. Are you sure, it's ok that I am here? I do not want to cause a problem. I may already be in trouble.'

"Roy it is ok, you are here as my guest. Why do you think you are in some trouble already?" I say.

"Well why else would I be called to be in the General's office, in full dress uniform no less." He says.

I answer, "It could be you did something right, could it not."

Roy looks at me like what do you know, 'Eric is something going on that I should know?"

"Roy I cannot tell you anything. Please don't ask." Everyone looks at me as if I have just let out the biggest, smelliest fart on record. To change the subject I tell everyone that I have a house on base now so we know I will be back soon. I tell them the address only to be told.

"Eric, that is over in the fenced in secure living area." Roy says.

Mike chimes in with, "Ok! Now I know something is going on. The only people that live there are the Generals, Colonel and any office involved with the ultra hush-hush stuff. Come on give, what is up."

With a total look of innocence, I say. "I do not know what you are talking about."

Roy looks at Mike, gives him a wink and says, "I would say he is in it up to his neck, wouldn't you."

Mike with a wink, answers, "We'd better drop it or he may have to kill us."

"Ok you guys drop it. You know if I knew, or could say, anything I would tell you." After dinner and a couple of drinks, we each go our separate ways.

Once back at my quarters, I call Debbie to talk with her. I tell her what has happened, about Mike in flight school, Roy now an officer and me coming home before going to the Pentagon for a short time.

Debbie asks me, "What happens after the Pentagon?"

I tell her, "I will be based here at Benning. General Lee has already set me up with a real nice four-bedroom house in very secure part of the base. I also tell her about the psychologist, and what he and I talked about. We talk for about an hour and end with "I love you. See you soon." As we are about to hang up Debbie asks a question that makes me stop dead in my tracks. She asks if I would like her and the children to move down here. I answer, "Yes of course I would. I also think we need to talk about that. Let's talk more about this when I am home tomorrow." We say our good-byes and hang up.

I go to bed and cannot help but wonder what brought that on. She has a very good medical practice in New York, and a very nice home that is paid for. Eric has been living in Kentucky now about 2 years, just like I did, and I know he is happy. Ingrid is in a private school not far from where they live and loves it. Ray will start school next year. Could it be Debbie just wants us to be a family? Well I will be home tomorrow and we can talk about it. My flight leaves Atlanta at 1300 and I will be home for dinner. I will have to leave here soon after meeting with the General.

I call Mike hoping Roy and Sunny have gone home. Mike answers the phone sounding as if he was half-asleep.

"Mike its Eric. Is Roy and Sunny gone?"

"Yes they left about an hour ago. Why?"

"Mike you have to keep this under your hat."

"Ok, I will. So what is up? While I was at Hunter-Stewart, I had a meeting with General Lee, General Shefler and two men from the Pentagon. In the meeting, I learned Lok had asked for help in being move to a safe place and we were the last team that spent anytime with them. The meeting was about my thinking on the Yard people and their problems."

"Ok Eric. So why the phone call?"

"Mike I just wanted to let you know the reason for Roy being ordered to be in the Generals office. You cannot say a word to anyone, not even Linda. Do you understand?"

"Yes Eric, I do. So what is it?"

I tell Mike, "I was asked if I thought Roy would make a good officer and if he could take a team back to Lok's village to help lead them out."

"Eric what did you say?" Mike asks.

"Well I told them yes to both questions."

"Eric why did they not ask you or I do it?"

"Mike first off I am just back on active duty and am going to the Pentagon to coordinate this and several other missions. Second, you have just been accepted in to flight school. We need good S.F. pilots now."

"Ok, I will buy that." Mike answers.

I go on. "The five of us that meet at Hunter-Stewart approved Roy's promotion, and General Rogers in the Pentagon signed the orders. Tomorrow morning Roy is being given a field promotion to the rank of Second Lieutenant. I just thought you might like to be there."

Mike answers with, "You know I will be there. I will not say a word to anyone. If Linda asks, I am meeting you. OK?"

"Yes sure. See you then."

Chapter 27

Morning comes early with little sleep. My mind kept racing about what was happening all around me at what was like the speed of light. This house is also fully stocked, so I fix myself some breakfast. At 0830, Lieutenant Hood comes and drives me to General Lee's office. We park in the lot behind his office.

As I am walking in, Mike catches up to me "Colonel, may I walk with you?" He asks.

"Yes you may Captain Danville."

"Thank you, Sir."

As we walk down the hall, Mike thanks me for letting him know what this is all about. We are using a back way in, so Roy will not see us.

I ask Mike, "How did you find me?"

"Eric I was sitting in my car at the north end of the parking lot watching to see when either you or Roy went in. I did not want Roy to see me, but wanted to meet you. If I had not seen your Jeep going around back of the building, I would have missed you. I ask what you would have done if you did miss me."

"I would have watched Roy enter and followed him, staying out of sight." As we arrive at the side door of the Generals' office area a Lieutenant stops us and closes the door behind him. He then states, "Excuse me Sir's. General Lee asked me to keep you out here until Master Sergeant Forestin is in a side room. The ceremony will be in the main conference room." There is a knock on the door behind the Lieutenant. We are escorted to the main conference room. In the conference room are several rows of chairs facing a platform. On the platform is a podium with seven chairs, four to the right and three to the left. Just to the right and slightly in front of the podium is an American Flag; to the left is the flag of the U.S.Army.

As we enter General Lee comes over to me followed by Captain Hicks and says, "Good morning Colonel Howard. Glad you could make it."

I answer, "Good morning Sir and thank you for inviting me. Sir I took the liberty to invite Captain Danville. He was my XO in Vietnam, and is a good friend of Master Sergeant Forestin. I hope that is Ok."

The General answers with, "Yes Colonel it is." The General turns to Captain Danville and says, "Good morning Captain Danville." I will have a chair added for him. General Lee tells his aide to add a chair next to mine. "Let's take our seats and let the poor Master Sergeant off the hook. I am told he looks as nervous as a virgin on her first date. We will be seated on the platform. We will take the four seats to the left of the podium looking at the audience. I have informed General Shefler, his aide and First Sergeant to sit to the right. Master Sergeant Forestin will be brought in and seated in the first row of seats in front of us. Colonel after the ceremony General Shefler wants a few words with you." As we walk on stage, I can see General Shefler and his people enter from the other side.

After we are all seated, two MP's escort Roy in from a room to the right of the platform. They guide him to his seat. He sits down, and the MP's take seats behind him. Roy looks up at me, then Mike. He then looks at General Lee. His eyes move from his right to his left, stopping briefly at each of the seven men seated on the Platform. General Lee stands and moves to the podium. One of the MP's taps Roy on the arm, and tells him to stand.

General Lee starts, "Master Sergeant Roy Forestin, you may be seated. Let me introduce the panel. First to my right are General Shefler, Captain McClain the General's Aide and First Sergeant Bailey here from Hunter-Stewart. To my left are Colonel Howard, Captain Danville, and Captain Hicks. We had hoped General Rogers from the Pentagon could make it, but he is unavailable. We are here to discuss a very delicate situation." The General then turns to me and asks, "Colonel, have you discussed the topic at hand with Captain Danville?"

"Yes Sir I have. Sir the Captain is fully aware."

"Good Colonel. Let me start with, Master Sergeant Forestin, this goes back to when you were in Vietnam working with the indigenous personal." I can see Roy is very nervous. He cannot sit still. "Master Sergeant Forestin, do you remember the people of the Ba-Choa village?"

Roy shakes his head "yes." The MP taps him again, with that tap; Roy stands and yells, "Yes Sir, I do Sir."

"Fine Master Sergeant, but you can just nod you head from now on." (In my mind, I can just imagine how Roy feels right about now. Here he is in front of all these officers. Sitting alone with two MP's behind him, watching every move he makes, not knowing if he is in trouble, being questioned by a General)

General Lee then asks Roy, "Master Sergeant, does the names Lok, Twan, Dau and Hi mean anything to you?" Roy nods his head in the affirmative.

"Is it not true you lived with them for several months? "Roy nods his head in the affirmative again.

"Are you aware of the situation they are now living under?" Roy nods his head in the affirmative with a tear in his eyes.

"Master Sergeant now the big question, with that the General just said. (Roy really looks like he could just jump out of his skin) "Master Sergeant would you like to have the chance to return to Vietnam and help save their lives?" I cannot tell by the look on Roy face if he is scared out of his wits, or pleased that he now knows he is not in any trouble.

Roy stands up, gives the General a salute and asks, "When do I leave Sir?"

Mike nudges me and whispers, "I knew he would. I just wonder how long it is going to be before he asks if we are going also." Before the word also could clear Mike's lips.

Roy asks, "Sir, I may ask a question?"

General Lee answers, "Yes you may."

"Sir, Am I returning with Colonel Howard and Captain Danville?"

"Master Sergeant Forestin no they are not. Now that brings us to the second part of this meeting. Please be seated Master Sergeant."

As General Lee continues, "Two days ago there was a meeting held at Hunter-Stewart in the home of General Shefler. General Lee acknowledged General Shefler. This meeting was attended by myself, General Shefler, Colonel Wallace of the Pentagon,

Lieutenant Colonel Marshall of the Pentagon, and then Major Howard. At this meeting, several options were discussed. After much discussion, a decision was made and approved by all present. A conference call was placed to General Rogers in his Pentagon office. After a short discussion, he also approved the decision we had reached. Then yesterday I had a meeting with Captain Hicks your commanding officer. He concurred with our findings. Now that brings me to the point of this gathering. Will the two MP's please escort Master Sergeant Roy Forestin to the platform?"

With an MP on each side, Roy mounts the platform, walks to the front of the podium and stands facing General Lee. (If I did not know better I could swear the front of Roy's pants was damp) With General Lee dismissing the MP's, Mike and I rise and stand behind Roy, General Shefler, his aide and the First Sergeant rise and move so as to stand behind General Lee.

"Master Sergeant Roy Forestin, it gives me great pleasure. In the company of these men present as witnesses, by an Act of the Congress of United States of America. You Roy Forestin are here by made an officer and a gentleman in the U.S.Army. Please raise your right hand and repeat after me.

With the oath done. General Lee says. "Colonel Howard. Please come forward." I walk around Roy, and stand next to General Lee. "Roy Forestin, I am here today to present you with this pair of gold bars as a symbol of your promotion to the rank of Second Lieutenant in the United States Army. Remember, as my father tells me often, It took an Act of Congress to make you a gentleman, now live up to it."

I can see by the look on Roy's face that he had no idea of what was coming. He has the look of a man just being pardoned from death row. After handshakes all around, General Shefler tells me to follow him. As we leave the stage, Mike tells me to come by his house when I am free.

"Ok I will" I answer. I see Captain Hicks take Roy by the arm, and follows General Lee out the other side of the room. I follow General Shefler to a room just across the hall from the conference room.

Once inside two men in civilian clothes meet us, "Coronel Howard, I am Thomas Baker and this is Nathan Ogoler. We are here from Langley VA. We need to speak with you."

"Ok, so what do you want from me?" I ask.

"Colonel, may we call you Eric? It would make this a lot easier."

"Sure why not." I answer.

"Eric we have some information that would make helping the indigenous peoples recovery effort more advantageous. We know you are going to the Pentagon to work on that situation, and want to help, Mr. Baker tells me.

"Mr. Baker, may I call you Tom?"

"Yes you may, and Nat is ok with Mr. Ogoler."

"Well Tom why don't you just tell the people in the Pentagon, instead of coming here to talk with me."

Nat then says, "Eric because what we have to say is extremely delicate. The people you will be working with in the Pentagon are not all Special Forces." With that said, General Shefler excuses himself from the room, and closes the door on his way out.

"Eric, as you are well aware Special Forces and the people we work for have had a close alliance throughout the Vietnam situation. What we have and know is not for public knowledge. That is why when our director received information that you were returning to active duty he asked to have you put in charge of this project. Your connection to the company and its working is to remain classified."

I spend about 45 minutes with them, and then start to leave for Mike's house.

"Eric what was said here is to go no further. You may contact us and we will be ready to help at anytime."

"Thank-you I will keep that in mind" I say as I leave. As I exit the room, an MP asks me to follow him. I do. We go to General Lee's office.

Inside General Lees office is General Shefler. As I walk in, they both stand and offer me a hand, "Colonel please take a seat. We wanted to talk with you before you left. General Shefler and I both want to thank you. We know the road ahead is going to be a long, hard and twisty one. In addition, one you cannot talk about with just anyone. When you return here to Benning, you will be on my direct staff. Your knowledge of Vietnam and its people has been recognized, all the way to the top. We need to keep you in the service of your country. I have arranged for your flight home to New York to be moved until tomorrow morning and your report time at the Pentagon has been changed to Tuesday. There will be a helicopter to pick you up on Tuesday morning at 0700. You will be notified as to the pickup point."

"Thank you sir. I need to let my wife know."

"That is fine, please use the phone in the First Sergeant's office, we will talk again soon Colonel." General Lee tells me.

As I move to leave, I say "Thank you." as I am headed to the First Sergeant's office my mind cannot help but think why the delay.

I call Debbie and leave her a message as to the changes in my travel plans, but nothing more. Once back at my quarters, I change into civvies and head for Mikes.

As I drive over to Mike's my mind is running 120 mph. What is going on? How can I head up a rescue mission? What about the other people in the Pentagon? How much do they know? What can I tell them? How much support can I count on? And what I think is most important, who do I report to once I am in Washington and what connection am I to have with CIA? Is General Rogers someone I can talk with? Is he in the loop as far as Langley is concerned? How many people know and what do they know? I am well aware working with the company you can become a spook real quick. Is that it? I have questions and more questions but no answers.

Deep in my thoughts, I drive right by Mike's house. As I am driving, it becomes clear that there are more then meets the eye going on here. Are we as a country going to lose our first war because of a group of old farts that cave to the pressure of a small but vocal percentage of the people? I hope not.

I am lost. How do I find my way back to Mike's house? As I come to a stop at a stop sign, there is an MP directing traffic. He signals me to proceed. As I am along side him, I stop and ask for directions. With anger in his voice, he tells me to move on as he bends down to look at me. It is the same MP that was at the gate, when I first arrived at Benning.

With a total change of attitude having recognized me, I hear "Sir if you turn left here, go six block then turn right for ten blocks and finally a right turn. This will put you about two blocks from where you want to be. Have a nice day Sir."

I say "thank-you" and turn left as he holds traffic for me.

I park in Mike's driveway and go to the front door only to be yelled at from across the street. I look to see who is yelling at me.

It is Roy, Sunny, Mike and Linda yelling for me to come over.

As I cross the street Sunny runs up to me and practically knocks me over. "Eric thank you, thank you. We are to move here now that we are better."

Roy comes up to me as I finally reach the grass and am out of the street. He takes Sunny by the arm, and tells her to go into the house.

With Sunny gone, Roy says, "Eric thank-you, I think."

"What do you mean think?" I ask.

"Eric I was happy as an EM. I did not have to think too much, just follow orders. It was easy state side. Now I will have to think."

"Roy, you are only a Second Lieutenant, the low man on the totem pole. Do not worry there will still be plenty of people telling you what to do." I say.

"Ok, Ok I have the picture." Roy answers.

"Now what is going on here?" I ask. As we walk up to the house, Roy tells me "General Lee has assigned me to the same B-team as Mike, so the housing office is moving me over here. I cannot stay in the EM housing area any longer. All our stuff will be moved here on Monday. We came over to see what the new place looked like, only to learn it was across the street from Mike and Linda. The house number is 106 numbers different then Mike's, so we did not think it would be this close."

Mike hears Roy say that and said "yeah too close." With many snickers from everyone, Mike says "Let's go across the street and have a cold beer to celebrate."

Sitting in Mike's living room, Roy asks me, "Eric how did this happen?"

"Roy if you are referring to your promotion, I think it was

overdue. You were instrumental in pulling our asses out of several jams in Nam. You were the one that knew the people we went to in Laos. If anyone has the lion share of saving Phil's life, it would be you. I had put you in for promotion then. However, in the infinite wisdom of the board, they only up graded you as an EM. From what I hear around base and from General Shefler you were ready sometime ago." I look to see if the wives are around and see they are in the kitchen making something to eat.

Therefore, I go on "Roy if it had not been for the problem with money you would have been is OCS by now, this way is easier." Roy looks at me like a kid that just found out he had passed a school exam, he thought he failed.

"Eric, so you did have something to do with all that is going on. Mike tells me.

"Yes Mike, I did. (Only as far as Roy and his promotion is concerned. I still do not want him to know I have a hand in the flight school thing) we will talk more about this later." I say as I see the Linda and Sunny coming back in to the room. Sunny asks what we are talking about; Linda knows better then to ask.

I tell Sunny," Oh, just some old war stories."

After about an hour of just general conversation, the phone rings. Linda answers it and tells me, it is for me. It is Lieutenant Hood. We talk and I hang up.

"Mike, you and Roy are to come with me. We have something to take care of."

As we drive over to the SOG office in the HHC building Mike asks, "Where are we going?"

"Mike we need to talk about something. There is a man from Langley waiting for us. I will tell you more when we are there."

The rest of the drive is in silence. In HHC, we go to an office marked S.O.G.

As we enter the door, Mike says, "Boy this is just like the old days. I did not even know this was here."

"Mike it is new. They opened this office a week ago. General Shefler told me to keep it on the QT. Inside the room are four desks set in a square in the middle of the room. The right side of the room is filled with file cabinets. The left side has six chairs by the wall. Beside each chair is a small table with a phone on it.

At one of the desks sits a man in civilian clothes. He stands up as we come in and asks, "May I help you."

I answer, "I hope so. I am Colonel Howard, this is Captain Danville and this is Lieutenant Forestin. I was called to come here."

"Yes that is correct. I am Laurence Baker. I was sent here to brief you on the latest situation changes in Vietnam. I was also told I there would be a Lieutenant Forestin with you. I was not informed about a Captain Danville."

"Mr. Baker, I want Captain Danville to be in on this. Is that all right with you?" I ask.

"Colonel Howard, it is fine with me, as you are the one in charge of this program." Both Roy and Mike have a look of amazement on their faces. "The director has assigned me as your contact within the Company."

We all take a seat at one of the desks as Mr. Baker hands out a folder to Roy and me "Sorry Sir, but I only have three sets of information with me. I did not know the Captain would be join-ing us."

"That is ok, those two can share" I answer.

After several minutes of looking over the maps and reading

the reports, it becomes clear the situation is becoming worse. We discuss what we have just read and after about an hour, I lean back, put my hands behind my head and close my eyes. In deep thought, it comes to me that we need to move and move quickly. I ask if everything is in place in Nam.

Mr. Baker answers, "Sir, all of our preparations are complete. The only thing outstanding is choosing the team going with the Lieutenant. General Rogers has a list of men for the team that Lieutenant Forestin is to select from. That list will be here in the morning. I will meet with you are 0800 in General Sheflers office to discuss the logistics. Sir's I must have the folders back." We hand Mr. Baker the folders back and he leaves.

Once the door is closed, Mike looks at me and asks, "So what the hell is going on?"

"Mike, I have been promoted and have been given the task of rescuing the indigenous people of Vietnam. I will have an office in the Pentagon and at Langley for the purpose of location and retrieval of the indigence personal. Our troops are pulling out of Nam according to the Paris Peace Accords. This leaves the Montagnard people in a very tenuous position. As we know both the North and South do not want these people around. It has fallen on me to help them. I asked Roy to work with me. Mike, you are here because I want to keep you up to date on what is happening. Once you are in flight, this will not be easy, as you will be at Fort Walters and then Hunter-Stewart. But General Lee, the base commander is aware and will help. Colonel Hunley, the commander of 1st S.F. Aviation is also aware. Colonel Hunley was my flight instructor."

Both Mike and Roy in unison say, "So you are a spook, a real spook. CIA cover and all."

"Ok, Ok, now just drop that spook stuff and let's go. Let's go have a drink now that Roy can be allowed in the O-Club. After a drink, I head back to my quarters.

Back in my quarters, I call Debbie. We talk for almost two hours about what has gone on. (But only what I could tell her) As I lay on my bed trying to sleep, my mind wanders back in time, back to a time in Loks village.

It was the first time we were in the village. This was just before we left the village after several months of living with them. Our last morning started as usual, just after sun up, we moved out on a normal patrol with Twan. Most of the villagers were doing what they do every morning, except there was something different in the air. Not something you could put your finger on, just a feeling and ill-defined pungency in the air. In our travels that day, we would come across people from neighboring villages, which was very unusual. For the most part things were quiet. We stopped to have lunch near a river. The beautiful landscape was always a comfort as well as a worry to me. It was so lush and green. That lushness made it a worry, because anyone could hide and not be seen until it was too late.

As the sun was going behind the mountains to the west, we started back to the village. Crossing the last ridge before heading down into the village, we could see the cook fires burning. There were more fires then normal. The closer we were to the village, the more voices we heard. There was a lot more voices then normal. They sounded friendly and like they were having a good time. The Montagnard people were a happy go lucky type of people. Lok's people could throw a party at the drop of a hat. Once about two weeks ago the situation was the same. We came back to find the village having a party for the birth of a new member of the tribe, a Water buffalo. Twan was in the lead. He was walking a little faster then I would have like him to have been. As we came down the trail in to the village, I recognize that Lok had put out people to watch the trails farther from the village then we did. As we entered the village, I could tell something big was going on. There were pigs roasting on two fires in the center of the village. There were pots of rice and vegetables cooking. There was Lok with the ceremonial Numpai Urn in front of the community hut. All the elders of the village were dressed in their ceremonial garb. The men had on their bright colored clothes and the women had their bright skirts on. (You know for the life of me I cannot remember what that skirt was called) There was music being played on the Montagnard instruments that included gongs, bamboo flutes, and stringed instruments. Twan told us Lok had decided to have a going away party for us.

After cleaning up, we were escorted to the center of the village. Lok was standing next to the large chair made of wood and greatly carved with symbols of his tribe and their history. We were guided to seven place mats placed on the front porch of the communal hut. Lok took his place and asked us to sit. Roast pig, vegetables, and an earthen jar of Nuoc-mam were placed in front of us on a low bamboo tables. Twan and his wife sat on the porch to our right and Lok was to our left. As we eat, the music restarted and the villager put on a traditional show. The show was a dance relating the history and victories over the enemies of the tribe. The people wearing them depicted man, nature and the animals of the area in costumes handmade. It was colorful and very exciting to see.

These people would do anything for you once they accepted you. We were made to feel like one of the family. Every so often Lok's wife would bring us a cup of rice wine from the ceremonial Numpai Urn. The wine was strong, but not as strong as moonshine. After about the third cup I started to feel a little lightheaded. The dancing and music went on well into the evening. I started to worry about the noise. Would it bring the NVA or Cong to see what was going on?

Twan saw the worry on my face and leaned over to me saying, "No worry we have sent out people to watch for Charlie." After the dancing and storytelling by the elders was over, or so we thought, Lok stood up "People of this village I would like to tell you about these men. You all know them, but the safety and freedom we have goes beyond their life with us."

He then tells the village several tales about things we have done beyond the village; some are a little exaggerated. When he is finished his last story he has us stand. With great pomp and ceremony, we received the traditional Brass Bracelet. The Brass Bracelet was a sign of friendship and we were made a member of the tribe. There is also a ritual; I am not at liberty to talk about. After the party was over, sleep came easily and the morning sun was not a welcome site. The two-hour hike to our pickup point was a sad one but we know we would be back. As the chopper came in low, we said our good byes with heavy hearts.

I am just about to wakeup when there is someone ringing my doorbell. I have to look for my robe, as I sleep naked. Once in my robe I answer the door to find Lieutenant Hood.

"Come in, what time is it." I ask him. "What are doing at my door in the middle of the night?"

"Sir it is 0730, and we have to be at the Generals office in a half-hour."

"Ok Lieutenant I will get dressed. Do you know how to make coffee?"

" Yes Sir I do."

"Good. Make a pot of strong coffee while I clean up and dress." After a quick shave and putting on my class A's, with a travel mug of coffee in hand we head out.

Chapter 28

We arrive just in time to see a General exit his car and enter the building. I look at Lt. Hood with a questioning look, and he tells me that is General Rogers. Two men in civilian clothes followed General Rogers into the building. I recognize one of them as Mr. Baker but do not know the other man. I know I have seen him, but cannot remember who he is.

As I am stepping out of the Jeep, Roy drives up and parks beside us.

"Roy, how are you this morning?" I ask.

"I'm just peachy Eric. All though, I did not sleep well. I had a dream about that the time we were made members of Lok's tribe."

"I did too." I tell him.

"Eric, I saw Mike on my way here, and he told me he had the same dream. Boy that is weird."

"Let's go in and see what is up. I just saw General Rogers going in." I tell Roy.

"Boy, all the big brass is here. I hope I know how to act in front of them." Roy says.

"Just be yourself, and you will be fine." I say as we walk into the building.

Once in the building, a Sergeant directs us to the auditorium. There are men standing guard outside each door. We are stopped at the door, and asked to identify ourselves. We show ID, and the guard opens the door for us to go in. Inside the auditorium, there are large maps and photographs set on easels behind a large table on the stage. In front of the stage, there is group of men talking with Generals Shefler and Rogers. Alongside the Generals, are Mr. Baker and the other man I cannot recognize. Seated in the front row are Captain's Wasnoski and McClain; beside them are Colonel's Wallace and Bates.

As Roy and I approach General Shefler, I am snapped back to the Nam. I now know the other guy in civilian clothes. I saw him before the mission that was a HALO drop over the Yunnan province of Red China that borders North Vietnam. It was to be basically a reconnaissance mission to photograph a North Vietnamese training camp for high-ranking officers. As I remember it took us five and one half months to walk out of there and then we only barely made it out with our lives. The same guy had a briefcase chained to his wrist.

General Shefler tells us good morning. He introduces General Rogers to Roy and I. General Rogers speaks "Good morning gentlemen. It is an honor and pleasure to meet the two of you. I have heard a lot of good things about both of you. Please, Let us take our seats."

We take seats across the aisle from the others. As we sit down the guy, I remembered from Vietnam takes the stage.

"Gentlemen, My name Amos Washington and I am with the

joint taskforce to help the people that worked so hard with us in Vietnam. Time is of the essence, and we know we cannot help them all. That is why we are working to help those that did the most first. The people of the villages of Ba-Choa and Ba-Ngu are the ones we will be speaking about today. Mr. Baker, please hand out the notebooks. As Mr. Baker hands out the notebooks, the lights go dim. For the next two hours, we watch films and look at maps. There are also many photos taken by aircraft.

When Mr. Washington is finished, he turns the program over to General Rogers. "Gentlemen the next part of the proceedings will be team selection. So let's take a break. General Shefler, Captain Wasnoski, Captain McClain, Colonel Wallace and Colonel Bates we will reconvene in one half-hour. Colonel Howard and Second Lieutenant Forestin, please stay. The rest of you are dismissed."

As every one but us leave General Rogers hands Roy a folder. "Lieutenant Forestin, this folder contains a copy of file on the people we think would be a good match for your mission. Please look it over. If you have anyone you would like to add to these choices, please let me know before we reconvene. Colonel Howard, I know you want to go home to your family, so if you would like you may fly back to Washington with me."

"I will be leaving shortly after we are done here. I would like that, but I have rental car I picked up in Atlanta to return and I am not packed."

"Colonel Howard, I will have First Sergeant McCoy take care of the car and there will be time for you to pack."

I answer. "Thank you, General Rogers, I would be more then happy to fly back with you."

"Ok, then be back in a half-hour, so we can get this completed."

With that said, he goes out of the auditorium. I stand up and look around, seated in the last row is Lieutenant Hood.

"Lieutenant Hood, would you come here please."

He walks up to me and salutes, "Yes sir, what may I do for you, Sir?

"Lieutenant would you please go back to my quarters, and pack my clothes. You may leave the things as they are in the bathroom, and what is on the desk. I will be going to Washington with General Rogers as soon as we are finished here."

"Yes Sir, I will take care of it for you." He answers and leaves.

"Eric, you are really coming up in the world, flying with Generals, living in the elite section of the post, and having an Aide."

I say, "Oh shut-up and let's have some coffee. I really need it and a smoke. "

"Eric I want to stay here and go over these files."

"Roy, just come with me." I tell him. We go out of the auditorium and down the hall to the office I have been told is mine. "This is my office please feel free to use it. You will be more comfortable here. I will be back shortly." In the area outside the General's office is a table with coffee and rolls setup. I take a cup and head out the door to think and have a smoke.

Sitting on the bench under a tree is Mr. Washington. He is looking at some folders. I do not want to intrude, so I go the other way. I do not go far before I hear. "Colonel Howard, please take a seat over here. I would like to talk with you."

"Ok" I say as I walk over and take a seat.

"Colonel Howard what would you think if I told you I want to go along on this mission that is being planned? Would you approve of my being part of the team? I was with Special Forces, before going to work for the Company."

"Mr. Washington, I do not have the power to approve something like that." I answer. His next statements to me almost knock me out.

"Colonel you will soon learn that the action to be taken, the personnel involved and the timetable for such action will be yours to decide. There are high-ranking officials that say you are the one to run the show. You will have only two people you will answer to and neither one of them are here.

As I light my second cigarette, I wonder what have I involved myself in now. "Mr. Washington, if what you say is true, not that I doubt you, I will give it a lot of thought." As I look up from staring at the ground and pile of pine needles, I have made with my foot, I see Roy waving at me.

As we enter the auditorium and take our seats, General Shefler comes over to us. We stand only to be told to sit down. The General asks Roy if he has looked at the files.

Roy answers, "yes I have. I have picked five men from your list and would like to add four new names."

"Ok, I will have their jackets pulled. The General takes the list from Roy.

I look at him and say, "I hope you did not put Mike and my name on that list."

"No Eric I didn't add you guys to the list. I know better then that. The names I added were of men I have worked with since we left Nam."

After a couple of minutes, General Rogers enters followed by the others. He takes to the podium and starts, "Ok Gentlemen, lets start. First can we drop the sir's and use first names to make this go faster?" Every one answers in the affirmative. This could be fun, as I do not know all the first names. "Gentlemen my name is Peter. This is General Wesley Shefler, Captain Johan Wasnoski, Captain Erin McClain, Colonel Ted Wallace and Colonel Erin Bates. When you have something to say, please start with your first name, as this will help in learning them.

"So let's start with Roy, Second Lieutenant Forestin. Have you met everyone present?"

"I am Roy, and no I have not formally, but I am aware of who they are."

"I am Peter, that will do for now."

"So Roy, what is your thinking on what needs to be done."

Roy still standing says, "First off, I need to meet with the people going with me. Then we need to set up our plan for the mission. I could use all the help I can have from Colonel Howard, oops I mean Eric."

"Roy, you will be meeting with the men you have listed later today, except for one of them. He is out of the country. We will discuss this later."

General Rogers then goes on with some of the logistics of what needs to be done. After about two and a half hours of a back and forth discord on how, what, when and where General Rogers stops the conversation.

"Gentlemen I think we have covered all we can at this point. If there are any further questions or comments please hold them until Tuesday. We, Colonel Howard and I, will be in Washington then. Please direct all correspondence to Colonel Howard as he has total responsibility from this point on. All questions concerns and requests must go through him. He will be the final word in all action. If he asks you for something, consider it the same as a request from the Joint Chiefs of Staff. All communications on this subject are to be considered a top security priority. Do not discuss anything that happened here or anything about this situation. If you need to put someone in the loop, Colonel Howard must clear him or her. No one other then Colonel Howard may add or remove someone from the loop. Is this understood?" A unanimous "Yes Sir" is heard. "Colonel Howard, General Lee could not be here for the meeting, but will be traveling with us today. He is aware of what was said, and done here today. You may call on him at anytime. Outside of those here now and the gentlemen that were here for the first session and anyone approved by Colonel Howard, no conversation is permitted on this operation. The Colonel will inform you of the code name and information you will need later. Have a good day Gentleman."

With that said, everyone leaves but me. Roy without thinking leaves the room. General Rogers comes over and sits beside me, "Eric I am sorry, I could not tell you everything before today. It was only this morning; I received the final ok to put you in charge of this."

"Peter, how do I answer? Why me? Who do I answer to?"

"Eric it was a decided in a joint meeting that you could do what needs to be done. Your name was at the top of everyone's list. As for you to you to answer to, I can only tell you that you will find out when you report to the Joint Chiefs of Staff on Tuesday. Now to answer an unasked question that I know you will think of later. Your friend and team member from Vietnam Captain Mike Danville is in your office now and you may talk with him. You must tell him that he is to have no conversation with anyone on this operation. No one is to know he is in the loop at this point."

"Thank-you sir" I say.

"My flight will be leaving in one hour. Your Aide knows where to take you. See you then." He stands and puts out his hand saying "welcome on board."

As I walk to the office I have been assigned, my mind wander to many flashbacks about the Yards. Their friendly nature towards those they know and trust. Their fear of those they do not know. The repugnance and mistrust they feel for those that have killed and tortured them over the years because they are Montagnard, both the North and South Vietnamese have wronged them.

As I enter my office, Mike looks like he is a quandary. He is standing at the window staring out at an empty lot, as if he is looking for something.

I speak up saying, "Mike we need to talk." He turns and stares at me saying nothing. "Mike, please sit down and take it easy."

"Eric I do not like what is going on around me. I think this is going to explode and we will be the ones injured. Am I correct?"

"Mike I am going to tell you everything, but first you must swear to me that you will have no conversation with anyone about what I am going to tell you. I must know that no one will ever hear about this. Even that you are in the loop at this point, that is if you want in at this point. Even Roy does not to know we spoke about this. What do you say Mike?" I ask.

"Eric you know me better then that. If I say I will tell no one or even hint that I know something, you can take that to the bank. Don't you?" Mike says.

"Yes Mike I do. But I hope you understand that I need to hear it from you and I need you to sign a statement to that fact for the brass" I answer.

"Yes I understand. It is just the normal bullshit we have to put up with. You know I will sign a statement for you and be assured I know not to say or hint at anything I am told not to. Don't you?"

"Yes Mike I do. We do not have much time so now that that is out of the way. Here is what is going on. We talk for almost an hour. I fill him in on everything, except the part about the people I will be answering too. We are just about done when there is a knock on my door.

I answer it to find Lieutenant Hood, "Colonel, General Rogers has asked me to tell you the flight to Washington has been moved back one hour."

I turn to Mike and ask him, "Did you drive over here?" Mike tells me he was driven over by two men sent by General Shefler. I turn back to Lieutenant Hood, and ask him if he had packed my belongings. He answers that he had and everything was in a car he checked out of the motor pool. "Good I say. Then would you drive the Captain and me to his house?"

"Yes sir I would be glad to."

The drive to Mike's was a silent one. We step out of the car at Mike's house leaving Lieutenant Hood in the car. I need to say my good byes but will not be long. I tell him as Mike heads up to the house. Inside the house are Roy, Sunny, Linda and the children waiting for me.

Roy is the first to speak, "Eric I want to thank you for this. I will live up to it. I must say I am a little scared."

"Roy you will do fine. I trust you. Both you and Mike are not only my friends, but also I think of you as brothers. Mike do you have a cold beer?" I ask.

"Yes I do and that sounds like a pregnant idea." Mike answers as he heads to the icebox.

As Mike leaves, Linda comes over and gives me a hug. Whispering in my ear, "I know you had a lot to do with Mike's acceptance into flight school, but I will not tell him." I try not to look shocked by this. Sunny then comes over to me, and gives me a hug. "Saying thanks you. Roy will be good as an officer." I tell her, "I know he will."

Mike is standing behind me with three cold beers. "Here you look like you could use this." He says as he hands me one. He gives the other to Roy and says, "Let's toast the Three Musketeers."

We tap our bottles and drink. I say my good-byes and start out the door. Mike and Roy follow me out. By the car, with Lieutenant Hood holding a backdoor open for me. Roy says, "So now we are Musketeers."

Mike answers, "Yeah that is the only thing that came to mind back there."

I answer that is "ok. Now the two of you know by the changes that have taken place. It will mean more time away from home and your families don't you?"

Both Mike and Roy simultaneously answer, "Yes we do and so does the family." We hug and I enter the car and drive away.

On the way to meet General Rogers, Lieutenant Hood hands me a role of mints saying you may want some of these.

"Thank you is it that obvious?"

"Yes Sir, I can tell you had a beer." I was a little surprised that Roy did not say anything about what happened after the meeting, because I know he could not with all those people around. The flight line building is the same as the time before except there is only one plane sitting alongside the building. It is a small executive type jet with U.S. Air force marking. The plane is closed up, and no one is around. So the Lieutenant and I head into the building.

Still sitting at the reception desk is Corporal Lovette. Lieutenant Hood walks ahead of me and up to her. She snaps to attention and salutes him. "Sir, May I help you sir?" She asks.

"Yes you may. The Colonel and I are here to meet General Rogers." She looks at me with a shocked look on her face. I think she remembers me.

"Excuse me Sir; I did not see you there." She says to me with a salute.

"That is ok" I answer.

"Colonel Howard, the General is in waiting room one. I will show you the way Sir." She states as she stands and leads the way. Just inside the hall that leads to Captain Drowns office, Corporal Lovette stops and knocks on a door marked with a large number 1.

A voice from inside asks. "Who is it?"

Corporal Lovette answers, "It is Corporal Lovette and I have Colonel Howard with me."

The voice answers. "Good, let him in."

I say, "Thanks" to Corporal Lovette and enter the room. The room looks just like any waiting room in an airport except the chairs here are well padded. There is a coffeepot on a table under the window; beside the windows that look out at the plane is a door. I see a large TV hung from one of the walls and several desks with phones on the other wall.

General Rogers comes over to me and tells me we will be leaving shortly. He then goes on to say, "If you need to use the phone go ahead."

I tell him "thank you" and head to the phone. Siting in front of the window looking out at the plane are General Lee and his Aide, Mr. Washington, Mr. Laurence Baker and a Major I have not be introduced to. After making a phone call to Debbie and only being able to leave a message, I go have a cup of coffee.

At the coffee table, the Major I saw comes over to me and says, "Colonel Howard I would like to introduce myself. My name is Alexander Stephens and I am General Rogers Aide".

"Nice to meet you" I say.

I have just finished making a cup of coffee, when an Air Force Major enters through the door to the outside.

"Gentlemen, we are ready to board."

I stay by the coffeepot trying to take a drink of very hot coffee. As General Lee is at the door, he turns to me and asks.

"Are you coming with us or have you changed your mind?"

"No Sir, I have not changed my mind. I was just trying to have a little coffee before we go." I answer.

"Coronel, the Air Force has coffee on their planes." I put my cup in the wastebasket and follow General Lee out and on to the plane.

Once airborne, Generals Lee and Rogers sit talking with each other in the front row of seats. The two CIA men are huddled in the last row and Major Stephens and I are about in the middle. I say to the Major. "I was told there is coffee on this flight. Where is the coffee?"

Major Stephens asks, "How do you take it? One sugar and a little cream I tell him with a question like tone. The Major stands and tells me" he will bring it for me."

After we land at Andrews Air Force Base, General Rogers takes me to meet the travel coordinator.

"Captain, this is Colonel Howard. We have arranged for him

to be flown to New York. Do you have the arrangements?"

"Yes General we do, I will tell his pilot he is here," the Air Force Captain answers.

General Rogers puts out his hand saying, "Colonel I will see you on Tuesday. Enjoy your weekend for all hell is going to break loose next week." I say "thank-you Sir" and shake his hand.

As he walks away, a strange thought pops into my mind, something I had read as a kid back Kentucky. It was from Dante's Divine Comedy; in the part called "the Inferno" was the inscription on the gates to hell. The part that hit home now was this, "ABANDON ALL HOPE YE WHO ENTER HERE" So is this my gates and am I entering the inferno?

Here I was so deep in my thoughts; I do not hear someone calling my name. I must have jumped three feet in the air when someone taped me on the arm. I turned to see an Air Force Captain looking just as shocked as I was.

"Sir, I am here to fly you to New York. Please follow me." After my heart rate is somewhat back to normal, I am told we are almost at McGuire Air Force Base, Wrightstown, New Jersey, and to buckle up. After we land, I transfer to a helicopter for the final leg of my trip home. I cannot wait to see my wife and children.

We land at La Guardia Airport just in time for me to see Debbie enter the waiting room. We run to each other and hug. I tell her how happy I am to be home, even if it is only for a short time.

The drive to our penthouse apartment is not an easy one, as New York traffic crossing from Queens to Manhattan is always heavy and it seems worse today. That could be, because I want to be home. My time at home goes by too quickly. We have talked a lot about what we will do when I am back at Benning. Debbie tells me that she has talked with her partners in the Medical Practice about her moving to Fort Benning and they told her she could keep her association with them as she has gained a big following. She has also been doing some checking on working with the hospital in Columbus, Georgia and at the base hospital. I tell her that I will talk with General Shefler about being associated with the base hospital if that is what she really wants.

Debbie tells me, "Yes Eric, that is what I want, and I think it would be the best for all of us. Now that Chucky is living with your Grandfather in Kentucky, we only have Ingrid and Ray at home for now. Eric Jr. will be born in July, and I would like to have him here in New York. We could then setup our home in Georgia just before school starts. Ray says he wants to go to VMI, but what does a five-year-old know."

I answer "Debbie he has spent the last two summers with Chucky and Great Grandpa and that could be playing a part in him thinking that way. You know what it is like down there."

"Yes I do" she answers.

The night before I am due in Washington the doorman rings the apartment, I answer. He informs me that there are two men that want to come to our apartment. I ask the doorman who they are. He tells me "they are from the Pentagon, I have checked their ID's and they say they need to see you."

I tell him "it is ok to send them up." I meet them at the elevator door. This elevator only has two stops. One stop is in the lobby, and the other in our apartment. I do not know them. They introduce themselves as Lieutenants Gigos and Henders. Lieutenant Gigos tells me that they will be back at 0700 to escort me to Washington.

I ask, "Why do I need and escort?" I am told because General

Rogers has some information I need to have before arriving in Washington. They will give the information to me in the morning to go over on my trip. I tell them "ok and I will be out front at 0700."

Lieutenant Henders asks me, "Sir would you please wait till we have your doorman call you to tell you we are here?"

I tell him, "Yes I will wait till then." As they enter the elevator and the door closes, I turn to see Debbie standing about 5 feet behind me.

"This is real cloak and dagger stuff isn't it?" She asks.

"I imagine so. But let's not think about that now" I answer.

Once in bed for the night I try to explain to her about what my job in the Army. In as easy a way as possible, I tell her about the covert nature of what Special Forces is all about. How from time to time we cannot tell those we love where we are going or when we will be back. I also tell her about the way we do not exist and how important it is that it stays that way.

Debbie asks one of the hardest questions I have had to answer, "Eric if something ever happened to you would I know?"

"Yes you would. You may not know right away or be told where, when or how. However in time you would have a good idea. I cannot tell you more then that. Just remember I love you with all of my being, and that will never change." Debbie gives me a big hug and kiss, with her holding me tight we fall a sleep.

At 0705, the doorman calls to tell me my ride is here. I tell him I will be right down. After I say "good by" to Ingrid and Ray, and give Debbie a big hug and kiss, I enter the elevator. As the door is closing, Debbie tells me to "be safe and come home soon." Once in the car Lieutenant Gigos hands me a large brown folder. I do not open it as we drive cross-town to La Guardia Airport. At the airport, we board a helicopter and fly to McGuire Air Force base to board a plane to Andrews Air Force Base. On the flight I open the folder, and review the photos, maps and reports it holds.

At Andrews Air Force Base, a car and driver meet us. He takes us straight to the Pentagon. Once in the Building, I am escorted to the office of General Rogers.

"Coronel Howard welcome. I am glad you are here. First, let me introduce Captain Martin Gray he will be your Aide while you are with us here at the Pentagon. He will take you for your photo and processing of the paper work you will need here. You will be given total access to all areas of the Pentagon, and to the briefing and situation room at the White House. Your office is just down the hall. After you have a chance to settle in, we will meet. You can meet the rest of your team. I am informed the processing take about three hours. So let's meet in the conference room near your office say at 1400."

"Sir may I have a word with you in private?" I ask.

General Rogers orders Captain Gray to wait in the outer office and then asks me "What do you want to talk about Colonel?"

I answer, "Sir, I would like to know whom I am working with and their background. I really do not think I could be comfortable with non-Special Forces personnel on this project. I do not mean to step on any toes. It is just the lack of training, I am concerned about. I had a real bad time with some Non-SF in Vietnam."

"Coronel I understand your concern, and let me assure you that the only people that are or will be involved other then low level people are all S.F. or CIA. There will be a chance for you to go over your staff records. At which time, it is your choice to keep or replace personal. The low-level personnel will only know a very small singular portion of what they are working on. Just enough to do what is needed of them and no more."

"Colonel Howard, are you aware of the fact that I'm not Special Forces personnel?"

"Yes Sir I am Sir." I answer.

"Does that worry you?" the General asks.

"No Sir, it does not because Generals Lee and Shefler tell me you are a good man and one that can be trusted."

"So what I am hearing from you is that you already checked me out. Is that correct Colonel?"

"Yes Sir it is." I answer.

"Good, I am glad to hear you did that and your honest enough to admit it. That is what I would have expected. It is that attention to detail, leaving very little to chance that brought you here," the General tells me as he opens the door to the outer office. In the outer office, General Rogers says, "Captain, take the Colonel to processing."

"Yes Sir."

"Colonel Howard, if there is anything you want or need ask the Captain and he will see to it. Have a good morning." He then turns and enters his office, closing the door behind him.

Major Stephens looks at me and asks, "Sir if I may ask what you said to the General?"

"Why do you ask?" I reply.

The Major answers, "Sir because, as he returned to his office he had a smirk on his face like I have not seen in a long time, well not at least since the situation in Vietnam turned so bad."

"Thank you for telling me that Major" I answer, as I leave the office.

As Captain Gray and I are walking through the building headed for the security office, I ask him about his background. He tells me he went through R.O.T.C. at the University of Kentucky, made it to the 49th week of Special Forces Training before he broke his left leg, and was sent to a Ranger brigade. He then spent one year in Nam with a LIRP unit; he was assigned to the Pentagon four years ago and wants out of here.

I ask him "why out of here."

"Because I want to return to a real Army unit." "A unit where I can do something besides push paper all day."

In my mind, I am starting to like this guy; maybe not everyone here is a REMF. I ask him if he had given any thought of going back to S.F.

"Yes Sir, I have, but I do not think I could requalify. The leg had to have a metal plate screwed to the bone to repair it. I tell him if he wants to go have the leg checked, and let me know what they have to say. The Captain tells me he will. The paper work takes forever. It is close to noon when we are finished. But I am not in the mood for food, there is some thing heavy going on, and I have a bad feeling about it.

Chapter 29

I ask Captain Gray to lead me to my office. My office is set up just like General Rogers. There is an outer office where Captain Gray has set up shop. The inner office is large with a huge desk set in front of the windows. There is a conference table to one side of the door that seats eight people. To the other side of the door is a seating area with six overstuffed chairs around a coffee table. Along one wall is a table with a coffeepot and ceramic cups with the emblem of the U.S. Army on them. There is sugar and cream set out next to the cups. A small under counter refrigerator and file cabinets are placed under the table. The opposite wall has file cabinets surrounding a door that leads to a private bathroom that has a shower.

Once in the office I ask the Captain to leave, until ten minutes before the meeting is to start. I want time to think and try to wrap my head around all that is going on in my life now. He tells me he will be at his desk and will call me when it is time for us to go. I say "thank-you" and close my door.

What a way to start a new chapter in my life. I am just back on active duty with a promotion, stationed in Washington, DC at the Pentagon, working with people that out rank me, only to have them answering to me. I do not know whom I answer to, or who will be my direct overseer. What position does General Rogers have in this, and is he one of the people I answer to. Exactly what roll does Colonels Tate, Coleman, Stone and Bates play in this, not to mention Laurence Baker?

I must have dozed off because the phone ringing causes me to jump for cover, just as if I was back in The Nam. Once I regain my composure, I pick up the phone. It is Captain Gray telling me we have to go now. I ask for a couple of seconds, as I need to prepare myself. The answer is we must leave in five minutes. I enter the bathroom; on the counter next to the sink are a toothbrush and a comb. In the cabinet above the sink is toothpaste, aspirin, antacid tablets, eye drops and mouthwash. There are hand towels on a rod by the sink and bath towels on a rod by the shower. The floor has a big bath mat that just about covers the floor. I wash my face, comb what little hair I have and brush my teeth.

Once out in the other office, Captain Gray asks me "if I am all right."

"Yes I am but why do you ask?" I say to him.

He answers with "You just look like you could use some sleep."

"Do I look that bad I ask?"

"No Sir, You just do not look as bright as you did."

"Ok then let's put this show on the road" I answer.

We walk down the hall a short way and turn left into a small room where two MP's meet us. I show my ID, and am allowed to enter, but Captain Gray is stopped. I turn to the MP's, and ask what is going on. The E-7 MP tells me that Captain Gray is not on his list as people that can enter.

"I ask him who gave him the list." He tells me it was General Rogers. I then ask, "If the General also told him who could add people to the list?"

"Yes Sir, I was told you and you alone could add to the list." The E-7 answers.

"Good then add the Captain."

"Yes Sir, he is added, Sir."

After we are in the room, Captain Gray asks, "Colonel, do you need me here?"

"Yes I do, I need you to take notes for me. Understand?"

"Yes Sir I do" was his answer."

"Now, you have been informed that what is said and done in this room and whenever you are with me is of the utmost secrete. I do hope General Rogers told you that."

"Yes Sir he has had me do the secrets act."

"Good" I answer.

The room has no windows and is set up with a large white board on one wall. The other walls are covered with wood with nothing on then. There is a slide and a movie projector on a table in front of the board. The chairs are set in two columns of ten rows facing the board. Off to the right side of the front is a podium with a mike and light placed on it. There is no one here but the Captain and I, so I walk to the back of the room and take a seat in the last of the ten rows of ten chairs each.

We just sit down when nine people enter the room. General Rogers leads the way followed by a Five Star General, a Three Star General and six men in suits. General Rogers goes to the podium as the others take seats in the second row. Military personal sit on the right side of the center aisle, with the men in suits taking the left side.

General Rogers starts by asking me "to please move to the front row". Both Captain Gray and I move up to the front row right side. General Rogers then starts by introducing the people present. "Gentlemen let me start with Colonel Eric C. Howard. Colonel Howard, please stand. This is the person in charge of all operations for a yet to be named program to help the indigenous people of Southeast Asia. Colonel, you may be seated. Next, we have General of the Army (five Stars) Douglas Southerfield General Southerfield is the Commander of the Joint Chefs of Staff. I am General (four stars) Peter Rogers; next we have Lieutenant (three stars) General Brodrick Belliome, Military Commander, Southeast Asia."

"On the other side of the aisle we have Mr. Kyle Kreis, Director CIA; next to him are Mr. Raymond Stearns, Deputy Director CIA, for Asian Affairs. Then we have Mr. Bertram Belford, Deputy Director CIA, Internal Affairs, Mr. Otis Collins, Deputy Director CIA, Military Affairs, Mr. Laurence Baker, Liaison CIA/Coronel Howard and lastly, Mr. Gary Sevenson, Office of the President of the United States."

"Now that we have that out of the way, let's go onto what we are here for. First, it is understood nothing said in this room is to be discussed with anyone not cleared to be privy to the information. Colonel Howard is the only person that is allowed to put cleared personnel on the list of from this time on. He also is the one who has the last word in who is to be removed from said list. Now Mr. Sevenson, would you like to say a few words?

"Yes I would and thank-you for asking. Coronel Howard on behalf of the President, let me thank-you for taking on such a big project. He has been informed of your record and is pleased you on are onboard. He would like to ask you to dine with him and the First Lady on Saturday, if time permits."

I tell him. "Thank-you and I would be honored too." Mr. Sevenson then returns to his seat.

General Rogers returns to the podium and says, "Gentleman as you are all well aware we have a situation in Viet Nam that must be resolved as soon as possible. Colonel Howard has already started the process by having one of his team from Nam start to build a team to return to Nam at this time. Lieutenant Forestin will be ready to jump off soon and needs our help."

"I would now like to have each of our members present say a few words about their section and its involvement in this operation. Let us start with General Belliome. General Belliome, please step forward."

As The General takes the podium, the lights go dim and a map appears on the screen. It is a map showing where the covert operation teams are located. By each team is a list of the personnel stationed there, the specialties and equipment of each station and the designation of that team. It shows all special operation teams, not only Army, but also all the other branches of service and other government assets available. General Belford takes about one half hour to go over the notes. The lights come up and he then asks Mr. Stearns to come forward.

Mr. Stearns goes to the board as a flow chart is displayed on the board. "Gentlemen this is a flow chart of our assets in Asia. As you can see, we are spread thin at this time. We will have a larger unit in Thailand within the next ten days. Their assignment will be to assist this operation. Our air units in the area will be at you disposal. I will go over that in more detail later. Now let's hear from Mr. Collins."

Mr. Collins walks to the podium, and starts "Gentlemen we have had a long lasting program of cooperation between the military and the company. That will not change as we are just as committed to helping our Allies as you are. Our work with the Army will not change. I have assigned Mr. Laurence Baker as our Liaison officer. Mr. Baker has had experience working with Special Forces and has spoken with the Colonel before on several occasions. Mr. Baker, Please stand up. I will now turn this program back over to General Rogers."

General Rogers takes the mike and says, "Now that we have all met as a group, Colonel Howard needs to meet with you, one on one so you can brief him on your parts in this. We will take a break after Colonel Howard has a few words.

As I stand up and move to the podium General Rogers tells me he will see me in my office in 30 minutes, and leaves the room stopping briefly at General Southerfield, Mr. Kreis and Mr. Sevenson seats taking them with him out of the room. I have no idea of what to say to his group of men. I am at a loss for words.

After a brief moment I start, "Gentlemen, we have a large task to perform. All I can ask of you is to discharge the work you are asked to do to the best of your ability. I have no question that each and every one of you is the best person for the job. I will give this assignment my all, and that is all I can ask of you. Secrecy is of the utmost importance on this, so let us keep it that way. I would like to see each one of you in my office as soon as your schedule would allow. My Aide Captain Gray, please Stand, here will have my schedule. Please call him as soon as possible to set up a time. Thank you."

As everyone leaves, they stop and shake my hand saying, "welcome on board." They also hand me a card with their name and direct, private, phone number.

After the room is empty Captain Gray says, "Sir I had no idea this was going to be an assignment with such a high level of people. I gather you will have to be very careful with what you say and do."

I answer, "Captain Gray, this is who I am, and I will not change. I do not kiss ass. Just to let you, I do not pull punches; I tell it like it is to anyone. Do not expect me to sugar coat anything, even to the President. If they do not like what I say or do to complete the job that is their problem. Is that clear?"

"Yes Sir, I was told you were a person that did what needed to be done and did not compromise."

"Good then, we understand each other and that will be no problem."

"Yes Sir! Now let's go to my office and see what is up there."

My office is empty when we arrive, but not for long. I enter my office and Captain Gray takes up his place behind his desk. A short time later, after I am having a cup of coffee, when Captain Gray call me on the intercom and tells me Major Stephens is here to see me. I tell him to "let the Major in."

The Major enters, and gives me a salute. "Sir, General Rogers and the others are on their way to the White House. I am here to drive you over there."

As we leave the Pentagon and enter the heavy traffic on the bridge, my mind is going 600 mph. What am I doing here? The White House, the Pentagon and all these people looking to me. WHY??? God did I do something wrong. Or on the other hand, maybe they think I can do something I do not think I can. What kind of shit am I in now? As we make our way through D.C., the traffic just keep going and going. Boy to be back home in the hills of Kentucky, where if you see three cars on the road at the same time, it is either a Wedding or a Funeral procession.

I am just a poor little old country boy from the hills of Kentucky. I am so deep in my thoughts; I do not even realize we have arrived. Major Stephens had the door open and snaps me back with "Sir, we are here."

After several I.D. checks and walking through several doors, we enter a large room. There are maps on all the walls, and TV sets everywhere.

As I enter, General Rogers comes over to me and says, "This is where we brief the President. He has an interest in what you will be doing, and we needed to show you this place. The President will be along later. Please take a seat on the right side of the table."

In the middle of the room sits a long table with six chairs on a side. At one end of the table is a large leather chair; behind the chair is a dark wooden door with the plaque of the President on it. As I move to sit in the most distant spot away from the head of the table, General Southerfield takes my arm and tells me to move down next to him, that puts me one chair away from the head of the table. He tells Major Stephens to wait outside, on the other side of the table is Mr. Kreis and next to him is someone I have not met as of yet.

General Southerfield turns to me and says, "Colonel Howard, I would like to introduce Mr. Loc Van Du. Mister Du is with the CIA. His family is from Thailand, and works for our joint operations team in Bangkok. (I do not like the looks of this but say nothing)

Mr. Du stands and bows to me then puts out his hand. I bow back, and shake his hand. His handshake is like a wet, limp dishrag (One more reason not to trust) He tells me clearly in English that he looks forward to helping in any way he can.

I ask him in Montagnard; "Do you think they will be able to escape?" His expression tells me he does not understand Montagnard language. With a pained expression on his face, he tells me that he did not understand. So in Vietnamese, I ask the same question, again he does not understand. This time I ask him in English, and he asks, "Can who escape?" Not a good answer goes through my mind, but then again, he may not know. Someone enters the room and asking Mr. Du to come with them.

Mr. Kreis looks and me and says, "Colonel Howard that was someone we wanted your opinion of. I know that was a very short time, but you will meet him again. We do not know if he would or could work out as a contact in Thailand.

"Sir, do you have a jacket on him?" I ask.

"Yes we do and it will be in your office when you return."

"I will also need to contact some people I know in South Bend, IN. They are people that were part of a special group of Vietnamese rangers; we trained our first year in country and had contact with throughout my time in country. They can be trusted. They are well aware of all the turncoats in the government and military service and kept a close eye on them. They would use the turncoats to feed bad intelligence to the North from time to time. I would trust these people. When I find out whom I can trust here, I will give you their names. Yes, I know how that sounds, but I still need to know. Mr. Kreis, if I am the one in charge of this operation, I must have no suspicions of anyone who has knowledge of where my men are or what they are doing. The people involved must be trusted beyond a shadow of a doubt. There are too many people in that part of the world that have a second agenda. I have also come to believe that we also have people in this country that may or may not have your back when it is to their advantage. Politics sometimes plays a big part in what side people are on. For me to trust without clear knowledge of what is behind someone's motives is hard to do. If I cannot trust the people involved, I can not do this job."

Before I could finish saying what was on my mind, the large door with the Presidential Seal opens and two men in suits walk in followed by the President.

The President walks over to me and says, "You must be Colonel Howard, as I know the others present."

I stood up and gave him a salute saying, "Sir. Yes Sir I am." He puts out his hand and tells me "Welcome."

He then takes his seat at the head of the table. He dismisses the two men that came in with him. After they left the room, he turns his attention to General Southerfield. "Doug, do you have anything to report as to progress in our predicament in Viet Nam?"

General Southerfield answers, "Yes Sir, I do. We have not been able to make contact with those we have a need too. Colonel Howard has requested we close the loop on those in the know. I have not informed him as to whom his supervisors are to be. I have given him total oversight as to the people below him. As of today, there are only sixteen people that have any enlightenment as to what the project is. Mr. President, it is of the utmost importance that we keep the operation on a need to know basis. The fewer people that have knowledge the better chance we have of completing what must be done."

The President put his hand up to stop the General. "General I am well aware of the sensitive nature of what is going on. I know you will keep the trust of the American people uppermost in mind. With public opinion as it is today, I do not want to inflame them anymore then is needed. No one outside of this room and only those who need to know are to have a full picture of what is going on. Colonel Howard, you are to be in charge of this Operation. You will only have to answer to Mr. Kreis and General Southerfield. They will inform me as to the progress of the operations needed to bring this to a close. I will not have anything to do with how, when or where it happens. As for the ultimate decisions, Mr. Kreis will make them. I want this to be a total covert operation headed by the CIA. As of this time you, Colonel Howard, you are assigned to the CIA. You will need the total cooperation of the Military. General Southerfield will be in the loop, and will give you any and everything you need to bring this operation to good conclusion. Is everyone in agreement? Since I hear no disagreement, this meeting is over. Gentlemen, let us resolve the problem. Colonel Howard, I will see you and your wife on Saturday at 7:00 pm." He then stands and leaves the room.

General Southerfield looks at me and says, "Colonel Howard, it is now up to you to bring home the bacon. I would like a list of the people you want involved at the start as soon as possible. Mr. Kreis will be taking you back to your office. I will see you in the morning." He stands and leaves the room.

That leaves just Mr. Kreis and me sitting in the room looking across the table at one another. As he is opening a large briefcase, my mind slips back to all the feelings I had about the spooks from the CIA and the trouble they caused us in the Nam. (Now here I sit, in the White House, across the table from the head of that group of spooks. It cannot be Halloween; it is only June, I think. Oh My God. The guys were correct, I am now a spook)

Mr. Kreis has put a stack of papers in front of me, and he has part of the stack too. "Colonel Howard, lets start with us calling each other by our first names. That will be quicker and easier in the long run that is when we are alone. OK?"

"Yes Sir, it will make this go a lot smoother." is my answer.

"Eric the first three pages in front of you are your orders assigning you to the Company. The next is an acknowledgement of the order for you to sign. Then you will find an agreement that you received a copy of the regulations of the Company for your signature. Then there are the rules and regulations for you to read. Finally, you will find an ID card and Pass Card for your office in Langley. A form for you to sign that you received the ID and Pass Card, then the form for the car you will use while here in this area. It has radio and other special equipment that will be shown to you when we arrive at the garage in Langley. You have no need to be in uniform from this point on, except when working in the Pentagon, but then only when you feel the need too. You now work for the Company. A new passport, a permit to carry a weapon and a Virginia driver's license will be issued to you in the next two days. We have a house for you half way between Headquarters and D.C. It has all the safety equipment needed and is in a very nice area. After we are finished back at Langley, Mr. Baker will show you the way there and help you settle in. Now please sign the forms marked with clips, and we can be on our way." I sign the forms and we leave for Langley. On the nine-mile drive, my mind is just spinning.

As we approach a large gate with a sentry box next to it, an armed guard steps out. He looks at the sticker on the windshield then comes to the driver side door. The driver opens the window and hands him some papers. As the guard is reading, Mr. Kreis opens his window, the guard looks in and steps back. With a wave of his hand, someone in the sentry box opens the gate for us to enter. Once in the underground garage, we park in a slot with a plaque that just reads Mr. K. Kreis. In the stall next to his, sits a black Chevrolet Suburban. The windows are tinted almost black. The plaque on the wall reads Mr. D. Howard. I say nothing as we exit the car, and head to an elevator. Mr. Kreis uses a key to start the elevator and up we go. As we exit the elevator, there is a man standing who takes the file folder from Mr. Kreis and asks me to follow him. As I walk away, Mr. Kreis says "Mr. Howard, be in my office in the morning that is when you get a chance, after your meeting at the Pentagon."

I am lead to a large office with a plaque that reads Mr. D. C. Howard on the wall next to the door. The man leading the way opens the door with a key. Once inside there is a large desk about ten paces in from the door. The wall behind the desk has an oil painting of Jungle scenes. Just to the right side of the desk between the painting is a door. The left side of the room has file cabinets. The right side of the room is set up with chairs and small tables. There is no one at the desk. We walk across the room only to have him use a different key to open this door. This room looks like set up for someone very important. There in front of me are windows that cover the entire wall. In front of the windows is a huge dark wooden desk. Behind the desk is a high-backed chair. The desk is set with what looks like an expensive set up. Wooden in and out boxes, pen and pencil set, a small American Flag and a telephone that looks like could be the instrument panel in a large aircraft. To the right of the desk is a cabinet that is more then likely a drink cabinet, next to it is a sideboard with a coffeepot, cups and glass holder for sugar, cream and spoons. To the left is a seating area of overstuffed chairs with a large round table. There is also a door that goes somewhere, as I find out later that it leads to a private bathroom complete with shower and sauna.

I am told to take a seat. I sit in one of the overstuffed chairs, and he sits down across from me. "Mr. Howard, my name is Thomas Pealer. I am assigned as your guide through the maze here at Langley. I will also be your Second Assistant."

"Thomas, may I call you Tom?" I ask.

"Yes you may, when we are not with the others around here, may I call you Eric?"

"Yes you may. Now I have question for you. What do you mean by Second Assistant? Who is tapped to be my first assistant?"

"Eric that is your choice within certain limits."

I say "and I bet I know what they are" I would like to have Captain Martin Gray. He is my aide at the Pentagon, and to have him here, would make life a lot easier."

"That is just what Mr. Kreis said you would say." Tom answered. "We will contact the Pentagon and see what can be done."

I answer. "When you contact the Pentagon tell General Southerfield that is what I want and will not take no for an answer."

"Will do. Now this is your office, here are the keys to this office, and to your car, which is in the garage below. This set is the keys to your house, and gate at your house. Do you have any questions? Or should we just head over to you house now?" We head to my new quarters.

The grounds have a high metal picket fence all around. There are metal gates across the drive. To enter you have to either punch in a pass code or talk into a phone that is in a case they are just short of the gates. Once inside the gate, the driveway curves up to the house. You cannot see the house from the gate. The house is a two-story colonial made of brick, not a bad looking house. I like the style.

As we arrive at the front door, a man comes out of the house and opens my door. He says, "Good evening Sir, May I take you bags?"

I was suddenly snapper to a realization. Where are my bags? When was the last time I saw them? Did they come with me from New York? As this is going through my mind, Thomas Pealer tells the butler the bags are in the back. Now I am confused. How did they wind up here?

Tom tells me, "Captain Gray had them sent over to the company earlier in the day."

Boy what is going on? I now have two offices, an Aide, a Second Assistant and a butler. What next…..?

As we enter the house the butler says, "Sir, I would like to introduce your house staff. My name is Harold. This is Rose the maid. Antonio is your cook and Alfio is the gardener."

"If you are hungry Sir, I will prepare something for you." Antonio tells me.

"No I am not I just want to take a shower and relax."

Harold tells me to follow him and he will show me to my room. As we head for the stairs,

Tom says, "Sir I will be in the library when you are ready to go over some things.

"Just give me a minute to change clothes and I will be back down. "After a quick shower and quick change into jeans and a sweatshirt, I return to find Tom in the library. As I walk into the library, Tom is sitting at a large desk with a stack of paperwork in front of him. We spend about an hour going over what is in the house and how to use it. I am to change the code for the phone system I am to use. I find there are three lines coming into the house. One phone line is for the help, one for the Company and one for the Pentagon. I ask which am I to use to make personal call. I am told I can use anyone I want. There is a scrambler on the lines for the Company and the Pentagon, which I can turn off with the code. I ask if either of those lines had someone recording them. I am told no, only if I ask, to have the call recorded.

Tom can see I am very tired, so he tells me that he will be leaving now. "Captain Gray will be here at 0730 to take you to the Pentagon." He then asks me to call him when I leave the Pentagon in the morning.

I say, "OK, I just do not have a number to call you."

I am told Captain Gray has the number. After he is gone, I wander around the house to find out the lay of the land. After finding the kitchen and taking a Pepsi, I head off to bed.

Chapter 30

Sleep does not come easy, as my mind will not stop going in circles. Now what have I done, and what will I do to fix this? If I am to do this job right, I must be able to trust all those about me. What happens if I can not trust General Southerfield, and even more so the President. I know the President is Commander and Chief of the Military, but he is also a politician who has to stand for re-election. So I know he will be the first to cover his ass if this operation goes wrong. From the beginning I have been taught that the only things lower then a snakes belly are politicians and lawyers, and they are usually one in the same for the most part, especially when they are Yankees.

I have just fallen asleep, when the phone next to the bed rings. Bleary eyed I try to figure out what the noise is. After a few seconds it hits me, it is the phone. Now where that is dammed thing? Oh it is on the table to the left. I must remember to move that to the right.

"Yes" I say still half asleep.

"Colonel Howard, This is Captain Gray. Can you be ready to

go to the Pentagon in one hour?"

I look at the clock to see what time it is only to see it is 0530. "Captain, why are you calling me so early? I am not due to report in until 0800."

"Sir, I received a call about 20 minutes ago from Major Stephens, General Rogers aide. Something had come up and you are needed. There is a situation update meeting scheduled for 0700."

"OK, I will be ready, call from the front gate and someone will let you in."

After finishing the phone call I take a shower and put on my uniform because I will be in the Pentagon. I then take a wooden hanger; place a suit, a shirt, and tie on it, then cover all of this with a travel bag for suits. I stop and stand in the closet thinking. I am missing something. Oh! Yes I also need to take shoes and socks. I cannot wear a suit with jump boot. As I am about to leave the bedroom the phone rings again and that makes me jump. I pick it up to hear a voice that is familiar but I cannot place it at first.

The voice is saying, "Mr. Howard, breakfast is ready? Do you need any assistance?"

Now I know you it is. It is Harold. I tell him no I am fine, I will be right down. On my way downstairs, I see Harold standing by the front door. He hears me coming, turns toward me, and asks, "Sir, are you expecting a Captain Gray?"

"Yes I am, please let him in." I then look down at my watch and see he is about 25 minutes early. Looking for a place to hang my bag I see Rosalie coming over to me and reaching out to take the bag.

"Sir, I will hang that up for you." she says as she takes the bag moves toward a door under the stairs. With my bag hung up, Rosalie asks me to follow her. I do and windup in the dining room. The head of the table is set with a pot of coffee, a tall pitcher of orange juice, and a plate of sweet rolls.

After I have taken a seat, Antonio comes out of the kitchen, walks over to me and asks. "Sir would you like some breakfast. We have bacon, and fried potatoes prepared. How would you like your eggs prepared?"

"Thank you, yes I would like some bacon, three scrambled eggs, potatoes, and two slices of burnt toast. Do we have orange marmalade?" I ask.

"No sir we do not. I will put that on my shopping list. Is there anything else you like for breakfast?"

"Thank you for asking, and yes there is, I like to have cooked grits with my breakfast. Buttermilk Biscuits with sausage gravy are also very good." I say.

"I am sorry Sir; I did not know you were a Southerner. I will make the corrections to the meal plan." Antonio tells me.

"Antonio, please do not change your menu. I like all types of food. I like almost everything, with one exception. That exception being peanuts, I have an allergy to them, just the smell makes me ill." As I am telling him, he turns around and says, "Rosalie, put the peanut butter away quick. We can not have it out; I will explain it to you later." He then turns to me. "Sir I am so sorry, we did not know."

With a look of surprise on my face, I ask. "We all work for the same company, don't we?"

"Yes sir we do." he answers.

"Then was the staff here not briefed about me? If not that is a real surprise."

As we are talking, Rosalie brings in a large plate of bacon, a bowl of fried potatoes and a plate of scrambled eggs. Harold tells me that all they were told was that I am an Army Officer, assigned to the Company on a hush, hush project and that I was to be shown every courtesy.

The door bell rings stopping our conversation. I ask Harold to answer the front door. Harold returns with Captain Gray in tow. I say to Harold, "We will finish our conversation later." then I say to Captain Gray, "Sit down, we have time to eat breakfast before we go. Would you like something?"

"No thank you Sir. I have eaten."

As I am about finished with my breakfast, Harold brings a phone to the table. "Sir it is a Mr. Kreis."

"Thank you, you may take the dishes" I pick up the phone and say, "Good morning Mr. Kreis, Mr. Howard here." (Boy it is going to take sometime and a lot of work to become comfortable with this civilian speak)

"Mr. Howard, this is Mr. Kreis. I will be meeting you in the situation room at the Pentagon. Do you have Mr. Pealer with you?"

"No Sir, I do not" I answer. I have not seen him since yesterday. He left here about 2100 last night Sir. He told me Captain Gray would know how to contact him, and I was to let him know when I was leaving the Pentagon for Langley."

Mr. Kreis answers, "Would you have Captain Gray contact him and have him met us at the Pentagon as soon as possible?"

"Yes Sir I will"

"Good I will meet you at the Pentagon in 30 minutes. " Mr. Kreis says and hangs up.

I tell Captain Gray to contact Mr. Pealer as we head out the door. Once in the car, Captain Gray tries to contact Mr. Pealer to no avail. The drive to the Pentagon takes longer then anticipated because of heavy traffic. We pull into the parking garage and head up to the Situation Room. Waiting in the Situation Room is General Rogers, Mr. Baker, Mr. Washington, Colonel Wallace, Lieutenant General Belliome, Mr. Kreis and Mr. Collins.

As we enter General Belliome stands and comes over to me. "Colonel Howard, please follow me. General Southerfield and Mr. Sevenson are waiting in the Generals office for us."

Mr. Kreis follows us out of the room and down the hall. At the Generals office Major Kyle Dorsen meets us. "Gentlemen please follow me the others are in the small conference room" we are told. As we enter the room, everyone stands and I am directed to a chair between General Southerfield and Mr. Sevenson. The rest are told to take a seat.

General Southerfield states. "Gentlemen, we have a situation" He then has an overhead projector turned on and an over flight photo is displayed. "This photo came in early this morning. As you can see the area in the center is devastated. Late last night the NVA mortared this area heavily and then overran an A-Team camp. This camp was to be the jump off point for our recovery of the indigenous personnel we have been speaking of. The team and their people did make it out but not without losses. We have lost contact with them since. "Colonel Howard, do you think your recovery team is ready? If not, how soon can we have them on their way?"

"Sir I have not been updated on their disposition since yesterday." "May I have the use of a secure line to check?"

"Yes you may."

"We will adjourn for one half hour."

"Major Kyle Dorsen, take the Colonel to the Communication Center, stay with him and then return to my office as soon as possible."

"Gentlemen please return to the situation room, we will be there as soon as we can."

"General Belliome, will you please bring the people in the situation room up to date on what we know?"

"Yes Sir I will. May I use the photos we have" General Belliome asks.

"Yes you may. Gentlemen we will be with you shortly." Everyone stands and leaves the room.

I follow Major Dorsen to the Como Room and am given a secure line to Fort Benning. I am connected to General Lee's office. After introductions and an exchange of pleasantries, I ask to speak with Lieutenant Forestin. I am told he is out in the practice area with the team and is not expected back till 1300 hours. I inform the operator that this is an urgent call. He needs to contact me in the Pentagon ASAP.

The operator answers. "Colonel Howard, I will send a runner for him." I thank him, and turn to Major Dorsen and ask, "Is there a secure line in General Southfield's Office?"

He answers. "Yes there is."

"Good, lets return there" I then go to the man in charge of the Como Center and tell him to put the call thru to General Southfield's office as soon as it comes in.

As we are heading back to the General's office, I ask, "Do you think the General will mind that I am having the call transferred to his office?"

"No Sir, I do not as he is very interested in this situation."

"Good let's get going." Why did he just not have me make the call from his office if he has a secure line?

The Major answers me with "Colonel Howard, the General had a call on hold that he was going to take when we left the meeting."

I say, "Thank you for letting me know."

As we are entering the Generals office, he stands and says, "Colonel Howard, here is your call. Please take it here." with that he hands me the phone and comes around from behind his desk.

I take the phone and say, "Hello this is Colonel Howard."

It is Roy and he asks. "Colonel Howard, is there a problem?"

I say. "Yes there is, can you hold a second." I turn to General Southerfield and ask, "General would you like to pickup the other phone to hear what is being said?"

He answers. "Yes I would if you do not mind?"

"No Sir, I do not mind just let me inform the Lieutenant, you will also be on the line, Sir." I return to Roy and tell him General of the Army Douglas Southerfield will be joining us on this line.

Roy says. "Is it that bad?"

General Southerfeild introduces himself to Roy. Roy in turn introduces himself to the General. The General then tells Roy. "Yes it could be that bad."

Roy with a slight quiver in his voice says. "Sir, May I ask why you are calling me?"

"Lieutenant, I will let the Colonel bring you up to speed."

I then tell Roy about what has happened and ask him how close he is to being able to jump off. There is silence on the other end of the line for sometime. "Colonel Howard, the team will be ready to go shortly."

I ask. "What needs to be done before you can jump off?"

"Colonel if I am may, the only thing holding us back is some of the people here not following through with their end of things."

With that said General Southerfield asks. "Is there anything we can do from this end?"

Roy answers. "Sir, the problem is in the logistics. As you are aware most people here do not know what we are doing, and that coupled with the fact that the ones that do know are so tied up with their normal daily operations, they let us slip thru the cracks. What would help us a lot is if someone here that is not going with us could do the logistical end of things, while we work on the preparation we need to complete."

The General then asks. "Lieutenant, if I were to have someone in place to take care of the logistics how long till you could go?"

Roy answers, "A day or two at the most. The final things that must be done can be taken care of on the flight over."

The General then tells Roy. "Lieutenant, thank you for your candor, I will take care of your problems. Someone will contact you shortly."

Roy answers. "Thank-you Sir" with that said the line goes dead.

General Southerfield turns to me and asks. "Colonel Howard, how would you handle this situation?"

I say. "We need a facilitator we can trust, someone that is experienced in this type of situation, and someone that knows the in's and out's of Benning. He must be Special Forces, and have first hand knowledge of the requirements."

"Colonel it sounds to me you are trying to sell yourself for this part of the job." The General tells me.

"Sir, no Sir I am not. If I were thinking of myself there would be more problems to solve. First, all the intelligence comes into Washington. Second, the people I need to talk with and receive information from are here. Third, I am still not settled in at the Pentagon or at Langley. The other side would be yes. I could possibly be the best person, because I know everyone there that could be of use to get the job done. After the team is in route, keeping the supply lines open would also be easier from Benning. But keeping updated with the Intelligence would be impossible, Sir"

"Colonel Howard, I understand what you are saying. This is a difficult position. If we are going to continue to have operations like this, they will need to be run out of a base set aside for just this type of operation. We have been discussing just that for several years. Part of what you were called in for was to be just in that type of base. Now let's go meet with the others and talk about to handle what is going on now."

"Yes Sir" I answer.

As we arrive at the Situation Room, we learn that some of the people that were there have gone for beverages. General Southerfield had his aide go and roundup everyone.

In just a short time, everyone is in the room and seated. General Southerfield stands at the podium and starts. "Gentlemen it appears we have a problem with logistics at Benning. There seems to be a snag in communications and follow-up between special operations and standard supply and logistics. As you know, we have talked about this before, and it appears it's not improving. The team we have setup for this mission is one to two days away from being able to commence the operation. The reason for the delay is the typical slow moving bureaucracy. The standard working needs of the line units are in the way of the special ops. Not that this is intentional; it stems from the workload. What we need to do is streamline the process. What are the ways to do this? Colonel Howard said something to me about this. Let's hear what the Colonel has to say."

I stand and start to speak only to have the General stop me, and tell me to come up to the podium.

At the podium I start again, "Gentlemen in my opinion we need someone we can trust, someone that is experienced in this type of situation, and someone that knows the in's and out's of Benning and its personnel. He must be Special Forces and have firsthand knowledge of the requirements and how to complete the mission, been there and done that kind of thing. He must be able to pull the loose ends together. Also most importantly, he must have the backing of those above him; those above him should only be the people in this room or their replacements."

As I am leaving the podium to return to my seat, I am stopped again by General Southerfield. He stands beside me and takes the microphone. "Gentlemen are there any questions or comments for the Colonel?"

Mr. Sevenson stands. "Yes, I have a question for the Colonel."

"Please state your question."

"Colonel Howard are you suggesting we form a special covert operational unit outside the arena of the Special Forces units? Also would this type of unit be made up of personnel from the other branches of the Military community?"

I answer. "I am not at this time suggesting forming any-thing other then having one person to augment the logistics of this operation. Although what you suggested is something we should think about, in my opinion that is. As you may be aware in Vietnam, we have a group known as Special Operations Group (SOG) that works outside of, not under, the military command of Southeast Asia. This system works well."

"Thank you Colonel" Mr. Sevenson says and sits down.

General Southerfield then asks if there are any other questions. "There being no other questions, gentlemen what are we to do now?"

General Brodrick stands. "General Southerfield while we were here waiting for you to return with the information on the extraction team, we talked about several options. One was if the team was delayed what could be done to speed it up. On the other hand, should we just cancel the operation? It was decided no matter what we need to go ahead. Now having heard what the Colonel had to say I am in favor of putting someone in Benning to pull it together ASAP. I would ask if there is anyone in opposition to this."

General Southerfield then asks. "Is any opposition to General Brodrick's suggestions?"

"None being stated then we will send an envoy to Benning for the purpose getting the mission underway." He then goes on. "Gentlemen are there any suggestions on who we send?"

General Rogers stands and says. "I would think the choice is obvious. I can not think of anyone better then Colonel Howard."

I answer. "Sir, as I have said to General Southerfield. There are pros and cons to that. Yes I could possibly be the best man for the job now and once the team is off. I say now because I know most of everyone there that could be used to get the job done. I say once the team is off, because to try to keep the supply lines open from here in Washington would be very difficult. Difficult because what may be needed by the team would be at Benning. The cons are all the information on the situation comes in through the Pentagon or Langley. The intelligence information to help the team once they are in the field would not be available as soon as it arrives. The lag between Washington and Benning could be deadly. The only way it could work would be either. One, there were two people involved one in Benning to get the team out, and one here to do the day by day follow-up work. The other way would be to have a fast way to have the information in Benning after the team is in the field."

Mr. Kreis then stands up and say. "There is a different way I would suggest. The man chosen would be in Benning to get the team out. Go with them to Thailand and setup in our command center there. All aerial photos and information go through there before coming to Langley. I also believe the safest way to insert a Covert Team for this mission is through Thailand."

I answer. "Mr. Kreis, The plan is to have the insertion of the team going through our base in Na Trang. Why move that to Thailand?"

"Colonel Howard, if a team were to be inserted from Na Trang could there not possibly be a leak? Coming from Thailand that would be lessened by time and distance."

I answer. "Yes it would, that is very good thinking. We still have to think about who to send."

General Southerfield then states, "Gentlemen, it is my suggestion we send Colonel Howard to Benning today to start the team on it way. We will then have him go with the team to Thailand and cover the rest of the rescue from there. Are there any questions?" He then looks at me with a look of not from you.

After a little time is spent on discussion, General Southerfield says. "Gentlemen there being no further discussion, it is decided Colonel Howard will be transferred to Benning today. There he will prepare and have the team out by 2300 tomorrow. He will then be transferred to the CIA station in Thailand for the remainder of the mission. Gentlemen, there being no further discussion I here by close this meeting. Mr. Kreis and Colonel Howard please meet me in my office. Thank you all for the input."

In General Southerfield's office the three of us take seat in the large overstuffed chairs. The General says to Mr. Kreis. "I am leaving it up to you to see that your people in Thailand are ready for what is coming their way."

Mr. Kreis answers. "I will have everything in place before your people arrive. I think the Colonel Howard and the team should go to Thailand as civilians, that way they will not draw suspicion. The needed equipment can go military. My people will meet them at Bangkok Airport. From there the team can go to the airbase. Colonel Howard will be taken to our office. Is that Ok with you Sir?"

I say. "Sir. I would think the team should go military that way the needed equipment will be with them at all times. I could go civilian."

General Southerfield thinks for sometime, and then says. "Mr. Kreis, I agree with the Colonel. The team will go military. Now as for the Colonel's travel planes. I will leave that up to him."

I ask. "If I go civilian are there less changes of blowing the cover on this mission, and do we know I if I am able to be booked on a flight to Bangkok?"

"Hold that thought." Mr. Kreis says as he reaches for the phone on the table next to him. The General and I get up and go to his bar for a drink. He fixes two bourbon and waters and hands me one. After a short conversation he hangs up. Mr. Kreis comes over to us and asks. "Colonel, can you be ready to leave from Atlanta by 2000 hours tomorrow?"

I answer, "Yes I can Sir."

"Good you are booked on flights to Bangkok. The only problem is the only seat I could book was in First Class from Los Angeles. You will be in coach from Atlanta to Los Angeles. Is that ok with you?"

In my mind, how do I answer this? Before I can say anything.

General Southerfield says. "That sounds good to me, now we have to fly the Colonel to Benning today. He calls his Aide into the room. "Major Dorsen, please make arrangements for Colonel Howard to fly Benning today at 1500 hours. The General then turns to me and asks. "Can you be ready by then?"

I answer "Yes Sir."

"Good that takes care of that."

Mr. Kreis tells me. "Colonel I will have a company credit card, ID, your new passport and weapons permit at your house in two hours. I think that takes care of everything on my end. What all taken care of I must get back to Langley, There is a lot for us to do. Good luck and good hunting Colonel"

I stop him and say. "Mr. Kreis, I have been informed by people I trust highly that Mr. Loc Van Du is a mole. Please do not inform him of anything we have spoken of."

"Thank you Mr. Howard, I will take care of this new problem." Mr. Kreis tells me.

As he leaves the room General Southerfield turns to me. "Colonel Howard, we will be expecting you back here when this is finished. If it is not too much would you spend sometime thinking about the Covert Operations System?"

"Yes Sir. I will."

"Good, Captain Gray will drive you back to your house." I salute the General and leave his office only to find Captain Gray in the outer office. He says, "Sir, Are you ready to leave?"

I answer. " Yes I am."

The drive to the house is silent, as I am thinking about what is to come, and that I have to call Debbie and tell her about what has transpired.

What has my life to bring now?

Glossary

A

A-TEAM A Special Forces Operational Detachment made up of a team of twelve men. In Vietnam, as well as other areas of operation, half teams of six or seven men are used on missions.

AIT Advanced Individual Training. The training soldiers get after basic. The schooling needed to learn the skills, or jobs the solders will do to be done.

AK-47 Russian or Chinese made Assault Rifle. Normally used by the NVA or Viet Cong. It was also preferred by some US troops, because it did not jam like the US made M-16.

Alpha Phonetic alphabet word for the letter A.

Ambush To attack or be attacked by surprise.

AN-109 Radio used by Special Forces for long-range communication.

A O Area of Operations

Arc Light B-52 bomber strike. The earth would shake up to 10 miles from the target area.

ARVN   Army of the Republic of South Vietnam. Also a nickname for South Vietnam solders.

ASAP   As Soon As Possible

B

B-52   American Heavy Bomber. Used to carry large payloads of bombs.

Ba-Choa   The Montagnard village we lived in.

Bennies   Benefits

Big Apple   New York City

Bird or Birds   Slang for the rank of Full Colonel

BOQ   Bachelor Officer Quarters

Browning M-35   Nine-millimeter automatic weapon favored by S.F.

Bravo   Phonetic alphabet word for the letter B.

Brig   Jail

Bush   The areas away from bases or base camps. Also anywhere you have little to no support.

C

C-130   A four-engine turboprop military transport aircraft which had a ramp under the tail that lowers.

C-4   A powerful plastic explosive. Can be used to cooking as well as a high energy explosive.

CH-47   Large twin rotors, twin engine Helicopter. Know as Chinook or by its slang name Shithook.

CH-57   The largest Helicopter. Strictly used for heavy lift cargo. Know as Skycrane.

Charlie   Phonetic alphabet word for the letter C. Also the slang for Viet Cong.

Chiev Hoi "I surrender" loosely in Vietnamese.

Chinook See CH-47

Chopper Slang for helicopter. Usually the UH-1. Also slang for a reworked motorcycle use by outlaw bikers.

Civvies Slang for civilian clothes.

CIDG Civilian Irregular Defense Group. Ethnic minorities trained by S.F. for village defense and commando operations.

Claymore Antipersonnel mine that fires a shaped charge of seven hundred and fifty steel balls with a range of fifty yards.

Como Slang for radio communications.

Como net radio (communications) network.

Cong Short for Viet Cong. Anyone you see by day could become a Cong by night and be your killer.

C.P. Command Post

C-Rats Combat Rations: Canned meals for use in the field.

Cricket Small metal child's toy that clicks when squeezed.

D

Delta Phonetic alphabet word for the letter D.

Demo Demolitions

DERO Date of Expected Return from Over Seas.

Dia-Uy Vietnamese for Captain.

Didi-Mau Vietnamese for Go Quickly.

Dink Slang for Asian.

Ditibag Slang for a cloth bag used for many purposes.

Dust Off To be flown out of the bush by Helicopter.

E

Echo   Phonetic alphabet word for the letter E.

E.M.   Enlisted Man.

E.T.S.   Emergency Transponder Signal.

F

F-4   Phantom Jet Fighter-Bomber. The workhorse of Tactical Air Support. Also called Fast Mover.

Fast Mover   See F-4

Fence   The borders of Laos, Cambodia, or the DMZ. These borders were not supposed to be crossed by Allied forces. Over the fence could be anywhere outside The Republic of South Vietnam.

Foxtrot   Phonetic alphabet word for the letter F.

Frag   Fragmentation Hand Grenade.

Freedom Bird   Slang for the flight that takes you back home after your tour is over.

Foo Gas   A mixture of explosives and napalm, usually set in a fifty-gallon drum

G

Garret   A thin piece of wire about two to three feet long with a wooden handle on each end. This is dropped over the head and snapped around the neck. If done fast and correctly the neck is severed and head may fall off.

GI   Slang for U.S. Soldier

Golf   Phonetic alphabet word for the letter G.

Gook   Slang for an Asian

Green Beret   See S.F.

Grunt   Slang for someone in the Infantry

H

HALO   High Altitude bailout, Low altitude Opening of para-chute. A technique of infiltration into an enemy controlled area. This is done mostly under the cover of darkness.

Hanoi Hilton   The main POW camp in Hanoi, North Vietnam. (PS not a nice place to stay)

HE   High Explosive

Hootch   A hut or small dwelling

Horn   The item used to make contact with someone. IE radio, phone.

Hotel   Phonetic alphabet word for the letter H.

Huey   UH-1 Helicopter. The workhorse of Army Aviation

Hump   To patrol the bush, to walk, to perform any arduous task.

HHC   Head Quarters and Head Quarters Company

I

India   Phonetic alphabet word for the letter I.

Incoming   A mortar attack. Also sometimes called incoming mail.

J

Jag   Judge Advocate Corp. The Army Lawyers

Jupiter   Phonetic alphabet word for the letter J.

K

Kelo   Phonetic alphabet word for the letter K.

KIA   Killed In Action

Klick   One kilometer

L

Leg   Airborne slang for Non-Airborne Servicemen

Lifer   Career Military Personnel, (a derogatory term)

Lima   Phonetic alphabet word for the letter L.

L.L.D.B.   Luc Luong Dac Bien. The South Vietnamese Special Forces. Sometimes referred to as Look Long, Duck Back.

L.U.R.P.   Long Range Reconnaissance Patrol Unit

Lt.   Short for Lieutenant

LP.   Listening Post. A two man post outside the camp to report on enemy activity.

LZ   Landing Zone. The place where a helicopter lands.

M

Mars   A radio system for call back to and from the United States. Ham or Government operated.

Mary   Phonetic alphabet word for the letter M

M-16   Standard issue assault weapon used by the U.S. Armed Forces. Sometime call Matte Mattel.

M-79   A single shot 40 mm Grenade Launcher. Sometimes call thumper because of the sound it makes.

MACV   Military Assistance Command, Vietnam

Medevac   Helicopter extraction of the sick, wounded, and the dead from the battlefield.

Mig   A Russian made Jet Aircraft.

Montagnard   The tribal people who inhabit the high lands of North and South Vietnam.

M.O.S.   Military Occupation Specialty. A job description.

N

Nancy   Phonetic alphabet word for the letter N

Napalm   A mixture of naphthalene, palm oil, and gasoline. The blast consumes hundreds of thousands of cubic feet of oxygen and burns with extreme heat. It will burn under water.

NDP   Night Defensive Position.

Nuoc-mam   A strong smelling fish extract used by Southeast Asians to add flavor to the food.

NVA   North Vietnamese Army

O

Oscar   Phonetic alphabet word for the letter O

OPS   Operational Control Center.

OCS   Office Candidate School

P

Papa   Phonetic alphabet word for the letter P

Paddy wagon   A large van used by New York City Police to haul people to jail.

PH   White Phosphorus mortar round use to light up an area

P.O.W.   Prisoner of War

PRR-9   Radio used in a Como net. Sometimes called a prick-9

P.S.P.   Perforated steel plate. Once used to build temporary runways for aircraft.

PT   Physical Training

Punji Stick   Sharpened Bamboo or other material stakes hidden to penetrate the foot when stepped on. Sometimes dipped in Shit.

PX   Post Exchange a small store where you could purchase daily needs.

Q

Queen   Phonetic alphabet word for the letter Q

R

REMF   Rear Echelon Motherfucker, slang for the personnel that work in the safe rear areas of the war and elsewhere.

Reup   To sign on for another tour of duty. Or to reenlist

R.O.T.C.   Reserve Officer Training Core

R.P.G.   Rocket-propelled grenade. A Russia made Grenade Launcher.

R&R   Rest and Relaxation. Time off give to personnel. Usually 10 days every year.

RTO   Radio Telephone Operator

S

S-1   Personnel Department

S-2   Intelligence

S-3   Operations

S-4   Supply

Saddle Up   An order to put on you gear and get ready to move out

S.F.   See Special Forces

Shiv   A Knife

Skid   Slang for a UH-1B Helicopter

S.O.G.   Official known as Studies and Observation Group. Also known as Special Operations Group

Special Forces   An elite highly trained unit of the United States Army. Activated at Fort Bragg N.C. on June 20, 1952 and first deployed to Vietnam in 1957. Each unit is made up of small teams of the best-trained solders. It takes almost 1 year of training after basic training to win the Green Beret.

Spook Slang term for CIA personal

Steel Pot Standard U.S. Army Helmet. The steel pot was the outer metal cover. It could also be used to bath in, shave in, cook in and other things.

T

T-10 A wing type parachute that can be steered like a hang glider.

Tracer A round of ammunition chemically treated to glow or give off smoke. This was done to follow the flight of the ammunition.

Turf Ones home, or any area around ones home that you control

U

UH-1 See Huey or skid

V

V.C. Viet Cong, South Vietnamese Communists

Viet Minh Shot for Vietnam Doc Lap Dong Minh. Also know as the League for The Independence of Vietnam. First started by Communists during the Japanese Occupation in WW II.

W

Waxed Killed

Web Gear Canvas Suspenders and belt used by solders to carry their gear.

Willie Pete A white phosphorus artillery or mortar round used for adjusting onto a target, for marking a target, for incendiary effects and for smoke screens.

X

X.O. Executive Officer or second in command

Y

Yard See Montagnard

Z

Zip Gun A small single shot home made pistol.

Numbers

60 M-60, Light machine-gun 60 caliber, or a U.S. Mortar round.

61 Communist Mortar

81 U.S. Mortar

105 105 mm Howitzer

1,000 yard stare A look that is as if you were looking 1,000 yard down the road and not at what is right in front of you. Almost a blank stare.

Military Rank

Enlisted

E-1	Enlistee
E-2	Private
E-3	Private First Class (PFC)
E-4	Corporal
E-5	Sergeant
E-6	Staff Sergeant
E-7	Sergeant First Class
E-8	Master Sergeant
E-9	Sergeant Major
E-9	Command Sergeant Major

Officers

O-1	2nd Lieutenant
O-2	1st Lieutenant
O-3	Captain
O-4	Major
O-5	Lieutenant Coronal
O-6	Colonel
O-7	1 Star Brigadier General
O-8	2 Star Major General
O-9	3 Star Lieutenant General
O-10	4 Star General
O-11	5 Star General of the Army

CPSIA information can be obtained at www.ICGtesting.com
Printed in the USA
BVOW011552030213

312227BV00007B/67/P